ENGL[...]
IN THE [...]

AND

A FAMILY FOR CHLOE

BY
LUCY CLARK

MILLS
BOON

ENGLISH ROSE IN THE OUTBACK

BY
LUCY CLARK

MILLS & BOON

Published in Great Britain 2016
By Mills & Boon, an imprint of HarperCollins*Publishers*
1 London Bridge Street, London, SE1 9GF

ISBN: 978-0-263-25447-1

Our policy is to use papers that are natural, renewable and recyclable
products and made from wood grown in sustainable forests.
The logging and manufacturing processes conform to the legal
environmental regulations of the country of origin.

Printed and bound in Spain
by CPI, Barcelona

Dear Reader,

I have to confess I've had a difficult time creating the town of Meeraji Lake. Small Outback Australian towns often contain a plethora of fun-loving characters, and to put all those eccentric secondary characters into this story would have left little room for us to really get to know Daisy and Oscar.

So I'll let you know that in this close country community are characters such as Erica and Glenys. These two women have been best friends since primary school. Both were raised in rural Victoria, but headed to the big city of Melbourne to do their training. Erica became a schoolteacher and Glenys became a nurse. And there's Bazza, a typical Outback bloke who loves the dust, flies and heat, but most of all a bit of a bar-room brawl on a Friday night. Needless to say he knows Oscar quite well from all the times he's needed stitches in his head or a bandage on his hand.

Tori and Scott are also wonderful characters, both of them not sure whether to move forward or to call it quits. Henry, the police officer, is a quiet, unassuming sort of guy, but when it comes to the time for him to break up a fight or protect the people of his town, this black-belted, ex-Army guy takes his duties seriously. There's Pat McGovern, too, a self-professed hypochondriac who always panics about his health. And Adonni and Bill and Sarah—excellent nurses, all of them—and of course Oscar Price, our dashing hero.

This is the fun-loving, caring community of Meeraji Lake that Daisy Forsythe-York finds herself working in. For Daisy it's as though a splash of colour has entered her life, but for a while she isn't quite sure how to respond. Thankfully Oscar is there to help her navigate the vibrant personalities of this little town, and in the process both of them run the risk of losing their hearts.

I do hope you enjoy getting to know Daisy and Oscar.

Warmest regards,

Lucy

For Tori and Scott

You've helped me, supported me and accepted me so
unconditionally that I don't know how else to thank you.
Hopefully dedicating a book to you is a small way to
show my heartfelt appreciation and sincere thanks. xxx

Phil 2:14

Lucy Clark loves movies. She loves binge-watching
box-sets of TV shows. She loves reading and she loves
to bake. Writing is such an integral part of Lucy's inner
being that she often dreams in Technicolor®, waking
up in the morning and frantically trying to write down
as much as she can remember. You can find Lucy on
Facebook and Twitter. Stop by and say g'day!

Books by Lucy Clark

Mills & Boon Medical Romance

Wedding on the Baby Ward
The Boss She Can't Resist
Taming the Lone Doc's Heart
Diamond Ring for the Ice Queen
Falling for Dr Fearless
A Socialite's Christmas Wish
Dare She Dream of Forever?
One Life-Changing Moment
Resisting the New Doc In Town
The Secret Between Them
Her Mistletoe Wish
His Diamond Like No Other
Dr Perfect on Her Doorstep
A Child to Bind Them
Still Married to Her Ex!

Visit the Author Profile page
at millsandboon.co.uk for more titles.

CHAPTER ONE

DAISY FORSYTHE-YORK PEERED out of the window of the small Cessna plane, which was coming in for landing. From what she could see of the patchwork ground below, it was generally different shades of brown with the odd spate of green here and there. They were passing over the small township of Meeraji Lake, although from where she sat there was definitely no lake anywhere to be seen. What she could see, however, were a few buildings, some made of brick, others were weatherboard huts and there were even a few just made of tin.

She gripped the edge of her seat as they seemed to be zooming rather too close for her liking to the buildings. Were they landing in the centre of the town? That was all right with her if that was the case as it would mean she wouldn't have far to go in order to find the hospital. Besides, she'd been in a variety of planes and transport carriers last year when she'd worked with the military and even though the pilot didn't even look old enough to drive, she had to put her trust in him.

Coming to Meeraji Lake hadn't been in her plan but, with the way things were with her family back in the UK, she was more than happy to be on the other side of the world for a while. A six-month respite would do her good.

'Go,' her mother had urged her just a week ago.

Daisy had been in two minds whether to accept the position in the Australian outback especially given her mother's health at the moment. 'Mother, I won't leave you.'

'You have to leave, Daisy. I need to learn to fight my own battles.'

'But Father is—'

Her mother had held up her hand, stopping Daisy's words. 'Your father is your father and always will be. He'll never change.'

'Come with me, then. Just leave him.'

Her mother had laughed without humour. 'Could you imagine me? In the Australian outback? I don't think my nerves could stand it.'

'But they can stand remaining here? He riles you up every single day, Mother. At least consider going back to Spain for a month or two. The winter here is going to be horrendous this year.'

But Cecilia Forsythe-York had shaken her head. 'I made vows, Daisy. To honour and obey your father. He has a busy few months coming up and needs me around to host his work events.'

'Mother—' Daisy had started to protest but once more her mother had stopped her.

'He wasn't always like this, Daisy. In the beginning, he was charming and loving and caring.'

'Father?' Daisy had looked at her mother in disbelief, but the reflective smile on her mother's lips had made Daisy wonder if somewhere, deep down inside, her mother was still in love with the man who had swept her off her feet.

Cecilia had taken her daughter's hands in hers. 'Go, Daisy. Have an adventure then come back and tell me all about it.' Then she'd let go and reached for a bottle of paracetamol.

Daisy had poured her a glass of water. 'Do you promise to call me if you need me?'

'I promise.'

'I've also set up that separate email account so I can email you without him knowing. Do you remember how to access the emails?'

'You've written down the instructions. I shall follow them.'

'Keep the instructions where Father can't find them. Put them somewhere he'd never look.'

'He'd never look in my bedroom.' Cecilia's voice had been filled with sadness and she'd lain back after swallowing the tablets and closed her eyes. 'He hasn't been interested in me in that way for many years now.'

'Oh, Mother.'

Cecilia had kept her eyes closed but reached out a hand to her daughter. Daisy had instantly accepted it. 'I'll be fine, dear, especially if I know you're not putting your life on hold for me. Go to Australia. Find yourself a nice man.'

Daisy had laughed and kissed her mother's cheek. 'That's hardly my main motivation for going, Mother.'

'I worry about you. You're thirty-eight, Daisy. Don't let the past dictate your future.'

'There's more to life than getting married, Mother.'

Cecilia had opened her eyes then, her voice small. 'I wish there had been in my day. Still, if things had turned out different, I never would have had you and John.' She had forced a smile. 'Well, enough of all this. You've had your Internet interview and the hospital in that small district sounds as though they need some class and distinction, so go and email that doctor back and tell him you'll take the job.' And because her mother had insisted—and because Daisy had really wanted to go—she'd done exactly that.

'Well, Mother, I'm here,' she said softly to herself as her thoughts were jolted back to the present as the plane's wheels made contact with the ground.

There was only one other passenger on the plane and he disembarked as soon as the door was opened. Daisy watched as he walked to a nearby tin shed and disappeared inside. Was that the airport terminal? She picked up her hand luggage and then climbed down the small flight of stairs onto the dirt airstrip, the heat almost swamping her.

She breathed in, the hot air seeming to singe her nostrils. Flies instantly started to gather around her and beads of perspiration started to form on her brow and down her back. She'd been warned that it was hot, often reaching in excess of forty degrees Celsius for months on end, but she hadn't expected it to be such a dry, burning heat.

She started to feel dizzy but forced herself to take a few more breaths, trying not to grimace as the hot air filled her lungs. 'I'll wait in the airport terminal while you collect my luggage,' she told the pilot and, without waiting for an answer, she mustered her dignity, stood up straight and headed for the tin shed.

The instant she stepped inside, she realised it had been a mistake. Where it was hot outside, it was sweltering in the shed. There was no one around, not even the other passenger on the plane. The shed contained a desk with an old landline phone, a thick book and pedestal fan next to the desk. Daisy instantly went over and pressed the buttons on the fan but it didn't work.

She was just checking to see whether it was plugged in when the pilot walked into the shed.

'Power's off outside,' he stated, dumping his logbook onto the desk. 'I'll go turn it on for ya.'

He disappeared, but a moment later the fan in front of Daisy started whirring. She stood in front of it and closed her eyes, allowing the air to caress her sticky skin. The clothes she was wearing were completely inappropriate for this weather but it had been freezing when she'd left London and she'd chosen this outfit because it didn't crease when she travelled. Off came her jacket and she unbuttoned the top of her embroidered shirt, holding it away from her skin in order to circulate the cooler air.

'Better?' The pilot's words jolted her and she quickly dropped her hands back to her sides and straightened her shoulders.

'Much. Thank you.'

'Is someone picking you up? It's a fair hike into town.'

'Yes. Yes, I think someone is picking me up. Uh... one of the doctors.'

'The *only* doctor. That'd be Oscar.'

'Yes.' Daisy fanned at her face, her mind exhausted, not only from the travelling, but the intensity of the heat. 'Do you...uh...have any water?'

The pilot shook his head. 'Sorry. Not in here and even if there was any water, it'd be boiling by now.' He swatted at a fly, then picked up his logbook. 'All righty, then. I've gotta refuel the plane and get it ready to return to Darwin.' The pilot indicated the shed. 'I wouldn't stay in here too long. You'll dehydrate and if you can just get Oscar to flick the switch on the power when you leave, that'd be beaut.'

'Thank you.' All she wanted was for him to leave so

that she could continue to cool herself down. What she wouldn't give for a cold shower and a change of clothes. As soon as the pilot left, she returned her full attention to the fan before her. Surely her new colleague, Oscar Price, would be here soon. They'd flown quite low over the town so no doubt he was aware the plane carrying his newest member of staff had landed.

Fifteen minutes later, she was a bit cooler but her mouth was starting to get very dry. She thought about changing her clothes but right now the ones she was wearing were sticking to her almost like a second skin and would be impossible to get out of.

'He'll be here, soon.' Comforting words. That was all she needed. The fact that she was starting to get annoyed wouldn't help her overheating problem. 'He'd better be here soon,' she growled between clenched teeth five minutes later. 'Or I may just get back on the plane and leave.'

'Tori! I need another bag of plasma in here.' Oscar Price pushed past two other patients who had come into Meeraji Lake District Hospital, pointing to some nearby chairs. One was cradling her right arm to her chest, the other had a nasty gash on his left leg. 'Sit down. We'll be with you as soon as we can.' There were so many people in the small emergency department it was difficult to get through to the treatment rooms.

'Tori?' His voice was louder, not because he was annoyed he couldn't find Tori, but because there was just so much noise. When he reached the triage sister's desk, he found seventy-one-year-old Glenys, writing down people's names and other medical information. 'Where's Tori?'

Glenys glanced up at Oscar. 'Hello, love. Tori's off

with a patient in room two. She asked if you could help her as soon as you were ready.'

Oscar closed his eyes and pinched the bridge of his nose, taking a deep breath to calm himself down. One doctor, five nurses and an ED filled with patients due to an explosion at an unauthorised distillery was not the afternoon he'd planned.

'It's all right, love. Lots of the able residents are on their way to help marshal the masses. Erica's making sandwiches and Ella is making the teas and coffees. We may be retired but we're not useless.'

'I appreciate that.' Oscar's smile was tight-lipped. He *did* appreciate it, but what he needed now was trained medical staff, yet getting doctors and nurses to agree to come and work in the Australian outback was almost impossible. Almost. 'I wish that new doctor was arriving today instead of tomorrow,' he muttered under his breath.

'Did I hear you yelling for plasma?' Oscar turned to see one of the maternity nurses who had come off the ward to help, holding out a bag of plasma to him.

'Yes. Room five. Can you deal with the patient?'

'I'm on it,' the midwife replied and headed off to room five.

Oscar pivoted on his heel and headed through the throng towards room two, but when he opened the curtain it was to find Tori giving cardio-pulmonary resuscitation to a patient who had a newly bandaged arm and leg.

'He just went into shock and decided to stop breathing.' She kept up the rhythm as she spoke. 'As if we're not busy enough. When's that new doctor getting here?'

Oscar was already grabbing the portable defibrillator before attaching the pads to the patient's chest. 'Tomorrow.'

'Darn.'

'Charging.' Tori kept her CPR going until the paddles were ready. 'Clear!'

The triage sister stepped back as Oscar put the paddles onto the pads and delivered the charge. Tori immediately checked the pulse. 'It's there but not strong.'

Oscar hooked a stethoscope into his ears and listened to the man's chest. 'Push fluids. Oxygen.' He checked the man's pupils as Tori gave a quick recap of the man's injuries. With the increased oxygen and fluids, their patient began to respond well. 'Get him to the medical ward. Tell Bill to keep a close eye on him.' Oscar knew he could trust Bill, as the other man was one of the best ward sisters the hospital had ever had.

'Oscar!' Someone shouted his name but the shout was filled with urgency. 'Treatment room one. Stat.'

Oscar looked to Tori. 'Get someone to take this fellow to Bill then help me in treatment room one. I'll go see what all the fuss is about.' He was pleased that the emergency department was now a little better under control, the volunteers doing an excellent job, but there were still so many patients who required attention. In treatment room one, he found a twenty-ish young dark-skinned woman who lay very still on the bed, eyes closed, a fresh padded gauze bandage on her head.

'She was hit by flying debris.' The woman who spoke stood by the bed. 'Unconscious for approximately twenty minutes, maybe more.' The woman's words were crisp and very British. Oscar knew a lot of people in this district but he most certainly didn't know her. She looked utterly exhausted and incredibly hot. Then again, she was wearing a navy blue trouser suit, which seemed to be sticking to her. He focused his attention on the patient.

'How did she get here? Did someone bring her in?'
Oscar removed the gauze pad and took a look at the
head wound.

'*I* did. I found her lying in the dirt.'

'Do you know her name?'

'No.'

'OK. Thanks for your help. If you'd like to take a
look in the waiting room, someone will see you as soon
as—'

'I'm not going anywhere.' The British woman turned
her back to him and started rubbing anti-bacterial gel
into her hands. 'This woman is my patient and I'll treat
her.' Her smooth but clipped words were enunciated
perfectly. Oscar stopped for a split second, the chaos
and franticness of the hospital around them disappearing. He looked at the woman opposite him, realising
that although she looked worn out, she was also clearly
determined.

She was quite tall and he could see she wasn't wearing high heels. Her brown hair was pulled back into a
tight chignon and any make-up she might have worn
had been sweated away. She looked sticky and uncomfortable yet still she persisted. As she reached for a
disposable gown to cover her clothes Oscar frowned.

'Listen, darl. Just because you brought the patient
in, doesn't mean you can help me treat her. If you have
a problem, go and sit in the waiting room and I'll be
with you—'

'For a start, I am not your "darl",' she interrupted.
'I'm Dr Forsythe-York.'

'Dr Forysthe-York? But you're not due until tomorrow.'

Dr Forsythe-York fixed him with a glare before opening and closing the cupboards, finding the equipment

she needed. 'Well, perhaps you'd like me to come back tomorrow because it looks as though you have things completely under control.' Even though her words were filled with a dry sarcasm, she still made them sound incredibly polite. He also had the feeling that she was extremely annoyed with him, or perhaps she was always this clipped and curt.

'I can deal with this patient,' she continued, 'as long as you leave me a nurse to assist.' When he opened his mouth to protest, she fixed him with a stern glare. 'This is hardly the time to be arguing semantics.'

'Are you dismissing me?'

'Yes. You know my credentials—we covered them during my online interviews. Now will you let me get to work?' The patient's eyes had opened and Dr Forsythe-York all but elbowed him aside, then spoke gently to the woman before performing the basic neurological observations. 'I'm going to give you a local anaesthetic because I'll need to debride your wound.'

'Will I need to stay overnight?' the woman asked. Dr Forsythe-York glanced over her shoulder at Oscar. 'Dr Price will evaluate you and decide but I would prefer it. Injuries to the head need to be monitored for at least twenty-four hours. Your cognitive function is good, though, which shows promise for a full recovery.'

Oscar was still stunned at the way she was just taking over but, then again, hadn't he just been whinging that he wished the new doctor was starting now rather than tomorrow? His brisk British buddy was right. Now was not the time to be arguing.

When Tori entered the cubicle, Oscar quickly introduced them, wishing he could remember Dr Forsythe-York's first name, but a lot had happened since he'd interviewed the woman online and read her impressive résumé. Plus, on the day they'd had the interview, he hadn't been able to get a visual image of her on his computer so, although she'd been able to see him, he hadn't been able to see her, just hear her.

'Right. Well. I'll get back to it.' With that, he left his new colleague in treatment room one to deal with the patient she'd brought in. No sooner had he stepped through the curtain than people were calling out to him.

'Oscar. Oscar, can you look at this?'

'Oscar? I need you over here.'

'Oscar, am I going to live? Break it to me gently.'

Oscar took a breath and tried to deal with each patient in turn. Two steady hours later and he'd lost complete track of his new colleague's whereabouts. He had no idea how she'd miraculously arrived at the hospital right when they'd needed her most but he wasn't about to look a gift horse in the mouth.

As the sun started to go down, bringing relief from the constant summer heat, Oscar and the rest of the staff at Meeraji Lake District Hospital were able to finally slow down, the emergency situation now under control.

'And many thanks to the Meeraji Lake retirees who were an amazing volunteer force in our time of need,' Oscar stated as many of the staff gathered in the small nurses' station. Some sat on chairs, other sat on desks. 'And while I have everyone's attention, I'd like to introduce you all to Dr Forsythe-York who will be working here for the next six months and who was an absolute godsend today.' He started clapping and everyone joined in, showing their appreciation.

'Dr Forsythe-York, would you like to say a few words?' Oscar knew she'd been trying to blend in, to stay at the back of the crowd, but now that everyone was looking at her she squared her shoulders and stepped forward.

'Thank you.' She waited for the applause to die down and wiped a hand across her brow. Although the air conditioners were on, Dr Forsythe-York appeared to be perspiring quite a bit. Then again, coming from an English winter to an Australian summer, especially dressed as she was in long trousers and a white shirt with embroidered flowers around the collar, it was little wonder she was hot. Thank goodness she'd had the presence of mind to take off her suit jacket.

'First of all, I'd like for you all to call me Daisy. Dr Forsythe-York does tend to be a bit of a mouthful.' She smiled and a few people laughed. Oscar, however, wasn't smiling back. Even though the smile was a polite one, it seemed to…soften her a little. She didn't appear as brisk or as starched. It made him wonder whether she used all that pomp and ceremony as armour. He knew from her résumé that she'd been in the army, working in a combat zone last year. She held a degree in emergency medicine and minor surgical procedures although, as she'd assured him in the interview, she was also quite proficient at adaptive medicine, too. In fact, Daisy Forsythe-York was almost too qualified for this job and could easily have taken up a position in one of England's leading hospitals. So why had she decided to come to the Australian outback?

'And Dr Price… I mean Oscar…did tell me in my interview that you were all very informal here.'

'Gotta be, love,' one of the volunteer retirees said. 'The outback is no place for fancy airs and graces. Just plain speaking.'

Oscar continued to watch as she pulled a handkerchief from her pocket and dabbed at her forehead. She acknowledge the comment and continued to say a few more words but he didn't hear any of them—instead he started looking at her as a doctor looked at a patient. Her face was quite pink but her lips were dry, even a little cracked. She swayed, a little unsteady, but shifted her feet in order to counterbalance herself.

He'd seen enough symptoms of heatstroke to easily recognise them. When Daisy swayed on her feet again, bringing her hand up to dab at her forehead, he noticed she was shaking. He stepped forward and placed a hand on her elbow to steady her.

'Tori,' he stated quickly to the nurse. 'Container, please. I think she's going to be sick.'

'What do you think you are doing?' Daisy demanded in her haughty tone, turning crazed eyes in Oscar's direction, but the swift movement caused her to wretch and within another moment Tori was by her side with the container as Daisy was ill. No sooner had she emptied the contents of her stomach than she looked at Oscar with what could only be described as a death glare.

'This is all your fault,' she growled before passing out and landing neatly in his arms.

'Let's find a camp bed for her as all the other beds are occupied,' he said, scooping her more securely into his arms and sitting down in a nearby chair. How was all of this *his* fault? 'Set it up in my office.'

'Poor doc. What a welcome,' someone else muttered as everyone started to disperse.

'Get an intravenous drip organised,' Tori instructed one of her nurses as someone else retrieved a cold pack from the freezer and placed it onto Daisy's forehead.

'Obs?' Oscar asked Tori, who was quickly gathering the different things she needed. The sister checked Daisy's temperature.

'Just under forty degrees Celsius,' Tori stated a moment later.

'Hopefully now that she's been ill, her temperature will start to decrease, but let's give her some paracetamol once the IV is set up.'

Tori continued to take Daisy's observations and, although Oscar was listening to the nursing sister, he was also well aware of how fragile Daisy Forsythe-York seemed to be in his arms. Poor woman. She'd come to a foreign country to help out and now she was sick. She was showing all the signs of heat exhaustion and if they didn't get her temperature under control as soon as possible, then her symptoms would get worse. He knew from her résumé that she was well trained and had an abundance of experience but what he didn't know was what sort of patient she would make. Usually, doctors made the worst patients, which was definitely true of himself. Would it be true of Daisy?

Soon, the camp bed was set up in his office and, like a hero at the end of a movie, Oscar stood and carried Daisy to her new, and temporary, abode. Although the doctors' residence was just two doors down from the hospital, until her temperature had broken she needed to be as close to treatment as possible. 'Can we get another fan in here, too, as well as a few bags of ice and a water-sprayer? We need to get her temperature down, stat.'

'Why don't you get that organised while I get her out of those heavy clothes and into a cotton hospital gown?' Tori stated. 'Go do a quick ward round as well.'

'But I shouldn't really leave—'

'I'll stay with her,' Tori promised before shooing him out of his own office.

Oscar shook his head, knowing his colleague was right, but while he did his jobs and assessed the plethora of patients who were almost causing the small thirty-bed hospital to burst at the seams he couldn't stop worrying about Daisy. Why had she blamed him? What had he done wrong? It would be terrible if the two of them couldn't get along as it would make the next six months almost unbearable, especially given the small population of the town. The best thing he could do for her now was to provide her with the best treatment and care.

It was close to two hours later when he was finally able to return to check on Daisy, pleased to hear from Tori that their patient's temperature had indeed dropped but was still a little high.

'Has she regained consciousness?'

'Yes. She was a little bewildered and extremely embarrassed about what had happened but I told her there was nothing she could do except to rest. I think she believed me because when she tried to get out of bed, she was astonished at how weak she was.'

'Has she been sick again?' Oscar asked as he listened to Daisy's chest, pleased her breathing was now more steady as she slept.

'No. I've given her paracetamol as well as a sponge bath.'

'Thanks.' Oscar waved goodnight to Tori before sitting in the chair behind his desk, watching as his new colleague slept the sleep of exhaustion.

Oscar sat and absorbed the peace and quiet, listening to the steady rhythm of Daisy Forsythe-York's breathing. What a mouthful. Forsythe-York, and yet it suited her straight shoulders, her firm gait, her aristocratic nose. However, her Christian name suited her even better. Daisy. He smiled and stood, walking over to sit beside her.

He picked up the cloth from the bowl of fresh water Tori had replenished, and squeezed it out before placing it on Daisy's forehead. She was still hot but the drip and the paracetamol were definitely doing their job. With any hope, she'd be up and about in a few days, restored to full health.

'We'll take care of you, Daisy,' he told her, sponging her down with a cool cloth. Now that it was just the two of them, he couldn't help but notice how flawless her skin was. Apart from still being red and hot, there wasn't a blemish on her face. He brushed back a few wisps of hair and sponged around the back of her neck and shoulders. It was then he saw the small tattoo, a little daisy flower with white petals and a yellow centre. 'Huh. I hadn't pegged you as being the type of woman to have a tat,' he murmured.

He had the impression there were many different layers to his new colleague. He grinned as he realised he was quite intrigued to discover them all.

CHAPTER TWO

DAISY SLOWLY OPENED her eyes, not surprised she felt a little uncomfortable. She wasn't exactly sure where she was but stayed calm and tried to think of the last thing she remembered. She was in a room, lying in a bed. A low bed, like the camp beds in the huts…but this was not a hut. She was at the base hospital. That made sense and she breathed a sigh of relief. Her deployment would soon be at an end and she could return to England and resign her commission.

As her eyes began to focus a bit more, she frowned. This didn't look anything like the army base hospital. There was no thatched roof, no mosquito net around her, no chirping of the birds outside. Lying still, she tried to gather a bit more information before she would give herself permission to panic. Listening closely, she could hear the sounds of someone else breathing, someone who was nearby.

Who was in the room with her, the room that appeared to be some sort of office? She could see a desk, bookshelves and a ceiling fan above her, whirring around softly. Well, that definitely meant she wasn't in the combat zone.

She thought hard, trying to grasp her last memory. She moaned as a plethora of images flooded her mind.

Flying to the middle of the Australian outback. Of no one meeting her at the airstrip. Of picking up her suitcase and beginning the trek into town in the scorching heat wearing the wrong sort of clothing, which was stuck to her like glue. She remembered coming across a woman who had been lying in the middle of the dirt footpath, slowly regaining consciousness. Daisy had pulled out the small first-aid kit from her hand luggage and applied a bandage to the woman's forehead in order to try and stem the bleeding. Then the two women had staggered arm in arm towards the hospital, Daisy still pulling her suitcase behind her. As far as initiations into a new culture went, this one had been pretty horrid.

If that hadn't been enough for her to handle, when they'd arrived at the hospital, it had been to find it in the grip of an emergency, which at least provided her with a possible explanation as to why no one had been there to meet her plane. Where she'd found the strength to push on, to offer her assistance, she had no clue but once the emergency had been brought under control, she'd started feeling incredibly dizzy. She'd started to perspire again, even though the hospital was air-conditioned. Then, to her absolute horror, her new colleague, the annoying Oscar, had singled her out and introduced her. That was when the shaking had started, her body protesting that she was asking even more from it…and then…and then…

'Oh, no.' She tried to speak but the words simply came out gurgled and it was then she realised her mouth was excessively dry. She needed water. She should get up and get herself a drink but the instant she tried to move, she felt shooting pains pierce her skull, causing it to pound with an excruciating pain.

'It's OK. Just lie still.' A deep, soothing voice

washed over her and a moment later she felt a cool cloth placed on her forehead. 'Good to see you're awake, Dr Forsythe-York.'

'Why—?' Her words dried in her throat as she tried to look around the room. She saw the drip, the tube going down into her arm. There were also several pedestal fans whirring around her, cooling the air almost to the point of freezing—yet she didn't feel at all cold. In fact, she still felt incredibly hot. She tried to swallow but her mouth remained dry. Thankfully, her new colleague was beside her in an instant, holding out a spoonful of ice chips.

'Here. This will help.'

Feeling utterly humiliated that she had to accept his help, especially as he had to feed her, she sucked on the ice chips, closing her eyes so she didn't have to look at him. Her first impressions of Oscar Price weren't at all flattering and she knew that if someone had met her at the airstrip then she wouldn't be lying here in this bed being fed ice chips.

'Why do I have a drip?' Her tone sounded haughty and ungrateful.

'You got heatstroke,' Oscar stated. There was no humour in his tone, merely concern. Well, she didn't want his concern. She just wanted to go to her new residence, have a shower and sleep.

'If you're in pain,' he continued, 'let me know and I'll give you some more paracetamol.'

'I don't want anything,' she tried to argue, tried to open her eyes, but the instant she raised her voice just a touch the pounding in her head became worse.

'Good thing it's not about what you want but rather what analgesics your admitting doctor prescribes, so shush. You're not a doctor at the moment, you're a patient—*my* patient.'

He didn't sound smug, as she'd thought he might, given that he most definitely had the upper hand in this situation, but instead he seemed to be genuinely concerned about her. How sick had she been?

'What's my temperature?' Her words were soft but she was pleased that her vocal cords seemed to be working properly again.

'Finally back down to normal. It was bordering on forty.' She could hear him moving around and realised that he was adding the liquid paracetamol to the drip.

'Celsius? That's—'

'Well over one hundred in Fahrenheit,' he finished. 'It broke only a few hours ago, so you'll need to take it easy for the next few days, give yourself some time to recover.'

'But I can't.'

'But you will.' This time there was a firmness to his tone that brooked no argument. 'I was wondering what sort of patient you would make.'

'And?' She risked opening one eye and found that at least the room wasn't spinning any more.

He chuckled then, a nice, warm, rich sound, which she realised she liked. Odd, especially as she didn't know him all that well. 'You're a lot like me. Bellyaching and miserable.'

'I'm not miserable,' she instantly contradicted. 'I'm uncomfortable.'

'In the bed? In the room? With me?'

Daisy felt quite ridiculous arguing with him when she was lying supine and he was all but towering over her as he took her blood pressure. 'Or all of the above.'

'That's right. I remember you saying, just before you passed out, that you blamed me for everything.'

She thought for a moment, trying to recall if she'd actually said that. She'd definitely been blaming him in her mind but she couldn't remember saying the words out loud. Clearly she had.

'Well…I do.' With that, she closed her eyes once more, unable to believe how exhausted she was.

She heard him chuckle once more, the sound relaxing her. 'Lucky for you, I don't argue with my patients.' He pressed a cold cloth to her forehead and she relaxed even more. 'Rest, Dr Daisy. Everything will be fine.'

Would it though? She'd travelled to the other side of the world when she probably should have stayed home with her mother. Would her brother support her mother? Help her? Would her father be his charming self, or his dark inner self? Would she be able to recover from this sudden onset of illness or was she going to be unable to work in her new job for the next week or two? Oscar had said that she'd need at least a few days' rest and clearly he'd dealt with heatstroke patients more than she had so she had no real option but to believe him. Right now, all she could do was to sleep and give her body time to recover.

The next time she awoke, there was daylight trying to peek around the edges of the blinds. She listened carefully but this time she couldn't hear sounds of anyone else in the room. Gingerly, she tried to sit up, pleased when her head didn't instantly pound. As the cotton sheet slipped down Daisy realised she was wearing a hospital gown.

How had she changed? When had she changed? She couldn't remember. The door to the room opened and Oscar came into the room.

'You're awake again. How are you feeling?' He instantly reached for her wrist and took her pulse before picking up the tympanic thermometer that she hadn't realised was on the small table next to her and checked her temperature. 'Still within normal limits. Any pain?'

'My pain is well within normal parameters.' There was a briskness to her words but she didn't apologise for them. 'How did I get into this hospital gown? How long have I been here? Did you undress me?'

A concerned look crossed Oscar's face at her questions. 'Do you remember waking up before? About eight hours ago? It was around three o'clock in the morning. We had a lovely conversation.'

His words confused her and she lay back down, pulling the cotton sheet up around her chin. 'I don't remember.'

'That's perfectly normal. Your body has been through quite a lot. You're exhausted.' He checked her blood pressure and nodded, clearly satisfied with the results. 'And as to undressing you...' He slowly shook his head. 'Tori, our senior nurse, took care of you.'

'Where are my clothes? My suitcase?' Oscar picked up some more pillows and gently leaned her forward before placing them behind her head. 'Thank you,' she murmured, appreciating his thoughtful bedside manner. Now at least she could sit up and talk to him without feeling too achy.

'Your suitcase and hand luggage are at the doctors' residence. I'll take you over later today once you've been off the drip for a while and I'm satisfied you're doing better.'

'Or we could go over now,' she prompted. 'After all, I can take care of myself.' She moved in the bed and only then realised she also had a catheter in. Why hadn't she felt that before? She glared at Oscar once more as though he were solely to blame for her present predicament. It didn't matter that she'd obviously been quite ill and dehydrated, otherwise she would have neither the drip nor the catheter.

'I know you blame me for your present predicament,' he said, uncannily echoing her thoughts and sitting down comfortably in the chair that was by the bed. Had her face conveyed her annoyance? 'However, once you've recovered from your jet lag and the heatstroke, I'm sure you'll see things differently.'

'Perhaps my annoyance has nothing to do with either of those factors and everything to do with being left stranded at an airport, which is nothing more than a tin shed, in the middle of the Australian outback.' She didn't raise her voice as she spoke but her words were clipped and controlled.

He thought on this for a moment, then rubbed his jaw. 'Fair enough.' He smiled at her and leaned forward in his chair. 'But I reserve the right to argue my corner... when you're fully recovered, of course.' Then before she could say another word, he stood and headed towards the door. 'I'll get one of the nurses to come and remove your drip and catheter. Once I've done my rounds, I'll take you home where you'll be prescribed lots of fluids and bed rest for the next few days.'

'I'm not one hundred per cent sure I agree with your diagnosis.'

'You can disagree all you like, so long as you do as you're told.'

'And if I don't?' She couldn't help it. His dictatorial nature was starting to grate on her nerves. She knew it was only because her father was an arrogant, high-handed man and that tone, that 'I'm better than you' tone, made her jaw clench and her insides bristle.

'Then I'll organise a roster of our retirees to stand guard over you so don't fight me on this.'

It didn't matter that she knew he was right, that she needed to rest, that it was the most sensible thing to do—her stubbornness, the one thing her father had always disliked, came to the fore. 'I'm a fast healer so I'll be fine to start work tomorrow. One good night's sleep and I'll be as right as rain.'

'I don't care. What I *do* care about is the smooth running of this hospital and, as hospital director, as well as *your* admitting doctor, my prescription is fluids and bed rest for the next two days. If you're stubborn and come to work before then, I will fire you.'

'What?' Daisy spluttered. 'You'll *fire* me if I recover faster than you presume?'

Oscar fixed her with a firm stare before shaking his head. 'You seem intent on arguing with me, Dr Daisy, and that is definitely not going to aid your recovery.' With an indulgent smile, as though he were humouring a child, he opened his office door. 'I'll send one of the nurses to help you.' Oscar closed the door behind him, then sighed. He made his way to the nurses' station where Tori was sitting writing up notes.

'How's the VIP patient?'

'Annoyed with me for some reason.' He sat on the edge of the desk. 'I think she blames me for leaving her at the airstrip yesterday.'

'But she wasn't due to arrive until today.'

'Dates have clearly been mixed up.' He shrugged. 'Can you remove her drip and catheter, and I'll take her over to the residence once I've finished doing a ward round?'

'Does she need a change of clothes? She might feel more comfortable heading out of the hospital in her own clothing.'

'Good thinking.'

'I'm almost done with my shift here so why don't I pop over and get her something to wear? Did you want me to stay and help get her settled in? After all, you do still have a clinic to get through this afternoon.'

'If you don't mind, Tori, that would be great.' For some reason, Oscar was a little concerned at leaving Daisy on her own. He knew she was a doctor and that she was more than capable of looking after herself, but it was *because* she was a doctor that he didn't want to leave her by herself. She would push herself too far, too fast and that was the last thing any of them needed. 'Hang on. Weren't you and Scotty supposed to be going out on a date tonight?'

Tori grimaced, then shrugged.

'Oh, no. Have you two broken up again?'

Tori looked as though she was going to cry but she quickly pulled herself together. 'I'll go get Daisy sorted out.'

'Scotty will come around. He's crazy about you.'

'He's crazy all right,' she snorted before walking down the corridor. Oscar shook his head, glad he wasn't involved with anyone. He'd had his fair share of relationship failures and he certainly didn't want any more. One busted marriage, one aborted engagement. Yep. He was more than happy to devote himself to his career for a while. Sure, he wanted to have a family one day but there were more than enough children in the district regularly visiting him and the midwives in the clinics to help keep that paternal instinct at bay.

'Life doesn't always turn out the way you expect

it to,' he murmured to himself, remembering how his sister, Lucinda, used to say that to him all the time. She was the reason he'd first come to live in Meeraji Lake. She'd looked after him when their parents had passed away in a car accident and he'd looked after her as she'd wasted away from cancer. It had been almost a year since her death and there wasn't a day when he didn't think of her.

He completed his ward round, managing to discharge several patients from yesterday's emergency, and then headed back to his office, pleasantly surprised to find Daisy sitting up in the chair, dressed in her own clothes. The dress was cornflower blue with small yellow daisies on it. Her hair was still up but not in the harsh chignon she'd worn yesterday but, instead, a simple high ponytail. She looked seventy per cent better than before and her statement at being a fast healer flitted through his mind. Perhaps she was.

'Where's Tori?' he asked.

'She said she was going over to the doctors' residence to make sure the air conditioner was on and the fans were whirring.'

'Good.' He handed her a cold bottle of iced tea. 'I snagged this from the fridge on my way here. You need to keep your fluids up.'

Daisy thanked him and accepted the drink, then read the ingredient label on the side. 'There's no tea in this.' She sighed. 'What I wouldn't give for a nice, proper cup of English tea.'

'No hot drinks for you at the moment,' he added as he lifted one of her wrists and checked her pulse. 'Normal. Good.' He pointed to the drink. 'Besides, this variety has electrolytes in it and we need to keep you hydrated as best we can.' He picked up the thermometer and took her temperature. 'Normal. Good,' he repeated.

'But having a cup of tea *will* cool me down,' she protested.

'You're a feisty little thing, aren't you?' he stated and she raised one eyebrow in his direction.

'I'm hardly "little".'

'Anyone shorter than me is little.'

'And that's not at all an arrogant comment,' she retorted, unable to keep the dryness from her tone. She was tired, annoyed and frustrated but she still braced herself for his retort, knowing she was being completely rude but seemingly unable to stop herself. Then, much to her utter surprise, Oscar started to laugh.

The sound was deep, rich and washed over her like a cool breeze on a hot Australian summer's day. It caused a mass of tingles to flood her entire body and her shoulders to relax a little. When he looked her way, she could see the mirth in his eyes.

'Are you laughing at me or with me?' she asked, which, for a moment, just made him laugh a little harder.

'Definitely *with* you. This whole situation, you arriving a day early, the explosion and the hospital being inundated yesterday, you getting sick—everything— there's no way any of it could have been planned. It's just one of those things and all we can do is to shrug our shoulders and get on with things.'

Before she could reply, he jerked a thumb over his shoulder towards the door. 'I'll just go get a wheelchair and then we can leave.'

'I don't need a wheelchair to walk out to the car. I can cope.'

'And that's great. I like this independent spirit of yours. However, we're not going to be driving the car because it's much easier to walk, hence the wheelchair because, for you at the moment, I don't even want you walking that far in the heat.'

'Walking? Where is it?'

'Two doors up from the hospital. The GP clinic rooms are in the middle.'

'So it goes hospital, GP clinics and then doctors' residence?'

'Yes.'

'Where do you live? In the next house or across the street?'

'I live in the doctors' residence,' he stated.

'There are two of them, I get that, but where is your place situated?'

'In the doctors' residence,' he said again. 'I'll just go get you that wheelchair.' He opened the door then stopped. 'Oh, and you look good. Comfortable.' He winked at her. 'We'll make an honorary Aussie out of you yet.'

Why had he winked at her? She wished he hadn't because it had certainly caused a flood of excited confusion to spread throughout her body. She wasn't used to men winking at her. Wasn't used to the relaxed manner of these Aussies. Besides, she'd probably only responded to him in the way she had because she was exhausted. Her usual defences were down but by the time he returned with the wheelchair, she had herself under better control. 'Are you sure I can't walk?'

'You don't need to exert yourself at the moment,' he said before wheeling her out of the hospital. As they went several people called out to let her know they'd all been concerned for her.

She was touched by the genuine emotion from people she didn't even know yet. She'd been wondering whether or not she'd made the right decision to come here but perhaps everything would turn out well in the end. There was one issue, however, that she wanted to get cleared up right now, as it sounded to her as though Oscar was being evasive.

'So which house is yours?' she asked as both blinding light and heat from the sun swamped her. Flies instantly buzzed around them and she swatted them away as best she could.

'That's the GP clinic.' Oscar pointed as he wheeled her past the weatherboard building that had been newly painted. 'And the doctors' residence is just…there.' When the residence, a brick house with a corrugated iron roof, came into view, he turned the wheelchair towards it and started up the driveway. 'I'll wheel you around the back so we don't have to navigate the stairs at the front.'

'I'm not that much of an invalid. I can manage a few—' She stopped, shaking her head as he just continued up the driveway to the rear of the property. He locked the wheels on the chair before opening a gate that had a large wooden fence around it.

Oscar unlocked the wheels, then pushed the chair around to the rear door, which was being held open by Tori.

'Welcome,' the nurse said. Oscar wheeled Daisy right through the laundry, kitchen and into the lounge room. Although the house had probably been built sixty or so years ago, it had been lovingly restored. The walls were freshly painted, the flooring had been recently replaced and the furniture was quaint and looked comfortable.

'This house is lovely. It'll be perfect for the duration of my stay.' Daisy nodded her approval.

'I'm glad you like it.' He parked the wheelchair beside a large wing-back chair and held out a hand to her. She was too preoccupied with looking around to refuse his help. Tori was on the other side of her and together they helped her into the chair.

'It is a nice house. It's been the doctors' residence for quite a few decades. All the doctors who have worked here in the town have lived here at one time or another.'

She settled herself thankfully into the chair and then opened the bottle of iced tea he'd given her earlier. She took a long drink, delighted at the way the cool liquid seemed to flood throughout her body. 'So...' She rested her head against the back of the chair. 'Where do you live now?'

Oscar raised one eyebrow. 'I live in the doctors' residence.'

'You've said that before, but what does that mean if *I'm* living in the doctors' residence?'

It was then that he smiled at her. One of those slow smiles that, for some reason, made her heart skip a beat.

'It means we share.'

'We *share*!' She sat up straight, deep brown eyes glaring at him.

He nodded. 'Howdy, neighbour.'

CHAPTER THREE

'I AM *NOT* living with you.' Daisy's tone was completely indignant.

'You're not living *with* me, you just happen to be living in a house that I live in also.'

'I'll get you some ice chips,' Tori stated and quickly headed back into the kitchen. Oscar walked over to the blinds and adjusted them so the light wasn't in Daisy's eyes.

'Better?'

'Yes. Thank you. Now will you explain to me what's going on?' She'd never had heat exhaustion before, but it *was* exhausting and she settled back into the chair again and took another sip of her iced tea.

'I'll just adjust the vents for the air conditioner. I don't want it blowing directly onto you.' He reached up and changed the direction of the vents. 'Better?'

'Yes.' She yawned. 'Now will you please just tell me what's going on?' There was exhaustion in her tone and she closed her eyes.

'Of course.' Oscar picked up the tympanic thermometer Tori had brought over from the hospital and took Daisy's temperature. 'Still normal. Good.'

Tori brought the ice chips in and put them on a small

table beside Daisy's chair. 'I'll just go make up the bed in Daisy's quarters.'

'Thanks,' he remarked and sat in the other wing-back chair opposite his exhausted new colleague. 'This house was originally built for the doctor of the town and his family and, believe me, back then, the doctors who worked here often had at least five or six children. Then, years later when times had changed, the doctors who came here were single and devoted to their careers. The town council decided to convert this house into smaller apartments but, instead of making them into fully self-contained apartments, they extended all the bedrooms so they included walk-in robes and en-suites as well as a small study area but left the rest of the house as it was. This way, there are four full bedrooms here and then the occupants share the living areas.'

When she didn't immediately respond, he looked more closely at her. 'Daisy?'

'I'm awake,' she said. 'I was just thinking. It sounds as though this house has been set up like one of the boarding houses that were around after the war.'

'Exactly.'

'Do only doctors stay here?'

'No. Several nurses and midwives have stayed here when they first came to town but people either only stay for a short period of time—like yourself—or they like the district so much, they buy their own residence and move out.'

'When you arrived, was there anyone else living here?'

'Er...yes.' He hadn't been prepared for that question and he most certainly wasn't going to go into details about the other emergency specialist who had been here when he'd arrived at Meeraji Lake. Deidre was a closed book and one he still wasn't quite ready to open again. 'One other doctor lived here and Tori.'

Daisy opened her eyes at this news. There was a touch of hesitancy in his tone and she idly wondered what had caused it. 'But Tori doesn't live here any more?'

'No.'

'And your bedroom is...where?'

'To the left of this room. Your room is on the right.'

'So we live on either side of the house with the lounge room between us.'

'Yes.'

'Do we share the household chores?'

'One of the residents at the retirement village cleans the house but if you want to share the cooking, I'm more than happy to do that.'

She sighed heavily again and took another sip of her drink before closing her eyes and resting her head back against the comfortable chair. The next time she opened her eyes it was to the sound of two people whispering. She couldn't see them but could hear them. The room was a lot darker than before and she realised that the sun had set. How long had she been sleeping?

'Are you sure you'll be all right with her this evening? I could stay if you thought she needed nursing.'

'She'll be fine, Tori. The fact that she's slept most of the day away is good, plus her temperature is cool and you've managed to get some fluids into her.'

Daisy looked down at the glass on the little table beside her, surprised to see her iced tea was finished and so was half a jug of iced water. She didn't remember drinking, or did she? She frowned, recalling hazy memories of a soft voice urging her to drink, or sponging her down, or taking her temperature.

'Thanks for staying with her, especially while I managed to get through my clinic and finish treating the patients from yesterday's disaster who weren't so urgent.'

'I'm awake.' Daisy had to clear her throat, surprised when her voice caught due to dryness. Oscar was immediately at her side, lifting the glass of water to her lips.

'I can do it,' she told him, but he clearly wasn't going to listen to her as he continued to hold it until she drank.

'How are you feeling?' Tori asked, putting the tympanic thermometer into Daisy's ear.

'Will the two of you stop fussing?' she growled and, instead of them being annoyed with her snappiness, the two Australians just grinned at each other. Honestly, they were so different from her other colleagues, who probably would have scolded her for being such an impatient patient.

'Let me help you to the bathroom before I go,' Tori said after showing Oscar the reading on the thermometer. 'Unless you'd rather Oscar helps you?'

Before Daisy could even answer, going to state that she would much prefer the nurse's assistance, Tori was already in position to help Daisy out of the chair. It was only then she realised the question was rhetorical and that Tori had simply been teasing. These Australians, with their easy humour, were very different from the people she'd worked with in the past. Within the British hierarchy in the hospital, she'd always understood her position, and even in the army, where she'd been required to fulfil a variety of duties on the spur of the moment, there had still been a strict command structure.

The natives she'd worked with in the combat zone; the patients in Britain; the way she'd been raised—it had always been clear and defined what people expected of her and yet, even though she'd only been in this country for a short time, she found everyone incredibly relaxed and jovial. And even though they worked extremely hard and offered first-class treatment to their patients, they all seemed to be very happy to do so.

Even as Tori assisted her, and helped her to get changed into lightweight cotton pyjamas, Daisy was surprised at how much the nurse seemed to talk about her own life, telling Daisy about her boyfriend, Scott, who had just called their relationship off for the second time.

'I want to get married and I know he does, too, but then he says that once we're married I'll stop him from doing all the things he loves and I won't. He can still go out shooting or go away for a few weeks to Darwin and go fishing or whatever he wants.' Tori helped her into bed and Daisy listened to her chatter, most of it going in one ear and out the other. She was still so incredibly tired, she just couldn't help it, her eyelids growing heavier with each passing moment.

'What do you think?' Tori asked.

Daisy smothered a yawn. 'It sounds as though the two of you are perfect together.'

'Do you think so?'

'Well, I don't actually know this Scott person you're talking about. However, from the way you've described him, he does sound like a nice, honest man.' Daisy wasn't sure whether her words were slurring or not, whether she was making any sense or not, but whatever she was saying seemed to be well received by Tori.

There was a knock at her open door before Oscar came further into the room. 'How's everything going in here? All settled?'

Daisy wanted to tell him she was fine, that she was healing nicely and that she didn't need him fussing over her all night long, but the words didn't seem to come out and she closed her heavy eyelids and listened to the muted conversation between Tori and Oscar.

Again Daisy drifted off to sleep and the next time she woke the clock by her bed indicated it was four o'clock in the morning. She listened for other sounds in the house but couldn't hear any. Gingerly she managed to get out of bed and go to the bathroom before lying back down in the bed. She'd done her research on Meeraji Lake and knew that sometimes, it could get very cold at night even though it was scorching during the day. Pulling the light blanket over her, she noticed a jug of cool water by the bed with a glass and a straw, along with a sticky note that urged her to 'drink up'.

She did as it suggested and then settled back down, surprised once more at how tired she was. It was then that she started to dream, to see herself floating through the sky, gazing down at the patchwork-like ground below, wondering what adventures were waiting for her. Daisy saw a face forming in the clouds and she stopped herself from moving and peered more closely. It took her a while to figure out whose face it was and when she realised it was Oscar's, she smiled.

There was something about the man that she liked, even though she didn't know him at all well. They hadn't had the greatest beginning to a working relationship but, as soon as she recovered from this illness, she intended to do her job to the best of her ability. She told him that. Told him that she liked his relaxed nature and she was happy to be here.

Annoyingly, he only chuckled softly then urged her to drink a little more. When she asked him if he was going to reply, if he was going to say something nice about her, he had the gall to shush her and tell her to go back to sleep.

Closing her eyes with annoyance, she felt a breeze start to swirl around her, lifting her loose hair from her nape and brushing it from her face. It felt nice and comfortable and once again she smiled at the fluffy Oscar cloud face before drifting back into a deeper sleep.

'How did Daisy cope last night? No problems?' Tori asked Oscar when he arrived at the hospital the next day.

'She slept well. I checked on her every two hours and managed to get her to drink a bit more, which was good.'

'She's very exhausted because she doesn't seem to completely wake up when you ask her to drink.'

Oscar crossed his arms and leaned against the desk, straightening his legs out before him. 'She sort of did—wake up, I mean. Around four o'clock. I heard her go to the bathroom so thought I'd check on her then, save me waking her up, but although she spoke to me she was sort of delirious, too.' He shook his head, a slow smile crossing his face. 'I doubt she'll remember it.'

She'd looked so relaxed, so at peace, especially when she'd told him she was glad she'd come to the outback. For a woman who liked to argue, she'd also looked incredibly beautiful lying back on the light-coloured pillow, her dark hair fanned out around her face. It was an image he wouldn't be forgetting in a hurry. Daisy Forsythe-York was become more and more interesting the longer he spent with her.

When he arrived home that evening, it was to find her sitting up in the wing-back chair, talking on the telephone. He waved to her, pleased to see she was looking even better than when he'd checked on her earlier that morning.

She acknowledged his presence with a brisk nod of her head before she returned her attention to her conversation. Oscar headed to the kitchen to make them both a cool drink and couldn't help but overhear the end of her conversation.

'I am so glad that you're feeling better, Mother,' she stated. 'Promise me you're not just saying that because I'm on the other side of the world.' There was a pause before Daisy sighed, a deep and heavy sound that seemed to be filled with anguish. 'Mother, please call John. Tell him you want to go and stay with him for a few nights, that way you won't be…' Daisy paused and sighed again. 'All right. I will stop fussing so long as you promise to call John. He's your son. He's supposed to be taking care of you.'

Oscar smiled, liking that Daisy cared so much about her mother. He finished making their drinks and took them into the lounge room as she disconnected the call. 'It must be difficult being so far away from your family,' he said as he handed her the cool glass.

'It is.'

'I didn't mean to eavesdrop,' he added as he sat down opposite her, pleased with the way she accepted the drink without making a fuss. 'How is your mother?'

'Doing all right, at the moment.' She added the last bit in a softer tone and he could clearly see the concern on her face.

'You obviously care about her a lot. Have you spoken to her much since you arrived?'

'Not really. That was the first real chat we've had.' Daisy sipped her drink but didn't make any effort at conversation. Oscar had the feeling Dr Daisy thought she could come here to Meeraji Lake, do her job for six months and then leave, but that wasn't how they did things here in the outback. They became embroiled in each other's lives, they supported each other through thick and thin, through drought and floods, through life and death. He eased back in his chair, settling in for a good old-fashioned conversation with his new colleague.

'You're fortunate your mother is still with you. My parents passed away when I was seven years old. Car accident.'

'I'm sorry to hear that.'

'Thank you. I was lucky, though. My sister, Lucinda, was fifteen years older than me so she took me in and raised me. I loved her so much.'

Daisy nodded and took another sip of her drink. Was she going to ask him questions? Was she just going to accept his words, surmising that, as he'd spoken in the past tense, Lucinda had passed away? Come on, Daisy, he silently encouraged. Engage. Converse. Loosen up.

'She's passed on?' she finally asked and he was pleased to see she was willing to make the effort to chat with him. Many of her patients would want to chat and all that chatting was usually a very important part of general health care, especially with their more senior patients. Even though they were a tight community, many people did still suffer from loneliness. Knowing that Daisy was willing to ask questions, even if she didn't feel like it, decreased his concern about her fitting in. Many people had been put off by the snobby tourists that occasionally came through their town, with their airs and graces, and Daisy hadn't exactly made the best first impression with her haughty attitude. Now, at

least, it was good to see she was starting to loosen up…
even if it was just a bit.

'Almost twelve months ago. Breast cancer. I moved
to Meeraji Lake to be with her, to help her through
until the end.'

'That's a difficult thing to do, to watch a loved one
deteriorate.' She sipped her drink.

'Have you had to do that, too? Your father?'

Daisy almost choked on her iced tea. 'No. No.' She
cleared her throat and shook her head. 'My father is
most definitely alive.' She clenched her jaw and he received the distinct impression that she wasn't too fond
of her father. 'No doubt he'll outlive us all.'

Oscar couldn't help but smile at the way she muttered
the last part. 'He can't be as bad as all that.'

'Huh,' was her only answer, which indicated that
she clearly did not agree with him. 'How was your day
at the hospital?'

'It was…far more relaxed than the past two days.
Clinic is still overflowing with patients but they've all
been seen and I get to be rewarded with a coldie.' He
raised his glass in the air, then took a long drink, noting
the way she'd changed the subject. Clearly she didn't
want to discuss her father any more.

'You don't go to the pub?' she asked.

'The pub?'

At his question, Daisy looked a little confused.
'When I was doing my research about Australia, I was
led to understand that the main hub of any outback town
is the local pub and that at the end of the week people
would often celebrate with what was called a "knock-
off beer". Is that correct?'

Oscar was utterly delighted she'd taken the time to
do a bit of research on their culture. 'That is one hun-

dred per cent correct, but as it isn't yet Friday it's just a knock-off iced tea for me tonight.'

'Knock-off? As in it isn't real? I wasn't quite sure what it meant.'

'It means you've finished work for the week. Clocked off. Knocked off. Time for weekend fun…or in our case weekend sport.'

'Oh? What type of sport?'

'Rugby. Australian Rules football. Cricket. You name it, they play it and we get to deal with the injuries from it.'

And then it happened. Daisy smiled at him. Not a polite smile but a genuine one. Her perfectly straight white teeth, her twinkling brown eyes, her head angled slightly to the side, her low ponytail sliding off her shoulder. The whole picture was one of pure beauty and he was by no means unaffected by it. His gut tightened and his breath caught momentarily in his throat. Did she have any idea just how stunning she was?

'Oscar?' She was looking at him with confusion now and he belatedly realised she'd asked him a question.

'Pardon?'

'I asked which sport you prefer.'

He couldn't think straight, couldn't get his brain to function properly so he merely shrugged one shoulder and said, 'I like them all but I'm always on call so can never really commit to be a part of the team.'

'Have you always been the only doctor here? Presumably before you came there was another doctor here.'

He looked into the bottom of his empty glass and nodded. 'There was. Deidre.' He cleared his throat, not really wanting to talk about his ex-fiancée, but he knew that, as nothing was kept secret in this town, Daisy would soon find out about his past.

'Where is she now?'

Oscar placed his glass on the table, then stood and walked to the window. 'She's in Canada, I think.'

'Were the two of you close?'

He turned to look at her over his shoulder. 'What makes you ask that?'

'You seem a little on edge, therefore it was an obvious question. However, if you don't wish to discuss it, that's quite all right.'

'Hmm.' He returned his gaze to the window, watching as some of the young children rode their bikes up and down the main street, calling to each other and laughing without a care in the world. 'We live in a small town, Daisy, and as such everyone knows everything so you may as well hear it from me.'

'OK.'

He paused for a moment, pleased when she didn't prompt him but instead waited patiently for him to speak.

'Deidre and I were engaged.'

'Oh?'

'In the end, however, she decided she didn't want to get married and left.'

'Just like that?'

'She'd spent twelve months here, her contract was up and I didn't want to go with her.'

'Especially not if you were here for your sister.'

'Yes. Thank you. So she left and I stayed.'

'And will you continue to stay?'

'Yes. This was Lucinda's home for at least ten years. When she first came to nurse here, they hadn't even built the hospital. Even before she'd had cancer, I'd come for visits every now and then when my schedule would allow. I would have moved sooner if I'd been able. It's quite…serene here.'

He seemed slightly preoccupied by what was going on outside the window as he spoke, his words almost as though he'd said them all before. Daisy sat up a little higher in her chair and looked out of the window through the open blinds.

'Do the children often ride around on their bikes of an evening?'

'It's just after six o'clock. No doubt they'll all be called in for their dinner soon.'

'It's six o'clock and it's still light?' She shook her head, bemused by the difference between this sunshine and the dark, winter climate she'd left behind in England.

'And stinking hot. Summer is probably the worst time for newcomers to arrive from the northern hemisphere. Scorching here and freezing there.' He sat back down in his chair and unsuccessfully smothered a yawn. 'How was your day? Did you rest as per your doctor's instructions?'

'I did. Although what I didn't need was a roster of people coming to check up on me almost every hour.'

'Every hour?' He chuckled at this. 'I only asked one or two of them to look in on you a few times.'

'More like four or five of them.'

'It's only because they care about you.'

'But they don't even know me.'

'They know you've come halfway around the world to offer your services. That's enough for them. Still, I hope you've managed to rest.'

'I have. I had all my meals brought to my chair, as well as a constant supply of iced drinks. Tori popped in at two o'clock and did my obs, pleased everything was normal.'

'I did receive that report.'

'Good. I hope you're satisfied with my progress because tomorrow I *will* be at work.'

'We'll see. Besides, at the moment, everything is quite calm.'

'No. Don't say that. That's a rather dangerous thing to say, Oscar.'

He smiled at her words. 'Superstitious, Dr Daisy?'

'It's perfectly fine if you call me just Daisy.'

'OK, Just Daisy, do you honestly believe that by me saying that things are calm, they're automatically going to go haywire?' No sooner had he finished his sentence than his cell phone rang.

'I rest my case.' She laughed a little and was amazed at how her body seemed to groan with the effort.

'Take it easy,' he remarked, obviously seeing her wince a little. 'As I've said, rest for the remainder of today and tomorrow, remain cool and drink lots of fluids. Then you'll be as right as rain.' He connected the call before she could say another word. 'Hello?' He listened for a moment, then glanced at the clock on the wall. 'Sure. What time will you be picking me up?' Another pause. 'Good. I'll be able to get about four or five hours' sleep so that's just perfect. Do you have all the equipment?' Pause. 'Excellent. See you then.'

He was just about to disconnect the call when he thought of something. 'Oh, and, Scotty, don't beep the horn when you pick me up.'

Clearly Scotty had asked why because Oscar continued with, 'Because the new doc has arrived from England and she'll be sleeping.' Pause. 'Yes she's a female. You knew that.' Another pause, one that had Oscar's eyebrows rising as he fixed Daisy with an intrigued glance. 'As a matter of fact, Scotty, yes, she is exceptionally pretty.' His lips curved up into a smile as he watched Daisy's eyes narrow with indignation. 'I'm not sure. I'll ask.' He took the phone away from his mouth for a moment, then asked softly, 'Are you single? If so, Scotty wants to know if you'd like to meet him in the pub for a drink some time this weekend.'

Daisy crossed her arms over her chest and huffed with impatience. 'Please inform this…Scotty person that I am here in Meeraji Lake to work. I am a medical health professional and I'm not the slightest bit interested in meeting anyone at the pub for a drink.'

Oscar completely surprised her by throwing his head back and laughing. A second later, he returned the phone to his ear. 'She said no, Scotty. Sorry, mate, and besides, I don't think Tori will take too kindly to you dating someone else and why you even broke up with her is beyond me. Tori's amazing.' Another pause. 'Fine. I'll drop the subject. See you when you get here— and remember, don't beep the horn.'

'So that was Tori's boyfriend, Scott?' Daisy slowly edged out of the chair, waving away Oscar's help. 'I'm all right.'

'Yes. That was Scotty.'

'She was lamenting about him when she came to check on me. It sounds as though he's not as serious about her as she is about him.'

Oscar shrugged. 'Scotty's a farmer, an outback farmer through and through. All his training in life is from the land, from his father and grandfather. Sometimes, I think he feels a little intimidated that Tori has a few university degrees behind her.'

'He thinks she's too smart for him.'

'Yes.'

She placed the empty glass on the table then slowly stood up, standing still for a while in order to steady herself. 'Other people's love lives allow us to be philosophers and to wax rhapsodic that we would never conduct ourselves in such a way.'

Oscar grinned at her and nodded. 'Well stated, Dr Daisy.' Now that she was standing, they were almost eye to eye.

'You really are tall.'

She angled her head to the side. 'Stating the obvious, Dr Oscar.'

His smile increased at the way she'd mimicked him and she really wished he hadn't because that smile of his was starting to have an effect on her fragile body. It was only because she was weak, only because she was still recovering, only because he'd been considerate of her, especially yesterday and today…and last night? 'Uh… strange question. Did you check on me last night?'

'Several times. You drank when I asked you to, swallowed paracetamol when I asked you to. All in all, you were a very accommodating patient.'

'Did you…did you help me to the bathroom?'

'I helped you to the door of the en-suite but you insisted you could manage the rest by yourself and you did.' He was instantly by her side as she started walking towards her part of the house, just in case she overbalanced. 'You don't remember?'

'Not really. Everything's sort of hazy. I remember dreaming that I was floating in a cloud and that your face was in the cloud.'

He chuckled. 'A cloudy Oscar. I like it.' When they reached her room, he switched on her overhead fan and checked the air vents, ensuring she wasn't too hot or too cold. 'Are you hungry? I'm more than happy to bring you in a tray of food.'

'I'm actually rather full. Every volunteer who came in to look after me insisted on feeding me something they'd spent all day making. It seemed churlish to refuse.'

Oscar seemed pleased by her response. 'You'll go far in this town, and no doubt you'll be getting a few more meals dropped in to help you out.' He rubbed his hands together. 'Which means there will also be enough for me. Good.'

As she lay down in the queen-sized bed, which was an old wooden frame with matching side tables, the fresh vase of flowers someone had brought her today filled the air with the relaxing scents of lavender and something else she couldn't quite distinguish. She pulled the light cotton quilt, which had clearly been handmade, over her, unable to believe how her eyes were already starting to close. 'You're clearly exhausted,' Oscar murmured softly. 'Sleep, Dr Daisy. I'll come by and check on you. Later, I'll run you a bath with some bath salts, which will help those muscles of yours to relax even more.'

'That's not necessary. I can take care of myself. I'm almost fully—' she yawned '—recovered.' Then everything went silent. She wasn't sure where Oscar had gone but what seemed like only a few moments later, she heard her name being called.

Daisy sat bolt upright in bed and looked around but there was no one there. She could hear water running. Had Oscar started running her a bath? She quickly walked to her en-suite to turn off the taps, but when she got there it was to find the bath completely empty but the water still running. He'd forgotten to put the plug in. When she turned to leave the bathroom, she almost doubled over in pain. She clutched one hand across her abdomen and reached for the towel rail with the other, trying desperately to steady herself but it wasn't to be. She was spinning around, falling towards the ground, the pain in her gut increasing. She was going to be ill again but when she looked around for a bucket, she found that the tiled bathroom floor had disappeared and in its place was hard, dirt ground.

When she looked up, it was to see the canvas roof of the temporary army surgery that had been set up so she could operate. The sound of a plane droned overhead and she and the rest of the staff in the operating room braced for impact. Thankfully none came. They were safe…for now.

Neglish made a comment in his native language and they all smiled, but for some reason Daisy couldn't understand him. That was odd because she spoke the language fluently—it was one of the reasons why she'd been stationed in this country.

She continued to operate on her patient, pleased she was no longer in pain, but when she looked at the patient's face she gasped and dropped the scalpel. It wasn't one of her usual patients. No. The face on the patient…was her own. She'd been operating on herself. Was that why her abdomen was sore? Had she been stupid enough to remove her own appendix?

'Daisy. Daisy.' The soft, insistent hand on her shoulder forced her to open her eyes. 'Wake up, sleepyhead. You were having a bad dream.'

'Where am I?' The words were a choked-out whisper and she couldn't disguise the terror in her tone.

'Meeraji Lake.' At the blank look he received from her, he continued, 'The Australian outback? You had heatstroke. Don't you remember?' Oscar instantly placed the back of one hand against her forehead. 'You don't feel hot.' He looked around the room. 'Where is that thermometer?'

'I'm fine,' she mumbled, her senses beginning to return. 'I'm fine.' Daisy waved away his words as her new world crashed down around her. 'I remember.' She swung her legs over the side of the bed and sat up slowly. Blinking a few times, she realised that Oscar had brought her in a tray of food that contained a piece of toast, some fresh fruit and a glass with what looked to be some sort of milkshake.

'What's that?' She pointed to the drink, trying desperately to ignore every single aching muscle in her body. 'You shouldn't be giving me milky things. I might be sick again.'

He raised one eyebrow at her haughty tone but didn't comment. 'It's actually a fruit shake with mango, ice, banana and manuka honey, topped up with still mineral water. My sister used to swear by this recipe for hangovers, sunstroke, sunburn, heat exhaustion and just plain old tiredness.'

Intrigued, Daisy lifted the glass to her lips and took a sip. It was nice and cool and refreshing. She took another sip, a bigger one, sighing as she felt the cool liquid spread throughout her body. 'That *is* nice.'

'Excellent. I've added some soothing mineral salts to the bath and a few bubbles. It's ready whenever you are.'

It was only then Daisy realised the water had stopped running. 'How long was I asleep for?'

'You call that asleep? I call it restless snoozing.'

Indignation pulsed through her. 'You were watching me sleep?' She stood from the bed, rising to her full height, almost staring at him eye to eye...almost. Good heavens, he was tall. She was trying to intimidate him, trying to put him in his place as she had with so many other men in the past. She was doing her best but she was failing miserably. She could see that twinkle in his eyes, his expression indicating he was both intrigued and amused with her actions.

'I was monitoring my patient,' he offered, but she'd had enough.

Clenching her jaw, she forced a polite smile. 'Thank you for the food, for the bath and for your care. I am now perfectly capable of taking care of myself and would appreciate it if you would kindly vacate my part of the house and return to your own quarters.'

'What was the bad dream about?'

Had he not heard her? Didn't he realise she didn't want to talk about it?

'I beg your pardon but I have just asked you to leave.' To her utter chagrin, he shifted his stance to a more relaxed position, still not moving from her room.

'I'm not one of your soldiers you can order around, Major Daisy,' he stated. 'You're my patient and, hopefully, my friend. I'm concerned about you. You won't recover properly from the heatstroke if your sleep is fitful and restless. Therefore, it's best if you just give in and let me look after you, ensuring you make a full recovery, because if you don't the exhaustion you're feeling could lead to chronic fatigue and none of us want that.'

'I *know* the prognosis, Oscar.' She sighed, feeling defeated and still unbelievably tired.

'Excellent. Then I'll be expecting you to eat, drink and then slip into your nice lukewarm bath. I'll be around for another few hours but if I don't think you're well enough to be left by yourself, I'll cancel my hunting night.'

'Hunting night?' She'd been inwardly annoyed at him but the last part had caught her completely off guard.

'Yes. There are a lot of vermin out here, destroying crops, stealing livestock and generally being a nuisance.'

'Do you go out often?'

'At certain times of the year, yes.'

'You're licensed?'

'Completely.'

'And tonight you're going to Scotty's farm?'

'Yes. Why?' He looked at her quizzically. 'Would you like to come one time?'

'Perhaps.'

He nodded, clearly impressed by her answer. 'I'll see what I can arrange but first—' he pointed to the tray of food and then the en-suite where the bath was waiting for her '—eat, drink and relax. OK?'

'Yes, Doctor.' Her tone was meek and mild but filled with irony.

'And that's the most sensible thing you've ever said to me.' He chuckled as he walked from her room and if she'd had the strength she would have thrown a pillow at the closed door. Since she'd met Oscar Price, she'd found him annoying, frustrating and arrogant. She'd also found him thoughtful, considerate and…fun to be around.

Fun. Her life had been so serious lately, had she forgotten how to have fun?

'It looks as though Oscar may help you remember,' she murmured to herself as she headed slowly to the bathroom, a relaxed smile on her lips.

CHAPTER FOUR

It was another two days before Daisy started to feel more like her old self, rather than someone who had been through the wringer. According to Oscar the jet lag coming from the Northern hemisphere to the Southern hemisphere was far worse than the other way around.

'Once, when I returned from a few months in the States, it took almost two weeks for the jet lag to settle down,' he'd told her.

The morning after Oscar had gone out shooting, she'd slowly walked into the kitchen to find him resting his head on the kitchen table, a lukewarm cup of coffee in his hand.

'Will you be able to work this morning?' Her words had penetrated his dozing and he'd sat bolt upright, spilling his coffee all over his hand.

'I'm awake,' he'd said, eyes open. She'd been unable to stop the bubble of laughter that had burst from her lips. Oscar's response had been to smile back, clean up the mess then head out of the door, giving her an easy salute as he went. 'Keep resting,' he'd instructed.

Once more, she'd been inundated with visitors throughout the day while Oscar had run himself ragged doing emergency-department work, clinics and ward rounds. It had made her feel guilty as this was the reason she'd answered the advertisement in the first place. 'Emergency trained doctor required for hectic small town outback practice.' And yet there she'd been, drinking iced tea and nibbling homemade biscuits, talking to the residents of Meeraji Lake's retirement village who seemed to have taken her on as their responsibility.

'Why don't you look at it from the point of view that you are indeed working,' Tori had said when she'd stopped by later in the afternoon to take Daisy's temperature. 'You're getting to know your new patients. Most of these people will be on your house-call list and, by the same token, they're getting to know you, to see if they can trust you when you prescribe a certain treatment for them.'

'Are you saying they've been interviewing me?' Daisy had been astonished.

'In a way, yes.' Tori had packed up the portable sphygmomanometer and grinned. 'From what I've heard, you've passed with flying colours.'

Oscar had come home late on Thursday night and, as someone had already dropped a meal in for dinner, he'd quickly eaten his portion, checked her temperature and then headed to bed, bidding her a subdued goodnight.

It had left Daisy feeling a little deflated as she'd been looking forward to having a chat with him, the two of them sitting in the wing-back chairs opposite each other, sipping cool drinks and talking about his day and the patients he'd seen. Clearly, though, he had still been recovering from his early shooting trip.

When she walked into the kitchen on Friday morning, she was surprised to find a bleary-eyed Oscar yet again.

'Did you go out hunting again last night?'

'You mean early this morning.' He nodded, then

frowned as he watched her move fluidly around the kitchen. She switched on the kettle and took out a teacup. Clearly whether it was hot or not, she was having a cup of tea. 'What are you doing up and especially looking that chirpy? I prescribed bed rest. You'll do as your doctor says.' He sipped his black coffee before resting one elbow on the table and propping his head on his hand.

'I've discharged myself,' she remarked as she went to the fridge and opened it. She stared into it for a moment, taking stock of the contents. 'As I haven't had any time to go to the market, I'm presuming it's all right for me to use the food provided?'

'Yes, yes, of course,' he snapped.

She raised her eyebrows and turned to stare down at him. 'No need to use that impatient tone with me.'

'Sorry,' he replied sheepishly.

'Clearly you've had little sleep—again. Perhaps it's my turn to look after you.'

His lips twitched as he continued to stare at her. 'Are you volunteering?'

Daisy sighed. 'Volunteering to boss you around? Most definitely.' She returned her attention to the open refrigerator, enjoying the coolness it was providing. Although she was dressed in a cotton skirt and light, short-sleeved shirt, it was still warm, even this early in the morning. She quickly removed eggs, tomato, asparagus, cheese and milk. There was silence as she moved around the kitchen, opening and closing cupboards, finding the utensils she needed, but she could feel Oscar's gaze upon her the entire time.

'You really do seem much better,' he remarked after a few minutes.

'Like I said, I'm a fast healer.'

'So I see.' She was cracking the eggs into a bowl and sniffing them to make sure they weren't rotten. 'They're fresh. Laid yesterday. So are the vegetables.'

'The vegetables were laid yesterday?'

He grinned and shook his head. 'Pedantic this morning, are we?'

'Perhaps I'm pedantic all the time.' She fixed him with a look, her tone dry.

His smile only increased. 'That'll make life more interesting.'

'So I'm presuming the eggs and vegetables have come from the retirees?' When he seemed surprised at her knowledge, she added, 'I've had several visitors over the past few days and all of them love to talk about their individual projects.'

'Ah. Yes. A lot of the residents of the retirement village have a hydroponics area they tend, because at times, being out in the middle of the Australian outback, it can be difficult to get fresh fruit and veggies.'

'They clearly have chickens, too.'

'Oh, yes. They may be "retired", as they term it, but they work incredibly hard providing for the entire community. We have a sort of farmers' market every week, depending on what's in season.'

Daisy was clearly impressed, and as she cut up the vegetables and grated a bit of cheese she could see that the ingredients were indeed fresh. She popped a bit of the tomato into her mouth and savoured the taste. 'Delicious. Much better than getting them from a supermarket.'

'We are spoiled. Of course, the plane comes in daily as well, bringing passengers—' he gestured to her '—and food supplies and the mail. We used to only get deliveries twice a week until one of the local lads got his plane licence and a plane and decided to provide this much-needed service for the community.'

Daisy poured the egg mixture into the pan, then slowly stirred it around. 'It's as though you have your own little army in this town, supporting each other in every way possible. Even down to the local doctor going on a hunting trip.'

Oscar growled into his coffee and took another sip. 'Foxes are vermin out here.'

'Foxes are vermin in England as well, hence why kings and queens have taken part in fox hunts for years.'

'You're not against hunting?'

She looked at him over her shoulder. 'I was in the army. Of course, the fox is an incredibly beautiful animal to look at but they have a vicious personality and will rip a lamb's head off if given the chance.'

'Huh.' He stared at her in astonishment.

'You seem surprised?'

'You're just not what I expected.'

'Oh? And what did you expect?'

Oscar breathed in deeply, savouring the flavours now beginning to waft through the air. Daisy added the vegetables and the cheese and stirred the contents of the pot again. 'I'll make the toast,' he said, not answering her question.

She didn't stop him and soon they were standing side by side in the kitchen, dishing up their first home-cooked meal together. Oscar had also laid the table and poured them both a glass of juice. 'I could get used to this,' he murmured after swallowing the first mouthful of savoury eggs.

'The food or me cooking for you?' There was that autocratic eyebrow of hers, raised in his direction.

'Definitely the former.' He forked another mouthful

of the delicious food into his mouth, chewed and swallowed. 'I'm very much an equal opportunities type of man. In my opinion, there is only one thing a woman can do that a man can't.'

'Give birth.'

'Exactly. There is no "woman's" work, or "men's" work. There is just work and the person best equipped for the task should take the lead.'

'Are you saying I'm a better cook than you, henceforth, I will need to do the cooking?'

This time, he couldn't help but laugh. 'Perhaps.'

'Well, then. I think you need to cook us dinner tonight and then we can judge who is better.'

'OK. Sounds like a plan.' He scooped up another mouthful and chewed his delicious food. When they'd finished, she stood and carried their dishes to the sink.

'Leave it. You cooked, I'll clean.' He stood and brought their glasses over.

She turned to face him, giving him her best 'don't argue with me' look. 'All right, but once you've done them you're to have a shower and go to bed. You need sleep, Oscar.'

'But, Daisy—'

'I'll head to the hospital,' she continued, ignoring his protest. 'And take care of the morning shift.'

'It's OK. I can—'

'Doctor's orders.' With one last glare she headed to the back door, took her hat off the hat rack where she'd put it earlier, and headed out of the door, leaving him standing there, staring at her as though he wasn't sure what had just happened. The knowledge put a spring in her step and a smile on her lips.

She couldn't remember the last time a man had made her feel this way. It wasn't as though she hadn't had relationships in the past but most of them had been well-suited matches, rather than based on attraction. During her senior years at a prestigious all-girls boarding school, she'd enjoyed flirting and laughing with the boys from the nearby prestigious all-boys boarding school. Even though the school had organised dances and other combined events, there had only been one or two of the boys who had taken her fancy.

Michael had most definitely been her favourite and they'd dated for at least a year. She'd often fantasised about marrying Michael, about travelling with him and running his charities. Then, in her second-to-last year of school, both male and female boarders had gone on a trip to Asia, where they'd learned how to build houses for those less fortunate. It had been an eye-opening time for her but Michael, although he'd excelled at everything they'd had to do, hadn't been affected in the same way. Daisy had wanted to do more and that was when she'd first become interested in studying medicine. Michael hadn't felt the same way and, even though she'd tried to convince him that they all needed to do more to help, his response had been to sleep with one of her friends, telling her that he was more than happy to keep dating her, to marry her even because she came from good breeding, but that if she wasn't happy with him living his own life, she would need to break up with him.

He hadn't felt at all guilty about the infidelity and it had been that attitude more than the act that had broken her heart. It was then she'd realised Michael had been cut from the same cloth as her father. From then on, she'd kept her distance from autocratic men and instead thrown herself into her studies. In her final year of medical school, she'd met Walter.

Daisy clenched her jaw at the thought of the man,

the man who had tricked her. No. She wanted to enjoy this sensation Oscar had evoked in her a little more. She didn't want to think about Walter, or Michael, or any of the other men who had let her down in the past. Right now, Oscar was making her feel light and happy and feminine. He was making her smile, was making her start to relax, and with all the pressures she'd faced during the past few years she needed to relax. Yes, perhaps Oscar Price really was the diversion she needed… for a while.

When Oscar finally arrived at the hospital it was almost midday.

'Sorry,' he said as he walked sheepishly towards where Daisy stood chatting with Tori. 'I didn't mean to sleep that long.'

'You obviously needed it,' Tori remarked.

'If you'd arrived here any earlier, I would have kicked you out,' Daisy told him, her words making Tori laugh with delight.

'Looks as though you've met your match, Oscar. She's as bossy as you,' the nurse joked.

'Hey,' he protested and put his arm around Tori's neck, playfully rubbing his hand on her head, just as an older brother would. Well, Daisy's older brother certainly wouldn't have behaved like that—ever. John had been born an adult and throughout Daisy's childhood he'd kept his distance, often complaining that she was too immature for him.

'But she's only seven years old,' their mother had told thirteen-year-old John. 'She's supposed to be immature.'

'No, she's not, Mother,' John had contradicted. 'Father says Daisy is to attend deportment lessons so she can have that tomboy streak knocked out of her because you certainly haven't been able to control her.'

Daisy closed her eyes as the thought entered her mind. Why had John talked to their mother in such a way? Why hadn't he shown her some respect? She knew the answer of course—because that was how he'd seen their father had always spoken to their mother, in front of their friends, in front of the staff, in front of their children. And her mother had allowed it because if she'd dared to tell John off, then he'd tell their father and then—

'Daisy?'

She opened her eyes and looked into Oscar's blue ones. 'Yes?'

'Are you all right?'

'I'm fine.' She drew in a cleansing breath and smiled politely at him. 'So, clinic this afternoon or house calls?'

'Both. Why don't you help me with the ward round as well and then we can head over to the clinic and I can explain things there to you and later show you how we organise the house calls?'

'OK.'

'I'll just stay here and monitor the entire hospital,' Tori remarked, sitting down in her chair, leaning back and putting her legs up onto the desk in a relaxed position. 'It's a tough job but someone's got to do it.'

With a shake of his head at Tori's antics, Oscar led the way to the ward. It was then Daisy realised he walked very quietly, no doubt a side effect from walking around wards at night in order to check on patients.

It was what he'd done to her the first night he'd gone out hunting. He'd crept into her room to check on her and, although she'd heard him, she'd pretended to be asleep. He'd lifted her hand and taken her pulse before pressing the backs of his fingers to her forehead.

'Good,' he'd whispered. 'In case you can hear me, I'm heading out on my hunting trip. I should be back around six-ish. Keep resting, Dr Daisy.'

Had he known she'd been faking? Had he just played along because he hadn't had the time to get into a full-on discussion with her? A few minutes later, she'd heard a car horn beep and Oscar's quiet footsteps moving through the house. 'I told him not to beep the horn,' he'd muttered before the front door had closed. Then she'd been left alone in a strange house, in a strange town, in a strange country.

Part of her had wanted to get up, to explore, to gather the lie of the land, but the other part had been far too tired. When she'd drifted off to sleep, she hadn't had a nightmare. Instead, there had been a man in her dreams, a man with a cheeky grin, a man with dark brown hair that was slightly greying at the temples, a man with twinkling blue eyes, a man who had looked a lot like Oscar.

After doing a ward round and being properly introduced to the ward staff, they headed back to the emergency department, half expecting to see Tori still sitting down with her feet up on the desk. Instead, they found her doing triage on two young children who had been brought in by one of the daycare workers.

'What's going on here?' he asked.

'Several of the children got into a sand-throwing fight.'

'Ah. Gritty eyes,' he remarked and picked up one of the young boys. 'I have just the superhero solution needed to fix your problem.' The young boy had been whinging and rubbing his eyes until Oscar spoke, but now he stared at the doctor, his little eyes red and clearly irritated by the sand and dirt.

'You do? Superhero solution?'

'Yes, I do,' he remarked, carrying the boy to room one. 'It's called super-saline solution.'

'Wow!'

'He's always been good with children,' Tori remarked. 'So sad it didn't work out between him and Magda.'

'Magda?' Daisy frowned. 'I thought his ex-fiancée's name was Deidre?'

'Oh. It was.' Tori seemed surprised. 'He's told you about Deidre?'

'Not much.' Daisy picked up the notes Tori had written about the other children with sand in their eyes, checking to see whether or not they had any allergies. It was all right for Oscar, who clearly knew every child's name and remembered their medical files off by heart, but she needed to read up on the notes first. Still, she glanced briefly at Tori, unable to stop herself from enquiring further. 'So, who's Magda?' And how many women had Oscar been involved with? If it hadn't been for Tori going on and on about how much she loved Scott, Daisy would probably have presumed that Tori was another one of Oscar's women.

'Magda was Oscar's wife,' Tori remarked, but that was all she said. 'Use room two for the twins.'

'They're twins?' Daisy remarked, looking down at the two boys who looked completely opposite. Clearly they weren't identical. 'Right.' She scanned the other set of case notes. 'No allergies, then?'

'No. Both clean,' Tori responded.

'Right.' Daisy looked down at the two boys. 'Let's get the two of you sorted out,' she said, the daycare teacher escorting her and the twins to room two. By the time she'd finished flushing out their eyes, helped along by quite a few tears, Daisy returned to the nurses' station to find Tori and Oscar chatting quietly. Clearly, from the way Oscar had his arm around Tori's shoulders and how the nurse was looking rather downcast, the topic of conversation was Scott.

'Everything all right?' she asked as she handed the completed case notes to Tori.

'I hate Scott,' Tori remarked and took the case notes to deal with them.

'What were you saying about it being interesting to be a spectator of other people's love lives?' He spoke quietly and shook his head. 'All I see at the moment are two of my friends in pain.'

'Do you think they'll be able to sort it out?' Daisy asked softly, watching as the nurse gave her complete attention to the case notes in front of her.

'I hope so.'

'Relationships aren't at all easy,' she remarked, wondering whether he'd mention his wife. Had she died? Had they divorced? Instead, he changed the subject.

'We'd better get to clinic. Otherwise, we'll be doing house calls at dinner time and we'll have to turn down all offers of food as you've tasked me to make dinner this evening.'

'Yes. I have, so please, lead on, Dr Oscar.'

As the day continued Oscar and Daisy did clinic for the rest of the afternoon, then headed over to the retirement village.

'How long do you usually allow for house calls?'

'Sometimes it can take all day.'

'All day?' She stared at him in shock. 'You have got

to be joking! This is another one of your little Australian jokes, isn't it? Scare the new doctor, type of thing?'

'I'm afraid not. There's at least sixty residents.'

'And we have to see all of them every day? Isn't there just a list of who might be needing medical treatment for that specific day?'

He grinned then and she realised he was teasing her once more. 'So this *is* another one of your jokes. I just want to know how giving me a heart attack counts as funny.'

'It's only because you're so easy to rile, Daisy.'

'Try and control yourself,' she responded dryly, and was answered with another of his deep chuckles.

'Sometimes house calls *can* take all day because we're not only general practitioners and surgeons, we're also occupational therapists, physiotherapists, counsellors and perhaps even a dentist. It all depends on what the issue is, how bad it is and how long it's going to take to transfer the patient to Alice Springs, or even, in some cases, Darwin. It depends on how much it's going to cost and—'

'All right.' She held up her hands. 'I get the point. We're a Jack of all trades.'

'Well, in your case, you'd be a Jill of all trades but that's just splitting hairs.'

'Yes, it is.' Daisy took a deep breath as they walked up the footpath of the first residential unit in the retirement village. 'Let's get started because I have a feeling this isn't going to be a quick introductory session.'

Oscar grinned at her attitude. Even though it might seem a daunting task, he was impressed with the way she squared her shoulders and tackled the situation. Given that throughout the entire time she'd been in

Meeraji Lake, she'd been sick, it was interesting seeing her as her normal, healthier self.

As Glenys opened the door Oscar stepped forward and spoke near Daisy's ear, his breath fanning her neck, making her aware of just how close he was. 'Of course, it'll take us a few days to get around to every resident properly. Fun times ahead.' Then he straightened and smiled brightly at Glenys. 'Hello there.'

'Ooh, goody. Am I first on the visitation list?' Glenys, who Daisy vaguely recognised as being one of the helpers during the emergency the other day, opened her door and ushered them both inside.

By the end of the day, they'd only managed to get around to five of the residents and afterwards Oscar insisted on taking her to the pub for a knock-off beer.

'It's all right. I don't need to go to the pub,' she told him.

'But it's an Australian legend and I wouldn't want all your prior research to go to waste. Surely you want to experience it at least once while you're here?'

'I don't drink alcohol,' she stated, expecting to be questioned, to have to justify herself. She stopped walking and crossed her arms over her chest. After everything her mother had been through, after everything she'd seen while growing up, Daisy was definitely a teetotaller. 'And I'd rather not go. Legendary or not.'

'You don't have to drink alcohol. In fact, I usually prefer an icy mocktail. That's a cocktail with no alco—'

'I know what a mocktail is, Oscar.' She started walking again, slowly at first. 'Do you drink alcohol?'

'Very rarely and usually it's only half a glass of champagne at a wedding or something like that.' He shrugged when she looked at him. 'I've been the only doctor here for over a year now. I don't have the luxury of being inebriated, even a little bit, not when a patient's life depends on my powers of deductive reasoning.' He lifted his arms out in front, mimicking a superhero.

'So why do you go to the pub?'

'To talk to people. To be sociable. In such a small town, it's just like going around to a friend's place and enjoying a drink while you're there. Even the local police officer, Henry, goes on a Friday. He doesn't drink either. Said he's seen too many drunks and what they can do to themselves.'

'Agreed.' They were passing the clinic and then she found herself stepping off the large gutter and crossing the wide road to get to the pub. 'Noisy already,' she remarked, bemused by the number of utility trucks and dirt-covered cars parked in the street.

'Welcome to a Meeraji Lake tradition,' he said as he opened the screen door for her. They found a table and, after she'd sat down, he immediately went to the bar to order their drinks. Several people called, 'G'day,' to her and she smiled politely and waved back.

When Oscar joined her again, he was holding two large glasses with straws and little umbrellas in them. She'd let him choose the mocktails and as she took her first sip she was pleasantly surprised at the fruity concoction. Oscar clinked his glass to hers and daintily pushed his umbrella to the side of the glass so it didn't poke him in the eye.

'Drinking the girlie drinks again, Doc?' one of the blokes at the bar called, the comment being received with raucous laughter.

'You need to get in touch with your feminine side, Bazza. Besides, you'll thank me for being sober the next time I have to put stitches into your head.' This time the raucous laughter was aimed at Bazza, who seemed to take the teasing in a good-natured way.

'Whenever there's a bar brawl, you'll find Bazza right in the middle of it,' Oscar explained to Daisy. He'd leaned closer to her so that she could hear him more clearly. Therefore, when she wanted to talk to him, she did the same, leaning nearer to his ear, trying desperately not to be so aware of his spicy scent or the way his hair was starting to curl around the back of his ear.

'I think it's too noisy in here for me. Besides, aren't you supposed to be cooking me dinner?' She could feel the warmth emanating from him and as she breathed in again she couldn't help the way his closeness made her feel. She felt protected, excited and nervous. These were not the emotions she wanted to have, especially when they pertained to her new colleague. After what had happened to her in the past, especially with her last disastrous relationship with Walter, which had almost tipped her precarious mother right over the edge and incensed her father, Daisy had decided that romantic entanglements weren't for her.

'Right you are.' Oscar nodded and drank the rest of his drink, indicating Daisy should do the same. It took her a few more sips than him but soon the icy liquid was gone. As they stood up Oscar placed an arm around her waist, more to guide her safely from the pub than anything else, and she had to say, with the number of farmers who seemed to be watching her every move, she was more than appreciative of his protective arm.

He dropped it back to his side once they'd crossed the road, then shoved both hands into the pockets of his shorts. It was odd, but right now she wouldn't have minded if he'd kept his arm in place, around her waist, drawing her close.

She had to admit that he wasn't what she'd been expecting. When she'd first arrived he'd been in the midst of an emergency and, even though she'd insulted him several times over, he hadn't been goaded into arguing with her. Then he'd cared for her, introduced her to people and generally been an all-round nice guy.

Yet all the while she had the distinct impression that he was definitely holding something back. He'd talked about Deidre. Tori had told her about Magda and it was clear he still felt the pain from the loss of his sister. Even though she was here to help, she was only due to stay for six months. What would he do then? Advertise again? Would he be lucky to get someone to answer the advertisement? Would he ever leave Meeraji Lake or was he planning to stay here forever? She knew it really wasn't any of her business but she was intrigued by the man.

As she watched him move around the kitchen, cooking a stir-fry for dinner, she couldn't help but notice his long legs, his lean body, his broad shoulders, his handsome smile. Rugged, good-looking and very capable. That was the best description for him.

'I think you're quite adept in the kitchen, Dr Oscar,' she told him as she ate the last delicious morsel of food.

'Thank you.'

'In fact, I'd say you're better than me.' Daisy placed her knife and fork together then laced her fingers and rested her hands in her lap. Perfect and poised, she sat there for a good ten seconds before he laughed and emphatically shook his head.

'Nice try, Daisy. There's no way I'm going to be able to do all the cooking.'

She smiled at him. 'Then I guess we'll just have to share.'

He raised his glass to her and when she did the same,

he clinked them together. 'To sharing,' he toasted and smiled that slow, gorgeous smile that turned her insides to mush. For some reason, she wondered whether he was talking about more than just the cooking. Did he have plans to share something else with her? Something to do with...romance? The thought warmed her through and through and, much to her surprise, she realised that the prospect wasn't completely distasteful. Not distasteful at all!

CHAPTER FIVE

DURING THE NEXT week Daisy slowly completed her induction to the retirement village, managing to speak to every single resident as well as being shown the hydroponics bay by several different enthusiastic gardeners, each one proud of their achievements.

'I don't know how many cups of tea I've drunk,' she told Tori as they worked a shift together. She'd been in Meeraji Lake for almost two weeks and she'd made a complete recovery from her heatstroke. 'But I've finally met everyone.'

'Even Mrs Piper was singing your praises in the ward this morning. She said you've managed to get her bumped up on the waiting list for her hip replacement.' Tori spread her arms wide. 'How did you manage that?'

'I know a plastic surgeon who works at Darwin hospital and he knows the orthopaedic specialist.' Daisy shrugged as though it were nothing.

'But Mrs Piper said she's being admitted as a private patient. She doesn't have the money to pay for private treatment.'

Daisy opened the next set of case notes that required her attention, not wanting to get too involved in this discussion with Tori just now. 'I know. It's being done as a favour to me.'

'Favour? Your request carries that much weight?'

'Apparently.' She pointed to the case notes. 'Can you remember whether this patient was transferred to Alice or Darwin? I can't find the transfer form.'

'Oh, that's because they're all here.' Tori handed her a pile of papers. 'I haven't had time to put them into the case notes. I was going to leave it for Adonni to do on the nightshift.' They went through the files, finding the correct form Daisy needed. She was thankful she'd been able to move the conversation away from Mrs Piper's hip replacement as the last thing Daisy wanted Tori—or anyone else in the town—to discover was that she had been the one to pay for Mrs Piper's private-patient privileges. After speaking to Mrs Piper during ward round over the past few days, Daisy had learned that Mrs Piper's sons had both been in the army, had both gone overseas as part of a peace-keeping mission, and had both been killed. Daisy had seen and experienced firsthand the devastation war could cause and, as the money didn't matter to her at all, it was the least she could do to ensure Mrs Piper experienced the best private-patient privileges.

'With me husband long dead, I only had me boys. Now I've got no one, except the people in this town. They're me family now.'

Daisy's heart had been filled with compassion for the woman and so she'd done everything she could to ensure Mrs Piper was not only bumped up the waiting list but also would receive the best treatment from the best orthopaedic surgeon at Darwin hospital.

'I've arranged for Glenys to travel with you,' Daisy had told Mrs Piper after it was all organised. 'That way, you won't be alone in a strange hospital and, with Glenys being an ex-nurse, she'll be able to help you out afterwards, make sure you're weight-bearing correctly.'

Mrs Piper had beamed so brightly, Daisy's heart had been warmed through and through and she'd slept very well that night, snuggling beneath the blankets as the evening temperature dropped. She was slowly getting used to the extreme temperatures of the Meeraji Lake district, with it being over thirty degrees Celsius during the day but then dropping to three or four degrees overnight.

Back at the doctors' residence later that evening, Daisy realised she was quite content with her decision to spend six months here in the Australian outback. Perhaps if things went well, they'd allow her to extend her contract. She might even be able to bring her mother out to Australia for a few months, to spend some time with her and to get away from Daisy's overbearing father.

With that thought in mind, she rang her mother and asked how she was feeling.

'I'm doing fine, Daisy,' her mother responded, her words firm and decisive. 'Stop fussing, dear.' Daisy closed her eyes and tried to stop the tears from springing to them. 'I'm absolutely fine. Great, in fact. Your father had a party last night and it was a lot of fun. I was the perfect hostess and an absolute hoot!'

Her mother cut the conversation short and Daisy didn't try to dissuade her from hanging up. She'd already received the information she wanted to know. Whenever her mother was self-assured, firm and confident, it unfortunately meant that she'd given in to the drink. Daisy couldn't help the tears that started to pour down her cheeks. It didn't seem to matter how many times she managed to pull her mother out of the quagmire, helping her into rehab, helping her to stay sober, her father would always find a way to destroy the good work and drive her mother to drink once more. Then, on top of that, he'd berate her for being weak and giving in.

When Oscar walked into the kitchen, she didn't even try to hide the fact that she'd been crying, she was that upset.

'Daisy? Daisy, what's wrong?' He was instantly by her side but she was too upset to answer him.

'It's…it's…' Even as she tried the words just wouldn't come. He put his hand on her shoulder and she flinched a little. He drew back, starting to feel uneasy, starting to worry about her. What on earth had made her so upset?

'Daisy? Can I get you a drink? Water? Tea? Iced tea?' What was he supposed to do? He tried putting his hand on her shoulder again and this time she didn't shrug off his touch. He gave her shoulder a little squeeze and offered her another tissue, moving the box closer to where she was for easier access.

'What can I do? Tell me. I want to help you.'

'You can't.' The words were wrenched from her and she shook her head. 'You can't help. *I* can't even help.' Her words were barely audible between her sobs.

Oscar gave her shoulder one more pat, then stalked to the cupboard, withdrew a glass and then went to the fridge, taking out the iced tea and pouring her some. If she hadn't already told him she didn't drink, he might have offered her something stronger to help steady her nerves. As it was, he needed to do something to help, trying to fix whatever small thing he could, and if that meant offering her a tissue and pouring her a drink, then that was exactly what he was going to do.

'It's all right, Daisy.' He put the drink in front of her but when she saw it, instead of stopping her tears, it only made her cry even harder.

'Don't be nice,' she mumbled between sobs and it took him a few seconds to understand what she'd said.

'Don't be nice? Why not? You'd be nice to me if the situations were reversed.'

'I don't know how to handle people who are nice to me.' She blew her nose and tried not to look at him.

'Why not?' He sat in the seat next to hers at the table and brushed some hair from her face. When she shied away, he started to worry. What on earth had happened to make her this upset?

'Don't look at me. I'm ugly.'

He smiled then, pleased to know the response to that statement. 'You are not ugly.'

'I'm all red and puffy and blotchy.' Her words were a little calmer now and she blew her nose again, catching her breath in hiccupping wisps. When she lifted the glass to her lips, he noted her hand was trembling slightly.

'You are a beautiful woman, Daisy Forsythe-York.'

'Don't call me that. Call me Dr Daisy. I like that. I don't want to be a Forsythe-York. I never wanted to be one.' She all but spat her surname then pushed the glass out of the way and slumped forward, resting her forehead on the table, her cell phone clattering to the ground. Oscar immediately picked it up and placed it next to the half-drunk liquid.

'What's happened, Daisy?' Surely she could see he was concerned about her. 'Has someone hurt themselves? Or worse?'

'No one has died, if that's what you mean.'

'I'm very pleased to hear that.'

She lifted her head and looked at him for a long moment before slumping back down onto the table. 'It's just…it's…stupid family stuff.'

'Ah.'

'I don't ever want to have a family of my own because that way I won't ruin my children the way my—'
She stopped then, lifting her head in shock, her eyes
wide, as though she realised she'd said too much. It was
only then Oscar began to realise that perhaps Daisy's
haughtiness wasn't due to her being rude but rather
was a type of defence mechanism to protect herself
from others. Had her childhood been bad? Had she been
abused? There were so many different types of abuse,
such as emotional bullying, and often people didn't even
know they were victims until much later in life.

'Daisy, it's all right,' he told her, placing a hand over
hers, thankful when she didn't shy away again. 'You
don't have to tell me anything you don't want to. I'll
listen. I won't pry and I won't try to fix your problems.'

'You couldn't even if you wanted to. If there's nothing I can do, then there's definitely nothing you can do.'
She dragged in another deep, shaky breath and stood
up, scooping up her phone from the table. 'I think I'll
go to bed.'

'OK.' He continued to sit at the table but Daisy didn't
move, still just standing there, as though weighing up
the pros and cons of whether or not to tell him what was
going on. He sat still, silent, patient. Then she picked
up the glass of iced tea and started towards her room.

'Goodnight, Oscar and…and thank you.'

'My pleasure,' he called as she disappeared into her
part of the house. And it was, he realised. His pleasure to have been a witness to that fragile, innermost
part of Daisy. He hadn't particularly understood what
she'd been saying, or why he wasn't allowed to be nice
to her, but she hadn't run away as soon as he'd entered

the room and he was going to count this as progress in getting to know her better.

As he lay awake in bed a while later, hands behind his head as he stared up at the whirring ceiling fan, Oscar couldn't help but replay the scene, trying to make sense of it. He hoped that Daisy was asleep, that she'd found some sort of peace. He wanted to go and check on her but, now that she was no longer sick, he didn't have any excuse for being in her part of the house.

Why had she been crying? Her cell phone had been on the kitchen table, which meant she'd just been talking to someone on the phone, but who? What had been said to upset her in such a way? Nothing made much sense only that, by some miracle, Daisy had actually accepted his support.

He knew of old, from his experience with Magda and Deidre, that women often had many layers to them. Daisy's outer layer seemed to be made up of an almost impenetrable hardness but inside…he was beginning to discover pure softness and that wasn't good. It wasn't good at all because he'd promised himself he would never become romantically involved with another colleague again. He'd already made two mistakes—*two!* Not only had Magda pulled the wool over his eyes, but Deidre had as well. Dating the women he worked with hadn't been successful in the past. What could possibly make him think it would work now with Daisy?

After he and Magda had married, she'd stopped nursing altogether, instead more than content for him to earn the money while she lazed around and did nothing. She had often told him that wasn't true, that she was networking behind the scenes, getting her nails done with the wives of other up-and-coming medical specialists. Magda had wanted the high life, the prestige of being a surgeon's wife. She'd never complained about the long hours he worked and she'd thrown great parties that had introduced him to several good contacts. However, in the end, it hadn't been what he'd wanted at all.

And Deidre? He closed his eyes and shook his head. He'd made a right ol' mess of that one. He'd ventured back into the ring of love and been knocked down and out. Why was it he seemed to choose women who had completely different agendas from him? Sure, they worked well, they laughed and they enjoyed themselves, but when it came to long-term life plans no one seemed to want what he wanted.

'And what do you want?' he growled into the dark, and a moment later a vision appeared of the doctors' residence being filled with children, his own children, the house bursting with love and laughter. It was the childhood he could remember, before his parents had passed away, his beautiful, fun-loving mother gone forever. Lucinda had done her best to provide him with a home but nothing had been the same ever again and now even his beloved sister had been taken from him.

All the women he'd ever cared about had left him, in one way or another. Was he cursed? Was he meant to be alone for the rest of his life, just him and his patients? Was he brave enough to step into the ring for a third time? Brave...or stupid? He wasn't sure which.

What he *was* sure of was the dream...the dream of staying here in Meeraji Lake, being a part of the community, of creating a stable and loving environment for his children, cooking a barbecue on the weekend, swatting flies, running around, playing games and all of it with the woman of his dreams at his side. The only problem was, he had no idea who the woman of his dreams was any more. It hadn't been Magda. It hadn't been Deidre. Could it be…Daisy?

'How's everything been going?' he asked the next day as he entered the ED. He'd just finished his Saturday morning clinic and Tori and Daisy were sitting at the nurses' station, going over some case notes.

'Apart from Mrs Piper still celebrating her good news, it's been fairly quiet,' Tori said, but a moment later the phone on the desk rang.

'Don't speak too soon,' Daisy and Oscar said in unison, then grinned at each other as Daisy picked up the receiver. 'Meeraji Lake District Hospital,' she stated. 'Dr Forsythe-York speaking.' She listened for a moment, then started taking notes. Tori handed Oscar two sets of case notes.

'Patients in rooms one and two just need you to review before admission,' she said. Oscar accepted the case notes and headed off to room one. It was five minutes later when he returned to the nurses' station to find Daisy still on the phone.

'Emergency,' she mouthed and handed him the piece of paper where she'd taken neat and meticulous notes. 'Yes,' she said into the phone. 'OK. So the helicopter…' She paused. 'Good. Thank you, Henry. I appreciate your assistance in this matter.' She disconnected the call and turned to face him. 'Henry's organising the police side of the emergency,' she told him, but Oscar wasn't listening.

He pointed to the piece of paper in his hand. 'Gracie? This has happened to Gracie Penderghast?'

'You know her?'

'I know everyone in the district.'

'I've requested her case notes and Tori is organising the rest of the emergency retrieval team.'

'And I heard you've already requested the helicopter so we'll have a meeting in a minute or two in the staff kitchen and you can give a debrief of the situation. Do you want me to take control of the team?'

'I think it's best given it's my first retrieval and, although I've read all the hospital's protocols, the staff—and some of the patients—don't have confidence in me yet.'

Oscar placed a hand on her shoulder. 'They will do. Things take time.'

'Things always take time.'

There was a hint of sadness to her words and Oscar angled his head to the side as he watched her. To say there were a lot of layers to the woman before him was an understatement. She was brisk, proficient and posh yet she'd gone above and beyond the call of duty several times since her arrival in Meeraji Lake.

'I'll go and get changed into the retrieval overalls and meet you in the staff kitchen,' she remarked before walking away. He stood there, like a fool, watching the way her hips moved, the way she swayed, the way her cool summery clothes made her look less austere than the suit she'd worn that first day.

When she disappeared into the female toilets, which also doubled as a changing room, Oscar knew he needed to concentrate on the emergency, to go through Gracie Penderghast's case notes, to check and see whether she was allergic to any medications and to prepare himself for the sight that awaited them. Gracie. Little seventeen-year-old Gracie! His sister, Lucinda, had been the midwife to deliver Gracie, Mr and Mrs Penderghast having given up any hope of ever having a child. She was their everything, and now she was hurt.

Oscar strode to the changing rooms, determined to do everything he could in order to save Gracie's life. When something drastic like this happened in the town, it didn't just happen to the people involved, it happened to everyone. They were a community and they stuck together like glue.

'We have to save her,' he muttered with determination as he came out of the changing rooms.

'We will.' Daisy spoke from behind him and Oscar spun around to face her. 'Sorry. I didn't mean to startle you.' They headed towards the briefing together but before they entered the room, Daisy surprised him further by slipping her hand into his and giving it a little squeeze.

'You're not alone in this, Oscar. I'm here to help. Whatever you need me to do, I'll do. I just wanted you to know that.'

He stood still for a moment and stared into her eyes. How had she known just the right thing to say? He'd momentarily forgotten that he wasn't the only doctor on staff now. He had back-up. He had help and Daisy was letting him know that she was there for whatever he needed. On a professional level, he appreciated the courtesy. On a personal level, it meant that Daisy Forsthye-York really was quite an extraordinary woman.

CHAPTER SIX

THE SCENE WHEN the retrieval team arrived at the remote part of the Penderghasts' property was not one of hysterics, for which Daisy was exceedingly grateful.

'You'll find that most country folk keep a cool and calm head in emergency situations.' Oscar's words were quiet as they started to gather up their medical equipment. 'They're a strong, tough, matter-of-fact breed of person.'

'Sorry?' Had she spoken out loud or could he now read her thoughts?

'Just in case you were wondering.' He kept his head bent as they left the helicopter and walked carefully towards the patient, who was sitting upright, knees bent helping to cradle her right arm and shoulder.

'Hello. I'm Daisy,' she remarked as she took off her medical backpack and knelt down next to Gracie.

'The new doc,' Gracie said.

'Good.' Daisy nodded and smiled, pleased with Gracie's cognitive function. 'That's right.'

'Hey there, Gracie.' Oscar knelt down on the other side of the teenager. 'Having a bad day, eh?'

Gracie laughed without humour. 'It's not my best, Oscar.'

'We're going to get you sorted out,' Daisy told her. 'I've dealt with this type of injury before.'

'And so have I,' Oscar added. 'So you are most definitely in good hands.'

'Well, that's good because I've almost ripped my right arm completely off,' Gracie said, seemingly not at all hysterical about her injury.

'You're very calm about it,' Daisy stated as she pulled on a pair of gloves and checked Gracie's right shoulder. 'Have you already been given something for the pain?'

'No. I've been injured before.'

'Yes, she has. She's broken her leg—'

'When I fell off my horse,' Gracie added.

'She's had a fractured jaw.'

'When I flew off the mechanical bull and landed on my face.' Gracie even grinned. 'I was almost fourteen then.'

'She's had her appendix out, is due to have her wisdom teeth out soon and has generally turned her parents' hair grey with her antics.'

Gracie grinned then flinched, her expression changing immediately when Daisy carefully touched her shoulder.

'Sorry. Sorry,' Daisy instantly said. 'Now you can add a dislocated shoulder to that list.'

'It's dislocated?' Gracie accepted the anaesthetic green whistle Oscar was holding out to her to breathe in. 'Oh, great. I love these things. They're the best part about getting hurt.'

Daisy frowned for a moment, concern touching her eyes. Had Gracie hurt herself on purpose?

'It's not what you think,' Oscar said as though he truly could read her mind. 'Gracie's just a typical outback kid. Rough as guts and tough as nails.'

'Yeah. I'm actually in a lot of pain,' she said, honesty in her eyes. 'But I knew you'd get here sooner or later.

Scotty wasn't going to leave me but he had no reception on his phone in this part of the land. Plus, I knew as soon as my parents found out what had happened—' Gracie flinched again and even whimpered a little '—that they'd be worried and so I told Scotty to stay at the house with them, that I'd be OK until you lot showed up.' She swatted at one of the many flies surrounding them with her left hand but then moaned in pain.

'Will you just sit still?' Oscar chided the teenager, a small smile on his face. 'Look, here comes Tori so you'd best behave yourself. You know she'll tell you off.'

Daisy couldn't help but smile herself as the nurse, carrying the portable stretcher and other equipment they'd need, took one look at Gracie and tut-tutted.

'What have you been up to now, Gracie Pend-erghast?'

'I was helping Scotty out here with the post-hole digging and got my arm caught in the auger.'

'That's the screw-like part which slowly digs down into the ground,' Oscar added for Daisy's benefit.

She raised a haughty eyebrow at him. 'I know what an auger is, Dr Price.'

'Of course you do,' he remarked with a slight hint of humour in his tone, his blue eyes momentarily twinkling with amusement. While they talked, or, more correctly, while they listened to Gracie explain what had happened, Oscar snapped pictures with his cell phone and took a bit of video as well. 'I think I've got it all,' he stated quietly to Daisy and nodded that they could start checking, debriding and bandaging the wounds as well as strapping the teenager's shoulder, getting her as ready for transportation as they could.

'Anyway, there was a lot of brush scrub in the way and we couldn't get the auger—' She gestured with her left hand and was once again told to sit still from both Oscar and Tori. 'Sorry. Well, Scotty didn't know I wasn't clear, or I think I'd yelled that I was clear but then I saw another bit I had to clear and went for it, thinking I had time but—' She glanced momentarily at her bloodied arm, her hand almost unrecognisable. 'But I didn't.' She paused for a moment, allowing Tori to offer her a drink of water. 'It's all a bit hazy and Scotty said it could have been heaps worse.'

Even when Tori put a neck brace around Gracie's neck, it still didn't stop her from chatting away and it was then Daisy realised that the chattiness was actually Gracie's way of dealing with the trauma her body was presently facing.

As Tori offered assistance to Daisy and Oscar, the two doctors worked exceptionally well together, putting in an IV line in order to boost Gracie's fluids, performing observations and reporting their findings to each other.

'Aren't you going to put my shoulder back into position?' she asked.'

'First we need to check you haven't fractured your shoulder, because if that's the case we can't relocate it. The X-rays will give us the information we need,' Oscar replied.

'I get to go in the chopper again. Am I going to Alice Springs hospital?' she asked Oscar as she took in another deep breath from the magic green whistle that contained midazolam. Chances were Gracie would hardly remember any of this but Daisy had to admit she would rather deal with a chipper, chatty teen than a screaming, sobbing one.

'You'll be going to Darwin,' Oscar remarked.

'Oh.' That stopped Gracie for a moment. 'But only

the really bad cases go to Darwin.' It was then Daisy noted Gracie's chin start to wobble and her breathing instantly increased, anxiety reflected in her eyes. Daisy glanced across at Oscar, read the matching concern in his own expression before returning her attention to Gracie, making sure she affected an air of nonchalance.

'Actually, you're only going to Darwin because I was the one to organise your transfer and one of my old army chums works in Darwin. He's the plastic surgeon there and he really is the best.'

'So you didn't know emergencies were supposed to go to Alice Springs?'

'Exactly and also because I really wanted you to have the best treatment and Timothy Hartfell is the best plastic surgeon I've ever met.'

'Oh, well, that's really nice of you, Daisy. Thanks.' Gracie's breathing seemed to settle down and Oscar breathed a sigh of relief, mouthing the words 'thank you' to Daisy. She felt so thrilled that she found herself doing something she'd never thought she would: she winked at Oscar, as though to reassure him that everything would be fine with their patient.

Oscar's answer was to smile so brightly at her that for one split second she actually forgot what she was doing, forgot where she was, forgot even her own name. How could he do that to her…and with just one bright smile?

'So how do you know this plastic surgeon Timothy dude?' Gracie asked, her question instantly snapping Daisy's attention away from the confusing way Oscar made her feel and back to the task at hand.

'I know, she's been in the country for the blink of an eye and already she's pulling strings and calling in favours.'

Daisy laughed and he felt as though he'd just been

punched in the solar plexus. She was stunning. So stunning, she took his breath away and he couldn't help but be dazzled by this incredible woman. How was it she was able to affect him in such a way with just a smile? Her teeth were perfectly straight, indicating braces in the past. Her eyes were twinkling with such genuine delight as she told Gracie how she'd known Timothy since medical school and that they'd both served in the army.

He tried not to be bothered by the radiance in her tone as she continued to chat with Gracie while they worked. He should be pleased she was keeping Gracie talking, keeping the girl's anxiety under control, yet for some reason he felt a pang of one hundred per cent jealousy at the mere mention of Timothy Hartfell's name.

He tried to push the sensation away, telling himself that Daisy was nothing more than a colleague—a stunning one, but that was all she was. Yes, he liked her. Yes, he found her attractive and yes, he wanted to get to know her much, much better.

Then they could hear a car engine in the distance and as it drew closer they realised it was Scotty. 'Docs, you're here. You're here. Thank God.' Scotty had barely brought the ute to a stop before he was out of the vehicle and racing towards them, dust and flies and the heat of the afternoon starting to descend upon them all. 'How is she? Gracie, honey? How are you?'

'How's Mum and Dad?' Gracie asked as Tori started setting up the stretcher.

'They're OK. I didn't tell them exactly how bad the injury was.'

'But it *isn't* that bad,' Gracie told him.

'Have a little bit more of the green whistle,' Oscar encouraged. They just needed to keep Gracie nice and calm for a bit longer. Once they had her in the helicopter, they could give her stronger analgesics.

'Bill was out and about doing his rounds so I managed to get him on the phone too and he's staying with your parents until we knew more about how you were doing. Your dad wanted to come out here with me but—' Scotty shook his head '—I said he'd be better off packing you a bag of stuff to take to hospital.'

'And you're sure Dad's OK?' Gracie's tone held concern for her father and Daisy wondered what had happened to Mr Penderghast in the past to put such wisdom into those young eyes of hers.

'Yes. Bill's checked his heart and everything's fine. He's not going to have another heart attack, Gracie.'

'Good.' At this news that her aged parents were indeed OK, Gracie sagged against Oscar.

'Scotty, help Tori with the stretcher then tell the pilot that we're almost ready to get going to Darwin.'

'Darwin? She's going to Darwin? She's not that bad, is she?' Scotty remarked but Tori hit his arm, telling him to be quiet. Daisy could hear Tori whispering briskly to Scotty and decided it was best to distract Gracie with more chatter.

'Tell me, Gracie. Do you still ride a horse?'

'Am I an Aussie?'

'That question implies that all Australians ride horses.'

'Perhaps all outback Aussies do,' Oscar added as they finished applying the top set of bandages and strapping to Gracie's arm.

'Then I can tick one box on my list,' Daisy told the teen.

'What list?'

'My list of what I need to do to become an honorary Aussie.'

Oscar chuckled then as Tori gave him the thumbs up that they were ready to get Gracie onto the stretcher. 'If you're going to become an honorary Aussie, Daisy...'

'Yes,' she drawled, raising one haughty eyebrow. Gracie giggled at the sight of the two of them teasing each other, then winced as though she remembered that her body really wasn't doing the best right now.

'Well...uh...then I think we're going to need to teach you how to speak with an Aussie twang. None of this upper-crust Britishness out here.'

'I beg your pardon. There is nothing whatsoever wrong with my accent.'

Tori and Scotty laughed, everyone trying to keep the atmosphere as light as possible so the teenager didn't go into shock.

'Don't worry, Daisy,' Gracie said just before they all got into position to shift the teenager to the stretcher. 'I'll teach you some Aussie words on the helicopter ride to Darwin.'

'Thank you, Gracie. That's exceedingly kind of you.' Daisy glared at Oscar, as if to teasingly imply that he wasn't being kind. He opened his mouth to reply but whatever he'd been about to say was drowned out by the drone of the helicopter blades.

They managed to get Gracie onto the stretcher but as they were strapping her in Daisy noticed that the look of panic was back. She glanced at Oscar but realised he'd seen it, too. With the sound of the helicopter making it impossible for them to continue to converse with Gracie, she was now starting to think more about what had actually happened to her, about what it might mean by being transferred to Darwin. It was a further distance away from Meeraji Lake, which would no doubt make it difficult for her parents to be with her for any length of time.

'Gracie. Gracie,' she called. 'What words are you going to teach me first?' she asked.

'Uh…umm.' Gracie's breathing was starting to increase and as they started carrying the stretcher towards the helicopter panic filled the teenager's eyes and she started to cry.

'Try and stay calm, Gracie. You've done an amazing job,' Oscar yelled, bending down to speak as close to her ear as he could, but it was difficult when they were all carrying the stretcher, plus having their medical bags on their backs and bending down as they drew ever closer to the whirring chopper blades overhead.

'How long is the flight to Darwin?' Daisy asked Oscar.

'Probably about an hour, maybe a little more,' he yelled.

'And how many bags of fluid do we have?' but her question fell on deaf ears as Oscar continued to watch the teenager, her eyes wide, her breathing becoming more and more erratic.

'Gracie? Gracie, can you hear me?'

She opened her mouth to speak but nothing came out and a moment later she started to shake.

'She's going into shock.' They were almost at the helicopter now, all of them walking more quickly but also being careful they didn't trip over any of the small branches and stringy bark that littered the ground around them.

'Adrenaline is starting to decrease.' Oscar's voice seemed to boom through the area and all of them knew that the sooner they got her into the helicopter, the sooner they'd be able to treat her. It took less than a minute to lift the stretcher into the waiting chopper but it seemed like an eternity to Daisy.

As Tori and Scotty locked the stretcher into place Oscar took his bag off his back and searched through it for the medication he needed. 'She's been so brave for so long,' Daisy stated as she started doing Gracie's observations, while Tori changed over the bag of plasma in order to keep Gracie as hydrated as possible.

'Scotty, wrap the space blanket around her,' Daisy instructed after reporting her observational findings to Oscar. When Tori had finished changing over the plasma bag, Oscar used the IV line to inject some morphine, knowing it would help settle Gracie down even more and keep her calm during transport.

'If you and Oscar take her to Darwin, I'll go back with Scotty and check on Gracie's parents and let them know what's happening,' Tori stated. 'I can organise a flight for them to Darwin so they can be by her side.'

'Thanks.' Daisy pulled off her gloves and put on her headphones, sitting in the seat next to Gracie's, and buckled her seat belt, noting Oscar was doing the same.

'Do you know if anyone has contacted Darwin hospital? And even if they have,' she continued before he had a chance to reply, 'do you think it would be at all possible if I could speak to Timothy before we land? I'd like to give him a fair assessment of what he'll be dealing with.'

Oscar nodded and spoke to the pilot through his headset microphone, asking when it would be possible to get someone from Darwin hospital on the radio.

'We'll be in radio range fairly soon,' came the reply.

'Thank you.' Daisy spoke into her own microphone as she watched Oscar hook a stethoscope into his ears and listen to Gracie's breathing. The teenager's previous agitation seemed to have settled down due to the morphine doing its job. 'It would be good if we could also send Timothy the photos you took.'

'I want to have a better look at them.' Oscar nodded. 'Do you think we'll be able to stay and assist with the surgery? I mean, is this Tim a decent sort or more of a get-out-of-my-theatre type of bloke?'

'Timothy—' she spoke his full name with emphasis '—is most definitely a decent sort of chap and I'm hopeful he'll allow us to at least be present in Theatre. I've assisted with this sort of surgery before and the last one we did took almost twelve hours for the initial surgery. With surgery that long, oftentimes you need to accept all the help you can.'

'We're in range now.' The pilot's voice came through their headphones. 'I'll try and make the connection.' As he did Oscar and Daisy kept monitoring Gracie closely.

'Go ahead, Daisy,' the pilot stated and a moment later Daisy heard Timothy's voice through her headphones.

'Daisy?'

'Timothy.'

'This is getting to be a habit, Dr Forsythe-York,' he stated in his clipped British tones, which seemed to sound perfect alongside Daisy's. 'First you call me about Mrs Piper and show off with your do-gooder generosity and now you no doubt want another favour…or two.'

'Oh, do shut up, Timothy. Listen, I'm bringing a patient to you. A young teenage girl whose right arm got caught in a post-hole digger. Multiple lacerations, dislocated shoulder and olecranon, multiple fractures and extensive tissue damage.'

'Ah. We had been notified of the transfer but I didn't realise you were the treating doctor.'

'One of the doctors,' she added, and continued to explain the situation, giving an update on Gracie's present condition. Oscar added his own opinion to the conversation and let Timothy know he'd taken photographs.

'Is it possible for you to send them to my phone? Daisy should have the number.'

'Still the same one?' she checked.

'Yes.'

'Splendid. We'll get them off to you directly.'

Had her accent become softer as she'd spoken to Timothy? Oscar had to admit that they did sound good together, relaxed, at ease but, then again, they had known each other since medical school so it was only natural they'd speak to each other as old friends because that was exactly what they were.

But were they more than just old friends? It meant nothing to him, of course. He was merely curious… curious about Daisy, about who she really was beneath that sometimes brisk exterior. Never before had a woman intrigued him so much and where that knowledge should have made him cautious, it merely continued to fuel the fire.

Daisy Forsythe-York was an enigma and it was an attribute he found incredibly alluring.

CHAPTER SEVEN

THEY SPENT FAR too many hours in Theatre, watching Timothy and his team perform a miracle. They were even allowed to step in and assist when one of the other doctors became too tired. At one stage, the situation didn't look good and there was a possibility that Gracie might actually need to have her hand amputated, but thankfully that didn't happen. At that moment, Daisy was glad that outback Aussies were as rough as guts and as tough as nails.

'Finally we're out of surgery!' Oscar shuffled out of the theatres, pulling off his cap. 'And that isn't going to be her last operation, poor kid.' Gracie was being wheeled to the intensive recovery unit where she would be closely monitored. 'I haven't done a stint like that since I was an intern.' He smothered a yawn.

'If you don't like it, then never join the armed forces.'

He frowned a little at the tone of her voice. 'I wasn't criticising,' he countered softly and was surprised to see Daisy look instantly contrite.

She closed her eyes for a brief moment before shaking her head. 'I didn't mean it like that.' She hesitated, biting the corner of her lip as she shifted nervously from foot to foot. 'Sometimes, Oscar, when I'm tired…' Daisy paused, forcing herself to say the words even though she already knew what the reaction was going to be. 'It sometimes comes across as being flippant or contradictory or rude. All I meant was that life in the armed forces can be a little…'

'Out of the ordinary?' he supplied and she instantly nodded.

'Yes. Exactly.' She held one hand out to him. 'See? You do understand.' She shook her head as she pulled off her theatre cap and tossed it into the appropriate bin. Then she took out the band and clips that were holding her hair into a loose bun.

Oscar gasped as she raked her fingers through the long locks to try and untangle them. She glanced surreptitiously at him only to find him staring at her in a way that said he most definitely found her attractive. He wasn't leering, he was…looking. And for some reason, she found she liked it. She quickly glanced away, unsure what she was supposed to do when he looked at her in such a way, his eyes saying that he wanted to take his sweet time kissing every inch of her face, to explore the delights she could offer, to savour the flavours of her mouth.

Daisy took a step towards the door. 'I think I'll get changed.' She was shocked to discover her own voice sounding husky and filled with a hint of desire. There was no denying that Oscar Price was an incredibly good-looking man, giving the cliché of tall, dark and handsome some depth of meaning. He was so incredibly different from her past boyfriends that she wondered if that was the reason she was feeling this attraction towards him.

'OK. I'll meet you in the doctors' tearoom and we can decide where we're going to stay tonight.'

Daisy glanced at him again and immediately wished

she hadn't. He'd taken a few steps towards the door and was reaching out past her to push it open. She stood, stuck to the spot, unable to move as she looked up at him, his body close to hers. Lifting her chin, she tried desperately to make her usually intelligent mind work yet all she was aware of was his warmth, his subtle spicy scent still evident even after the long and hot day they'd endured. He exuded everything that was the epitome of masculinity. She edged further away, trying desperately to have her legs compute the signals her brain was sending but all she felt when she moved were more tingles, more awareness of just how much Oscar's closeness was affecting her. She needed to either get out of the room, or throw herself into his arms. That thought alone helped her to snap her mind back into gear.

'Well... I shall go and get changed and...er...meet you in the doctors' tearoom where we can continue with the conversation about where best to stay this evening.' With the politest smile she could paste onto her lips, she continued to back out through the open doorway, desperate to ensure not one part of their bodies touched. When she was clear, she all but sprinted back towards the female changing rooms, unable to believe everything that had happened in the past five or so minutes. She caught a glimpse of herself in the mirror and stared in shock. Her cheeks were indeed red, her eyes were dark with a repressed desire and her lips looked plumper than she'd ever seen before. Her loose hair was in a wild mess around her face and shoulders, making her look nothing like the poised finishing-school graduate that she was.

Why had she felt the sudden urge to throw herself into Oscar's arms? Was it because the other night, when he'd comforted her, she'd felt as though he'd really cared? He'd listened to her blubbering, he'd fetched her a drink, he'd been attentive and kind. He'd supported her and she hadn't had that kind of support… especially from a man she found attractive…for a very long time. There was no use denying to herself that she was attracted to Oscar. She'd lied to herself many years ago, believing her family life was a normal one, and when she'd realised the truth she'd vowed never to lie to herself again. However, although she might accept that she was attracted to Oscar, she also knew there was really nothing she could do about it. At the end of her contract here, she would need to return to the UK, to make one more effort to get her mother into rehab again.

Her mother. Daisy sighed and shook her head. How was she supposed to support her mother effectively from the other side of the world? It was so difficult and gut-wrenching to watch someone you loved waste away from such a disease, especially one that could be helped. She bit her lip and closed her eyes for a split second, remembering how upset she'd been just after speaking to her mother on the phone. Poor Oscar hadn't known what to do and Daisy hadn't known what to say. She *couldn't* tell him. She'd made that mistake years ago with Walter and it had—

No. She wouldn't rehash the past. She'd made a mistake once and she'd learned from it. Talking about her family life was taboo and, besides, she doubted Oscar needed to be bothered by her personal problems. So long as she did her job well, so long as she supported him with the medical needs of the town, then that was all she had to be concerned with. She most certainly didn't need to be distracted by the way he made her feel, by the way he would sometimes stare at her mouth as though he wanted nothing more than just to gather her close and kiss her senseless. Even at the thought, Daisy had to sit down on the bench in the changing rooms because her knees had suddenly decided to give way. Oscar Price was gorgeous. She couldn't deny that and the more she got to know him, the more she liked him as a person.

But they came from very different worlds. His life was clearly here in Meeraji Lake and her life was… At this moment, she had no idea where her life was. It didn't seem to be in England or working with the army or living in the outback. She was in limbo and she didn't like it one little bit.

Daisy started to feel exhaustion setting in. She'd been running on adrenaline ever since they'd received the call about Gracie, but as she changed out of the theatre scrubs into her own clothes and tidied her hair back into its neat bun again she couldn't seem to stop yawning.

Wherever Oscar was planning to stay, she sincerely hoped it wasn't too far away and when she met him in the doctors' tearoom, she still continued to yawn.

'Good thing we're not planning to head back to Meeraji Lake. You're wrecked,' he said.

'Sorry, I'm…' She yawned. 'I'm trying not to yawn.'

'Go ahead.' He yawned as well and she couldn't help but smile. 'How about we stay across the road in the emergency medical accommodation?'

'We wouldn't be putting other doctors out of a bed, would we? I'm happy to stay at a nearby hotel or something.'

'I'll give the place across the road a call and see what the score is.' Oscar headed to the phone on the wall and dialled the appropriate extension. As he organised their accommodation, she went to the sink and had a glass of water. She was still supposed to be keeping her fluids up after the heatstroke, but after such a gruelling long stint in Theatre it was no wonder she was feeling a little dehydrated.

'All done. Plenty of room with beds to spare for others who may need them. They're also organising for some meals to be sent over.'

'That's very nice.'

'It appears young Gracie is something of a celebrity in medical circles. After all, it isn't every day someone comes in with such an injury and requires extensive surgery to put them back together and, therefore, the doctors who have been looking after her are also entitled to the celebrity treatment.'

'Excellent.' Daisy yawned again and in the next instant realised Oscar was by her side with his arm about her waist.

'Let's get you across the road. You need food and sleep.' They left the doctors' tearoom, Oscar keeping his arm firmly around her waist in case she should collapse. She really was that tired and she was annoyed with herself for feeling so vulnerable when he was around. She needed to keep her guard up, especially when she was this exhausted.

'Could we possibly organise a toothbrush from somewhere, do you think? I can't sleep properly without brushing my teeth.'

'I remember,' he said softly.

'Pardon?'

'That first night when you were delirious from heat exhaustion, you kept asking for your toothbrush.'

'I did?' Embarrassment flooded through her. 'I'm terribly sorry I was such a nuisance.'

'You weren't a nuisance, Daisy. Far from it.'

'Are you laughing at me?' she asked as he led her from the theatre block, calling a few goodbyes to people he knew. Daisy wasn't sure it was a good idea for the two of them to walk through the area with his arm firmly around her waist but at the moment she also wasn't sure whether she could walk unassisted.

'Not at all.'

'Why is it that since I landed in this country, I've been nothing but tired?'

This time he did chuckle. 'Probably because you've been pushing yourself too far, too fast.'

'I always do that. It's my thing.' Her words were barely audible as she yawned twice while speaking.

Daisy wasn't sure of which way they were going but she trusted Oscar to get her where she needed to be. It was odd to be trusting someone she barely knew, but she did. She did trust him. She wasn't sure she'd ever trusted anyone so quickly and she'd had to work in war zones where she'd been reliant upon other people to protect her life. She'd trusted them—in the end—but in the beginning she'd been concerned they wouldn't be able to keep her safe.

Oscar ensured she ate something and then, much to her surprise, he produced a toothbrush and tiny tube of toothpaste from behind his back like a magician. She laughed and gratefully brushed her teeth before slipping between the cool, cotton sheets, the ceiling fan whirring gently overhead.

When Daisy awoke the next morning, she had no idea where she was. She lay still, eyes opened, taking in the surroundings of the room. The whir of the ceiling fan helped her to remember she was in Australia and she relaxed, knowing that it would only take a few weeks before she could wake up and not be alarmed by that feeling of not knowing where she was.

Closing her eyes, she snuggled deeper beneath the sheet, the heat of the day already trying to sneak in behind the closed curtains. It was only then she realised that the light was coming in from a different direction. How was that possible? The curtains in her room were on the left and these curtains were on the right.

She opened her eyes and sat bolt upright in the bed, looking around the room. Then it all came flooding back to her. The emergency with Gracie, staying overnight in Darwin. Oscar! She glanced at the other side of the bed but he wasn't there. She listened carefully. Was he in the en-suite bathroom? She'd been so utterly exhausted the night before, she couldn't remember much of what had happened. Exhaustion had always been her Achilles heel. When she was tired, she became a little delirious. Now, though, she was wide awake and very alert but still couldn't hear any sounds from the bathroom.

Flicking back the sheet, she stood, pleased to see that she was still dressed in the clothes she'd worn beneath her retrieval overalls yesterday. Creeping around to the bathroom, she listened at the closed door for a moment. No sounds. She knocked. No answer. She tentatively opened the door but the room was empty. She quickly made use of the facilities and, when she exited the bathroom, she jumped with surprise at finding Oscar in the room, setting down a tray of food.

'I didn't hear you.' She placed a hand onto her chest in a vain attempt to still her erratic heartbeat. Was it beating so erratically because he'd surprised her? Or because he looked incredibly handsome and refreshed? He, too, was wearing the clothes he'd had on under his retrieval overalls but his hair was slightly damp and his eyes were glowing with a refreshed delight and…and… the man simply looked absolutely gorgeous.

'Is it raining outside?' she asked, knowing that, as Darwin was in the tropics, it would often have torrential rains and still be over thirty degrees Celsius with exceptionally high humidity.

'I had a shower before I went out.'

'Oh. I didn't hear anything. Guess I really was sound asleep.' As she spoke she started to plait her hair, needing to have it out of the way. Oscar wished she wouldn't because she had looked absolutely incredible with it flowing so freely around her shoulders. It had given her a more ethereal look, one of peace, one of contentment.

Last night, she'd woken after sleeping for two or so hours and sat up in bed.

'What's wrong, Daisy?' he'd asked, still a little dozy.

'Hair. Hurts. Need to take it out.' And then her clever fingers had quickly unwound her hair from its usual bun. Her eyes had still been closed and he hadn't been at all sure she was fully awake.

'Are you awake?' he'd asked.

'Of course I'm awake,' she'd replied in that haughty way of hers that he now found so incredibly charming. Daisy had been running her fingers through her now loose strands, tilting her head this way and that, her eyes closed. Good heavens, the woman was beautiful. Had she had no idea of just what she'd been doing to him, sitting there with her perfectly straight back? Tilting her head this way and that and exposing delicious glimpses of her perfect neck? Parting her lips and breathing out a perfect sigh of relief?

With her dark hair spread around her head on the white pillow, she had looked like the perfect vision of loveliness. It had been too much for him. Too much beauty. Too much perfection. Too much... Daisy—the woman who seemed to never be leaving his thoughts. He'd needed to get control. To stop thinking about her in that way. Yes, he was incredibly attracted to her, an attraction that seemed to increase with every passing day he spent in her company, but there could be no future for them. She had her own life to live and he doubted she would want to live it in Meeraji Lake. He wanted the dream, the fairy tale of house, wife, children. Family life. He wanted the typical family life and he felt certain that, for perfect Daisy Forsythe-York, that sort of life would be too mundane.

He'd swallowed, his throat dry. 'Did you want a glass of water?' Without even waiting for her reply, he'd flicked back the covers and stood, walking to the en-suite.

'What are you wearing?'

He'd turned as the words had seemed to burst forth from her, then glanced down at his boxer shorts. 'My underwear. You might choose to sleep in your clothes but it's not my thing.'

Daisy had frowned at him even more. 'Can't you at least put on a robe?'

'I would, Daisy, if I had one. You're lucky I'm wearing these. I usually sleep naked.' He'd had his drink of water, then returned to the bed. It had been dangerous. Feeling this way about her, lying so close to her, and even though he'd known it was foolhardy, that Daisy would leave Meeraji Lake after her contract was complete, he hadn't been able to stop himself from shifting onto his side and propping himself up on his elbow to look at her.

It was only then he'd realised she'd fallen back into

the deep slumber she'd been in before. 'Daisy?' He'd whispered her name. 'Daisy? Are you awake?' His answer had been a small, soft snoring sound and he'd realised that she had indeed been very much asleep.

Lying back down, he'd exhaled a sigh of frustration. She was so close yet so far. Wasn't that the story of his romantic life? Wasn't that what had happened before with both the other women he'd loved? Loved? He didn't love Daisy. He knew that. It was just physical attraction and that was at least something he could control.

'Oscar?'

He blinked once, twice, then pushed aside the memory of last night and focused on her face. 'Sorry? What were you saying?'

She'd finished plaiting her hair and had wound it out of the way into a bun, securing it with another hair band. How it stayed in, he had no idea but all he knew was that she looked so incredibly beautiful first thing in the morning.

'I asked what was for breakfast, seeing as you've clearly gone to the trouble of obtaining it.'

'Uh…yes.' He lifted the warming covers off the food he'd brought in. 'First of all, we have a full English breakfast. Then orange juice, coffee and croissants with jam.'

Daisy peered at the food on the plate. 'Baked beans, scrambled eggs and bacon isn't exactly a full English.' Her stomach chose that moment to gurgle and she grinned. 'But it will definitely suffice.'

Any awkwardness she might have felt from him standing there, staring at her for a good thirty seconds, began to disappear and that comfortable camaraderie they'd established during the other breakfasts and dinners they'd shared seemed to return.

They discussed Gracie and Oscar told her that, while he'd been at the hospital heading to the cafeteria, he'd called by the intensive care unit and checked on the teenager. 'They're keeping her in an induced coma at the moment, in order for her body to recover from the shock of what really happened yesterday.'

'She was so brave. So incredibly stoic about everything.'

'But now reality is looming and she has to face the fact that if she develops complications throughout her recovery period, she may end up losing at least one or two fingers. Timothy, however, is amazing.'

'I know.' Daisy nodded as she took a sip of her coffee. 'He's always been that way. Always knew he wanted to specialise in plastics and to do that minutiae surgery.'

'So why did he go into the army? And what's he doing here in Australia? He could be earning a fortune in the States or in Britain.'

Daisy shrugged. 'Money and prestige aren't that important to him.'

That haughtiness was back in her tone but it was laced with annoyance. What had he said to upset her? 'Are they important to you?'

'No. Most definitely not.'

Well, that was at least something that was different from both Magda and Deidre, he realised.

'You're saying you're not driven by the need to make money?'

'No.' She shook her head and frowned at him. 'Money's not that important.'

'Aha. Only people who have money say that.'

Daisy clenched her jaw and glared at him, then stood from the table, carrying her coffee cup over to the window and most definitely giving him the cold shoulder.

'So you're telling me there's nothing going on between you and Timothy? You've been friends for years,
served in the army together and yet there's no romance
there?'

'Why does there need to be?' She threw the words
over her shoulder. 'Why can't two people simply be colleagues? Why does everyone expect there to be something romantic between us just because we've known
each other a long time?'

'Why are you getting so worked up over this?' Oscar
eased back in the chair. 'It's a simple question.'

'I haven't heard any question, only supposition and
allusion.'

'OK, then. Are you romantically involved with Timothy?'

'Why do you need to know?'

'Come on, Daisy. I just asked you a straight-out question and you're still not going to answer it?' When she
didn't immediately respond, still standing there at the
window with her back to him, he couldn't help but prod
a little further. 'It's not such an unusual question—
after all, you did come to Australia around the same
time he did.'

'That was completely coincidental.' She drank the
rest of her coffee and turned to glare at him. 'I don't
see what any of this has to do with you.'

'It's just seeing the two of you together, seeing how
you work well with each other, having your own shorthand to convey what it is you need the other to do—'

'We worked together in very difficult circumstances
in a very unsafe environment. Developing the shorthand
was necessary and came out of constant experience.
And besides, he is one of my closest friends. Probably

my oldest friend, if truth be told, and I actually don't have that many friends.'

'You don't?'

'No.' She walked towards the table and started clearing up their breakfast dishes.

'Do you want to talk about it?'

'No.'

'Does it have anything to do with the way you were crying the other night?'

'What? No.'

'Well, it's difficult to get a read on you, Daisy. You're so incredibly closed off. You keep yourself to yourself and, while that's generally fine in a large medical setting, at Meeraji Lake it's impossible to keep your distance from others without feeling ostracised by the township.'

'I understand that and I have actually been opening myself up to others.'

He shook his head at this. 'You've been receptive to others telling you things about themselves but you most certainly don't open yourself up to others. I've asked you a simple question and yet you've gone and blown it all out of proportion.'

'No. You were fishing. Wanting to know if there was anything romantic going on between me and Timothy because you have feelings for me.'

He raised an eyebrow at that.

'Oh, don't deny it. I've seen the way you look at me.'

'And I've seen the way you look at me,' he countered. 'So is there anything, other than friendship, going on between you and Timothy?'

'Why?' She spread her arms wide. 'Why is it so important for me to tell you the most intimate details of my life when I'll be gone in less than six months?'

'Why indeed?' he growled and, without another word, picked up the tray of dirty dishes and headed for the door.

'Where are you going?' she asked, but received no reply except for the room door closing behind him.

CHAPTER EIGHT

DAISY PACED AROUND the room, fuming with annoyance and swamped with regret. It wasn't fair to Oscar that she'd exasperated him by not providing him with the answers he wanted but, at the end of the day, it really wasn't any of his business whether or not she was involved with Timothy or anyone else for that matter.

Except that perhaps he'd been trying to ask her whether she was single, whether she was available for a...for a what? For a relationship that lasted for the duration of her contract? What sort of relationship did he want? She had to admit that the thought of getting closer to Oscar wasn't entirely unpalatable but what would be the point? She needed to return to the UK, to check on her mother, to do whatever it was that needed to be done to ensure that Cecilia didn't end up drinking herself into an early grave. Starting something with Oscar, especially when she knew it wouldn't end well due to the fact that they lived on opposite sides of the globe and wanted different things from life, would be ludicrous.

At least she thought they wanted different things from life. She hadn't really asked Oscar what he wanted but she was sure that, as he seemed to be a strong family-man sort of chap, a man who counted every person in the town and the surrounding district of Meeraji Lake as his family, he would most definitely want a family of his own. Was that the reason why he'd been married once and engaged the next time? His only problem, as far as she knew, was that he'd chosen the wrong women.

Daisy sat down at the table where they'd eaten their breakfast and slumped forward. It was such an unladylike pose and one she'd been told off for many times during her younger years at home. Even though she was thirty-eight years old, she could still hear her mother's admonishing voice, telling her to sit up straight, shoulders back. That was the way a lady sat. Daisy still hated the fact that the rules her parents had drummed into her seemed to resonate at the most inopportune moments.

When the door to the room opened, Daisy immediately sat up straight, her finishing-school training kicking in.

'Still here, eh?' Oscar walked into the room and headed to the bathroom to wash his hands.

'Where else was I supposed to go? I've already spoken to the hospital and received an update on Gracie. I don't know the city, I don't know where the airport is and I don't know how we're supposed to get back to Meeraji Lake.'

He came out of the bathroom, hand towel in his hands as he thoroughly dried them. 'I apologise, Daisy. I shouldn't have walked out on you. It's just that sometimes—' He threw the towel onto the bed and crossed his arms over his chest. 'Sometimes you drive me crazy.'

'The feeling is mutual.' She stood and faced him, mimicking his stance and crossing her arms over her chest. 'But…' She relaxed for a moment, dropping her hands to her side. 'You weren't totally blameless for what happened. I'm sorry, too. I didn't mean to rile you up.'

'It's just sometimes that—' he held out a hand towards her '—Britishness of yours really grates on my nerves.'

'And that Aussieness of yours does the same to mine. I don't have to tell you about every aspect of my life, Oscar. The residents of Meeraji Lake may like everyone knowing their business but I'm British. We don't talk about our feelings even when we want to.' She spread her arms wide. 'I've been raised to repress that natural urge to share, to discuss. I was told it wasn't ladylike to prattle on about one's problems or the mundane nuances of my life. I was warned that no one would be interested.'

'I'm interested.' He raked his hands through his hair. 'I *want* to know all about the mundane nuances of your life. I want to know if you have a boyfriend, a fiancé, a husband. I want to know what your favourite foods are, what colours you like, what plans you have for your future. I'm interested, Daisy.'

'Because you like me?'

'Yes!' He laughed with exasperation, then shook his head.

'Timothy is not my boyfriend. Not now, nor in the past and never in the future.'

'You can't be sure of that.'

'Oh, I can. You see, he's gay.'

Oscar stared at her for a moment, then blinked one long blink. 'I didn't...er...realise.'

'Not many people do. He likes to keep it quiet. He hasn't "come out" as they say nowadays. He's a respected surgeon, a brilliant surgeon and, believe it or not, his personal preferences can and will affect his career if it becomes common knowledge.'

'I won't say a word.'

'Thank you.'

'And thank you.' When she raised her eyebrows in question, he added, 'For trusting me.'

She smiled at him then and began to relax a little, sitting down at the table. 'What's happening with our transport back to Meeraji Lake?'

'I'm waiting on the Royal Flying Doctor Service to call me. They'll be able to take us back, it's just a question of when. In the meantime,' he said, going to the cupboard and taking out the teacups and electric kettle, 'why don't we have another cuppa and you can tell me some of your tales about your time in the army?' He looked thoughtful for a moment. 'I've thought about joining the army.'

'You?' She couldn't help the laughter that bubbled up with the word.

'Why? What's wrong with me going into the Army?'

'Uh…lack of discipline for a start. You'd have to be the class clown, wouldn't you?'

'What's wrong with enjoying a laugh every now and then?'

'Having a laugh, as you call it, might jolly well get your head blown off.' Oscar laughed at her words and she shook her head. 'You're pulling my leg, aren't you?'

'Yes.' He pointed to the cups. 'Tea?'

She nodded and while she watched him make them both a drink she talked with enthusiasm about her work in the army.

'How isolated were you?' he questioned.

'Most of the time, we were in compounds. We worked alongside a lot of Americans as well as Australians and New Zealanders. It wasn't safe. It wasn't pretty. It was difficult operating in a tent, especially when patients were in such life-threatening situations. One time, there were big trucks rumbling past not too far away from where Timothy and I were trying to operate, removing bullet fragments from a soldier's chest.'

'It must have been frightening.'

'Working with Timothy?' She wilfully misunderstood.

He smiled, pleased to see her sense of humour was definitely intact. 'Yes.'

'It was terrifying,' she replied, her smile big and bright and absolutely beautiful. Oscar tried not to sigh from just staring into her eyes. The more time he spent with her, the more he was liking her…wanting to kiss her…wanting to hold her close and never let her— He stopped his thoughts before his mind could finish that sentence.

'Why did you go? What made you sign up for duty?' The moment he spoke, he saw her jaw clench and she glared at him.

'Do I need a reason?'

'Don't give me that look,' he retorted with light humour, shaking his finger at her. 'It's a fair question. The army doesn't suit everyone, as you've so aptly pointed out.' He indicated himself as he spoke.

'True. I think I needed to prove something.'

'To yourself? Or someone else?'

She thought for a moment. 'Perhaps it was a bit of both.'

'Your…father?' Her quick look told him he was correct. 'Did your father want you to go into the army to toughen you up or didn't he think you could handle it?'

'The latter but now I have to wonder if he didn't

goad me into it.' She closed her eyes and shook her head slightly. 'When I'm not staying with them at the big house, he has full control over my mother. Then again, maybe I felt guilty after what I'd done.' She opened her eyes and shrugged. 'I guess we'll never know.' She was still sitting quietly, clearly lost in contemplation.

'Would you like to talk about it?' he asked, hoping against hope that she would.

'Talk about what? My father? My mother? My life in the army?'

'Whatever it is you want to tell me. I'm interested in *all* aspects of your life,' he stated and she looked at him with surprise. The fact that Oscar was interested in her, that he wanted to know more about her, was willing to listen to what she had to say, was such a nice thing that she found herself wanting to tell him.

She bit her lip, then stood and walked over to the window, looking out through the lace curtains at the bustling city outside. So much was going on, cars speeding up and slowing down, traffic lights changing, seagulls squawking. She watched them all unseeingly as she spoke, her tone quiet.

'If you think I talk all posh, then you'll find my parents almost over the top.' She was trying to inject a bit of humour into her words and he wondered whether that was because she was nervous at opening up to him. 'My father rules the roost, controlling everyone and everything that happens in his house.'

'What about your brother? Does he live close to your parents?'

'John? Yes, he and his family live on the estate.'

'You have an estate?'

She shook her head and looked at him. 'My *father* has an estate. *John* has an estate. John's *son* has an estate. It's inherited through the first-born male. My father is most definitely stuck in the past, not moving with the times and intent on upholding tradition.'

'Tradition is clearly important to him.'

'It's how he was raised. At any rate, he was pleasantly surprised with my grades from medical school and seemed quite pleased his daughter was a doctor. It was an accomplishment.'

'That's a good thing.'

'You'd think that.' Daisy pursed her lips. 'Once I'd completed my training and was qualified, he decided I should go into practice with an old friend of his who had been our family doctor since…well, since before I was born.'

'That wasn't what you wanted?'

She spread her arms wide. 'No, but did that matter to my father? Not in the slightest. I was to do as I was told.'

'How old were you? Mid-twenties?'

'Yes, but as far as my father's concerned I'm a woman and so I couldn't possibly make up my own mind or know what's good for me. He's a dictatorial control freak and I—' She stopped and closed her eyes, forcing herself to take some calming breaths. 'My mother encouraged me to leave home, to try working overseas.'

'She was on your side?'

Daisy looked at him and nodded. 'She didn't want me to end up living the same life she'd been forced into. Of course, after I left, my father blamed her for corrupting me.'

'He doesn't sound like a very nice man.' Oscar held up his hands in apology. 'Sorry. I know I don't even know him, but—'

'You're right, though. He isn't nice. He's manipulative and exceedingly arrogant. If he can't control your life, he'll make it a living hell.'

'But you've escaped?'

'To a point. My mother isn't…um…in the best of health.' She was choosing her words carefully and he received the distinct impression that there was more to the situation, especially where her mother's health was concerned, than she was letting on. 'Because of that I have to keep going home to help her.'

Oscar reflected on the conversation he'd overheard. 'And your brother? Does he help your mother?'

'More out of duty, rather than because he's concerned about her.' She laughed without humour. 'Both he and my father always say I'm overreacting.'

'But as a medical professional, you clearly have knowledge that they don't.'

'Exactly. Thank you. I'm not overreacting and my mother's condition… I've tried to get her help and she'll accept it, to a point but then—' Daisy stopped and sighed as though she was exhausted from even thinking about it. She crossed to the bed and sat down, relaxing a little. 'If I stay too long at home, my mother often tells me to leave. In the nicest way, of course. Besides, I can only take so much of my father and his autocratic behaviour.'

'So you ran away and joined the army?'

She grinned. 'I didn't exactly run away. Timothy was already in the army reserves but then when they were calling for full-time medical doctors to head into the combat zone, I figured that if I could handle my father, I could handle anything.'

'Stubborn?'

Her smile increased and she nodded. 'I am.'

'I know.'

'Hey!'

'Have you already forgotten that you were ill when you first arrived? You were stubborn to the point of annoyance.'

'*I* was annoying? Ha. I think it was the other way around,' she told him, her eyes twinkling with mirth as she pointed her finger at him. He moved to sit beside her on the bed and grabbed her finger.

'Point that thing back at you.'

She laughed, a sound he could most definitely become addicted to...if he wasn't already. 'I think we should agree to disagree on this point.'

'Or agree that we're both as stubborn as each other,' he added, lacing his fingers with hers. The action caused her to tremble a little and she quickly looked into his eyes, nervousness mixed with excitement bubbling through her. They were sitting so close, his hypnotic scent filling her senses and causing butterflies to churn in her stomach.

He was sitting so close. Smelling so good. Driving her crazy. They shouldn't be looking at each other like this. They were colleagues. They were...friends? She certainly didn't tell just anyone about her family. Oscar was someone she'd come to trust but she'd made the mistake of trusting the wrong person before and she couldn't make it again. She swallowed as she continued to stare at him. How was it that he could set her insides on fire by just looking at her, by visually caressing her face? How was it that she wanted him to kiss her, to press sweet and tender kisses on her cheeks, her eyelids, her forehead? She couldn't remember the last time she'd been so attracted to a man, as quickly as she'd become attracted to Oscar.

She swallowed again, her lips parting to allow the

pent-up air to escape. She glanced at the clock beside the bed and cleared her throat, trying to deny the senses he was awakening. 'We…uh…should probably head over to the hospital.'

'Daisy.' Her name was a caress upon his lips and somehow he'd shifted even closer to her, or perhaps she was only now realising how easy it would be to lean over and press her mouth to his. Her breath hitched when he put his other hand beneath her chin, smoothing his thumb over her parted lips.

'Daisy.' How could he say her name in such a way that caused desire to rip through her, desire for him to want her, need her, kiss her? She wanted Oscar to kiss her. She'd dreamed about it and now the moment was here, the moment when she could find out how this wonderful man could make her feel. Instinctively she knew it was going to be good. It just had to be. Oscar was handsome and intelligent and delightful to spend time with.

She closed her eyes, feeing his light breath fan in her face. He was going to kiss her. Oscar wanted to kiss her! Her lips opened a little further in anticipation, her heart pounding wildly against her chest, her senses on alert as she waited…waited…

His lips brushed hers in an exceedingly light but delicious way and she all but melted towards him. 'Mmm…' Had that sound come from her or him? He didn't try to deepen the kiss, didn't try to rush, instead he seemed more than content to brush another small kiss across her lips, their breaths mingling and dissolving together.

His hand at her chin slowly shifted around to rest just below her ear, cupping her cheek while his other hand tightened around hers, the actions showing her his restraint at not allowing himself to get carried away. It was as though he wanted to treasure her, wanted to let her know that this wasn't something he did every day, that she was special.

Whether or not Daisy was reading too much into the way he was treating her, she had no idea, but just as he eased back, opening his mouth to hopefully deepen the kiss, to give them both what they appeared to want, his cell phone rang, piercing the air around them. Daisy instantly jumped with fright at the sound and pulled away from him.

Oscar growled and removed his phone from his pocket, turning his back to her as he answered the call, saying a few clipped words here and there before hanging up. He tossed his phone onto the table and shoved both hands into his pockets. He looked her way but didn't hold her gaze. What did that mean? Did he regret what had happened between them?

'That was the Royal Flying Doctor Service. They have a plane heading to Meeraji Lake in thirty minutes with room for two passengers.'

'That's good news.' Daisy needed to do something, needed to be busy, to find a way to distract her thoughts. She stood and started pulling the coverings off the bed they'd shared.

'What are you doing?'

'What does it look like I'm doing?' Her words came out in that haughty way of hers even though she didn't mean them in such a fashion. 'I'm removing the sheets from the bed.'

'But they have cleaners. They can do it,' he stated, looking at her as though she was a little crazy.

'And just think how that person is going to feel when they walk into this room and see one less job they have to do. It might just make their day and if that's the case, then I'm happy to do it.'

'Huh.' Oscar nodded. 'I hadn't thought about it that way before,' he said and immediately picked up a pillow and removed the pillow case.

The truth of the matter was that being near him, having kissed him so tantalisingly, had made her more nervous than a long-tailed cat in a room full of rocking chairs. Daisy had needed to do something to expel the nervous energy zipping through her and doing something practical had been the solution.

'Where do we need to meet the plane?' she asked, picking up the edge of the blanket and starting to fold it. Oscar immediately grabbed the other end and helped her.

'We need to take a taxi to the airport and head to the RFDS airstrip.'

'And we only have half an hour to do that?' She folded the blanket with him, then automatically walked towards him to grasp the two ends together. It was a mistake. Their fingers touched and her body pulsed with a longing and need she'd had no idea she possessed. Her heart rate increased as they stood there, close once more with a neatly folded blanket between them. Daisy hugged the blanket to her as she watched him swallow, before meeting his gaze.

'It will only take about ten minutes to get there.' His voice was soft, deep, intimate, just as it had been before when they'd kissed. Daisy closed her eyes, unable to really understand what was happening to her. Why did he have to smell so good? Why did the pheromones exuding from both of them mingle perfectly together to make one highly potent concoction?

'Ordinarily I can control my emotions.' Her words were as soft as a whisper but she knew he could hear her. Their senses were overly attuned to each other, heightened, sensitised. 'I was raised to quash all emotions and, between medical school and the army, I've learned to compartmentalise everything.'

'Including what you want? What you need?'

Daisy opened her eyes and looked at him. 'Yes. Honour and duty come first. To the monarchy. To family. To the armed forces.'

'You're not in the UK now. Your family is not here either and you're no longer in the army.' Oscar reached out and brushed his fingers across her cheek before lifting her chin a little higher. Then, before she could say or do anything else, he lowered his head and brushed his lips across hers, this time with a little more pressure. It was as though he intended there to be absolutely no doubt that he wanted to kiss her, that he wanted to be near her, that he was attracted to her.

Daisy started to shake, her breathing coming so fast she thought she might hyperventilate. Thankfully, Oscar made no further effort to deepen the contact between them, seemingly content to repeat the gentle, sensual action again and again. It was as though he was trying to memorise every contour, every nuance, every flavour she provided.

Never before had any man treated her in such a way that made her feel precious and treasured and appreciated. That was what he was doing. He was appreciating her mouth, appreciating *her*.

Daisy stepped back, her heart pounding wildly against her chest, her blood thrumming through her body so much, the sound was reverberating in her ears. She dropped the blanket but didn't bother to bend down and pick it up. Instead, she stared at Oscar as though he was something too good to be true. It was always the way.

In the past, when she'd been interested in a man, nine times out of ten he'd been more interested in her family money, or the prestige her family name might provide. However, if what she was feeling for Oscar, especially having only known him for such a short time, was this powerful, hungry desire, then something had seriously been lacking in her life. The question now remained, what did it all mean? What did it mean to him? Did he want money? Did he really find her attractive? What were his motives?

Licking her dry lips, Daisy took a few deep breaths, trying to get her wayward breathing to settle into a more even rhythm. 'We'd...' She cleared her throat when her voice cracked. 'We'd best get to the plane.'

With that, she bent to pick up the blanket and continued to tidy the room. Oscar just stood there, watching her as though he really didn't understand what was going on. When she was done, she walked to the door, not waiting for him. There was a taxi rank across the road outside the front of the hospital and, leaving him to gather his personal items and lock the door behind them, she continued across the road to flag down their transport.

When he joined her in the taxi, sitting in the back seat while she sat in the front with the driver, Oscar seemed his usual jovial self, chatting and laughing with the driver as though they were old friends instead of two people who had just met.

At the airport, he was the same with the RFDS staff, although, she discovered, he really was old friends with most of them. He introduced Daisy to everyone, ensured her seat belt was correctly fastened before take-off and showed her every courtesy as though nothing weird, crazy or sensual had happened between them.

All it did was confuse her even more.

CHAPTER NINE

WHEN THEY RETURNED from Darwin, Oscar continued to be his usual polite self towards Daisy. He behaved this way because he had no idea what he was meant to do after kissing her. Should he kiss her again? Hold her hand in the taxi? Whisper in her ear during the plane ride back to Meeraji Lake?

He'd been so unnerved by the way she'd responded to him, by the way she had smelled so sweet and delicious. Why had he kissed her? When he'd taken the breakfast tray back to the hospital cafeteria, he'd been so incredibly annoyed with her, wondering why she hadn't been able to trust him, to open up and then…when she had, it had stirred all his protective instincts.

It was then he'd realised that her reticence, her reluctance to discuss her life with him, was more attributed to her repressed upbringing than not wanting to confide in him. He also couldn't deny he'd been pleased to hear that she wasn't Timothy's type and, while he had nothing against the brilliant surgeon, it had been a relief to know that Daisy wasn't attached to him. None of this, however, explained why Oscar had finally given in to the urges he'd been fighting so successfully up to that point and kissed her!

Because he hadn't been able to stop himself. The

woman had managed to get under his skin, to become a part of his dreams and after lying next to her all night long, and with their heightened emotions, when the moment had arisen he'd grabbed it with both hands. The only problem with his actions was now that he knew how wonderful she felt in his arms, now that he knew how perfectly her lips seemed to meld to his own, now that he'd tasted the delicious flavours of her mouth, he most definitely wanted more. Much more. And that was indeed a major problem.

Daisy would leave at the end of her contract and now he knew why. Looking after and supporting her mother was a noble cause. He could also understand why she'd previously said that she never wanted to have a family herself, because her own family life hadn't been a happy one. His upbringing, although filled with sadness when his parents had passed away, had still been a happy one. He'd been encouraged, he'd been supported and he'd been loved.

From what Daisy had said, she'd had very little of any of those things, and it pained him to think of what she might have been through in the past. All of this, however, meant that kissing her had been the absolute wrong thing to do. He knew he wanted to stay here in Meeraji Lake, to get married and raise a family. Yes, he was concerned about getting involved with a woman again, opening his heart up once more and risking it being broken, and with Daisy he was almost ninety-nine per cent sure that would happen. If he continued down his present path, of wanting to spend more time with her, of wanting to talk more about her past, of learning everything there was to know about Daisy Forsythe-York, then he would definitely end up with another broken heart.

Surely it would be best for both of them if they forgot all about those kisses and went back to just being colleagues. Wouldn't it?

A week later, Daisy still had no idea what was really going on in Oscar's head, not where the attraction between the two of them was concerned. When they'd returned to Meeraji Lake, Oscar had been his usual kind and considerate self. He'd made her breakfast every morning for the next week, had helped her cook dinner in the evenings and had brought her a cup of tea just before she'd headed to bed. They would often sit and chat about movies they both liked as well as discussing different books, offering recommendations or lending each other the title.

When he said goodnight to her, he would politely kiss her hand then bid her sweet dreams before disappearing down to his end of the house. He'd made no reference to the kisses they'd shared nor had he made any other effort to drag her close and plunder her mouth once more…even though she'd continually dreamed he would.

It was as though those kisses had never happened and she could only conclude that he now regretted the impulse and wanted to forget about it. She tried not to let that knowledge bother her, tried not to take it personally, to compartmentalise her feelings, but at the end of it all he was making it quite clear he only wanted a professional relationship with her. Well, if that was the case, she could be just as nonchalant about it, just as dismissive of it and just as kind and polite to him as he was to her.

So why did he still kiss her hand every night and look

at her with eyes that were filled with repressed desire and bid her sweet dreams?

'What's going on between you and Oscar?' Tori asked her one day after clinic had finished. Daisy had walked into the hospital to find it almost eerily quiet so had sat down to catch up on some of the paperwork.

'You tell me and we'll both know,' she stated with a sigh.

'Do you *want* something to happen between the two of you?' Tori persisted.

Daisy put her pen down and looked at the nurse with confusion. 'I don't know. I'm only here for a six-month contract and then I'll be leaving. Is it really worth starting anything up with him?'

'Fair point. That's what happened between him and Deidre. He thought she'd stay permanently, in fact we all did, but then, when her contract was up, she decided to leave instead. She was more than happy for him to come with her but she wasn't going to stay in the outback for any longer than she had to.' Tori shook her head. 'She had us all fooled.'

'She'd given him no indication she was going to leave?'

'None whatsoever. They were engaged and she was talking about their wedding here and starting a family and then—' She shrugged. 'I don't know. Something just happened and she left.'

'And you don't know what it was?' Daisy asked.

'I do,' a deep male voice said from behind them and they both turned to see Oscar standing near the door to the ED. Daisy was instantly embarrassed and quickly looked away, annoyed with herself for gossiping about him. Tori took one look at the scowl on his face and made herself scarce. 'It's all right, Oscar. You don't need to tell me.' Daisy cleared her throat. 'Tori mentioned Deidre.'

'It's OK. I don't mind. The truth was that Deidre received a better offer.' Oscar walked over and pulled up a chair, sitting next to Daisy. 'Because of her outback medicine training and experience, she was head-hunted—at least that's what she told me, but I have a feeling she'd applied for the job—for the position of consultant to the minister of health, particularly concerning the health of native Australians. Three times the pay she was getting here and a lot more prestige.'

'That must have been incredibly difficult for you, Oscar,' Daisy stated.

He nodded. 'She even offered to give me the engagement ring back but I didn't want it. I didn't have time to grieve over the breakdown of the relationship as Lucinda was really ill by then and needed all my attention.'

'And being the true hero that you are, you gave her everything she needed.'

'Just as she gave me everything I needed when our parents passed away.'

'You're fortunate to have had that one special person in your life.'

'True. She was a great sister and I still miss her.'

'Of course you do.' Daisy's heart was breaking for him and, without thinking, she reached over and took his hand in hers. 'I'm so sorry for what you've been through.'

He met her gaze, hopefully realising she was genuine in her words. 'I'm becoming quite adept at recovering from being abandoned.' He tried to inject humour into his words but ended up sighing with a heaviness of heart. 'First my wife, Magda, decided she didn't want to be with me any more and left me for another man, someone who could give her more money than I ever could. Then I move here and Deidre breaks my heart and then my sister dies.'

'You really have been through the wringer.'

'Well, from what you've said, your life hasn't exactly been a picnic.'

She grimaced and nodded. 'We all have our crosses to bear.'

He gave Daisy's hand a little squeeze then let it go, standing up and walking to the other side of the desk. Was he trying to put distance between them? To keep her questions at bay?

'If you don't want to talk about it, Oscar, I completely understand.'

'It's all right, Daisy. I probably owe you some sort of explanation.'

'For what?'

'For kissing you and then keeping you at arm's length.'

'It's all right—' she started to say, but stopped. She did want to know what he was thinking and as he was offering to talk to her, she'd be stupid to refuse him. 'Actually, tell me whatever you feel comfortable telling me.'

He smiled then, causing a mass of tingles to flood through her at the sight. 'OK.' He still kept his distance, standing on the other side of the desk, arms crossed over his chest. It seemed to take a while for him to gather his thoughts but eventually he spoke. 'Kissing you... I shouldn't have done it.'

Daisy bit her lip, mainly to keep it from wobbling and to hold the threatening tears at bay. It was one thing to think it, to come to that conclusion on her own, but to have him come right out and say that he regretted kissing her—

'That doesn't mean I didn't enjoy it,' he added quickly and she wondered whether she'd been adept at controlling her expression or whether he now knew her well enough to read her face accurately. 'I did. Oh, I did.'

'I did, too.' Her words were a whisper.

'But it can't be, Daisy. Surely you see that.'

'I'm leaving at the end of my contract.'

'Yes.'

'I *have* to go back to England and check on my mother, try again at another attempt to get her to leave my father but...but she loves him and takes all his—' She stopped, realising every muscle in her body was tense. She forced herself to relax. 'But that's not what we're discussing.'

'I admire you for caring for your mother, for being so concerned about her that you effectively put your own life on hold until you can be sure she's OK. That's what family is all about. Being there for each other.'

'Yes. I guess it is. My brother sees it merely as doing his duty.'

'And that's where you're different from him—you care, genuinely care for your mother and her well-being. That's, as I said, admirable and therefore I can't even get mad at you for leaving.'

'Were you hoping to talk me into staying longer?'

'That was my initial plan when I advertised the position.'

'Why not advertise it for twelve months, then?'

'Well...partly because it's difficult to get doctors out here at the best of times and offering only a six-month contract provides more chance of success at filling the vacancy.'

'And the other part of the reason?'

'Because of Deidre. She was here for twelve months, she told me she felt locked into it and although she had planned on staying, said she liked it here, when that other job offer came up, it was only then she remembered what her life had been like before she'd come to Meeraji Lake. Does that make any sense?'

'Yes.' She smiled. 'I can see how being here feels as though you're in another world. I love it.'

'And, in the end, Deidre didn't.'

'So what will you do when I leave? Advertise for another six-month position?'

'More than likely.'

She thought on this for a moment. 'Did your wife—?'

'Magda.'

'Did Magda ever come to Meeraji Lake?'

'Magda?' He laughed without humour. 'No. No, this wasn't the place for her.'

'What was she like? Er…do you mind me asking?'

'No.' He raked a hand through his hair with frustration. 'Magda was…duplicitous. That's probably the best word to describe her.' He shook his head. 'I was so blind. She was beautiful and funny to work with. I was living in Brisbane, that's in Queensland,' he added and she nodded, indicating she knew where Brisbane was. 'Anyway, Magda was a nurse on the ward where I was working and she was absolutely lovely.' He re-crossed his arms over his chest. 'In hindsight, I've realised she was more of a chameleon, changing the way she was in order to get what she wanted.'

'And she wanted you?'

'She wanted a doctor who had prospects, who could keep her in the lifestyle she'd always wanted. One time, she even confessed to me that she'd only completed her nursing training because she knew it was the best way to secure a rich doctor as a husband. It wasn't until after our honeymoon that she began to change. First, she decided to go part-time at work and then she quit altogether.'

'That didn't bother you?'

He looked past Daisy, as though he was looking back into his past, his tone filled with regret. 'She told me she had a better chance of falling pregnant if she wasn't so stressed because of work.'

'She didn't get pregnant?' Daisy surmised.

'She was taking birth-control pills the entire three years of our marriage.' He sighed. 'Her expenses started to increase, she'd go shopping, have lunch with a lot of the other surgeons' wives. It was an exclusive club to her and because she was married to me, she'd gained access.

'Then she encouraged me to apply for a job in Sydney and I was successful. It was longer hours but more money.'

'What she wanted?'

'All along. We bought an enormous house, far bigger than we needed, but it had a pool and a tennis court and was good for entertaining and holding networking parties...which she did.'

Daisy nodded, thinking of her father's estate, which was more than three times the size of what Oscar was describing. 'Were you happy?'

'I thought I was. I did meet a lot of influential people, which helped me to secure more money for my research projects.'

'Not what you know but who you know?'

'Exactly, but it reached the point where I was working long hours all week at the hospital, working at home, sleeping less, stressing more and then having to be the host at one of Magda's networking parties on the week-ends. It was all just too much and when I asked her to stop—at least for a while—she exploded.'

'Not literally, I hope.' Daisy grinned and was thankful when Oscar returned her smile, and the tension that had tightened his shoulders as he'd spoken of his ex-wife visibly started to decrease. 'So things just sort of fizzled out between the two of you?'

'Sort of. Lucinda was diagnosed with breast cancer and, although she had a double mastectomy, the chemotherapy would only hold it at bay for a while. I instantly resigned from my job and made arrangements to move here to Meeraji Lake.'

'Magda wasn't too thrilled?'

'If I thought she'd exploded before, it was nothing compared to how she reacted to that news. It was then she told me that she'd been taking birth-control pills throughout our entire three-year marriage, that she'd had several affairs with other men and that as far as a husband who could provide reasonably for his wife was concerned, I was a failure and she was moving on.'

'She filed for divorce?'

'Yes.'

'And you moved to Meeraji Lake?'

'Yes.'

She pondered his words for a moment before saying softly, 'Life's a strange thing, sometimes. The connections we make can either bring us joy or disaster.'

'Have you had many relationship disasters?'

'There are always bad relationships in everyone's history,' she stated and he could see her clamming up.

'Not quite ready to talk about it?'

'Is anyone ever ready to talk about their failures?'

'I just did.'

'Why? Why did you?'

Oscar came and sat back down next to her. 'Because maybe I'm crazy. Maybe I'm making a mistake, opening up to you instead of pushing you away.' He reached for her hand. 'I've been trying so hard to fight it, Daisy, but when it comes down to the bottom line, I'm attracted to you.'

'And you don't want to be.' She nodded and slowly pulled her hand back. Oscar looked up at the ceiling and exhaled harshly.

'I don't know, Daisy. You make me feel like I haven't felt in a long time. You make me believe in a future when for quite some time I was more than content just to go from day to day. So much has happened to me, two women I've loved have let me down. My parents and my sister passed away. I don't know if I'm the sort of man who needs to be married, who needs the stability of a wife beside him and, if I am, perhaps that comes from being orphaned at such a young age.'

He looked deeply into her eyes. 'All I know is that when I'm around you, I'm happy.'

'Being happy is good.' She nodded and found that for a long moment she simply couldn't look away. What was it about him that she found so compelling, so exciting, so hypnotic? She agreed with everything he was saying and yet she knew deep down inside that there couldn't possibly be a happily ever after for the two of them together. They lived on opposite sides of the world; they had different priorities in their lives. Daisy had vowed that, after her previous disastrous relationship, she wasn't going to venture back into that ring for quite some time. She was going to focus on her career; she was going to look after her mother and hopefully start a new life for the two of them somewhere away from her father.

'Right?' His gaze dropped to her lips and she felt her heart rate instantly increase. 'So when you find someone who makes you happy, why should it be the right thing to pull away from them?'

Daisy couldn't help but lick her parted lips, watching him watch her. The tension between them was so real and as vital as breathing and yet it was a hopeless situation. 'Because there's no hope for a future together.' Her words were barely above a whisper but she knew he'd heard them as he closed his eyes, almost as though he was trying to block out the vision of her sitting there before him.

'Daisy.' He breathed her name. 'Those kisses…'

'Oscar, don't.'

He looked at her. 'Denying the way you make me feel is making me ill. I'm not sleeping properly, I'm only eating well because we eat two meals a day together and I really like spending that time with you, getting to know you a bit better even when I know I should be putting more distance between us.'

'We have to work together, live in the same house together. To have that fraught with tension—'

'It's already fraught with tension.'

'Negative tension,' she clarified. 'To live like that would be unbearable for the duration of my contract. I don't want that.'

'Neither do I, which is why a professional and light friendship seems the best way to go and yet when you laugh, or unplait your hair and—' He stared at her mouth once more and sighed with longing.

'Should I move out?'

'No.' The word was instant.'

'Do you think we ought to…?'

'What?' he prompted when she stopped.

Daisy dragged in a deep breath then blurted out what she was thinking. 'Do you think we ought to discuss those...' she cleared her throat '...those kisses we shared?'

'I've thought about that.' He moved his chair a little closer to hers and reached out to take her hand in his, entwining their fingers just as he had before the last time he'd kissed her. 'I just didn't think it was a good idea to discuss it at our house.'

Our house? Even those words caused her heart rate to flutter. 'Why not? We're alone there and less likely to be interrupted.'

'That's why. Because we're *alone* there and I'm not sure talking about kissing you is sensible when I'm then able to kiss you and hold you close and then...' His voice had become thick and husky with repressed desire as he'd spoken the quiet words and her eyes half closed, as though she was quite capable of imagining the perfect conclusion those kisses might reach. 'Daisy.' Her name was a caress upon his lips. 'I can't ignore any more the way you make me feel.'

'Feel?' The word was so soft she wasn't even sure she'd spoken it out loud.

'Yes.' He shifted closer, bringing his chair right up against hers. Daisy was too stunned, too overpowered by her wayward emotions, by the heated tingles that ran from her fingers, up her arm to explode throughout her entire body. Her breathing had increased, her mouth had gone dry and even her knees were weakening at his touch. Why was it that she turned into a hormonal teenager at one simple look from him, or one gentle touch, or one absolutely incredibly sensual kiss?

'We do need to talk about it but perhaps the middle of

the emergency department isn't exactly the right place. So, how about tomorrow night?' he suggested.

'T...tomorrow night?'

'Saturday night. There's a movie showing at the town hall. Haven't you seen the flyers up for it?'

'Uh...yes. Yes.' She eased back, surprised at her reluctance to let go of his fingers. She crossed her arms over her chest but rested one hand over her heart, as though trying to protect it from getting hurt. 'It's an outdoor cinema and everyone sits on rugs and eats food. Yes. I've seen the flyers.' As she spoke she was trying hard to keep her mind off the fact that he was still so incredibly close.

'Let's go together.'

'I'm... I'm on call.' Being alone with Oscar, planning to talk about the sensations he evoked within her... Could she do that? Feelings were to be kept personal, not telling anyone how you really felt because the public façade was more important to maintain for the sake of the family. That was what had been drummed into her by her father and nannies and her brother and everyone else in the social circle she'd been raised in. But she wasn't in those circles any more. She was on the other side of the world and perhaps it was time for her to make new rules for herself.

'I know, but the majority of the district is going to be at this event so if there's going to be any medical emergencies, chances are they'll happen there so we'll be in the right place at the right time.'

'So you want to go to this event together?'

'Yes. And I mean "together", as in a date.'

'A date?' Even the words caused her heart to race. Daisy pursed her lips in an effort to control the riotous sensations of unbelievable dread and excited anticipation that flooded her. 'Oscar! We've spent the past week trying to ignore this chemistry which seems to exist between us and now you want to embrace it?'

'Ignoring it clearly hasn't worked that well for either of us. Don't you think it's worth trying to sort things out? To talk about the "what if"s'?'

Daisy tentatively shook her head. '"What if"s can be dangerous. What if I tell you something that you don't like? How will you treat me after that? What if I confide in you and you let me down and I treat you differently?'

'And what if we figure out what this really is between us and sort it out? If necessary, I'll move out of the residence.'

She frowned at the thought of not seeing him all the time and felt a pang of regret. 'That'll set tongues wagging.'

'So let's discuss it later. Let's sort it out because I've lived in limbo before, Daisy, and I don't much care for it. Talking plainly, figuring things out. That's good.'

'And what if we decide to pursue this...this...'

'Frighteningly natural chemistry which exists between us?'

'Yes. That. What do we do then?'

'We'll figure it out. We're two very intellectual people, Daisy.' He raised her hand to his lips and brushed a kiss across her knuckles, just as he had every night since Darwin.

'Uh-huh.' She was completely unable to speak.

'And to save us from both tearing each other's clothes off while we discuss such a sensitive topic—'

'Shh.' Even hearing him say those words was starting to cause a warmth to flood throughout her entire body. 'Someone might hear you.'

'Tomorrow night, we'll be able to sit near the back

of the crowd, out of the way, and pretend to enjoy the movie while we sort this attraction out.'

She stared at his lips for a long moment before slowly shaking her head in bemusement. 'You've got it all sorted out, eh?'

'Absolutely, mate.' He winked at her and she momentarily found it difficult to remember to breathe. Why did he have such a devastating effect on her equilibrium?

Daisy closed her eyes and forced herself to breathe deeply because when he looked at her like that, as though he wanted nothing more than to forget all their responsibilities and simply spend the rest of the day kissing her, her mind turned to mush.

'OK.' She kept her eyes closed as she spoke. 'Movies. Tomorrow night. We can talk.'

'Good.' When he brushed a light finger across her cheek, her eyelids snapped open and she quickly pushed his hand away.

'Someone might see.' She looked around but the ED was still very bare. 'Things may be relaxed and informal out here in the middle of nowhere but not for me.'

'And it is for that very reason that I bid you farewell.' He stood and affected a mock bow before turning and walking from the ED. Daisy knew she should follow, knew she had a few patients she needed to see in her afternoon pre-operative clinic, but, due to Oscar's flirting, she was now unable to move her legs.

'Darn that man,' she mumbled. Why did he have to be so incredibly wonderful?

Now he wanted to take her on a date? It seemed so odd to be organising a date with him when they lived in the same house. *Our house.* Even remembering him saying those words was enough to cause a fresh bout of tingles to flood throughout her. Why, oh, why couldn't she control her emotions? And what was she supposed to do when he started asking difficult questions?

Agreeing to go on this date meant she'd need to open up to him, especially as she really did want to figure out where this attraction might lead. She hadn't expected anything like this to happen when she'd accepted the job but now that it had... She'd lived a lot of her life not knowing what was going on, not understanding why her parents argued or why she was sent out of the room, or off to boarding school or generally overlooked. Was she ready to tell him more? To tell him about her mother's alcoholism? About how, until her mother decided to get permanent treatment, Daisy's life would never really be her own? Would that make a difference to Oscar? Would he try and sell the story to the papers, just as her last boyfriend, Walter, had?

What if she and Oscar started a relationship only to have it go sour? What would happen then? He'd clearly been burned before so she doubted he'd want to try that again. Was that what he wanted to talk about? Was he only interested in a short-term affair with her? Was she capable of giving him that? Would they be able to share the same house? Work alongside each other? Continue to provide expert care to their patients if things went wrong and they ended up disliking each other?

Daisy leaned her head into her hands and whimpered. What had she done? She couldn't go on a date with Oscar! It was ridiculous. Nice things didn't happen to her. Nice things happened to other people and, as such, she knew she had to put a stop to the ridiculousness that there could ever be anything between herself and Oscar other than a professional working relationship.

She'd seen it happen time and time again in the army,

when colleagues had started a relationship only to have it fail and yet they'd been in the middle of a jungle, expected to work together. The tensions in the surgery tents had been hopelessly fraught and had made the working environment unbearable for everyone.

No. She couldn't let that happen here. Not when she'd been accepted as part of the community. No. She and Oscar would remain colleagues with a professional friendship. Nothing more.

With that resolved, she breathed in deeply before standing and straightening her shoulders. Now that she had her priorities straight once more, now that she hadn't let him talk her into doing something she wasn't ready for, she could concentrate on her work. Her patients awaited and, with a firmness to her stride, she headed towards the clinic rooms next door, finally feeling more like herself.

Oscar and the unsettling way he had made her feel were now completely behind her. Once and for all.

CHAPTER TEN

THAT EVENING, IN order to avoid being alone with Oscar in the house, Daisy suggested they go to the pub for dinner. She'd also planned to tell him she couldn't go on the date to the movies with him, that she'd had second thoughts, but they'd been interrupted by a bar-room brawl of epic proportions, with Bazza in the centre of it, and the two of them had spent the next three hours in Emergency, treating the foolhardy farmers who had enjoyed one too many 'knock-off' beers.

On Saturday morning, Daisy had headed off early to her clinic, feeling so incredibly self-conscious about the house space she shared with Oscar. It was happening already, the strange awkwardness she knew would come if they acted upon their attraction. Surely when she told him the date was off, he would understand, as the confused tension that already filled the house seemed to be rapidly increasing.

At the end of her clinic, she finished writing up the notes and then returned them to the filing room. Oscar had told her he had plans to computerise the entire practice but sometimes things took a lot longer to deal with out here in the middle of nowhere. The room she was in was floor-to-ceiling shelves with patient files on either side.

When Oscar walked in to return his own case notes, she felt his presence before she saw him. Breathing in deeply, she turned around to face him.

'All done?' he asked, putting his armful of case notes on the ground.

'Yes. Just have to file this last set of case notes and I'm done for the day.'

'All ready for our date this evening?' He was edging closer, his gaze dipping to look at her lips before returning to meet her eyes.

'About that—' she began but then realised how he was looking at her. 'Why are you looking at me like that?' she asked, trying not to look back at him, trying instead to concentrate on putting the last set of notes into place, but she was having difficulty due to the trembling that seemed to have flooded through her body at his nearness.

'Let me help you with that.' He put his hand over hers and together they slipped the file into place. The instant he touched her, she gasped and looked up at him. She licked her lips, unable to stop herself, and she was delighted when he didn't let go of her hand but instead drew her closer. 'I have been completely aware of you all day long, from the moment you woke up this morning until right now.'

As he spoke he slid his arms around her waist. 'You're driving me crazy.'

'I know,' she whispered, her heart hammering wildly against her ribs. He shifted in the small area so that he was standing as close to her as possible and, because of the confined space, Daisy slid her hands up to rest on his chest, not sure whether she should push him away or pull him closer.

'You smell so good. Your perfume drives me wild.'

'Mmm-hmm,' she responded, her senses working on overdrive as she breathed in his own glorious scent. 'Likewise.'

'My perfume...' he started bringing his head closer to hers, his words barely above a whisper '...drives you wild?'

'Mmm-hmm,' she repeated, licking her lips again.

'I want to kiss you, Daisy. Really kiss you as I've been longing to do ever since last week when we were in Darwin.'

Even just hearing the words from him was enough to cause a thousand tingles to flood throughout her body, making her tremble with excited anticipation.

'I know we're going to talk tonight, that we're going to figure things out—' He bent his head and brushed a kiss to her cheek. 'But if it turns out we decide just to be friends—'

He slowly shifted around to the other side, his breath mingling with hers as his lips passed hers. He didn't kiss her though; instead, he brushed a kiss to her other cheek and it was all Daisy could do not to sag completely into his arms, her body filled with a want and need that only he could satisfy.

'I don't want to miss this...opportunity.'

No sooner had he said the last word than he gave them both what they so desperately wanted and pressed his lips to hers. Daisy gasped at the contact and then instantly slid her hands further up his chest to wrap them around his neck. Oscar was kissing her. It was what she'd been wanting all morning long, to have him really kiss her, not just the light, teasing tastes they'd shared in Darwin.

His mouth was on hers with a gentleness that only caused more tingles and heightened her awareness of him. She opened her mouth when he nibbled at her lower lip, matching his urgency, needing him to know she wanted this as much as he did.

There were all sorts of logical thoughts springing to her mind, such as what did this kiss mean? What would happen when it was over? What did Oscar want from her? Daisy closed her eyes tighter and pushed those thoughts away. Just because she'd been raised to always consider the logical consequences of her actions, didn't mean she had to follow that rule now.

The way Oscar was making her feel as he deepened the kiss, as he drew her closer to him, as he seemed to ignite every nerve ending in her body, was something she'd never felt before. Good heavens! If she'd known that kissing him was going to be like this then she would have done it that first morning after she'd woken up with thoughts of him in her head.

Now, it was as though being close to him was a drug and one she'd become addicted to in next to no time. Her heart was pounding against her chest with such force that she was positive he could hear it. Her breathing had increased and she knew that if she didn't ease back from the glorious sensations he was creating with his lips pressed so perfectly to her own, she would probably suffocate. At the moment, she couldn't think of a more delicious way to go!

Oscar moved back a bit and looked deeply into her eyes before tucking a stray wisp of hair behind her ear, his fingers both soothing and caressing her skin, causing a fresh round of tingles to spread throughout her. 'What is it?' he asked, looking at her with curiosity.

'Pardon?'

'You're frowning, Daisy.' He brushed his fingers across her forehead, smoothing out the lines, delighted he was allowed to touch her in such a familiar way. His mind and body were still reeling from that kiss. The woman before him was so amazing, so incredible. She came across as all pompous and hoity-toity but in reality she was as vulnerable as the next person.

'I am?' She instantly smiled up at him and he couldn't resist brushing his lips across hers, deepening the kiss for another moment before actually putting her from him and taking a few steps backwards, almost tripping over the files he'd left on the floor.

'It might be better if I stand over here.'

A cautious look immediately came into her eyes. 'Why? Have I done something wrong?'

'What? No. No.' He shook his head instantly. 'I want nothing more than to hold you close, to kiss you again and again, but if I do I'm not sure I'd be able to stop my urges.'

'You have urges?'

Her words were clipped, her vowels perfectly rounded and where a few weeks ago he would have thought she was making fun of him or simply being thick, he now recognised that small twinkle in her eyes, caught that minute twitch of her lips as the corners curved upwards. She was teasing him and flirting with him and he liked it—a lot. He grinned at her and raised an eyebrow.

'Where you're concerned? Absolutely.' He crossed his arms over his chest as she slowly closed the distance between them. 'Playing with fire, Dr Daisy?'

'I like a bit of danger in my life. It allows me to feel truly alive with every fibre of my being.'

'So now you're saying I'm dangerous?' His words were spoken softly as she now stood toe to toe with him. She was wearing flat shoes today so he was slightly taller than her but in many respects they were still almost eye to eye. He clenched his jaw as her sweet floral scent wound itself around him.

'How is it possible that you can smell as fresh as a daisy all the time?' His gaze dipped to her lips and he swallowed, wanting so badly to pull her back into his arms and kiss her with such abandon that the only conclusion would be to sweep her off her feet and carry her back to their place where they could be truly alone.

But Daisy wasn't 'some woman'. No. Daisy was special. He wanted nothing more than to be with her, to get to know her better, to build a relationship with her, but what would happen when her contract was up? Six months. She'd come here for six months and while there was the possibility she could renew her contract, would she? If things went wrong between them—

Fear suddenly gripped his heart. He'd been down this road before. It was the whole reason why they were supposed to be discussing things tonight, but he hadn't been able to stop himself from pressing his lips to hers, from seeing whether this attraction between them really was as incredible as he thought it might be. It was... *more* so than he could ever have imagined.

'Are we taking it in turns to frown? Because you seem incredibly lost in thought,' she said quietly as she reached out and touched her fingers gently to his forehead, reciprocating his earlier action.

Oscar uncrossed his arms and took her hands in his, mainly to stop her from touching him, because that one simple caress was enough to start unravelling the tight control on his emotions he was trying to maintain.

'I like what's happening between us, Daisy.'

Her smile was instant—and delightful. 'So do I.' She shrugged one shoulder. 'I was going to tell you I couldn't go to the movies with you tonight, that deciding to spend more time together—in a personal sense—was probably a bad move and one we might end up regretting.'

He chuckled. 'I think we're both over-thinkers.'

Daisy relaxed at this, seeing that he, too, had his concerns. 'Oh, good.'

Oscar chuckled again and shook his head before leaning forward to press his lips to hers, unable to resist kissing her after she'd sounded so formal, pompous and nervous all at the same time. When she started to deepen the kiss, he put his hands onto her shoulders and eased her back. 'I really should put my files away and then go help out in the ED.'

'Yes. Yes.' She cleared her throat. 'I really should go and start house calls.'

'And I should really tell everyone what I just saw!'

Oscar and Daisy instantly turned towards the doorway where Tori stood, gaping at them with a goofy grin on her face. 'How long has this been going on?' She waggled her finger at the two of them as she walked towards her desk.

'About ten minutes,' Oscar said as they both came out of the file room. He placed a protective arm around Daisy's shoulders, pleased when she didn't shrug him away or deny what was happening between them.

'Well…I think it's been building up for quite a few weeks,' Daisy added, smiling at him. That one look gave Oscar courage. She was invested in…whatever this was that existed between them.

'Do you think you might be able to keep it on the down-low, at least until after the movie tonight?' he asked Tori.

'Are you kidding me?' Tori spread her arms wide.

'The whole district has just been waiting for the two of you to realise how perfect you are for each other. In fact, Erica's been running a betting pool on it.'

'Huh.' Oscar thought for a moment. 'Are you in the betting pool?'

Tori's eyes widened as the reality of the situation dawned on her. 'Ooh. I could make a lot of money here. Who else knows about the two of you?'

Oscar shook his head and slipped his arm off Daisy's shoulders, taking her hand in his. 'Come on, Daisy. We'll do house calls together and leave crazy Tori to take care of the ED by herself.'

'It's quiet anyway,' Tori called after them as they left the clinic, heading out to walk in the sunshine. It was then that Daisy started to feel an enormous weight lift from her shoulders. She couldn't remember the last time she'd done something just for herself.

The fact that they did the house calls together certainly raised a few more eyebrows and really set the tongues to wagging. Daisy was certain that by that night's movie session the entire community would have settled their bets.

'We are most definitely the talk of the town,' Oscar said to her as they headed home to shower and change for the evening's festivities. 'I wouldn't be surprised if they all cheer and clap when we arrive together, hand in hand.' He took her hand in his and gave it a little squeeze.

Daisy smiled at him, caught up in the brightness of his eyes. She wasn't sure if she would ever get tired of gazing into them. Oscar really was such a handsome man and one who seemed to understand her completely. It seemed odd that they'd only known each other for such a short time and yet it seemed as though she'd been waiting for him her whole life. He'd gently but firmly smashed down the walls she'd erected over the years to protect herself and now he looked at her as though she were the most beautiful, wonderful and incredible woman in the world. How could any woman not be affected by that?

She started to laugh, unable to stop the giggles.

'What?'

'It's nothing.'

'You're just laughing for no reason now?'

Daisy couldn't help it. Her smile increased and she giggled again. 'It's just that...well...I'm happy.'

His smile was wide and bright and he leaned forward to kiss her. 'I'm sure you deserve to be.' He opened the door to their residence. 'After you, Lady Daisy.' He affected a small bow.

Annoyance hard and fast burned through her, destroying her happiness as though someone had smashed a glass window with a hammer. 'Please don't call me that.' Even she heard the haughtiness of her tone and when Oscar gave her a puzzled smile, she shook her head. 'Sorry. I didn't mean to sound so snappy.'

'It's OK.' As they headed into the cool of the house Oscar sensed it wasn't the right time to press her for answers. Oscar was taken with her, even though he'd done his best to fight it. He knew he needed to ease the tension he could see in her shoulders and he quickly started talking about the food everyone would bring to tonight's barbecue.

'We're bringing a salad,' he said. 'So chop-chop, Dr Daisy. Literally,' he said, handing her a bunch of carrots. Slowly, as they worked side by side, the tension in her shoulders began to ease and the smile began to reach her eyes once more.

Oscar continued to chat, to tell her about the delicious goodies other people in the town would bring.

'Glenys is making her famous all natural ice-blocks. My favourite is peach and blueberry.'

'Ice-blocks?'

Oscar nodded. 'Of course. Being from England, you wouldn't often eat ice-blocks, now, would you?'

'Hey!' She scolded. 'It gets hot over there. Not as hot as here, but it still gets hot enough that we eat iced lollies.'

'Well, you'll love these. Glenys purées fruit, mixes it together and then freezes it in her moulds so you have the perfect ice-block on a stick with no added nasties. It's like perfect sunshine in an ice-block. You love strawberries, right?'

'How do you know that?'

'Uh…because I've seen you eat them and you seem to savour them in the same way that my sister used to eat chocolate.'

'Oh.' She'd had no idea he'd been observing her. She couldn't blame him though, as she'd been observing him as well. She knew he didn't like mushrooms but was more than happy to cook them for her in the morning when he made breakfast. She knew he drank his coffee black with two sugars and she knew he had a marvellous baritone voice because he often sang in the shower.

They talked a bit more about the fruit ice-blocks Glenys made and the home-made lamingtons Erica would be bringing and by the time they were changed and ready to walk down to the town hall, Daisy's stomach was already grumbling.

True to Oscar's description, there were tables laden with food, the ceiling fans and air conditioner in the hall working overtime as they all joined together, laughing and eating and having a brilliant time.

Naturally, Daisy and Oscar were subjected to a lot of knowing looks and smiles and pats on the back and handshakes regarding the change in their relationship from colleagues to…more than colleagues.

Even Daisy wasn't one hundred per cent sure what was going on between them. They'd kissed. They'd held hands. They didn't seem in any hurry to be separated from each other and she liked that he appeared to enjoy being around her all the time. However, deep down inside, she knew it would come to an end. Things always did for her. Nothing ever worked out the way she envisioned it and the fact that they were living in the same house, working at the same hospital and now attending functions together meant that, sooner rather than later, she half expected Oscar to get sick of her company.

'Ready to come and sit outside and watch the movie?' Oscar asked her after the sun had gone down. Police officer Henry and a gaggle of others had set up a large screen behind the town hall in order to screen the movie. The flies had all disappeared and the mosquitoes seemed to be giving them the night off, even though several people, including Daisy, sprayed themselves with repellent.

'Well, I do declare,' Oscar stated as he came to sit beside her on the rug he'd spread for them. 'You are becoming quite the local, Dr Daisy.' They were sitting near the back of the gathered group, some people sitting on beanbags and others having carried sofas and rocking chairs down to the hall from their own houses. Daisy was pleased with the community feel, delighted at the acceptance she felt and thrilled that Oscar thought she was turning into a local.

'You're all set. Got your repellent on. Using your event programme as a makeshift fan to cool yourself down and relaxing back on a rug finishing off an ice-block.'

'This was my third,' she said softly, whispering her words near his ear. 'You were right. They're delicious.'

Her face was tilted towards him, her lips slightly parted, as though begging him to kiss her. He didn't disappoint and captured her mouth with his. 'Mmm... Strawberry and apple,' he remarked after tasting her cool lips. 'My favourite.'

'I thought you liked peach and blueberry.'

'I wasn't talking about the ice-block,' he murmured and captured her lips once more in another kiss, this one slow and teasing and igniting the need deep inside Daisy she was finding difficult to ignore. He then shifted closer to her and was delighted when she leaned her head on his shoulder as they watched the movie with the rest of the town.

After the first hour, Daisy eased back, lying propped up on one arm. She'd seen this movie several times before and loved the storyline of how the main protagonists had to work together to solve the mystery...falling in love as the story progressed.

'If only life were that simple,' she whispered, and as he heard the pain in her words his protective instinct began to flare. Who had hurt his Daisy? And would she ever trust him enough to tell him about it?

CHAPTER ELEVEN

'WHAT DID YOU think of the movie?' Tori asked. 'I know most people have seen it as it's a classic but there's just something about sitting out here together as a community and watching it as one big happy family,' she continued, not giving Daisy a chance to answer.

'Oh, I doubt she and Oscar were watching much of the movie,' Glenys remarked as she walked past. 'Too busy canoodling, from what I could see.' She laughed as she carried her picnic rug and chairs to her car.

'Don't mind Glenys,' Tori said as Oscar finished folding up their own picnic rug. 'The gossip is always rampant when something new and exciting happens in town.'

'Was Scotty here tonight?' Oscar asked but Tori shook her head.

'He's still in Darwin with Gracie and her parents, helping out. He calls me regularly with updates.' The nurse seemed very pleased that she and Scotty were back on speaking terms.

'That's right. I thought he was coming back in time for the movie night.'

'No. Gracie's doing well, as you both know, but her parents still rely on Scotty to help them out.'

'Of course. Anyway,' Oscar stated, slipping his hand

into Daisy's, 'time to get some sleep, I think. Who knows what sort of emergency we'll encounter next?' It was just after midnight as they headed back to the doctors' residence and Daisy was having a hard time controlling her yawns. 'Do you realise, my delicious Daisy…' she chuckled at his name for her '…that when you're tired and sleepy you're even more irresistible?'

'I am?'

'Yes. I remember that very first night you arrived. I watched over you as you slept, making sure your temperature didn't spike.'

'You did?'

'Of course I did. I couldn't have my new doctor checking out before she'd really checked in.' He pulled her into his arms and looked into her eyes. 'I love that you're almost the same height as me. I love the way you throw yourself into whatever situation you face, family, war zones or outback problems. You just…confront whatever is in your own way and I admire that quality in you.'

'Admire it, please, but don't love me, Oscar.' She closed her eyes and rested her forehead against his. 'Don't love me,' she whispered.

Initially, he'd only used the word as a throwaway line, in a non-serious context, but seeing her reaction caused him to question further. 'Why not? You'd be so easy to love.' And he meant it, he realised. The knowledge should have scared him but, instead, he felt a peace settle over him that holding Daisy close to his heart was the right thing to do.

'I wouldn't be easy to love because my life is not a normal one,' she stated, pain in her tone, but she was more than happy for him to capture her mouth with his, more than happy to lose herself to the sensations he could evoke within her. She tried so hard to kiss him back the same way, to let him know that he made her happy, that she thoroughly enjoyed being with him but...love? How could she possibly know what love was when she wasn't sure she'd ever received it from anyone else?

'What's love got to do with it?' her father had ranted when she'd begged him to help her mother, the woman he was supposed to cherish and care about.

'You don't love Mother?' she'd questioned.

'I'm exceedingly fond of her, Daisy, but love is for people with no real power. We have position, integrity and breeding to uphold. Your mother's antics are disgraceful and, as such, she should deal with them and not drag me down to her level. She can host my parties, but apart from that she can keep out of my way until she can get herself under control. She's so weak.' He'd said the last three words with such distaste and at that moment, Daisy had hated her father. He had no compassion, no understanding. All he cared about was how the situation looked to the outside world. It was why he'd been more than happy for her to study medicine because bragging to his friends that his daughter was a qualified doctor had been impressive.

'Love only brings pain,' her mother had said when Daisy had once more tried to get her into a rehabilitation facility. Cecilia had already been to one in Spain and for almost a year it had worked. She'd been strong and kept off the alcohol, but when she'd discovered Daisy's father was having an affair with the woman who had purported to be Cecilia's best friend she'd returned to the bottle.

Love only brings pain. The words kept repeating

over and over in Daisy's head. Her parents were living proof that the statement was true.

If she dared to allow herself to love Oscar, to really love Oscar, would it bring her pain? Every time she'd tried to love the people in her life, her parents, her brother, her friends…it had indeed brought her nothing but pain. So she'd held herself aloof, wanting to concentrate on her work, on using the skills she'd gained in order to help others. That had certainly brought a sense of satisfaction but here with Oscar, here in his arms, in their lounge room, she wasn't sure she could take those final steps towards supposed happiness.

She broke free, her breathing ragged as she looked into his eyes. 'Oscar, where is this going?'

'Well…' He raised his eyebrows suggestively. 'Your room's probably cleaner than mine.'

'No, not that. Of course I realise that on an attraction level, on a sensual level, we are indeed compatible, but what's next? We sleep together? What then? We work closely together. The health and well-being of this town rests on our shoulders. We were scheduled to have this discussion this evening and yet all we've done is ignore the conversation we really should have been having.'

'Daisy.' He kissed her forehead, then led her over to the lounge, which contained the two wing-back chairs. They sat down together, Oscar holding both of her hands in his. He paused for a moment, then spoke clearly but quietly. 'I've been hurt twice before, my heart ripped up into little pieces, and I swore to myself it would never happen again.'

'And yet tonight you mentioned love,' she felt compelled to point out.

'I know. It stunned me as much as it stunned you but,

at the end of the day, the heart wants what it wants even if logically the decision isn't a sound one.'

'You'd risk getting hurt for a third time?'

'If it meant I had memories with you?' He thought about it for a moment then nodded. 'I think I would.'

'But…there's still so much about me you don't know, so much that I haven't told you.'

'I know enough.'

'Really? You'd still feel the same way about me if I told you that my family is very wealthy?'

'Are they?'

'Yes.'

'Good for them.'

Daisy let go of his hands and took a few steps away from him. 'Oscar, my father is an earl. He's Lord Forsythe-York. My mother is Lady Forsythe-York.'

'Titled, eh?'

She spread her arms wide at his blasé attitude. 'How can you not care about this?'

'Because it doesn't change the person *you* are right now, the woman standing in front of me, the woman who paid for Mrs Piper's surgery.'

'You know about that?'

'Timothy told me when we were in Darwin. All it did was make me admire you more.'

'So it wouldn't bother you that my official title is Lady Daisy Philomena Sarah Forsythe-York?'

'Ah.' It was as though a light bulb clicked on over his head. '*That's* why you didn't like it when I called you Lady Daisy. Fair enough, too.' He grinned at her. 'Pretty name. So you really are a lady?'

'I am.'

'And you have certain societal responsibilities that your family expect you to uphold?'

'I do.'

'And yet you've stood your ground and demanded that you go to medical school. You worked overseas, you joined the army and went to war! Daisy, you're amazing and brilliant and brave and so many other things that this news doesn't change my opinion of you at all.'

Daisy threw her arms up in the air. 'Why are you being so accepting and complacent about this?'

'I'm not being complacent, Daisy, I assure you. The last time we had a big turnout to a movie night like that was about three weeks before Lucinda passed away. Tonight brought back many memories of her telling me to find myself again, to not let myself be squashed by my mistakes of the past, to enjoy the life I had. "Life is for living, little brother—so live it…for yourself and for me." That's what she said and tonight I remembered that. Tonight, I experienced what those words meant. Sitting there with you, watching the movie with the town, I don't know… I felt—' He shrugged one shoulder. 'I felt happy.'

'And you haven't felt that way in a long time?'

He nodded. 'See? We're not so different, Daisy.'

'Yes, we are! How can I make you understand the very real differences between us?'

'You like strawberries. I hate mushrooms. Yes, we're different, but that's also what makes us unique. However, when we are together, when I hold you in my arms…' He stood and started walking slowly towards her. She stood her ground, wanting him to be near to her but also wanting to find a way to get it through his thick head that they came from completely different backgrounds.

'Oscar.' She put up one hand to stop him advancing but all he did was take it in his and kiss it. 'Your parents passed away when you were young. You were raised by your sister. You've had pain and loss all throughout your life.'

'I know this.'

'If you insist on becoming involved with me, then you'll continue to have pain and loss.'

'I disagree,' he murmured, cupping her face and lowering his head to capture her lips. He was rewarded with a sigh and her arms entwining around his neck. How could she say this was wrong? How could she say that what existed between them was only going to bring pain and loss?

'Something that feels this right,' he whispered against her mouth, 'couldn't possibly be that wrong.'

'Shut up and kiss me,' she demanded and he grinned before complying with her wishes. It was only the ringing of her cell phone that stopped them. At this hour of the night, it was imperative they answer all calls.

'Emergency?' She extracted herself from his embrace and walked to the table beside the wing-back chair where she'd left her phone.

'You get the phone. I'll get the emergency bag.' He spun on his heel and headed towards the kitchen. He heard her answer the call, 'Dr Daisy speaking,' and couldn't help but smile that she was now calling herself that. She was becoming more of an honorary Aussie every day. Not that he wanted her to lose her haughty Britishness, as he loved that part of her.

Loved. There was that word again. Until tonight, he hadn't allowed himself to think of her in such a way, but since they'd given in to the need to touch and caress and kiss, he hadn't been able to stop the word from springing to mind...or his lips.

'Don't love me,' she'd said, and yet she'd still to give him a decent reason as to why not.

Oscar grabbed the emergency bag then went back into the lounge room to find out what the situation was. What he found was Daisy sitting in the chair, her face almost deathly pale, just hanging up the phone.

'Daisy?' He received no reply from her. 'Daisy?' His senses heightened to full alert. 'Daisy, what's wrong? What is it?' He knelt down in front of her and stared into her face.

Slowly she looked at him but her eyes were glassy, not seeing him at all. 'It's my mother. She's in a coma.'

CHAPTER TWELVE

'WHAT?' OSCAR STARED at her, then gathered her close, or at least he tried to. This time when she put up her hand, she kept it up, using her strength to push him away.

'Don't hug me.'

'What?' he said again. 'Why not? I'm here for you. I'll do whatever you need.'

'I need you not to hug me.' Her words were clipped, her expression was controlled and, although she still had very little colour in her face, her eyes were huge and expressive. It showed her concern, her worries, her fears. 'If you hug me,' she continued a moment later, 'I'll crumble and right now I don't need to crumble, I need to be one hundred per cent in control of my faculties.'

'All right.' He held up his hands but still stayed kneeling in front of her. 'No hugging. What can I do to help you?' For a while he thought she wasn't going to answer him, her eyes still staring unseeingly past him, her mind clearly working fast. Her mask, the one he'd seen her wear that very first day she'd arrived here in Meeraji Lake, came back into place. She had herself under control. If that was what she needed in order to function, then so be it.

'A cup of tea, please.'

'As you wish,' he stated and immediately stood and

headed into the kitchen. While the kettle boiled, he could hear her on the phone and realised she was making a few calls of her own. When he returned with her cup of tea, she was just dialling a new number.

'Thank you,' she remarked and eased back in the chair, pulling her feet beneath her, protecting herself and at the same time shutting him out. He remembered when she'd first arrived and how she hadn't wanted to accept anyone's help, how she'd wanted to get better all on her own. That woman, the one who had survived terrible situations in the heart of a war-torn country, came to the fore. Still, he wasn't just going to walk away and leave her alone. Whether she liked it or not, he was going to stand by her.

'John,' she said a moment later into the phone. 'I wanted you to give me an update.' Her beautiful eyes swam with tears as she listened to her brother. 'John! Mother is in hospital. I've just received a call from her physician to tell me she's in a coma. How can you not know this?' A pause. 'I don't care if you're in Scotland. I'm on the other side of the world and it will take you far less time to get to her than me.'

As Oscar listened unashamedly to her side of the conversation, equally astonished at her brother's lack of concern, he started to realise what she'd been trying to tell him earlier, about how her family was very different from his.

'Get on a plane. Drive in your car. I don't care. Just get to the hospital.' Another pause. 'I'm presuming Father knows as he's the one who's no doubt caused all this with his constant berating and emotional bullying of her.' Daisy gritted her teeth. 'No, I'm not going to call him and, yes, you *do* have to go.' She closed her eyes. 'Because she's your mother, John. Think of how it will look if the papers get a hold of this story. You'll be the doting son. The one at her bedside. Helping her through this situation.'

Her family were newsworthy? He guessed an earl's wife being admitted to hospital in a coma might very well be newsworthy. Apparently Daisy's latest attempt to shift her brother into gear had worked because she sighed and opened her eyes. 'Thank you, John. I've booked a flight but I still won't be there for another two days—at the earliest.'

'You've already booked your flight?' Oscar asked after she'd hung up.

'Of course.' Daisy stood and headed to her bedroom, where she got out her suitcase and put it on the bed.

'Do you need to pack right now?' he asked.

'Yes. I've called Henry and he's organising for the emergency chopper to fly me to Darwin. I'm booked on the mid-morning flight to Heathrow airport.'

'Then I'm going with you.'

She stopped and stared at him as though he'd grown an extra head. 'You're going to come to England with me?' Her tone was laced with sarcasm and he so desperately wanted to tell her that that was exactly what he was going to do; however, both of them knew that was impossible.

'I can go with you to Darwin. I can check on Gracie while I'm there.'

'Oscar, I don't think that's wise.'

'I don't care what you think,' he stated and pulled his own phone from his pocket and called Tori to let her know that he and Daisy would be leaving to go to Darwin so she was first point of call for any emergencies.

'There.' He shoved his phone back into his pocket. 'All organised. I'm just as stubborn as you, remember?'

Daisy's answer was to grit her teeth and toss more of her clothes into her suitcase. For a woman who was usually meticulous, she didn't seem to care all that much about the contents of her suitcase. 'How will you get back from Darwin?' she asked. 'I've told Henry I'll pay the cost of the chopper taking me to Darwin. Are you going to pay for your own ride home?'

'I can hitch a ride with the RFDS, as you well know,' he stated. 'I'm not backing down, Daisy. You need to go and see your mother. I understand that but your attitude of trying to shut me out, of making it seem as though this situation has nothing to do with me—'

'It doesn't have anything to do with you,' she interrupted, raising her tone. 'This is *my* family. *My* life.'

'I thought things had changed between us. I thought we'd moved past this professional acquaintance, past being just friends.' He opened his arms wide, almost wanting her to see that this was him, stripped raw, willing to throw himself at her feet. 'Daisy. You know how I feel about you. Let me help.'

'There's nothing you can do.' She enunciated every word meticulously and he dropped his arms back to his sides. 'Excuse me.' She sidestepped him and removed the clothes from her closet.

'OK. If that's the way you want to play it, I'll help you pack. Let me get your toiletries for you.'

Daisy glanced at him, clearly wondering if he was now trying to get rid of her, but thankfully she could see his genuineness and started to soften a little towards him. For one split second, Oscar thought he might have reached her, might have broken through that tough diplomatic exterior she was wont to wear, but as fleetingly as it came, it disappeared.

'Thank you.' She continued to pack and Oscar knew

his only course of action was to stand his ground, to not let her quash his efforts to become a part of her life. He wasn't even sure when he'd realised he *needed* to be a part of her life—no matter what. He would even leave Meeraji Lake and move to England if it meant he could be with her and he most certainly hadn't felt that way with either of his previous relationships. All he knew right now was that he needed to support her and if she couldn't tell him what she needed from him, then he would do his best and muddle through.

He returned with her things and handed them to her. 'Thank you,' she replied again, ever polite, and as he watched her move about the room in a stiff and controlled manner he realised, for the first time, that he was actually looking at Lady Daisy Philomena Sarah Forsythe-York. Here she was. The groomed aristocrat... and he still loved her. It didn't matter whether she was Dr Daisy, Major Daisy or Lady Daisy, at the end of the day, she was *his* Daisy.

'What wrenches my heart,' he murmured as she zipped the suitcase closed, 'is that you think you need to go through all of this alone. You don't, Daisy.'

'I do.'

'No.' He caressed her cheek, pushing her hair behind her ear. 'You don't. I'm here. I'm here for you. In whatever capacity you require.' He cupped her cheek, wanting to exude as much love and support as he could. When she didn't immediately pull away from his touch, he leaned forward and kissed her, wanting to let her *feel* just how much he cared for her.

'Oscar.' His name was a whisper of pain, then she eased away from him and shook her head. 'Don't come to Darwin with me.'

'Daisy, I—'

She held up her hand. Didn't he understand how difficult this was for her? Couldn't he see the extra pain he was causing her?

'Can you at least tell me why? Why don't you want me to come with you?'

'Because saying goodbye to you here is hard enough.' It was then that her voice broke and tears filled her eyes. 'I've been so happy. I want to keep those memories. Please? Please, Oscar?' she pleaded and he knew he'd give in, knew he'd give her whatever she wanted even if it almost killed him to do so. 'I want these last memories to be happy ones, not ones of us arguing.'

He frowned for a moment. 'Daisy, this isn't goodbye.'

'Oscar, my mother is in a coma. Her physician couldn't tell me much over the phone in case his phone is tapped.'

'Tapped? What sort of world do you live in?'

'One very different from here.' Her words were sad and she hefted her suitcase from the bed and started wheeling it towards the front door.

'Can I at least drive you to the helicopter?' he asked as he took the suitcase from her, which, thankfully, she allowed him to do. Again, she shook her head.

'Henry's giving me a lift.'

Oscar couldn't believe his life had gone from happiness to misery in such a short space of time. 'Will you at least call me? Let me know you arrived safely?'

She nodded. 'Kiss me, Oscar. Kiss me goodbye.' She wrapped her arms around his neck, pain filling her eyes. 'Make it memorable.'

'I'll make it memorable, all right, but this isn't goodbye, Daisy.' He gathered her close, knowing she was concerned for her mother, knowing she was going to have a hectic few days of travel ahead of her, knowing she was going to be standing alone, fighting the battles yet to come by herself. He wanted to pour the love, a love that seemed to be increasing with every passing second, into her, wanted to shower it over it, to protect her, to let her know that he was always with her, loving her.

He kissed her with purpose, with reason, with promise until a car horn beeped from outside and Daisy pulled away, slightly breathless. 'I love you, Daisy.'

She shook her head slowly as though she didn't really believe him. 'I'll call you when I'm safely in England.'

'Thank you.' She was so polite, almost impersonal, and he wouldn't have believed it if it hadn't been for her slightly swollen lips, which let him know that she'd enjoyed those kisses as much as him. 'I'd better go. I don't want to keep Henry waiting. Stay inside. Please.'

He pursed his lips for a moment before nodding and forcing a little smile. 'OK, but only because you asked so nicely.' With that, he winked at her and she forced a smile of her own in return.

'Goodbye, Oscar.'

'See you later,' he responded in the typical Australian farewell. Within another moment, she'd walked out of the door and closed it behind her. Another moment later, he heard Henry's police car pull away and drive off into the distance.

How long he stood there, he had no clue. All he knew was that the house smelled like Daisy, like the woman he loved, and although she'd thought she was saying goodbye to him, she had another think coming.

CHAPTER THIRTEEN

'HAVE YOU HEARD from Daisy?' Tori asked him two days later as they dealt with a busier than usual emergency department.

'She called to say she's arrived.'

'Any news on her mother?'

'She didn't give me any details.'

'Have you tried calling her?'

'Yes, Tori, I have,' he snapped. 'She probably hasn't been able to get back to me because she's at the hospital looking after her mother.'

'Do you know what happened to put her mother into the coma?'

'Just stop with the all the questions and go and see the patient in room two.' He picked up a set of case notes. 'I'll be in room one.' He stalked off to deal with his patient, wishing everyone would stop asking him about Daisy.

It would be fine if the woman would answer his calls, and if she didn't have the time to do that she could at least send him a text message, or email him but Daisy seemed intent on maintaining her radio silence, as it were.

A week later, there was still no news, not from Daisy. Scotty had returned from Darwin, giving them a firsthand account of Gracie's progress and even showing Oscar photographs he'd taken with his cell phone of the wound site.

'That is a great improvement,' he said, handing Scotty's phone back to him.

'Timothy, her doctor, said she's going to make a full recovery although there may be a slight restriction in the movement of her little and ring fingers.'

'Fantastic news. And her parents? Are they home yet?'

'They're going to stay in Darwin until Gracie can be transferred here to Meeraji Lake. It'll make it easier on them.' Scotty continued to talk about his experiences in Darwin but Oscar wasn't listening. Whenever he wasn't with a patient, a part of his thoughts was on Daisy, wondering why she hadn't called him, wondering how her mother was progressing, trying to figure out what her father could possibly have done to send her mother into a coma. Whatever it was, had they managed to keep it out of the papers?

Another week later, he still had no answers and was even more worried than before. He'd been determined that when she'd left, it hadn't been forever, that it wasn't a real 'goodbye', but with the way she seemed to be refusing to return his calls, was ignoring his emails and generally snubbing him, he was starting to wonder whether she hadn't been right.

Was this the end of his relationship with Daisy? Was he willing to let this one go?

'No!' He paced around his house, the house that seemed to be far too empty. Now, when he dreamed about having a wife and children, filling this house with laughter, his wife's face was clear and distinct because it belonged to Daisy.

Whatever he'd felt for Magda or Deidre was nothing compared to how Daisy made him feel. She was his other half, his soulmate. So why was she insistent on causing both of them so much pain?

Another two weeks later, with absolutely no contact, and he was finally starting to believe that last kiss had really been their goodbye kiss. The only correspondence he'd received from Daisy was her letter of resignation. It stated that due to a family emergency she would be unable to fulfil the full terms of her contract, that she was willing to pay any damages and that he should get in contact with her attorney to settle the details.

Didn't she realise, it wasn't about the money? Did she think that she could just buy him off? What sort of person kissed him the way she had and then left without a word? She thought she had to go through this crisis alone and even though he'd tried to reassure her, to let her know that he was here for her, she'd still rejected him.

It was that that hurt the most, the lack of trust, the disbelief that he could support her, that he would do anything for her. How could she do this to him? How could she kiss him in such a way that clearly indicated she'd had very strong feelings for him, and then just cut him off without another word?

What added fuel to his already annoyed and burning fire were the whispers that seemed to stop the instant he walked into a room. His friends would smile at him, in that sad, pathetic way they had in the past when Deidre had left.

'Poor Oscar,' he'd heard them whisper. 'That's *three* women who have rejected him now. I can't understand why. He's such a nice, handsome bloke.'

Three women. One had left him because he didn't

earn enough money. The other had left him because her career was more important and the last... He shook his head. She'd left him because she was stubborn and that was just plain stupid. Daisy was stupid and he was stupid too because he still loved her, even more than when she'd left.

As he sat in the kitchen, drinking a hot cup of tea even though it was still very warm outside, he allowed the pain from his breaking heart to fill his entire body. When someone knocked at the door, he wasn't sure he had the energy to tell them to go away.

'Hello?' Tori called and a moment later she and Scotty walked in together, followed by Glenys, Erica and Henry. 'Are we disturbing your dinner or aren't you bothering to eat food any more?'

'What do you all want?' He sighed and finished his cup of tea, clattering the cup down onto the saucer.

'This is an intervention,' Scotty said, resting his hand on Oscar's shoulder.

'We care about you too much to see you going through this again,' Glenys remarked.

'So,' Erica said with glee, 'we've bought you a ticket to England.'

'A what?' Oscar looked at them all as though they'd gone stark raving bonkers.

'A plane ticket. For you to go to England.' Tori spoke to him as though he were five years old.

'We all chipped in,' Henry remarked as he handed over the piece of paper that indeed confirmed that Oscar was booked to travel overseas the day after tomorrow.

'It's a nice gesture but I can't go.'

'Why not?' Tori asked.

'Why not?' He stood and spread his arms wide. 'Because unless you can find another doctor hiding somewhere in this building, I can't go. I can't leave Meeraji Lake without a doctor for that length of time and Daisy knows it. She knows I won't come after her and therefore she can maintain her resolve not to speak to me because I can't do anything about it except get frustrated and annoyed and—' He stopped and covered his face with his hands.

'But that's where you're wrong,' Scotty said.

'He's right. I've managed to find a locum for you,' Tori stated. 'Her name is Harriette and she's arriving tomorrow so you'll have a one-day hand-over before you head off on your overseas adventure to bring our Daisy back home.'

'What?' Oscar dropped his hands from his face and stared at the smiling, nodding faces of his friends.

'It's true,' Erica said.

Glenys clapped her hands with excitement. 'Daisy's going to be so surprised to see you.'

Oscar stared at the travel details as the reality of his situation slowly sank in. He was booked to go overseas. A locum would look after the town. He could go and see Daisy.

The question was, would she want to see him?

The phone from the gatehouse buzzed and Daisy walked across the polished marble floors to answer it. She'd been back in England for four weeks and she couldn't believe how oppressed she felt. Her time in Australia, in Meeraji Lake, seemed like a mirage, something she could see, could remember, but would never be able to touch again.

Her mother, thank goodness, had woken from the coma the day after Daisy had arrived back in England and was now convalescing at home, under Daisy's watchful eye. Daisy's father was home but keeping his distance from the situation as best he could. Upon arriving home, Daisy had discovered her father had insisted upon installing his mistress permanently at the house, that he expected her mother to be civil to the mistress but keep up appearances that everything was perfect in the Forsythe-York household. It had been the last straw for Cecilia and she'd taken to the bottle as though it were her only hope.

Daisy had thrown herself into doing everything she could for her mother, organising for a private nurse as well as handling the press when she'd needed to, and she'd done it all with the firm intention of not focusing on Oscar. She hadn't allowed herself to think about him and how much she missed him because she knew, if she did, she'd end up in a state almost as bad as her mother's. Oscar Price and the way he'd made her feel were in the past. She'd been used to disappointment her entire life so why should now be any different?

She picked up the phone. 'Yes, Gibson?'

'Sorry to bother you, Lady Daisy, but there's an Australian gentleman here who says he knows you. Says he's a doctor, not a reporter. He's becoming more and more agitated the longer I refuse to let him through. He demanded that I ring up to the main house to speak to you.'

'Give me that phone,' Daisy heard a familiar deep voice say and a moment later he spoke.

'Daisy? Daisy, is that you?'

'Oscar! What are you doing here?'

'Not getting past your bulldog. Let me in.'

The last three words were ground between clenched teeth and she had the sense that if she didn't give Gibson the all clear to let Oscar come up to the main house,

Oscar would probably find a way to jump the fence and trip every alarm in the place. Then the police would be called, not to mention Gibson and the rest of his security staff weighing in on the misdemeanour. In other words, a complete nightmare.

'Daisy!'

'All right. All right.' A moment later, Gibson came back on the line and she told him to allow Oscar access. The moment she put the phone down, her entire body began to tingle with confusion, excitement and dread. If Oscar was here, then there would be no way she would be able to protect him, to shield him from the overbearing attitude of her family, to ensure her father didn't spend hours interrogating him. Why had he come? What could he possibly hope to gain from—?

The front doorbell rang and she quickly headed across the entry hall, calling to the butler that it was all right, she'd answer the door.

'What are you doing here?' she demanded as soon as she'd opened the large wooden door and stared at Oscar standing opposite her. She hadn't meant to be so direct, so rude, but he'd caught her completely off guard and…and…how could a man look so amazing, so handsome, so…? Her brain shut down and she could think of nothing else except the way his mouth was enticing her to taste, to…to…

And then, as though unable to restrain himself at all, Oscar stepped forward, dropped his bag and gathered her into his arms, pressing his mouth firmly to hers. Daisy wound her arms around his neck and kissed him back with abandon.

Even though he was groggy from the exceedingly long flight, tired, angry and frustrated, all that disappeared in an instant. Daisy. *His* Daisy. She was all he needed and he could stand here kissing her forever.

'Wait. Stop. No.' Daisy wrenched herself free and took two huge steps back from him. 'What are you doing here?' she asked again. Her breathing was as erratic as his and he stepped closer, needing her.

'I would have thought that was obvious.' When he reached for her again, she held up both her hands and he stopped.

'You can't be here.'

'Well, I am.'

'Oscar!'

'Daisy!'

'Shh.' She looked around them, knowing they were probably being observed, whether by the butler, who reported everything to her father, or one of the maids, who, although having signed non-disclosure agreements, wouldn't be above making money off this story. Closing her eyes for a moment, Daisy reached out and grabbed his hand, dragging him through the high-ceilinged rooms, around a few twists and turns, heading further back into the estate home, which was most definitely a mansion.

'Where are we—?'

'Shh!' She put a finger over her lips for emphasis, then opened a door and dragged him inside. He looked around the room, the walls covered with display cabinets containing pieces of patterned china and other ornaments.

'Whoa.' He quickly looked around the room as she let go of his hand and went to close the door. 'I wouldn't want to be the person responsible for dusting this room.'

'Oscar. You shouldn't have come.'

'Then you should have returned my calls, responded to my emails.'

'I thought it best to make a clean break.'

'You thought wrong.' He stepped forward and kissed her again, loving the way she responded to him, as though the time they'd spent apart had done nothing to decrease the attraction between them, but had intensified it instead. When they broke apart, she shook her head and walked over to sit in the only chair in the entire room.

It was an old fashioned tête-à-tête seat, designed in the eighteen hundreds. He sat on one side and Daisy sat on the other. Their faces were incredibly close and he couldn't help but breathe in her scent.

'How's your mother? Is she out of the coma? Improving?' He hoped all the answers were in the affirmative because if things had gone tragically wrong…

'Yes. She's home now, upstairs in fact and starting to eat.'

'She wasn't eating?'

'Not really.' Daisy looked down at her hands, knowing that now he was here he would find out the truth. Even by reading the papers, if he hadn't already, he'd discover what was going on. 'My mother is…an alcoholic. My father has finally installed his mistress in the house and my mother tried to drown herself in drink.'

'Oh, Daisy. Is that what you couldn't tell me?' He cupped her face and kissed her. 'Did you think I wouldn't understand?'

She kissed him back but then slowly shook her head. 'I ruined our family's reputation once before. I couldn't do it again.'

'I don't understand. How did you ruin the reputation of your family?'

'In my final year of med school, I met a guy called Walter. We hit it off right away and we fell in love, or so I thought.' She sighed and shook her head sadly.

'He turned out to be someone different?'

'In a way. He turned out to be someone who wasn't past trying to make some money selling a story to the papers.'

'Ah.' It all made sense now. 'You told him about your mother,' he stated and she nodded.

'Walter and I had been together for five months, we'd planned to get married and he'd given me a toy ring from a vending machine as a makeshift engagement ring.' She smiled at the memory. 'I'd loved it because it wasn't flash or an enormous diamond. It was...fun.'

'Did you bring him home?'

'To meet my father. Yes. He insisted on doing everything right. Asking my father's permission to marry, meeting my mother, becoming best friends with my brother. He was eager to please.'

'Did he know who your family was before you met?'

'I don't know.' The smile slipped from her face and she shrugged. 'Still to this day, I don't know if he targeted me or not. My father said he must have because when Walter discovered my mother was a recovering alcoholic, he didn't hesitate to try and sell the story to the highest bidder.'

'What happened then?'

'My father has spies everywhere. Especially at different newspapers. He got wind of the story and paid Walter off. Walter received more money than he could ever have hoped for and completely disappeared from my life.'

'And your father blamed you for the entire thing? For "ruining the family"?'

'Yes, but he also emotionally abused my mother for a long time after that. He said that if she hadn't been drinking, Walter never would have had a story to sell. He calls her a disgrace. He berates her and criticises her at every opportunity.' She was gritting her teeth again and he could quite clearly hear the disgust in her tone. 'He kept everything out of the papers and still ensures that his PR team handle anything and everything to do with information about the family.'

'So why wasn't he able to stop it this time?'

'Because he didn't want to, because he wants my mother to be disgraced, to paint her as the reason he wants to divorce her and marry his mistress.'

Oscar shook his head in disgust. He could see how upset Daisy was and he knew that no matter what happened between them, he needed to tell her the truth, to be completely honest with her.

'I have to confess I did try to look you up online and, apart from some very flattering pictures of you dressed in your army uniform and one of you in a very flash ball gown when you were younger, there really isn't that much about you I didn't already know.'

'You looked me up online?'

Was that disgust or disbelief in her tone? 'You weren't giving me *any* information, Daisy. I wasn't sure if your mother had passed away or whether you were still safe. I was beside myself with worry. I had to do *something*.'

'I thought you'd be angry with me.'

'I was. I still am. Very angry. Don't you ever try and cut me out of your life like that again because I will find my way back into that inner sanctum you keep so tightly locked up.'

'Giving me orders, Dr Price?'

'No, Major Forsythe-York. Making you a promise.'
He leaned over and kissed her, wanting her to feel,
rather than rely on his words, just how much he adored
her. When they broke apart their breathing was ragged.
'I've missed you so much,' he whispered against her
lips before kissing them once more. A moment later,
she pulled back and looked at him. 'Wait a second. How
could you leave Meeraji Lake? Who's looking after the
patients?'

'Tori found a locum. Her name is Harriette and she's
happy to stay there for at least the next twelve months.'

'Oh? Well, that's good news, for the town. I do miss
everyone. Oh, how are Scotty and Tori? Back together,
I hope.'

He smiled and nodded. 'They are. And now *we're*
back together because, crazy woman, I'm not letting
you go, ever again.'

'Wait. Wait. Are you saying that…you're staying?
Here? In England? With me?'

He tightened his grip around her and dropped a kiss
to her nose. 'That's what boyfriends do.'

'Boyfriend?' She giggled nervously at the word.
'You're my boyfriend?'

'Yes.' He grinned, loving her reaction.

'Do I get a say in this?'

'No.'

'Oh.'

'Got a problem with that, Your Ladyship?'

'If I do, am I allowed to register a complaint?'

'No.'

Daisy smiled, then kissed him soundly on the lips.
'You are amazing.'

'I love you, Daisy. That's the amazing thing. I never
thought I'd feel this way again and this time, with you,

everything is magnified. Where I thought I was happy before, I'm ecstatic now.'

'Oscar, I—'

'You don't have to reply. I'm not trying to put you on the spot. I'm here for you, Daisy. I think you don't really know what it's like to be loved so I'm going to give you very clear examples of what that means.'

'Like travelling halfway around the world to support me?'

'Exactly. See, you're a fast learner.' He kissed her and she responded with such abandonment, as though she was trying to express the way he made her feel with actions because she wasn't sure how else to show him.

After a moment, he drew back, both of them breathless and filled with desire. 'Perhaps this isn't the best room in the house to have a reunion.'

Daisy nodded, overcome with emotion. Her lower lip began to wobble. 'Thank you. Thank you so much, Oscar. Thank you for coming, thank you for pushing through my stubbornness, thank you for…for…loving me.' She started to choke back the tears but Oscar shook his head.

'Let it out, Daisy. You've been carrying far too much on your shoulders. Together we'll deal with this.'

'How?' She sobbed.

'Well, why don't we take your mother someplace else? Somewhere she likes. Perhaps your mother will finally be ready to leave him.'

'I hope so. Will you come and talk to her with me? Help me to convince her? Is that sort of thing part of the boyfriend description?' She pulled back and looked at him, hope in her eyes.

He smiled warmly. 'Of course it is.'

Daisy thought for a moment, then nodded slowly. 'She likes Spain.'

'Then Spain it is. We'll rent a place where the three of us can relax and talk and find some sort of peace.'

More tears gathered in her eyes. 'Is this what love is? Being kind? Thinking of others? Being supportive?'

'And all of it completely unconditional.'

'Oh, Oscar. If that's true, then I love you. I love you so incredibly much that it feels as though my heart is going to break through my chest.'

He brushed the loose tendrils of hair back from her face and kissed her lips. 'Mine, too. I love you, my beautiful Daisy. You've brought so much sunshine to my life and I hope you continue to do so forever.'

She nodded earnestly. 'Yes. Yes, I will. It won't be easy, Oscar. You know that, don't you? My family is—'

'Your family is *me*. And Tori and Scotty and Glenys and Erica,' he added. 'And all of the Meeraji Lake district.'

'And my mother?'

He nodded. 'Let's hope so.'

Daisy smiled and kissed him. 'I'm liking the sound of this love thing, this family thing…this you-and-me thing.'

'Do you think "this you-and-me thing" might end with a wedding?'

Daisy couldn't help but laugh, a rich sound of pure happiness. 'Oh, it had better because now that I've found you, Dr Price, there's no way I'm ever letting you go.'

'I like the sound of that, Dr Daisy.'

Then he stood and gathered her to him once more, kissing her soundly, both of them more happy than they could ever have imagined.

EPILOGUE

DAISY AND OSCAR stood barefoot on the beach in Spain in the cool of the day, a small marquee erected over their heads. Scotty stood beside Oscar as his best man and Tori stood beside Daisy as her maid of honour. Daisy's mother sat in a wheelchair on the other side of her daughter, the two of them holding hands.

It was far more than Daisy could ever have dreamed. For the past eight weeks, she had come to know her mother as she'd never thought possible. There had been no objection from her father or her brother when she'd told them she was taking her mother to Spain. In fact, her brother had seemed more relaxed at this news as it meant he would no longer be hounded by reporters.

Thankfully, Cecilia had finally realised that the life she was living was no life at all and that she did deserve better. In Spain, her mother had relaxed more and, through Oscar's coaxing and relaxed Aussie manner, had started to open up, just as Daisy had. The two women had talked and cried for past hurts and lost opportunities.

'Oscar is an absolute delight,' her mother had said just that morning. 'At first I thought him rather rustic and uncouth but now I understand. I most definitely see the appeal and I could not be happier that it is *him* you are marrying.'

'Thank you, Mother.'

Her mother had become rather emotional then but, rather than shying away from her emotion, she embraced it and held Daisy's hand in hers. 'I've never said this before and it's long past overdue but I'm so proud of you, Daisy. You have done things I did not have the courage to do. You have stood your ground, gone head to head with your father and shown him that you cannot be bullied. And now look at you. You are so beautiful. A bride, waiting to be united with her knight in shining armour.'

Daisy had had a difficult time choking back the tears. 'Oh, Mother. Thank you.'

'And Oscar said that if I continue to improve, I'll be able to return to Meeraji Lake with you.' Cecilia said the town's name slowly and carefully as though she'd been practising it. 'After all, if I'm going to be a grandmama in the future—a real one, who plays with her grandchildren and feeds them lots of sugary stuff and buys them too many toys—then I need to get better.'

'Of course you do.' Daisy had laughed through her tears and hugged her mother close. 'I love you, Mother.'

'Oh. Oh.' The two women had been choked up, those very precious words never having been expressed between them before. 'Well. Well, then.' Speech had been difficult for a moment and when Cecilia had looked at her, she'd shaken her head. 'Daisy, you'll need to redo your make-up if you don't start to control those tear ducts.'

Daisy knew that haughtiness was a front for feeling uncomfortable and she laughed once more. 'Then I'll redo it. Moments like this don't happen every day.'

And neither did standing beneath the marquee with the man of her dreams looking at her as though she were the most precious, most wonderful, most incredible person in the world. What she'd done to deserve a man like Oscar, she had no clue, but there was no way she was going to let him go now. She knew he missed his life in Meeraji Lake and so did she. After all, it really was their home.

Now, as they stood before the celebrant, they held hands and looked into each other's eyes. 'There are so many things I want to say to you,' Oscar began. 'But I've realised that I have the rest of my life to say them, to show you how incredibly happy you've made me. I never thought I'd find love again but I was wrong. For a long time, I wasn't sure if you were Major Daisy, Dr Daisy or Lady Daisy, but now I know, with one hundred per cent clarity, exactly who you are—you're *my* Daisy and I promise to love you forever. Work beside me. Walk beside me. Communicate with me. Laugh with me. Cry with me. Listen with me…and I promise to do the same, with all my heart.'

Daisy's lower lip had started to wobble as he'd spoken and she sniffed and quickly looked at her mother. 'I may need to redo my make-up yet again.' They all laughed but then she turned her full attention to the man before her, her heart swelling with a love she'd never known possible but was more than happy to accept.

'Oscar.' She gave his hands a little squeeze and he immediately smiled at her. 'I *love* you.' She paused. 'It really is that simple. I *love* you and I have never loved anyone until you. Because of you, I can now love others.' She smiled at her mother and then at Scotty and Tori, so pleased their two friends had been able to travel to Spain to be here for their special day. 'You have given me so much and I want nothing more than to make you happy. Thank you for saving me.'

Oscar gathered her close. 'It has been my absolute pleasure.' Then he kissed her, even though they weren't really up to that part in the ceremony yet. No one seemed to mind, though. This was their day and they could do whatever they wanted.

* * * * *

Look out for the next great story in
Lucy Clarke's OUTBACK SURGEONS *duet*
A FAMILY FOR CHLOE

And if you enjoyed this story,
check out these other great reads
from Lucy Clark

STILL MARRIED TO HER EX!
A CHILD TO BIND THEM
DR PERFECT ON HER DOORSTEP
HIS DIAMOND LIKE NO OTHER

Available now!

A FAMILY FOR CHLOE

BY
LUCY CLARK

MILLS & BOON

Published in Great Britain 2016
By Mills & Boon, an imprint of HarperCollins*Publishers*
1 London Bridge Street, London, SE1 9GF

ISBN: 978-0-263-25447-1

Our policy is to use papers that are natural, renewable and recyclable
products and made from wood grown in sustainable forests.
The logging and manufacturing processes conform to the legal
environmental regulations of the country of origin.

Printed and bound in Spain
by CPI, Barcelona

Dear Reader,

Welcome to the second story in my Outback Surgeons series. Harriette and Felix certainly make an interesting couple, and I loved getting to know them.

I knew I wanted to write about a heroine who has an adult son, and the relationship between Harriette and her son Eddie is based on the great friendship I share with my own adult son. Added to this mix is a very strong, some would say stubborn, little girl who is almost four. Miss Chloe Jane McLaren was an absolute hoot to create and write about, because when you're almost four years old you know *everything*…except how to juggle! Poor Felix often feels as if he's floundering in a world he knows nothing about, but with Harriette's help, and support from the rest of the crazy characters in the small Outback Australian town of Meeraji Lake, he finally finds his happily-ever-after.

During the writing of this story my beloved father passed away from cancer, which often made my creative times harder to find. I can't thank my editors enough for their patience as I worked through my grief. There are many aspects of this story that pay homage to my dad and what he taught me and my siblings—the main thing being that family really is so very important. Harriette helps Felix to realise this, and to understand that what is past is past and all we can do is learn from our mistakes and move forward with a positive attitude.

A Family for Chloe will always hold a special place in my heart… I hope it finds one in yours, too.

Warmest regards,

Lucy

To Erica, Tim, Ella and Chloe—wonderful friends,
thank you for allowing me to peek into your lives.

Hebrews 4:16

**Praise for
Lucy Clark**

'A good and enjoyable read. It's a good old-fashioned
romance and is everything you expect from medical
romance. Recommended for medical romance lovers and
Lucy Clark's fans.'

—Harlequin Junkie on
Resisting the New Doc In Town

'I really enjoyed this book—well written, a lovely
romance story about giving love a second chance!'

—Goodreads on
Dare She Dream of Forever?

CHAPTER ONE

'HARRIETTE? HARRIETTE JONES?' Felix McLaren stood in the middle of the Meeraji Lake District hospital's emergency department and looked around for Dr Harriette Jones, the doctor he was supposed to contact, the doctor who was supposed to be in charge of the small outback Australian hospital. Apparently, she wasn't here. In fact, there didn't seem to be anyone in the entire ED. How could a hospital—one located in the middle of nowhere—be completely empty? He found the notion impossible, especially as he'd always worked in bustling, hectic hospitals.

Felix looked around, astonished to find all the treatment rooms and emergency bays set up and ready for whatever emergencies might befall the small community. What on earth had he got himself into? He'd thought the decision to work in the Australian outback, in a small sleepy town, the right thing to do given his present circumstances; that working here would afford him more leisure time, but this—this was absolutely absurd. He'd expected things to be quiet but not *this* quiet.

He hitched up the sleeping almost-four-year-old girl in his arms and walked towards one of the treatment rooms. 'Hello?' he called as loud as he dared so as not to wake the child. The last thing he needed right now was for her to wake up. He looked around to see if there was a bell or something he could ring in order to alert someone to his presence. 'Hello? Harriette? Tori? Anyone?' Still he received no answer. He'd been told by his friend Oscar Price to speak to either Harriette or Tori but neither was to be found.

'They'll be on hand to help you with whatever you need,' Oscar had told him. Well, Oscar had been wrong. Felix shook his head with complete incredulity at the situation. What if there was an emergency? What were the patients supposed to do then? Treat themselves? He could only hope the drug cupboard was locked up tight.

Surely there had to be *someone*, somewhere within this thirty-bed hospital, which boasted a small surgery, one ambulance and, from what he could see, two very well-stocked emergency treatment rooms.

He walked back to the nurses' desk and availed himself of a chair, sinking into it with relief. Chloe resettled herself in his arms without incident. Ordinarily she wouldn't have had a bar of him but as she was so completely exhausted, she probably had no idea she was now sleeping in the arms of the guardian she didn't like.

And he knew for a fact that she didn't like him because she'd told him so, in no uncertain terms. The words, 'I hate you' had left her lips several times during their short acquaintance and although he recognised them as the words of a child, that she couldn't possibly comprehend the magnitude of her situation, they'd still cut him deep.

It was the main thing he'd quickly discovered about becoming an instant parent—when it came to the child's feelings about a person, place or thing, they told the absolute, honest to goodness truth. For Chloe, her new guardian was someone she one hundred percent did not like. As far as she was concerned, he was 'dumb'. She'd called him the word because he'd told her he wouldn't be able to help her find her mummy and daddy.

For the most part, though, Felix thought he wasn't doing such a bad job. He usually managed to cope fairly well when she was asleep, but when she was awake Chloe Jane McLaren was more than a handful. Not that he blamed her. The poor little girl had been through more than enough during the past three months. Shunted around, confused, abandoned and now he'd brought her halfway around the world.

Although she'd been born in Lancashire to an English mother and an Australian father, apart from him, Uncle Felix, she really had no other relations. Of course there was Felix's father, but the two men had been estranged for decades. Not only had Felix had to deal with the deaths of his brother, David, and his sister-in-law, Susan, but now he'd become an instant parent.

He was doing his best, trying to give Chloe some sort of normal life and, as such, he'd realised he needed to downsize his own workload. It had been a difficult decision because his career had been his life for so long. He'd worked incredibly hard and incredibly long hours to achieve the success as a respected and sought-after general surgeon. He'd won fellowships, been appointed to boards, written several published papers and been involved with new and innovative inventions designed to make the surgeon's life that much easier. He was considered, amongst his peers, as a brilliant mind. Now... he sighed and shifted the sleeping child a little in his arms. Now, he was responsible for a little person and he'd never felt more out of his depth.

That was the reason why he'd agreed to take the job here, in outback Australia. He'd hoped it would pro-

vide him with time. Time to get to know Chloe, time
to come to terms with his grief, time to figure out what
on earth he was going to do in the future. Would a year
here make a difference to his career path? Could he be
a respected surgeon *and* a parent? Should he employ a
full-time nanny and housekeeper to give Chloe more
stability? Or would that make her feel as though she'd
been abandoned by yet another person in her life? He'd
been so conflicted that when he'd bumped into his old
friend Oscar Price, who had been temporarily in England, Felix had found himself confessing he'd no idea
what to do. Oscar, as it turned out, was director of Meeraji Lake District Hospital in outback Australia but was
presently on leave with his new fiancée, Daisy.

'Why not go to Meeraji Lake for a while?' Oscar had
suggested. 'A locum, Harriette Jones, is there holding
down the fort but it's a two-doctor hospital and I hate
leaving everyone in the lurch. At the moment, though,
family comes first and Daisy's mother has been ill—
we're planning to head to Spain so she can enjoy the
warmth. My focus has to be on my family and now that
you have a family, that needs to be your first priority.
That little girl needs you, Felix.'

Felix had frowned for a moment, his mind working
fast as he'd thought through a plan. He could take a
twelve-month sabbatical from his present position and
spend it in a less stressful working environment while
figuring out how to be a parent. It could work. 'You're
sure you don't mind me going to Meeraji Lake?' he'd
asked.

'Mind?' Oscar had chuckled. 'Mate, you'd be doing
me a big favour.'

Oscar had told him of the tight-knit community, of
the excellent day-care centre, of the doctors' residence

that was only two doors down from the hospital. Everything was nice and close. Felix could spend whatever free time he had with Chloe and, when he weighed it up against his current job where he was at the hospital more often than not, it had sounded brilliant.

However, Felix also wasn't ignorant of the many dangers he would face with raising a wilful young child in such a barren environment. What if she decided to run away? She could dehydrate within a short space of time. Or what if she didn't understand that the snakes and spiders in Australia were some of the deadliest in the world? Felix shuddered at the thought, realising he'd have to keep a close eye on her. How was he supposed to do that and—?

The side doors to the hospital burst open and a gaggle of voices greeted him. Felix instantly opened his eyes and stood; the sharp action combined with the plethora of urgent chatter woke Chloe and she immediately began to cry. A paramedic stretcher was being wheeled in, the patient on the stretcher moaning and groaning with pain.

'Shh... Shh...' He started jiggling Chloe up and down while stroking her lightly on the back.

'Tori, get an IV in. Adonni, get the portable ultrasound machine into emergency room one. Pat? Patrick? Can you hear me?' The woman, a redhead with her mass of long curls pulled back into an extremely haphazard bun, continued giving rapid-fire instructions to the rest of the staff. 'Bill, get Theatre prepped.'

'You're going to do the surgery here? You don't want to transfer him to Alice?'

'There's no option but to operate. We don't want Pat to end up with peritonitis,' the redhead answered before the man she'd addressed as Bill headed off in a different direction.

Chloe started to cry louder at the ruckus around her, as though completely indignant that anyone should disturb her sleep. At the sound of the child's cries, the redhead, who was dressed in scrubs, turned to look at Felix. 'Is she all right?'

'Pardon?' he called back as the stretcher disappeared into emergency room one. The redhead was patting her supine patient's hand but called out louder to him.

'Is your daughter sick? Does she require urgent treatment?'

'Uh. No. She's uh…'

The front door to the hospital opened and in walked three men, all of them looking the worse for wear with bloodied hands, bloodied faces and sheepish grins.

'What now?' The woman glared at the three of them then pointed to the waiting area, shaking her head, the loose messy bun bobbling around on her head. 'Sit. Don't move and if you dare start to fight again in here, I'll have Henry lock all of you up for three days.'

'You can't do that,' one of the men said, his tone indignant.

'Oh, yes, I can, Bazza, so don't try me.' Her tone was determined, brooking no argument.

'Er…perhaps I can help?' Felix spoke up louder as Chloe cried louder. 'If there's somewhere I can put her down so she'll settle…' He looked around at the vacant ED treatment-room beds.

'Pardon?' The redhead quickly walked over to him. 'If you could just take a seat in the waiting room, I'll be with you as soon as I can. I have an emergency appendectomy to deal with and—'

'I'm Felix McLaren,' he interrupted and when she

still looked at him with a blank expression, he added, 'The new doctor. Oscar's friend. I'm here for the next year. Ring any bells?'

Patrick's moans and groans from emergency room one were getting louder. The woman took a few steps away. 'If you know how to do an appendectomy, you can most definitely help out.'

'Then I'll help out.' Again he angled his head towards the unsettled child in his arms; her cries were slowly subsiding but he could tell that the slightest noise could set her off again. 'Here. You put Chloe down somewhere and deal with the brawlers and I'll start scrubbing.' He handed Chloe to the redhead. 'I wouldn't usually offload her like this but we don't want that appendix to perforate and, besides, Oscar told me you were great with children.'

'He did?' Staring at him with big green eyes filled with confusion and a hint of annoyance, the redhead had no option but to accept the child he was thrusting into her arms.

Felix paused for a moment and fixed her with a firm look. 'Are you Harriette or Tori?'

'Sorry?' She had to raise her voice as the child hadn't enjoyed being handed off to a stranger and was making her displeasure known.

'Who are you?' he asked, leaning in towards her so his words could be better directed towards her ear. His warm breath fanned her exposed neck and she was treated to a hint of his subtle spicy scent. It was nice. It was good. It was disconcerting. Why the action should cause a burst of goosebumps to flood down the side of the body, she had no idea. She pushed the unwanted reaction to his nearness aside and met his gaze.

'I'm…um…Harriette. Harriette Jones.'

'Harriette. Good.' He nodded and took a step away, then shook his head and pointed to the door the man called Bill had gone through. 'I'm presuming it's that way to Theatres?'

'Yes, but—' She shifted the child in her arms and started jiggling up and down in an effort to help comfort the little girl, but anything else she might have said was useless as her new colleague had disappeared through the door that led to the wards and the operating theatre.

Harriette tried not to be completely miffed at the man, at his high-handedness, at the way he'd simply abandoned his daughter to the care of a stranger and waltzed off in search of *her* operating theatre. Of all the nerve!

'Then again, Harriette…' Her little internal voice of reason spoke up. 'You did say if he could do an appendectomy you'd be grateful of his help.'

'But I hadn't expected him to actually be able to do it!' her irrational side answered. It had all happened too fast. She hadn't asked him for any identification, hadn't checked his medical credentials. He could be just anyone about to embark on a surgical operation that might affect Patrick's health.

She kept jiggling the child in her arms as her mind whirled with a thousand different thoughts at once. Oscar had called her to say his friend Felix McLaren would be arriving to locum for twelve months and Harriette had been glad of the help. She just hadn't expected to be faced with an emergency, brawling idiots, her new colleague and a crying child all at the same time.

Harriette dragged in a breath and assessed the situation as she patted the little girl on the back, doing her best to ignore the cries and figure out the triage of her patients. Bazza and his bar-room brawling mates were starting to argue again and Patrick, the town's resident and self-proclaimed hypochondriac, was moaning even louder than before. At least this time Pat's symptoms were genuine. Shifting the child to free up one hand, Harriette reached for the phone on the desk and called Henry, the town's police officer.

'Can you come and give me a hand, please?' She spoke as loudly as possible, trying to compete with the little girl with the big brown eyes and exceptionally good set of lungs. She called out to Tori, the senior nurse, who was still caring for Patrick.

'I'm just going to go to the ward,' she yelled over the din. As she headed towards the ward Harriette tried to remember what her new colleague had called the little girl. What was it? It had started with a C. Chloe? Yes, Chloe.

Harriette immediately tightened her grasp on the now squirming little girl. 'Shh, Chloe,' she tried to soothe. 'It's going to be all right.' But even as she said the words, Harriette wasn't so sure she was telling the truth. On the ward, after she'd located ward sister who had just finished cleaning up after a patient, Harriette quickly explained the situation and asked if she could leave Chloe here. The poor child was now screaming and thrashing about as though she were some feral animal and Harriette's heart went out to her. The overtired toddler had lost all sense of reason and comprehension.

'Ordinarily I'd be fine with her,' the ward sister stated, 'but I'm run off my feet.'

'Call Erica. See if she can come and take care of Chloe.'

'Good idea.' While the ward sister placed the call, Harriette took Chloe over to a spare bed and sat down with the little girl. The child scrambled from Harriette's grasp and bunched herself up near the pillows, wanting to get away from the stranger. She was still crying but, thankfully, not as bad as before, now that she wasn't being held tightly.

'My name is Harriette. I'm a doctor here.'

Chloe was breathing quickly, hiccupping a few times, and once again Harriette's heart went out to her. 'I'm so sorry, Chloe. Things are a bit crazy here at the moment but one of my friends, Erica, she's going to come and stay with you. She has puppets and colouring in and stories and all sorts of fun things for you to do while you're waiting.' Chloe's breathing was still fast but was starting to settle as Harriette spoke.

The ward sister came over. 'Erica's on her way. I'll stay with Chloe. You go.'

'Thanks, Sarah. I appreciate it.' She stood and waved to Chloe, not taking it personally when the little girl turned her head away, not wanting to look at anyone.

Harriette headed off to first check the ED, then head to Theatres. What she hadn't expected was to walk directly into a hard male chest as she pushed open the door.

'Sorry.' They both spoke in unison. Felix was exiting as she was entering and her hands immediately came up to his chest, in a reflex action, to belatedly protect herself. His hands landed on her shoulders. Their gazes met and held for a split second and in that second the rotation of the earth seemed to slow down completely.

Harriette was even more aware of his spicy scent mixed with earthy human sweat, a scent she found very pleasing indeed. She was also aware of the warmth tingling through her fingers as they rested against his cotton shirt and the firmness of his body beneath the clothing. He wasn't wearing a tie and the top button of his shirt was undone. His neck was smooth and she watched his Adam's apple slide up and down as he swallowed. Had his shirt been like that before?

She lifted her gaze back to his, her lips parting slightly as she belatedly realised he seemed to be watching her as closely as she was watching him. Her new colleague was all male. She appreciated his help and hoped it meant Felix McLaren was a good man, because he was definitely a sexy one. She smiled nervously and immediately dropped her hands, her fingertips still tingling from the touch. Time returned to normal and Felix nodded politely at her, shoving his hands into his pockets.

'Going to the changing rooms,' he mumbled. He started to walk off when her brain clicked back into gear.

'Uh... Felix?' The sound of his name on her tongue was foreign but nice at the same time. He turned on his heel and looked at her, his brow furrowed, his gaze flicking down the corridor to where he could hear Chloe crying. 'We're going to get Erica to come and look after her. Erica runs the day-care centre and is a retired teacher.'

'Good.' He turned again, seeming not to care that much about Chloe's needs, but perhaps his thoughts were on the surgery he was about to perform. Still, Harriette should at least get some sort of identification from him, to check he really was who he said he was.

'Felix.' She stopped him again and this time he gave her a look that said he didn't like being waylaid. 'I was...uh...' Good heavens. Why was she stuttering and finding it difficult to speak? She knew it couldn't have anything to do with the fact that her fingers were still tingling from touching his chest, nor that his face had been so incredibly close to hers, nor that his spice scent was continuing to tantalise her tired mind.

'What is it?' His tone was brisk and impatient, as though she were a first-year medical student daring to speak to the high and mighty surgeon. It was enough to snap her from the trance their accidental contact had created. Harriette squared her shoulders and lifted her chin.

'I'd like to see some identification, please. After all, you're about to operate on a patient here and quite frankly you could be any Tom, Dick or Harry who just says they're a doctor.'

His jaw clenched. 'That's ludicrous. Besides, I thought small hospitals didn't care so much about red tape.'

'I'm not asking you to fill in a mountain of forms, Felix.' Her own exasperation was starting to rise. If he was who he said he was, why couldn't he just show her a driver's licence to put her mind at ease? And why should he make her feel guilty about protecting her patients? 'I'm asking to see some identification, which I don't think, given the circumstances, is at all unreasonable.'

Exhaling harshly, he shoved his hand into the back pocket of his trousers and pulled out his wallet, opening it to reveal his Australian driver's licence, which had his name, address and date of birth as well as a picture that most definitely matched the handsome man before her.

'Satisfied?'

'Thank you.'

'Can I go now?' He jerked his thumb over his shoulder towards the corridor where the changing rooms were situated.

She bit her tongue as a thousand answers came into her mind of where she wanted to tell him to stick his overbearing and dictatorial attitude. 'Yes. I'll be assisting you in Theatre.'

'Fine.' He rubbed a hand across his forehead, then turned on his heel and headed towards the changing rooms. Was it strange for him, to just walk into a strange hospital and then operate in a strange theatre? She knew he would have come in on the daily flight to Meeraji Lake but where had he travelled from? Had today's journey been a short hop from Darwin or Alice Springs or had he been travelling for days?

'What do you think of the new doctor?' Tori asked Harriette when she returned to the ED to assess Bazza and his brawling mates. Henry had arrived and thankfully his police presence was stopping the men from starting anything else.

So many thoughts went through her mind at Tori's question. She thought Felix was exceptionally handsome but also brisk to the point of rudeness. Of course if she'd confessed that to the nurse, who was counting down the weeks until her wedding day, Tori would have plied her with excited questions and then tried to matchmake them. Why did engaged couples feel that every unattached person around them needed to be paired off?

'I don't think anything,' Harriette responded. 'Patrick's been taken to Theatre?' she asked in an effort to ensure they didn't remain on the topic of the new surgeon.

'Yes.'

'Good. If you're OK to finish cleaning and stitching the wounds of our bar-room brawlers, I'll head over there.'

'Go. I'll keep the ED under control.'

'Thanks, Tori.'

Harriette did her best to keep her thoughts one hundred percent strictly professional as she changed into theatre garb. She was also conscious that Chloe didn't seem to be screaming the hospital down any more. Clearly Erica had arrived to lend a hand, so that was another problem dealt with. 'Two down, one to go.' She left the changing rooms and headed to the anteroom, joining Felix at the scrub sink.

'What did the ultrasound show?' she asked Felix.

'Confirmed enlarged appendix.' He finished scrubbing and elbowed off the taps, grabbing a sterile towel to dry his hands. 'I'll see you in there.'

Harriette watched him with curiosity as he headed into Theatre, hands upheld, back to the swinging door in order to push it open and keep his hands sterile. He was clearly focused on what needed to happen with the operation, which was a good thing, but in some respects she'd expected him to ask about the three bar-room brawlers or at least to ask how Chloe was.

Perhaps it wasn't so strange that Felix hadn't asked about Chloe or the brawlers. Perhaps it was just Harriette's way of thinking as she'd worked the majority of her medical life in small district hospitals. She'd only done two years at a major teaching hospital and that had been enough to make her hurry back to the small country hospital that had been her refuge for so many years. A small community where she'd been able to figure out her life, to get the help she'd needed when her parents had—

'Now is not the time to think about that,' she chided herself softly as she finished scrubbing, and by the time she entered Theatre she had forced her mind not to think about the bar-room brawlers, not to think about little Chloe, not to think about the other patients who were presently undergoing treatment or recuperation in the ward. Her mind was always so busy that getting it to focus on one solitary thought really did require her concentration.

'Are you fine if I take point?' he asked as she stood on the opposite side of the table to him. Patrick was draped, prepped and sedated. Bill stood beside Felix in order to provide immediate nursing assistance and Adonni, one of the nurses who was also trained in anaesthetics, was monitoring Patrick closely. They were ready to remove the offending appendix before it perforated and caused them more problems.

'Absolutely. I'm sure Pat would be honoured to be your first surgical patient here in Meeraji Lake,' she said.

'You've got that right,' Adonni added.

'I prefer not to think of my patients by name while they're on my operating table,' Felix stated.

'Really? I've always found it helps me to concentrate better, to know that Pat needs my full attention, that I need to do my best for him. That sort of thing.'

'I do not and I'd kindly thank you to refrain from speaking in such a way because the last thing I need now is to lose my concentration.' There was a crispness to his tone that brooked no argument. Harriette glanced at Adonni, the two of them sharing a brief look before apologising.

Thankfully, the surgery went well, with no complications. Felix managed to remove the appendix before it perforated. 'At least Pa...er...the patient won't be faced with a case of peritonitis thanks to your careful and brilliant skills, Dr McLaren,' she stated as he started to close the wound. 'Has it been a while since you've removed an appendix via laparotomy rather than laparoscopically?' she asked as they finished up.

'No.' He gave Adonni the nod to reverse the anaesthetic.

'Oh. That's surprising. I thought the majority of big hospitals now only remove the appendix via—'

'What if the patient's allergic to the gas used to inflate the stomach as required for laparoscopic appendectomy?' he interrupted.

'Ah, of course. Then the patient would require a laparotomy.'

'Precisely.' Felix stepped away from the table and started to degown. Adonni began to reverse the anaesthetic and Bill gave her a nod, indicating he was ready to take over monitoring Patrick.

As they were degowning Harriette decided that even if Felix was all gruff and grumpy it was no reason for her to act in the same way. She smiled at him.

'Thank you for operating, Felix.'

Felix didn't bother to look at her and she clenched her jaw, forcing her smile to stay in place.

'Good. Now, if you wouldn't mind showing me to the doctors' residence, I'd like to get settled in.'

'Of course but uh…' She frowned and pointed in the direction of the ward. 'What about Chloe? Your daughter?'

Felix stared at her blankly for what seemed like a few long seconds. 'Yes, yes. Chloe.' He frowned as though he really had forgotten he had a child. It begged the question of what had happened to the child's mother. Had she passed away? Had they divorced? Was she due to arrive in Meeraji Lake at a later date? At any rate, it did strike Harriette as a little more than odd that he'd forgotten he had a daughter. 'Of course I have Chloe to consider but I thought it best if I could get set up at my new digs before bringing her across. If that's OK with the ward sister and...er...whoever you said was going to help look after her.'

'Erica. I'm sure it'll be fine.' Harriette pulled off her cap and tossed it into a recycle bin. 'Just let me change into a fresh pair of scrubs. Won't be a minute and I'll show you where you're staying.' She turned and spun on her heel, sprinting to the change rooms before he could say another word. Within a minute she was back before him, beckoning him to follow her.

'Feel better now?' he grumbled, as though her changing had caused him great inconvenience. 'I also need to check my bags have been sent to the residence from the airstrip. The pilot told me that he would take care of it.'

'Dale's a good lad and a good pilot. They'll be there and if they're not, we'll just chase them up. In a town this small, it shouldn't take us too long to find a few suitcases.'

'Hmm.' He frowned again, trying to control the surge of irritation and impatience coursing through him. He was beyond exhausted and all he wanted now was to find his bed and sleep, but of course he had Chloe to consider, his bags to find, a thousand things to think about before he could give in to the need to sleep. It wasn't as though he wasn't used to this sort of tiredness—he was—but travelling with a small child and dealing with her tantrums had wiped him out. Give him a hectic operating schedule any day rather than dealing with a three-year-old.

'Are you ready to head over now?'

'I'd like to change out of my scrubs.' And to have a shower and something to eat and drink, he wanted to add, but that information was irrelevant and, besides, he wasn't sure he had the reserve energy to do any of those things.

Harriette shrugged, her disposition still cheerful. Did the woman have any other setting? He wasn't sure he could work around someone who smiled too much. 'I prefer to wear them most of the time when I'm working at the hospital.' She chuckled and the tinkling sound washed over him, soothing him a little, which, he had to confess, surprised him. How could a person's laughter be relaxing? He'd certainly never felt anything like that before. He looked at her lips, her perfectly formed pink lips, which, even as she spoke, seemed to be curved upwards in a smile. 'You go change. I'll check on Chloe and let the staff know you'll be collecting her later. Meet me on the ward.'

'Fine.' He turned on his heel and went to the changing rooms, needing a bit of distance from happy Harriette. Felix resisted the urge to sit down on the chair in the changing room, knowing if he did, he'd probably fall asleep right there and then. Instead, he went through the automatic motions of changing.

He headed to the ward and found his new colleague standing at the bottom of Chloe's bed, watching the child sleep.

'She's an angel,' Harriette murmured softly.

'They managed to get her to settle again?'

She chuckled and the sound soothed the pain around his temples. He resisted the urge to massage the area with his fingertips, knowing it would alert her that he was tense. The last thing he wanted was to play twenty questions with his new colleague as to exactly why he was so tense. He hadn't realised Harriette would be so chatty, as, it seemed, were most of the staff.

Harriette pointed to where two women were chatting

quietly at the nurses' station. 'Erica's a genius when it comes to children and Sarah's an excellent nurse.' The two women saw them looking and waved before resuming their conversation.

Felix had never worked in a small hospital before and the informality everyone seemed to exhibit was completely foreign to him. Still, he had to make it work. He had to try the hardest he'd ever tried in order to fit in with this community, to make these next few months full of transition and peace.

He had to get it right. In the past he'd only had himself to contend with but times had changed. He was responsible for Chloe. He was her guardian and, although he was still annoyed with his brother for doing this to him, he wasn't the type of man to shirk his responsibilities.

Chloe was an innocent little girl and as he looked down at her, her breathing peaceful and trusting, he knew he couldn't let her down. He'd taken a risk by coming here and he was now desperate for it to pay off because if it didn't…the consequences didn't bear reflection.

CHAPTER TWO

BY THE TIME Harriette went to bed that night, it was well after midnight. Although it had been great having Felix perform Patrick's surgery, his arrival had left her feeling highly confused. It wasn't the fact that she now had to share a house with him. She'd lived in shared housing before and she'd been fine. Nor was it the fact that he had a child who would also be under the same roof. She'd lived in the same house as a child for a very long time. No, it was more to the point that her new colleague was already causing conflicting emotions within her and she wasn't at all happy about it.

This was supposed to be *her* time…the time in her life when she didn't need to worry about anyone else except herself. For so long she'd given everything she had for other people and, while she didn't regret it one little bit, she'd been holding onto the day when her time really would be her own. So the last thing she wanted was to be thinking about her new and exceedingly handsome colleague and housemate!

Naturally she appreciated his skills as a medical professional but she couldn't say she was all that impressed with his 'big city' attitude towards the patients. They were just a number to him, not people with names and families and real-life problems. She'd once been told by a big-city doctor that she was a fool to pursue surgical training for that very reason. She was too emotionally involved with her patients, she couldn't be objective, might falter and fail when it counted most because she couldn't effectively distance herself.

'The great surgeons, the truly *great* surgeons, always detach themselves from their patients. Provide first-class treatment? Of course. Be polite and understanding? Most definitely.But overly sympathetic? Empathetic? No. Not if you want to be a great surgeon.' That was what she'd been told when she'd chosen to specialise in surgery.

If Felix McLaren continued to treat every patient in Meeraji Lake with the same professional distance he'd shown to Patrick, then she feared she might have a revolt on her hands. If patients refused to see Felix because of his standoffish attitude, that would mean more patients on her own list—both clinical and surgical—and she'd still be run off her feet. If the purpose of him coming here was to lend a hand, and if he wasn't prepared to relax his usual policies regarding patient care, then he might as well leave because he wouldn't be doing anyone in the town or district any good—no matter how brilliant he was.

Harriette shook her head as she brushed her teeth. There was no room for that big-city attitude out here in the middle of the Australian outback. She would never succumb to the professional distance she'd been advised to maintain but would Felix? The main flaw with the entire argument, as far as she was concerned, was that she had no desire to become a *great* surgeon; she just wanted to save people's lives. What was so wrong with that? She wasn't interested in climbing the hospital hierarchy ladder, wasn't interested in having her accomplishments written up in medical journals. Naturally she wanted to be a *good* surgeon but having her opinion sought after by other doctors was not on her radar. Was Felix? Had he been on his way up the ladder? Sought after by his peers? If so, then why on earth had he chosen to come here?

Harriette knew she needed to put Felix and his professional behaviour out of her mind. She had more than enough to keep her thoughts occupied. At the end of this year, she would sit her final exam in general surgery and then she could continue to work in small communities like this one, to help out, to make a real difference where it was needed most.

She'd worked for so long, she'd worked so hard and she'd done it not only for herself but for Eddie. Her darling Eddie. How she loved him. Even at the thought of him, she felt a lightness start to settle over her, her shoulders relaxing. Harriette glanced over at her phone and when she'd finished brushing her teeth, she sent him a text message, knowing he'd just be starting work over in Paris. She finished her message with lots of lovehearts and smiley faces and kisses.

Feeling more calm and with thoughts of her new colleague replaced by thoughts of Eddie, she lay down in her bed, sighing with happiness when she received a reply message from Eddie, which consisted solely of emoticons of funny faces plus a love heart at the end. Her Eddie loved her and as far as she was concerned, it meant that everything was perfect with her little world. She didn't need to worry about her new colleague or his daughter. It didn't matter what sort of day she'd had at the hospital, good or bad, so long as she could rely on Eddie to always be there for her, she could cope. Harriette closed her eyes and allowed the bliss of a well-deserved sleep to settle over her.

The loud scream that pierced the air had her up and out of bed like a shot. Dressed only in a pair of cotton short pyjamas and matching T-shirt, she rushed towards where she thought the scream might have originated, her heart pounding wildly against her chest.

She heard crying, the sound of a little girl, clearly frightened. Harriette stepped into the shared lounge room of the doctors' residence and turned on the light, intending to head to the other side of the house, which was where Felix and his daughter, Chloe, had their rooms. Harriette was on one side of the house, the two of them on the other. Separate bathrooms but shared lounge, kitchen and dining rooms.

As soon as the light illuminated the room the little girl screamed once again and it was then Harriette realised the child was standing in the middle of the room, fear filling her eyes. 'Mummy! Mummy!' Her cries were becoming louder, her voice strained, her beautiful British accent conveying her distress.

'Shh, sweetie. It's all right.' She headed towards the child.

'No. No.' Chloe held up her hands towards Harriette as though fending her off. 'Leave me alone. Leave me *alone*! I *want* my *mummy*!' She actually stamped her foot and Harriette's heart melted.

'Of course you do, darling, but she's not here right now.' Harriette sat down on the floor a little way off from the child in an effort to bring herself more to Chloe's height and to hopefully not cause any more distress. 'I'm Harriette. Remember?'

'I want my mu…mu…mummy.' The words hitched

in her throat and Harriette's own emotions started to be affected by Chloe's distress.

'And you're Chloe.' She knew she needed to distract the child long enough to calm her down. Even though the child didn't answer her, Harriette continued. 'That's a very pretty name. How old are you? Are you two years old?'

At this deliberate affront, Chloe's eyes cleared for a moment and she fixed Harriette with the same glare Felix had used when they'd first met. 'I'm not. I'm nearly four,' she replied with firm indignation.

'Wow. Such a big girl. I'll bet you're going to have a great birthday party, with presents and cakes.' It was clearly the wrong thing to say as the vulnerability immediately returned to Chloe's eyes, mixed with distress. 'Do you know where you are, Chloe?' Harriette asked softly, wanting to reach out to the little girl, but she knew if she did she risked alienating Chloe even further.

'Where's my mummy?' At least this time Chloe didn't scream the question but her lower lip began to wobble. 'I *want* my *mummy*!'

'I know, darling. Why don't we go and find your daddy?' And give him a dagger look for not waking up to his daughter's screams.

'Daddy?' There was a thread of hope in her tone. If she couldn't have her mother, then her father was the next best thing.

Harriette nodded and stood, beckoning the child to follow her. She didn't make any effort to touch the girl, nor to wipe away the tears, nor hug her close, which was what she really wanted to do. The poor little angel was clearly frightened and yet her tears had started to subside at the thought of her father. Chloe was still watching Harriette cautiously but at least she'd stopped the loud screams and hysterical crying. How could Felix have slept through them? He was a surgeon. He was used to being woken up in the middle of the night, of sleeping deeply but waking quickly when an emergency arose.

'Daddy's bedroom is this way.' Harriette took slow steps towards Felix's part of the house, patiently waiting as Chloe slowly followed. 'I'm surprised he didn't wake up when he heard you crying.' In fact, she was surprised the entire town hadn't woken up as Chloe's screams had been that loud...or had they? Perhaps Chloe hadn't been crying too loudly after all and perhaps it was simply Harriette's well-honed instincts that had instantly kicked in...or the fact that she hadn't yet slipped into a deep sleep.

When she reached Felix's closed door, she listened for a moment and could hear the sounds of faint snoring on the other side. Annoyance ripped through her. Why wasn't he looking after his daughter? Wasn't he interested in her well-being? Not only was he distant with the patients, he was distant with his own daughter? The knowledge didn't endear him to her one little bit. Working alongside a man who didn't seem to have any sort of bedside manner, both in his professional and private life, would only make things more difficult.

'Let's go wake Daddy up so he can give you a cuddle and make you feel better. Yes?' She waited for Chloe's nod of approval before knocking firmly on the door and opening it.

And there he lay. Sleeping diagonally across the double bed, his hands and feet still hanging over, he was so tall. The overhead fan was whirring on low and the floral bedcovers were bunched around the centre of his body. His snoring indicated his breathing was deep and even. He was clearly in a good REM cycle and she knew, after travelling and then operating, as well as dealing with a child, it was only natural he'd be so exhausted. Still, Chloe was his daughter, not hers, and as such he should be the one to settle her down. It was the duty of a parent—no matter the circumstances.

'Felix? Felix?' She called his name as she walked closer to the bed. 'Felix? Wake up!' She turned and looked over her shoulder, surprised to find Chloe sill standing in the doorway, shaking her head vigorously from side to side.

'That's not my daddy.'

'Felix?' Harriette spoke a little louder, hearing the hysteria beginning to rise in Chloe's tone. She walked to the head of the bed and put her hand on his shoulder, surprised to find his skin quite cool. She flatly ignored the way her fingers were tingling from where they'd made contact with his flesh. Annoyed with her own reaction, she shook his arm more firmly. 'Felix. Wake up.' Her voice was insistent. 'Chloe needs you.'

'That's *not* my daddy. My daddy is called David. That's *not my daddy*!' With that, Chloe turned and ran away, her crying starting all over again.

'What?' Harriette was now thoroughly confused, so she shook Felix even harder, calling to him. 'Wake up, Felix. There's an emergency.'

As though she'd said the magic words, Felix shifted and sat up so suddenly, he fell out of the bed, knocking Harriette over in the process and landing on top of her. She felt instant pain in her back and left arm but it quickly began to subside. She dragged a breath in, belatedly realising her mistake. That thing the world did, of standing still whenever she was within close proximity to Felix, happened again and her mind seemed to be gathering as many details about the firmness of his body, of his crazy, gorgeous scent and of the way her hands felt on his smooth, bare shoulders as she tried to shift him off her.

It was ludicrous of course. There was no way she could be physically attracted to a man she wasn't even sure she liked. In fact, during their short acquaintance, Felix McLaren had annoyed her far more than any other emotion and if she was mildly attracted to him, it was simply physical. The fact that she hadn't been this close to a semi-naked man in a rather long time meant it was her libido she had to control and nothing else. Her head was far stronger than the weaknesses of her body. She could and would control herself.

'What? What? Where am I?'

'Meeraji Lake,' she squeezed out. 'Chloe. Chloe woke up. She's upset.'

'She's awake?' There was almost the sound of dread in his voice. Was he scared of his daughter? He scrambled to his feet but not before he'd accidentally head-butted Harriette in the process.

'Ow.' She rubbed her head. 'What *is* it with you?'

'Sorry. Discombobulated.' He stood and it was then she realised why all she'd been able to feel when she'd been trying to extricate herself from beneath him was hard, male flesh. Felix McLaren was dressed only in a pair of boxer shorts, his perfectly broad shoulders appearing much broader from where she sat on the floor, looking at him silhouetted against the light that was coming in from the lounge room.

Control. Self-control. That was all she needed...and not to keep staring at his gorgeous...firm... Harriette forced herself to look away and cleared her throat. So Felix was a perfect male specimen. She'd seen several, more than several in fact, during her time. She was a doctor. She was used to seeing the male form and... Harriette tried a few deep breaths to bring herself better under control. If she didn't look at him, then that should work. Instead, she rubbed her head once more and tried to focus on what he was saying.

'Where did she go?'

'I don't know,' Harriette grumbled as she rubbed her head and slowly stood to her feet. 'She ran away, saying you weren't her daddy. Her daddy's name is David.'

'Her father's name *is* David,' Felix stated as he reached for a T-shirt and headed out towards the lounge room.

'She's probably hiding somewhere.'

'Chloe? Chloe? It's all right. I'm here to help you.'

Harriette followed him but when she reached the lounge room, it was to find no trace of the child. 'Where is she? Chloe?' she called. Felix was now starting to search behind curtains, under tables.

'Can you check your part of the house, please? She has the tendency to either hide or run away when things go wrong but thankfully, as the doors to the house are locked, she can't have got far.'

A prickle of apprehension washed over her and she slowly shook her head. 'The doors aren't locked,' Harriette stated slowly, then, as though the reality of the situation dawned clearly on both of them, she rushed into her part of her house and started to search, calling the little girl's name as she went.

'What do you mean they're not locked? Didn't you lock them when you came back from the hospital?' She could hear the censure in his tone and she didn't appreciate it one little bit. How dared he imply that this was her fault? How was she to know that Chloe had a tendency to run away? How was she to know the child would wake in the middle of the night, crying for her parents who clearly weren't anywhere to be found? And more to the point, if Felix wasn't Chloe's father, then who was he and why did he have charge of the little girl? No wonder the child was distressed.

Gritting her teeth once more, Harriette pushed the questions aside and focused on the more important task at hand—finding Chloe as quickly as possible. She checked in every small space where a child could hide, in the closets, beneath the bed, in the spare room, the bathroom—everywhere—but Chloe wasn't to be found. Harriette grabbed her mobile phone from the bedside table. If Chloe wasn't in the house, it meant she was outside and for that they would need help.

She returned to the lounge room where, for some reason, Felix was lifting the cushions on the chairs as though desperate to find Chloe beneath there. 'You haven't lost your car keys,' she stated. 'You've lost a child.'

'*I've* lost a child? How could *you* not lock the doors?' He spread his arms wide with astonishment, his voice indicating *she* was a prime imbecile for not doing such a simple, mundane task.

'We live in the middle of nowhere, Felix. Crime is basically non-existent. No one locks their doors and I had no idea Chloe was the type of child to run away!' Tensions were increasing to the point where soon they would be embroiled in a slanging match, rather than focusing on finding the girl.

As though Felix realised this as well, he rubbed both hands over his face before pushing them through his hair, causing the follicles to stand on end, making him look vulnerable, confused and incredibly sexy. Harriette actually shook her head, pushing the thoughts away. Focus. They needed to focus.

Felix strode to the back door, which was in the kitchen, and pointed. 'Did you leave the door like this? The main door open and the screen door closed?'

'No. I shut the main door.'

'But you didn't lock it.' Again, there was that tone of his, calling her stupid without actually saying so.

Harriette didn't bother replying. Instead, she grabbed the emergency torches from the cupboard and slipped on a pair of flip-flops. 'Here. Start looking. I'll call Henry.'

'Henry?'

'The town's police officer. He can help organise a search.'

'Search?' The word stopped Felix in his tracks for a split second and Harriette saw deep fear and concern flash across his face. 'Surely we won't need to go that far? Surely you and I can find her? I mean, it's far too late to wake the entire town in order to find a stubborn three-year-old, right?'

'This is the outback, Felix. Things can turn from bad to worse in a split second.' Before he could say another word, she punched a pre-set number into her phone and put it on speaker phone.

'This is Henry,' a sleepy male voice said a moment later.

'It's Harriette, mate. The new doctor's daughter...' She paused on the word but shook her head and continued as Felix headed past her, his torch on, looking around the back of the house. There wasn't much grass, nor were there fences between the properties. 'She's upset and confused and she's gone out of the house. We're not sure where she is but she can't have gone far.'

Felix listened with half an ear as Harriette spoke to the local cop, all the while flashing his torch around the area, calling for Chloe. She really couldn't have gone too far, right? She was confused, frightened and upset as well as being forthright, determined and stubborn. The problem was he had no idea what was going through her head and even if he hadn't been still groggy from jet lag, he still wouldn't have been able to predict where she might go. He felt so helpless. He didn't know Chloe. She didn't know him. It was why he'd come here in the first place, to try and be a father to the little girl, but as he had no idea how to be a father and as she clearly didn't want him in the role it was making life incredibly complicated.

He knew it wasn't Harriette's fault the door hadn't been locked. She was right. How was she to know that Chloe had a tendency to run off? Felix closed his eyes for a brief second and rubbed a hand across his temples. He was exhausted, jet-lagged, running on the last shred of his energy reserves and he honestly didn't know how much longer he'd last.

'You'll continue until you find her,' he told himself sternly. Chloe was his responsibility and he knew— or at least he hoped—that within the next few months they'd be able to find a footing where they could both appreciate the situation they were in and make the best of it. He did care for the child. He had a familial love for her and it was that that had spurred him forward to become her legal guardian. His heart ached for the pain and confusion she must be feeling.

'Chloe?' He called her name as he checked behind a native shrub. He didn't call too loudly as he didn't want to wake people up, nor scare the child.

'Chloe?' Harriette yelled as she came out of the house, her voice booming in the dark.

'Shh. She can't have gone far,' Felix said, feeling self-conscious and worried and confused and completely out of his depth.

'She won't hear me if I don't yell and you're wrong that she couldn't have gone far. When a three-year-old decides to run, their little legs can be pretty fast.'

'Even if she does hear you,' Felix hissed, keeping his curt words low, 'she still might not answer.'

Harriette ignored him and shone her torch around the area, looking down the path that led to the clinic and the hospital. 'There's no point in arguing semantics, Felix. Where do you think she might have gone? Maybe she went back to the hospital? After all, there are lights to pave the way and she might have just followed them, still unsure where they led.'

'I don't know.'

'Chloe!' she yelled again and listened for a response but nothing came. 'You don't have a clue what she might do?'

'No.'

'How often has she run away like this before?'

'Twice.'

She gritted her teeth, knowing he should have taken better precautions to ensure Chloe's safety, but what mattered now was finding Chloe before something else did. There were plenty of four legged predators out at night as well as snakes. True, they usually didn't come this close to the town but there were always exceptions. Harriette hoped tonight wasn't one of them.

'I'll check the hospital. You check down the path that leads to the retirement village and community centre.'

Harriette shone her torch in the direction he should go. 'Have you got your mobile phone with you?'

'No. It's inside. I'll do a double-check in there again in case we missed a hiding spot and pick it up. Then I'll head to the retirement village.' He spoke the words as though he was getting things clear in his head, as though he really wasn't capable of coherent thought right now and was happy she was making the plans.

'Good. Call me if you find her.' Harriette headed off down the path towards the clinic and the hospital.

'Wait. I don't know your number.'

'Ask anyone you meet. They all have it,' she called, before disappearing around the side of the house and out of his view. Felix frowned as he headed back into the house, grumbling to himself.

'What if I don't meet anyone? They're all asleep so what am I supposed to do—?' A sound stopped him and he paused, then said clearly and firmly, 'Chloe, if you're hiding in here, you need to come out immediately. You're starting to worry me…and soon, there will be lots of people trying to find you and really, well, we all just want to know you're safe.' And he did. He wanted to know he hadn't failed his brother by not being a good enough guardian.

Nothing else seemed to matter now. The past was the past and even though he and David had managed to patch things up a few years ago, they still hadn't spoken much. The best thing he could do for his brother now was to care for Chloe. *That* was how he would make peace with the pain piercing his heart. Chloe had to come first.

'Chloe?' He called her name everywhere he went as he rechecked every nook and cranny in the house, including Harriette's side. The little girl really wasn't anywhere to be found. He picked up his phone, slipped on his Italian loafers, then headed on the path towards the Meeraji Lake retirement village and community hall.

Surprisingly, as he drew nearer to the community hall, he was astonished to find quite a few people coming out, many of them retirees, laughing and joking together.

'What are you all doing out so late?' he asked, switching off his torch, the light outside the community centre casting enough light for him to see their faces.

'Who are you?' one of them asked.

'Dr McLaren. Oscar Price's friend.'

'And what might *you* be doing up so late and dressed as such?' one of the ladies asked, waggling an arthritic finger at him and giggling. Felix looked down at his attire of T-shirt, boxer shorts and loafers. Clearly this wasn't how he'd wanted to meet the townsfolk but there was nothing he could do about that now.

'My…er…child—Chloe. She's three, nearly four. She's run away.'

'Why didn't you say so first off?'

'Has Henry been called?'

'Where's Harriette? Does she know?'

'How long ago? Are we talking hours or minutes?'

'Er…' He tried to compute all the questions that were spoken in unison. 'Only a few minutes ago.Five. Maybe five minutes by now. Harriette's checking the clinic and hospital. Henry's been called.'

'Good thing the council meeting ran rather late tonight,' one of the men said. 'What did you say her name was?'

'Chloe. She's almost four years old.' And just like that, they all started helping. No other questions, no forms of censure. Nothing. Some of them switched on their mobile phones, using them to light the way, others started calling more people to come and join the search. They were a community. They cared. They had no idea who he was, they hadn't even met Chloe and yet here they were, immediately offering assistance. Felix was… humbled as well as appreciative.

'Chloe? Chloe?' They all started calling and spread out, helping him to look for her. Felix hoped the child wasn't in any danger. She couldn't be, could she? The poor thing had already been through enough in her short life. She didn't need more. The concern he'd felt earlier doubled as five minutes turned into ten.

Henry was now on the scene and Harriette had checked the clinic and the hospital, alerting the night staff of the situation.

'It's all right, Felix. We'll find her,' Harriette reassured him after she'd spoken to the people who were awake and helping them search. He'd also lost count of the number of times people had asked him where he thought Chloe might have gone and his helplessness increased when he simply had to shrug and say he had no idea.

'The next step is to raise the alarm and wake the volunteer firefighters so we can get some big lamps set up and cars heading up and down the main roads with their spotlights,' Henry said.

Felix sat down in the gutter outside the hospital and put his head in his hands. How had this happened? He clearly wasn't fit to be a parent to the child. Surely tonight proved that.

'We'll find her,' Harriette said again as she sat down next to him and put her hand on his shoulder.

'I can't do this. I can't.'

'If you need to go back to the house, that's fine.

We all understand. We'll get the search party organised and—'

'I meant I'm not cut out to be a parent.'

Harriette processed his words for a moment before asking softly, 'Who's David?'

'My brother.'

'So…Chloe's your *niece*?'

'Yes, and until my brother and his wife were killed in a car accident four months ago I had no idea I was listed as her guardian.'

'Chloe's parents have passed away?' Harriette's words were filled with sadness and compassion.

'Yes.'

'And you're her guardian?'

'Yes, but I—' He stopped and shook his head. Around them people were talking and organising and planning. He felt incredibly helpless. 'I don't know how to be a parent.' He hung his head after speaking the words out loud. 'Clearly I'm no good. I didn't even realise she was upset and then I didn't check the doors were locked and she hates me and she cried almost the entire time on the plane—and it's a long flight from England to Australia and—' He buried his face in his hands, his tone filled with anguish. 'I have no idea what to do. I don't know. I just don't know. And now she's lost. Lost in a strange place. Not knowing anything or anyone and…oh, Harriette…she must be *so* frightened.'

Harriette listened to him, her heart going out to him and the little girl who had been orphaned. She had many questions but now was not the time. What Felix needed right now was reassurance. Time was ticking by and although it felt as though hours had passed since they'd started to search, that wasn't the case at all.

Harriette sniffed and cleared her throat and when

Felix turned to glance at her, he could see a tear sliding down her cheek, the light from the street light above making it glint in the darkness. 'We'll find her, Felix.' She took a deep, cleansing breath, her words now filled with determination. 'We're a strong community and when something like this happens, we all band together, leaving no stone unturned. We support and—'

'Found her!' came a loud female call from the very far end of the street.

'What?' Felix was on his feet like a shot and Harriette wasn't far behind him. They sprinted towards where the woman's voice had come from and, in the dim lights from around them, they saw a woman coming towards them, carrying a small child in her arms.

'Oh, Erica. You absolute legend.'

When Erica reached Felix, he immediately took Chloe from her and hugged the child close.

'Where was she?' Harriette asked.

'At the bus stop. Waiting.'

'Oh, the poor love. The bus stop is quite a way from the house but clearly she was determined to get out of here.'

'Chloe. Chloe, you had me scared out of my wits.' Felix's words were soft and filled with emotion. He tried to ease her head back but she'd buried it in his neck, her little arms holding him tight. 'I was so worried about you.' He sniffed, exhaustion, stress and relief all mixing together.

Chloe pulled back a little and looked at his cheek, lifting her chubby hand to wipe at the tears. 'You're crying?'

'Because I'm so relieved you're OK. I need you to be safe, Chloe. I need to know where you are. I need to keep you *safe*,' he reiterated.

'Why?' the child asked softly and Harriette found herself holding her breath.

'Because we're family,' he returned and the answer seemed to settle the child somewhat. 'Let's get you home,' he said.

'To England?' she asked with hope.

'Just back to our new house.'

'With Harriette?' Chloe asked.

And it was as though Felix had even forgotten his new colleague was there because he shifted the child in his arms so he could look at his housemate. 'Yes, Harriette lives there, too.'

'I want to sleep with Harriette,' the child declared and held out her hands towards Harriette, lunging so quickly, Felix had no option but to let her go. 'I want to sleep with you. I used to sleep with Mummy when I had bad dreams.'

'I think you need to get used to sleeping in your own bed,' Felix started, but before he could say another word, Harriette interjected.

'Of course you can sleep in my bed,' Harriette said as they started walking back, most of the searchers now having been told that the child had been found safe and well. Felix shook hands with everyone but the women were having none of this hand-shaking business and pulled Felix close for a hug. Harriette had to smile at the look of shock and confusion on his face. Confusion at what? At being so warmly and readily accepted by the community? This same community he'd previously been determined to keep at arm's length? Soon he would realise that in a district this small, it was inevitable to make relationships with the people who were also your patients. There were no case-file numbers here. There were only people, people who needed a holistic approach to medicine and that involved having relationships with them.

Erica, the woman who had looked after Chloe while they'd been operating on Patrick, the woman who had eventually found Chloe at the bus stop, gave Felix a big, warm hug.

'You bring her to see me at the day-care centre tomorrow. We need to get Chloe mixing with other children in the district, to let her know she has friends here so that she feels secure and loved,' Erica told him, and Felix nodded in agreement.

'I'm just so glad she was found and that she's OK,' he said quite a while later as he stood beside Harriette's bed. Chloe was lying snuggled next to Harriette, sound asleep. 'She *is* OK, isn't she?'

'She's a little shaken but that's to be expected. Psychologically, I think tonight pales in comparison with what she's already been through.'

'I'll say.' He walked over to pick her up.

'What are you doing?'

'I'm putting her into her own bed.'

'Why?'

'Because she's asleep now and all the parenting books say that the children will only learn to sleep in their own beds if they sleep there every night, regardless of where they may have fallen asleep.'

'Oh, hang the parenting books.' Harriette shook her head and placed a protective arm over Chloe's little body. 'She's fine where she is. You go and get some sleep. We'll be fine.'

'Hang the parenting books? How can you say that?'

'Because I know more about parenting than any parenting book, mate.'

'You do? Do you have kids?'

Harriette fixed the covers over Chloe before turning out the bedside light. 'Make sure the doors are locked before you turn in. Thanks, Felix,' she said, smothering a yawn.

And just like that, he was dismissed.

CHAPTER THREE

THREE DAYS. FELIX had been in Meeraji Lake for three days and it seemed as though Chloe preferred Harriette to him. In fact, Chloe seemed to prefer anyone to him. She'd willingly gone to the day care that was run by Erica; she'd willingly played with other children at day care; she'd gleefully told him in that posh little voice of hers that she liked *all* of them better than she liked him. Yesterday, after day care, he'd been running late in the ED and so Tori had taken Chloe around to the ward so she could visit with some of the patients. When Felix had finished his work, he'd headed to the ward to find Chloe sitting at the end of Patrick's bed, chatting with him and laughing and entertaining all the other patients on the ward.

The child simply preferred anyone and everyone to him. It was as though she was trying to punish him in some way, showing him that she was more than capable of loving, of showing affection, but that she simply *chose* not to show any to him—the man who was her guardian. He knew logically that, deep down inside, she didn't mean it. She was hurting and she was taking it out on him but, illogically, he couldn't help but be hurt by the little girl's actions.

Instead of doing the sensible thing and talking to

someone about it, Felix quashed all the emotions he was feeling way down deep and focused on his job. He was getting to know the Meeraji Lake protocols, getting to know the patients who seemed to drive for miles just for a check-up. He realised Harriette, who seemed to always be happy and jovial and willing to listen to anyone who was talking, might have had a point—that here in such a small and intimate community, patients were people, not just a diagnosis.

That morning, as he and Harriette sat at the table having cereal for breakfast, he discovered the reason why the hospital ED had been vacant when he'd arrived in the town three days ago. Apparently, Patrick had collapsed at the community centre and, rather than sending an ambulance, it had been easier to just take a barouche down to the community centre, treat Patrick and then wheel him back. The ward sister had been in charge of the hospital, but at the time he'd walked into the ED she'd been caring for a patient who had just been ill all over the ward floor.

'It happens,' Harriette said after explaining the situation to him. 'When it doesn't rain it pours. All the drugs are securely locked up as well as any patient information. Plus we're fortunate that the nursing staff are happy to rotate through the different positions as well as using their specialist skills when needed.'

'I don't follow.'

'Well Sarah is a trained midwife, Adonni is trained as in anaesthetics and Bill holds qualifications in geriatric nursing. Tori's trained in emergency nursing and is also hospital administrator so she's the one who does a lot of the paper work. They're our full-time nurses and then they all rotate throughout the other positions of working in the ED or theatres or being ward sister or doing immunisation clinics. It's a very different system to a large hospital but it seems to work.'

'And what if there are emergencies? Four nurses and two doctors surely isn't enough to handle a big emergency?'

'There are quite a few trained part-time nurses in the district so they come in to cover leave and days off or when there's a big emergency."

'You sound as though you've been working here for quite a while yet I could have sworn when I met with Oscar he said you were covering for them while he and Daisy were looking after her mother.'

'I am. I've been here a total of almost ten weeks.'

'That's not long.'

She shrugged and poured herself a glass of iced tea. 'Is that a problem?'

'No. No. It's just that you seem so…integrated into small-town life.' He frowned, not sure he was making much sense. 'What I mean is—'

'I know what you mean,' she interrupted. 'Perhaps I'm simply brilliant in any environment?' She looked at him over the rim of her glass as she took a sip.

'Perhaps.' He said the word slowly, as though he wasn't quite sure of her mood. Was she teasing him? Was she being serious? Was she fishing for compliments?

'Or…perhaps I'm related to half the people in this town, which means it's easier for me to…integrate.' She raised one eyebrow at him, which only made him lower two of his into a confused frown. He simply didn't know Harriette well enough to know when she was teasing or when she was being serious. He decided to remain cautious as, right now, anything and everything she was saying might be true.

'Perhaps,' he repeated.

'Or…' As she drawled the word she raised the glass to her lips and, although she was talking, he found he was completely captivated by her actions. He was all too aware of the way her perfectly formed lips parted to accept the cool liquid, her perfectly smooth neck as she swallowed, the tip of her pink tongue sliding out to lick her lower lip as though eager to retain every drop of the delicious iced tea. Felix drew in a deep breath, forcing himself to look away, to focus on what she was saying.

This wasn't how he treated female colleagues. He didn't ogle them. He didn't stare at them in an impolite manner. He respected them. He admired all his colleagues, regardless of gender, for their intelligence and abilities, and during the past three days he'd come to admire Harriette—her ease and friendliness with the patients as well as her professionalism.

It was true that on a physical level he found her attractive, especially with the way her beautiful auburn locks seemed to have a mind of their own, never allowing themselves to be tamed into the hairstyle she chose. Or the way her green eyes seemed to sparkle with emotion, whether it was anger, annoyance or mirth…as was being displayed at the moment. She was teasing him and he liked it, even though he couldn't remember what it was she'd just said.

'Felix?' She was looking cautiously at him now, a slight furrow of concern creasing her brow. 'Earth to Felix?' She snapped her fingers in his direction in order to get his attention. When he met her gaze, she smiled. 'Are you all right?'

'Yes. Sorry. Too many things on my mind. So you're not related to half of the town?'

'No.' He could see the twinkle in her eyes, the corners of her mouth curving upwards.

'Just a small girl from a small town. Big cities give me the heebie-jeebies so when I was asked to come and help out, I was more than happy to transfer from Melbourne city to outback Australia.'

'Where did you say you grew up?'

She shrugged and took another sip from her glass before standing and walking over to the kitchen bench, needing a bit of distance from him, especially if she was going to successfully avoid talking about herself. 'Small towns in South Australia and Victoria. We... uh... I moved around a bit.' This was no time for her to launch into an explanation of just why she'd ended up in small towns, or why she'd moved so often. Even though her situation was more acceptable nowadays, she still didn't like to discuss it with someone until she knew them much better.

'So I guess that explains why I can be here for six weeks and appear as though I belong. I'm used to tight-knit communities. I'm used to not locking my doors at night. I'm used to seeing my patients as people, rather than just another case-file number.' She leaned against the kitchen bench and sipped her tea, watching him closely. 'You're such a big-town man, Felix. That was evident from the first time I saw you.'

'You make it sound like that's a bad thing?' He finished drinking his coffee, then stood and started clearing the table, not just his own dishes but hers as well. She appreciated that. Chloe hadn't wanted to eat anything other than a banana and was presently supposed to be in her room putting her shoes on. The little girl clearly knew her own mind and Harriette couldn't help but smile at the long road ahead that Felix would need to navigate.

'Not at all.' She finished her drink, adding it to the pile of dirty dishes in the dishwasher. 'All I'm saying is that I can understand why it might take you a while to settle in here.' She checked the digital clock on the microwave and grimaced. 'We're going to be late. You'd better get Chloe to day care or you'll be late for clinic.' Harriette picked up her sunhat and bag before heading towards the door.

'Can't you take her?' Felix called. 'She hates me.'

Harriette's answer was a chuckle. 'She doesn't hate you, Felix. She's been through so much pain, and seeing you reminds her of that.'

'Is that why she's friendly and happy with everyone else in the town except me?'

Harriette nodded. 'She's just behaving the way she's behaving because that's how she behaves. She's three years old.'

'Well, there's sound logic for you,' he replied with a snort of derision. 'What am I supposed to do?' Even he could hear the desperation in his tone.

Harriette smiled warmly at him and once again Felix felt that tightening in his gut. She had a lovely smile. 'Just be there for her. She'll come around.'

'When?'

'When you stop reminding her of her father. Thankfully, she's almost four and it's very rare children have crystal-clear memories from a time before they start pre-school. She'll settle down.'

'I don't want her to forget her father, or her mother for that matter.'

'Of course not. That's not what I'm saying.' Harriette angled her head to the side, a few tendrils falling loose from the messy half-bun she'd wound it into. She stared at him for a long moment, long enough that it made him feel a little self-conscious. 'Did you and David look alike?'

'A bit. Same height. Same dark hair, brown eyes.'

'That's what I mean. You *remind* her of her father but you're not him. That's got to be confusing for her. Just wait it out.'

'That's it?' He spread his arms wide. 'That's your advice? Wait it out?'

Harriette laughed, the sweet tinkling sound washing over him and having a strange calming effect on him at the same time. He cleared his throat, unable to look away from the alluring image of the woman before him. 'Just love her, Felix. It isn't that hard to do. She's a gorgeous girl.'

'For you, maybe.'

Harriette laughed again, the sound following her as she put her hat on and left the house.

Love her? That thought stayed with him for the rest of the day. Sitting in the ED later that afternoon, he looked blankly at the paperwork he was supposed to be filling in, not at all sure how he was supposed to *just love* Chloe. When he took her to day care in the mornings, it was like pulling teeth to get her to wear her hat, something it was necessary for her to do in such an incredibly hot climate. When it was nighttime, she seemed to hate every food there was and preferred to eat a banana or a cheese sandwich. In fact, yesterday all she'd eaten for breakfast, lunch and dinner had been a cheese sandwich. He'd made her a bowl of cereal. She'd thrown a tantrum. He'd made her some toast. Another tantrum and not just stamping her foot and being defiant, but a full-on yelling, screaming match that had had him throwing up his hands in despair and going to his room.

When he'd come out, it had been to find her sitting at the table, quietly eating a cheese sandwich that Harriette had made for her.

'You gave in to her?' he'd questioned and received such a death stare from his new colleague, he'd immediately backed off.

Felix leaned his head back and shut his eyes. What was he doing here? He'd brought a child he didn't know to the middle of nowhere and now was being ostracised by said child for bringing her to the middle of nowhere! How could a three-year-old possibly understand the ramifications of what was happening? How could she possibly make him feel so guilty for trying to do what he thought was best for her? What had made him think he could be a parent? He'd never wanted to have children. His own childhood had seen to that and now he was stuck with a recalcitrant three-year-old who was running rings around him.

What Felix *had* wanted was to climb the hospital ladder, to be well published, have the respect of his peers, to become an incredible surgeon. He'd wanted to make an important discovery, to have accolades and awards lavished upon him and he'd been doing very well heading towards that goal before David had died and changed his destiny. Felix groaned and shook his head, looking unseeingly at the paperwork before him. He shouldn't have any ill feelings towards his brother. David clearly hadn't planned to die in a car accident.

'That's a firm look of consternation you've got going on there,' Harriette said as she came and sat down next to him, dumping a load of case notes onto the desk.

'Pardon?' He looked at her unseeingly for a moment, not having fully computed what she'd said.

'You look deep in thought.'

'I am.'

'About…' She paused and checked the case notes he was writing up. 'Mrs Donovan or about Chloe?'

Felix sighed and quickly added a few words to Mrs Donovan's notes before signing his name and closing the file. 'Mrs Donovan's concern over her heart palpitations and her need for further investigation in the clinic are indeed concerning but not my most pressing concern at the moment.'

'So… Chloe?'

Felix leaned back in his chair, turning the pen over and over in his fingers. 'I can't figure out why my brother even named me as guardian. You see, David was six years younger than me and after our mother's death…' He paused. 'Well… I was at medical school, David lived at home with our dad and…' He stopped again and shook his head. 'We didn't talk for a long time. It wasn't until after he married Susan that we finally connected again.'

Harriette angled her chair towards him, giving him her full attention. The ED was quiet for the moment so if Felix wanted to get a few things off his chest, she was more than happy to listen. She remained silent, not wanting to interrupt his train of thought. He seemed to be speaking as though it was necessary for him to get his thoughts out of his head, needing to vent, needing to try and make sense of why he'd been made guardian of his niece. He looked unseeingly at the pile of case notes before him.

'I guess, as Susan didn't have any family, I was the logical choice. I'm Chloe's biological uncle.' He heaved a sigh. 'I was working overseas in Tarparnii. It took the solicitors weeks to track me down, to let me know of the accident.'

'Where was Chloe during this time?' She couldn't help the question and when he raised his gaze to meet hers, she wondered if he'd stop confiding in her. He looked at her for a long moment before answering.

'With a foster family.' He tossed the pen onto the desk and stood, raking both hands through his hair. 'It was a short-term thing but she seemed happy there. Then I arrived, the uncle she'd never met, and her life changed again…and she hates me for it.'

'She doesn't hate you,' Harriette reiterated yet again.

'Oh, really.' Felix crossed his arms over his chest in a defensive gesture and glared at her. 'She's told me so. Right to my face. I. Don't. Like. You.'

'She's three years old! It's what three-year-olds do and I'll bet you any money she used to be just as vehement with her own parents. She's a smart little cookie but she's also only three years old.'

'Almost four,' he corrected and rolled his eyes. 'She likes *you* to take her to day care. She likes *you* to sleep with at night.'

'You can have her sleep in your bed if you like.' Her words were wry and filled with humour. 'She kicked me three times last night and she hogs all the covers.' Harriette emphasised the point by rubbing her lower back.

'And more to the point, she should be sleeping in her own bed. She should be eating a healthier diet rather than cheese sandwiches for breakfast, lunch and dinner with the occasional banana thrown in for good measure. She should know that she can't throw a tantrum anytime she doesn't get her own way and giving into those tantrums and doing what she wants isn't going to help her out in the future.'

Harriette spread her arms wide. 'For heaven's sake, Felix, cut the kid some slack. Her parents have died. She's been brought halfway around the world to a different country. The climate is different and she's not used to wearing a hat every time she goes outside. The first time she gets sunburnt, she'll learn that lesson for herself. And the fact that she's eating the same thing day in, day out, isn't bad because at least she's eating and trying to establish some sort of normalcy for herself. A cheese sandwich isn't going to let her down, isn't going to leave her. It's going to taste delicious and make her feel happy. What's so wrong with that?

'And she may not be sleeping in her own bed but at least she's sleeping. Her jet lag seems to have gone, which is more than I can say for yours, and she won't be sleeping in my bed forever, just for now. Chloe's not sick—that's a good thing. She's eating, she's sleeping, she's physically healthy. Psychologically, that little girl has been put through the wringer and the last thing she needs right now are a bunch of rules and regulations which really only exist to make *your* life easier.' She paused for a breath. 'Ditch the parenting books and go with your instinct and common sense.'

'Are you equating me with common sense?' He tried to joke but it came out flat.

'Yes, I am. I mean, you're what…in your early forties?'

'Forty-one, yes. What's your point?'

'Don't you want to have children of your own? I know it's different for men, you don't have biological clocks ticking, but surely you've thought about having children at some point in your life, right?'

'No.'

She frowned at him. 'What do you mean, "no"? You didn't want to have children or you just haven't met the right woman to have the children with?'

'I met the right woman. We married. We fought. We divorced. I devoted myself to my career.'

'And then your little brother ruins your plans by saddling you with a child.' He frowned at her words but didn't comment because the expression on his face indicated she'd hit the nail on the head. 'You don't have to feel guilty for feeling that way. Life is what it is, Felix, believe me, I know. I had loads of plans for my life but then things change. However, the one thing I've discovered is that those changed plans, the plans you hadn't even considered, sometimes turn out to be the best thing that ever happened to you.'

'Something happened to you?'

'"Something" happens to everyone. Mrs Donovan didn't expect to come to the ED today with heart palpitations. Patrick didn't expect his appendix to attack him. Oscar didn't expect to fall in love with Daisy. You didn't expect your brother to die and leave you as sole guardian of his three-year-old daughter.'

'Almost four,' he murmured softly, mimicking Chloe's words every time someone mentioned her age. It was as though she was desperate to turn four, that when she was four things would be better. Felix wasn't about to squash that feeling and fervently prayed the little girl was right.

'Don't blame your brother for doing what he thought was the right thing. He probably never thought he'd die so soon after becoming a father. The fact that he chose you means he thought you could handle it.'

'Boy, was he wrong.'

'But you *are* handling it. Don't you see?' She sighed and shook her head as though she wasn't sure what else she could say to convince him. The phone rang and she immediately reached out a hand to answer it. 'ED, Harriette speaking.' She listened, then picked up a pen and started scribbling down some notes. 'What time is the plane due to land?' She glanced up at the clock on the wall. 'That's in ten minutes.' She listened again. 'Yes. OK. We'll come down to the airstrip and meet the plane.' She put the phone down and stood.

'Apparently a patient on the daily plane to Meeraji Lake has taken ill. The pilot radioed in and said the passenger's been vomiting and it appears to be more than just airsickness. The patient has a temperature and is sweating, complaining of pains in their abdomen.'

'Doesn't sound good. What's the protocol?'

'Usually we'd get into retrieval gear but the airstrip isn't far and we don't have a lot of time. The best thing to do is to drive the ambulance down and deal with whatever we find on the spot, stabilise the patient and then bring them back here. I'll let Tori know to cover the ED while we're gone and get Bill to prep the operating theatre just in case.'

'Where is Tori?'

'In clinic giving immunisations but that can all wait for now.' While she'd been talking Harriette had located the keys to the ambulance, which was always stocked and ready for any type of emergency, and slipped on her sunglasses. She quickly made calls to the relevant people, also letting the ward sister know that until Tori arrived, the ED was unmanned.

It wasn't until they were in the ambulance that Felix hit her with the question she'd always hated, always done her best to dodge, and today was no exception.

'So…what about you? Have you ever tried the married-with-children thing?'

'Does it matter?' she asked, trying to keep her words light and impersonal.

'Er…no.' Felix frowned, surprised at her reticence to talk. 'It's just you seem to know a lot about parenting.'

'I've done quite a bit of paediatric work in the past.'

'I didn't mean to pry. I just thought we were getting to know each other a bit better. I mean, you just asked if I was married—'

'No. I asked if you'd thought of having children. *You* were the one who volunteered the information about being divorced.'

'Then you're not married?' he guessed.

'What brings you to that conclusion?'

Why was she being so cagey? It only intrigued him even more, making Harriette more of an enigma than he'd first realised. What was her story? Why had she lived in a lot of small towns? Why did she hate big cities? Why was she always so incredibly happy and optimistic? Was she hiding something? Plus, when they'd been talking about her living in small towns, she'd used 'we', then changed it to 'I'. What was she hiding?

'The fact that most women, when asked if they're married, usually say yes if they are but try and dance around the question if they're not. Now you'll probably give me some information about how you don't need marriage to define you, that you're an independent woman, that you're more than happy with your life the way it is—'

'I *am* happy with my life the way it is and I'll have you know that I've worked very hard for it to become that way. At the end of this year, I'll sit my final exams and then I'll be a qualified surgeon.'

'You're still a registrar?' he queried, clearly more surprised at this news than discovering she wasn't married. 'I didn't realise.'

'And besides, just because I may not be married, it doesn't mean I don't have a special someone in my life whom I love and adore.'

'Oh, so there *is* someone.'

'Of course there's someone. Everyone needs a special someone.'

'Where is this mysterious "someone"?' He thought for a moment. 'Is it Henry? The police officer? You two seem quite easygoing with each other.'

'Henry is married, to Sarah, one of our midwives.'

'OK, so who do you text all the time? Who texts you back?'

'You've been watching me?'

'I live in the same house as you, Harriette. Sometimes it's difficult not to notice the way you get a text, then smile that cute little smile of yours.'

Harriette raised an eyebrow and glanced over at him. 'Cute little smile?' She smirked at his words then shook her head and concentrated on getting to the airstrip. Felix thought her smile was cute? That was nice and the knowledge warmed her although she wasn't entirely sure why.

'You know what I mean.' He seemed embarrassed.

'Uh, not really but…whatever.' She slowed down to turn the corner into the entrance to the airstrip. She brought the ambulance to a halt, as close as she could to the airstrip. The plane's wheels had just touched the ground and Harriette jumped from the vehicle, immediately swatting flies as she went. 'Let's see what we're dealing with.' She opened the back of the ambulance and took out one of the emergency backpacks.

She handed it to Felix, who slung it over his shoulder, then she pulled out two pairs of gloves. 'Here you go.'

It wasn't too much longer until the plane stopped and another moment more before the steps were lowered. They both headed over, pulling on the gloves so they were ready for action. Harriette was about to head up the steps in order to check on the patient, but before she had one foot on the bottom step a tall, handsome young man came bounding out of the plane.

'Surprise!' he called and opened his arms wide. In another second, he'd barrelled down the stairs and scooped Harriette up into his arms, spinning her around.

'Eddie!' She wrapped her arms around him and gave him an enormous kiss.

Felix watched, taken aback by this turn of events. Here they'd just been talking about Harriette's special someone and, clearly, the man who was holding her close, who was kissing her cheek, who was laughing at her surprise was Harriette's special *someone*.

Why he felt a thread of annoyance surge through him, Felix had no clue. No clue whatsoever.

CHAPTER FOUR

SHE HUGGED EDDIE close and kissed his face several times, clearly so incredibly happy. Felix looked away from the radiance of her smile, the way her beautiful red hair started to come loose from the haphazard bun, her tinkling laughter filtering through the air as though she had not a care in the world.

'What are you doing here?'

'I thought I'd surprise you,' the young man replied, his voice deep. In Felix's opinion, this Eddie person really did have a baby face and he couldn't help but notice that Harriette seemed quite a bit older than the man she had her arms wrapped around. Perhaps Eddie was older than he looked. Perhaps Harriette was younger than she looked, although, as he knew, she was finishing up her surgical training. That meant she had to at least be in her early thirties.

Well, some men preferred older women and some women preferred younger men. Who was he to judge? What he was more concerned with, and what Harriette seemed to have clearly forgotten in light of her surprise visitor, was the sick patient still on board the aeroplane. Felix edged past the happily reuniting couple, determined not to give them a second thought, and walked up the steps of the plane, peering inside.

'There's no one here,' he stated, looking over at the pilot in complete confusion.

'That's right. There's no emergency.' Dale, the pilot, finished filling in his logbooks and gathered his headphones and other bits of paraphernalia so he could disembark. He grinned at Felix. 'Eddie wanted to surprise Harriette so we decided to get her to the airstrip under false pretences.'

'You *faked* an emergency?' There was disbelief and censure in Felix's tone. 'You took the only two doctors in town away from the hospital's emergency department, which therefore required our senior nurse to leave the immunisation clinic in order to staff the now vacant ED, and you thought this was a good idea?'

The young pilot had the grace to look guilty at Felix's words. 'We didn't think—'

'No. Clearly you did not. What if there had been a real emergency, an emergency which required the ambulance and the attention of the doctors?'

'Was there?'

Felix paused for a moment before reluctantly admitting, 'No. But there might have been,' he added quickly. 'Emergency service call-outs aren't some sort of joke, young man.' With that, Felix exited the aeroplane, stalking briskly to where Harriette was now loading Eddie's duffel bag into the front seat of the ambulance.

'You can ride in the back,' she told him, her smile still wide and happy. 'But don't touch anything.' She waggled a finger at him, then stared at him a moment longer as though she really couldn't believe he was standing in front of her. 'Put your seatbelt on,' she remarked as she took the backpack from Felix and stowed it back in place. She shut the rear doors of the ambulance and went around to the driver's side.

'That's it?' Felix asked. 'Put your seatbelt on?'

'What?' She waved goodbye to Dale, then looked across at Felix. 'What's wrong?'

He looked into her face and his breath caught in his throat. He'd known she was an attractive woman but right now, the way she looked so incredibly happy, as though she could take on the world and knew she would win, brought out her inner radiance. She was... stunning.

'Uh...' Felix tried to think of what he'd been saying but his mind was blank.

'Are you ready to go?' she asked as she climbed into the ambulance. 'We should get back to the hospital asap and let Tori know it was a false alarm.'

As he walked around to the passenger side his brain seemed to click back into gear. 'They could be charged,' he remarked softly while he put his seatbelt on.

'Who?'

Felix glanced back towards where Eddie was sitting. 'Eddie and Dale?'

'Yes. They've radioed in a false emergency, removing valuable resources which may have been needed elsewhere.'

'But we weren't. We'll be back at the hospital in a few minutes and everything will be back to normal. Henry won't charge them.'

'Won't he?'

'No. He and Eddie get along really well.'

Felix frowned. 'Eddie's a local?'

Her smile increased. 'He is now, aren't you, sweetheart,' she stated, raising her voice so Eddie could hear them.

'What am I? I can't hear you properly back here.'

She laughed as though Eddie had just said something hilarious. 'Felix here wants to know if you're a local.'

'Ah. *This* is Felix. Sorry. We weren't properly introduced. I'm Eddie. I'm—'

His words were cut off as Harriette's phone buzzed. 'That'll be Tori wanting an update,' she remarked. 'Just as well we're almost there. She is going to be gobsmacked to see you, honey.'

Felix rolled his eyes and looked out of the window. No one seemed to care that Eddie had disrupted the smooth running of the hospital and clinics. It was as though the prodigal son had returned back home and everyone was getting ready for a feast in his honour. The odd thing was that in the three days he'd been in Meeraji Lake, he couldn't remember Eddie's name ever being spoken—not once. Eddie, however, seemed to know exactly who he was.

'How's Chloe been sleeping?' he asked from the back. 'Getting any better?'

'How do you know about Chloe?' Felix glared at Harriette. Had she been telling her 'special someone' all about him? About Chloe?

'Here we are,' Harriette stated as she pulled into the hospital driveway and drove the ambulance back into the garage. No sooner had she stopped the vehicle than Eddie had opened the back doors and loped inside the hospital, leaving Harriette to grab the duffel bag before heading inside. 'Come on. We'll miss Tori's reaction.'

'I'm fine,' Felix muttered, not particularly caring about Tori's reaction to the energetic Eddie. What was so special about him? Felix checked the ambulance was locked up, then caught sight of his reflection in the window, only then realising he was scowling. He wasn't too keen on this Eddie bloke because Eddie had disrupted the calm Felix had only just managed to achieve.

True, there was still a lot of turbulence in his life, mainly thanks to Chloe, but with Harriette's help even that had started to settle down a bit. Now Eddie had come into the mix and the search for calmness would need to start again because no doubt Harriette would want Eddie to stay at the doctors' residence. The entire situation was exactly what Felix didn't need right now, and neither did Chloe. This would create more disruption in her life. Couldn't Harriette see that?

When Felix entered the ED, it was to find Harriette with her arm around Eddie's waist. Eddie looked as though he was tolerating the embrace.

'What a scamp, eh?' Tori remarked when she saw Felix. 'Can you believe what Eddie did in order to surprise Harriette? Crazy.' Tori didn't wait for Felix to answer but instead bid them farewell, heading back to clinic.

'OK,' Eddie said, extricating himself from Harriette's arms. 'I'm gonna go get settled in, then say g'day to some people.' He picked up his duffel and slung it over his shoulder, looking every bit like a handsome superhero, with his blond hair and blue eyes, tanned skin and perfectly straight white teeth.

'Make sure you see Erica. She'll be mad if you don't.'

Eddie grinned and winked at her. 'Yes, Mum,' he said in a teasing tone before walking out of the door. She laughed again and once more Felix found the sound to be like music to his ears. What he didn't like was that Eddie had been the one to make her laugh. Why this should bother him, he really wasn't sure. He only knew that it did and that simply made him mad at himself.

Harriette sighed and sat in the chair, looking very relaxed and at peace. Her eyes were bright, her pink lips held the faint hint of a smile…a smile he wouldn't mind tasting. Felix blinked and immediately looked away from her, one hundred percent confused as to where that thought had come from. Why on earth would he be interested in tasting Harriette Jones's lips? In kissing her? She clearly had that avenue of her life all sorted out thanks, once again, to her special Eddie.

'We will be eating well tonight, my friend,' she remarked, rubbing her hands together with glee.

'Pardon?' He glanced at her and thankfully didn't experience any immediate pangs of jealousy or the need to gather her close and kiss her senseless. Good. He was a grown man and, as such, was more than capable of controlling his libido.

'Dinner tonight. Eddie's going to cook.'

'How do you know?' It also appeared there was no changing the subject from the latest arrival in Meeraji Lake. He opened the next file in the pile and tried to study it, displaying an air of nonchalance as he interacted with Harriette. 'Did he say something?'

'No, but he always cooks the first meal whenever he comes to see me. It's a rule.'

'A rule? Whose rule?'

'Mine.'

Frowning, Felix eased back in the chair and looked at her. 'You make him cook dinner for you whenever you see him?' he clarified, as if trying to make sense of the conversation.

'Yes. I didn't pay for him to go to culinary school for nothing.'

'You paid for—?' Felix held up his hand. 'Wait. What? You paid for your boyfriend to get his qualifications as a chef and in return he has to cook you a meal whenever he comes to—' He stopped again, because Harriette had started laughing again, but this time it was definitely something *he'd* said that was making her crack up.

'What? What did I say?' His words only made her laugh harder. In another moment, she had tears in her eyes and was wiping them. 'What's so funny?' His earlier annoyance and frustration returned and he tossed the pen back onto the desk before sighing with exasperation.

'Oh. Oh, Felix. Thank you. I'm incredibly flattered.'

'Why?' He was totally lost now. Had no clue what she was going on about.

'You think Eddie's…' she stopped, another bout of laughter bubbling through her '…my…my boyfriend?'

Felix frowned, now knowing he'd definitely missed something. She'd kissed Eddie. She'd hugged Eddie. She'd called him sweetheart and honey. How was he *not* to think Eddie was her boyfriend? 'Your…brother? Nephew?'

She laughed again, sniffed and wiped at her eyes. 'No, you absolute ninny. Eddie's my son.' She reached for a tissue and dabbed at her eyes before chuckling again.

'Your *son*! How old are you?'

Harriette's answer was to laugh again, then stand from her chair. 'He even called me "Mum".'

'I just thought he was being ironic.'

Another burst of laughter. 'Well, as we're all quiet here, I think I'll give Tori a hand in the clinic with the immunisations.'

'You're going to tell her, aren't you?' Felix stated, shaking his head with slight embarrassment. 'You don't have to, you know. It was an honest mistake.'

'Yes, but it was a hilarious mistake.' With that, she sauntered out of the ED, still chuckling to herself.

'Her *son*?' he mumbled as he tried to focus on the paperwork before him. How was that possible? Either she was much older than he'd thought or Eddie was much younger than he looked. Or both. It also put the prank at the airfield into better perspective. The son, eager to see his mother, to surprise her, doing a crazy stunt without thinking through or considering the ramifications. It also explained why Harriette had been so happy.

'He was her son.' He shook his head in bemusement. 'It was an honest mistake,' he grumbled as he once again tried to focus his thoughts on the paperwork before him. When he'd finished at the hospital that night, he headed to the doctor's residence, already having received a call from Harriette to check it was all right for her to collect Chloe from day care. As he walked in the door his senses were filled with the most delicious aroma, along with the sound of laughter.

He went into the lounge room and found Eddie lying on the floor on his back, his knees bent, his feet on Chloe's hips and his hands holding her firmly as she stretched out her arms as though she were flying, giving her an aeroplane ride.

'Look at me! I'm flying!'

Harriette sat next to them clapping her hands. Her hair was loose, freed from its messy bun, and when she glanced up at him, the red shoulder-length tendrils curling a little at the end, softening her face and making her look even younger, Felix felt a tightening in his gut. How was it possible that this woman could have a grown-up child? And how was it possible he was no longer in control of his senses? Clearly his self-control required even more work than he'd thought.

'All done?' she checked and he nodded, momentarily unable to speak, he was so captivated by her beauty. 'Doesn't dinner smell delicious? I told you Eddie would cook something brilliant.' Chloe was calling to him, demanding his attention, demanding he comment on her excellent flying skills. Felix obliged, making sure he put the correct amount of enthusiasm into his tone because he'd discovered the hard way that if he didn't, she'd get cross with him and a cross Chloe was not something he had the energy to deal with right now.

'Glass of wine?' Harriette asked as she walked into the kitchen, taking another glass from the cupboard and putting it next to the two wine glasses already on the table.

'Eddie's old enough to drink?'

Her answer was to laugh but not provide him with an answer so he simply had to presume Harriette's son was either over the legal drinking age or she simply didn't care. She poured Felix some wine and handed him the glass, picking up her own and clinking it gently to his. 'Cheers.'

'Cheers,' he returned and they both sipped their wine. 'Mmm. This is delicious. What is it?'

'Burgundy,' Eddie called. 'Perfect to go with the boeuf bourguignon.'

'You've made boeuf bourguignon?' Felix's mouth started salivating at the flavours he knew would come.

'Yes, sir,' Eddie replied.

'I haven't had that for...well, for quite a while.'

'Eddie's been studying in France. Paris, actually, on a scholarship. I'm so proud of my boy.'

Felix sat down at the table, watching as Eddie now crawled around the floor with Chloe, pretending to be lions in the African jungle. 'Does everyone get along with Chloe better than me?' he grumbled.

'It's not like that.' She smiled at him and again he felt as though he'd been kicked in the gut and winded. She was so caring, so positive, so optimistic. 'Just give Chloe a little longer. That's all it's going to take and then she'll be fine.' She grinned then. 'Well, not *fine*, per se. She's almost four, and four-year-olds know absolutely everything about the world. That's what she told me earlier on.'

'She knows everything?'

'That's what she told me when we were walking home from day care. She said, "Harriette, I already know about everything in the world," then she paused and looked quite quizzical before adding, "except juggling. I don't know how to juggle." I couldn't help but crack up laughing. She's quite the comedienne,' she finished.

Felix couldn't help but smile at hearing this exchange. 'Chloe said that?'

'She did. She's very intelligent for her age and her vocabulary is extensive. Quite a smart little cookie.'

'I'm not a cookie,' Chloe called out.

'Nothing wrong with her hearing,' Harriette mumbled with a smile.

'Hey, Chloe,' Eddie said a moment later. 'Do you want to come and help me finish unpacking my bag? There might be a present in there for you.'

'A present? For me?' She clutched her little hands to her chest, her eyes wide in astonishment.

'Yes. Come on. Let's go find it.'

'Yay, yay, yay.Presents!'

'He brought her a gift?' Felix asked.

'Looks that way.'

'Clearly you've told him about me…er…and her…about us…er…being here and—'

'I chat over the Internet with Eddie as much as I can or else we text or call each other so, yes, of course I told him you'd arrived. He was getting worried that I was working myself into an early grave. Naturally, I told him I'd been through worse and being the sole doctor in town was nothing new to me.' She took a sip of her wine before continuing. 'I think if he hadn't come and helped me move here, meeting everyone and seeing I would be well supported, he might never have accepted the scholarship to study in Paris.' Harriette shook her head in bemusement. 'I still can't believe he's here. He's travelled all that way just to see *me*. Now that type of action definitely warms a mother's heart.'

'You're…friends with your son?'

'Of course. It's always been just Eddie and me so there was no other real alternative but to get along.' As she spoke, her expressions and tone filled with pride and happiness as well as pure maternal love for her son, Felix once again found himself staring at her in awe. Parenting was hard. That was a fact he'd always known, especially from the way his own parents had often clashed with him and his brother, but seeing the man Eddie had clearly become, seeing how he clearly adored his mother, how he was accepted by the community and how quickly Chloe had taken to him, was a testament to how well Harriette had raised him. She deserved to be proud of him.

Would he be proud of Chloe one day? Would she want to spend time with him when he was old and grey? Humouring him? Surprising him? He honestly hoped so. It was an odd thing to realise that he *wanted* Chloe to like him, that he wanted her to one day love him. Did he love her? He most certainly cared about her otherwise he wouldn't be here, doing what he was doing.

Felix paused, wanting to ask her a lot of private questions, wanting to know more about her past. Would she find them too invasive? Well, he'd soon find out. He took another sip of his wine, then cleared his throat. 'How old were you when you had Eddie?'

'Sixteen. I got accidentally pregnant on my sixteenth birthday. My boyfriend dumped me the moment I told him about the baby and my parents kicked me out when I refused to get an abortion.'

'Your parents *wanted* you to get an abortion?'

'Yes. They said that having a child so young would ruin my life and that I'd never get into medical school, which was all I'd ever wanted. They called me a disappointment and a few choice other names, then told me to pack my bags and never come home again.'

'While you were pregnant?'

'Yes. Four weeks pregnant. Not even showing but, still, I was a disgrace.'

'What about Eddie's father? He didn't support you in any way?'

'No. He's never wanted anything to do with Eddie. He's married now, with a young family of his own, but still refuses to have anything to do with his oldest son, still declares that Eddie isn't even his.' Harriette shrugged as though she didn't really care but Felix could read between the lines. Eddie's father was a coward, who had taken the easy way out, not only shirking his responsibility towards his son but accusing Harriette of sleeping around. Felix clenched his jaw at the injustice.

'So you were kicked out of home and left to raise a child on your own?' Felix stared at her, completely in awe of the woman before him.

'Yes.'

'And you not only did that but somehow managed to get a medical degree?'

'Yes, I did. The degree took a bit longer than the average medical student but I got there in the end.'

'And now you're almost finished your surgical training?'

'Oral exams at the end of the year and then I'm a bona fide general surgeon. Had to pull a few strings to get my supervisor to sign off on me finishing my registrar training here in Meeraji Lake.'

'And how old is Eddie?'

'Twenty-two.'

'You're thirty-eight? You've raised a child, put yourself through medical school and now surgical registrar training and you're not even forty?'

'What can I say? Some people in the world are clearly over-achievers and I'm one of them.' Harriette took another sip of her wine and he could see he was starting to make her feel a little embarrassed.

Felix stared at her, quite unashamedly, regarding her with appreciation and awe. 'Wow.'

CHAPTER FIVE

'Wow?'

Felix grinned. 'Not a word I often use, Dr Jones, so count yourself fortunate.'

'OK. I will.' Harriette looked at him in confusion, not quite sure how to deal with him in such a mood as this. It wasn't that it was bad seeing him like this; in fact, it was quite the opposite. It was good. Good to see Felix smiling and relaxing a bit and using words he didn't usually use. However, seeing him smile in such a way, seeing the way his eyes seemed to relax from their constant state of stress, seeing the lines soften around his brow, only made him even more appealing and that really was the last thing she needed. Admitting he was a handsome man was one thing, constantly staring and ogling him was another. She shook her head slightly in order to clear her thoughts. 'But what do you mean by...*wow*?'

'It means I've always thought I had a rough life. My father had undiagnosed post-traumatic stress disorder after serving in the military and my mother did everything she could to hold things together. Then she...er... died and Dad blamed me for her death. I transferred to a different medical school. I needed distance from my father's constant tirades and left David behind—or at least that's how he saw it.'

'What happened?'

'With David?' At Harriette's nod, he hesitated for a moment then shrugged as though keeping silent really wasn't such an issue. 'David was... David was headstrong, right from the start. If there was a kid in the neighbourhood who would come a cropper, then it was David. Fell off his bike, fell off the swings, ran into a tree, got into a fight.' He chuckled. 'Broke his arm, broke his nose, skinned his knees, twisted his ankle. Mum was always taking him to the hospital to be patched up.' Felix spread his arms wide. 'If there was trouble to be found, David found it before anyone else.'

'Sounds as though you were close back then?'

'We were...brothers. We fought, we argued but we'd stick up for each other when it counted most. Until I went to medical school.' He looked up at the ceiling, as though trying to peer back into his past. 'All I could see was an escape from my father's constant berating, constant emotional negative abuse. David saw it as me deserting him. Then when Mum died... David was left to deal with Dad on his own and, from what David told me, Dad was a constant mixture of anger, aggression and antagonism.'

'But you were able to forgive and reconnect, right?'

'To a point. We met up after he married Susan and he sent me a picture of Chloe when she was born. Apart from that it was birthday and Christmas cards.'

Chloe and Eddie had come back into the lounge room, Chloe very eager to show both Felix and Harriette the colouring-in book and pencils Eddie had given her as a gift. 'And I know that I don't draw on the table but only the paper and Eddie's going to colour in with me, aren't you, Eddie? And then we can show you the picture and it's from France!' She flicked open the book and, sure enough, there were a few words here and there in the colouring-in book that were in French. 'And Eddie's going to teach me what they say. That one—' She pointed to one next to the black outline of a princess. 'That one means "beautiful". *Belle,*' she repeated, glancing across at Eddie as though to ensure she was correct. When he nodded, she said the French word again then raced away to kneel down at the coffee table, settling herself comfortably so she and Eddie could colour in.

'And do you still think you've been dealt a horrible hand?' she asked softly so Chloe couldn't hear. 'Becoming guardian of Chloe?'

Felix sighed thoughtfully and sipped his wine and she could see the shutters starting to come down on his expression. 'I did in the beginning.'

'And now?'

He leaned back in his chair and took another sip of his wine. He wasn't used to speaking so openly about his life, his plans, his past. He kept himself to himself and that was the way it went. If people didn't like it, they could lump it. He was a good surgeon, focused on his job and now he was expected to play happy families? It still didn't sit well with him, especially as Chloe seemed to accept other people far more easily than she'd accepted him.

'I'm just taking it one day at a time. I know more about this parenting caper than I did yesterday.'

She nodded. 'One day at a time. Good concept.'

Felix stood and walked to the kitchen window. He could almost feel Harriette watching him, waiting patiently for him to talk. He didn't want to talk. Didn't want to open up. In the past when he'd allowed himself to be vulnerable, he'd ended up being hurt. He'd loved his mother and she'd died. He'd loved his ex-wife and she'd left him because he'd worked too much and didn't want to have children. Then his last relationship had ended because he'd become guardian to a bereaved three-year-old. Now, though, no matter what he did, for the next fifteen years at the least his first priority would need to be Chloe.

Felix looked at her over his shoulder. 'How did you cope? Young, single mother…how did you cope?'

Harriette shrugged. 'I don't know. I just did.' She thought for a moment more. 'I guess I chose not to let it beat me. I chose to look on the bright side, and that bright side was Eddie. He was my everything. Still is. Without him, everything I do in life has no meaning. I like being in small communities rather than big cities because it allowed me to spend more time with my son. When he's not here—which is still a huge adjustment for me—I focus on getting through the day so I can share it with him over the phone or via email.' She raised her arms in the air. 'Thank God for technology!'

'Are you always this optimistic?'

She chuckled, then shrugged a shoulder. 'I guess so because I couldn't bear to be the alternative.'

'A realist?'

'Nice try. I meant a pessimist. I am a realist—sometimes. If I wasn't, Eddie wouldn't be living on the other side of the world but I know he needs to walk his own path. I guess it all comes down to deciding whether the glass is half full or half empty; whether you're facing struggles or challenges? Perspective. It does make a difference.'

'Chloe's eating and sleeping.' Felix nodded. 'She's healthy and safe.'

'Exactly.'

'Were you always this positive? Even before you became pregnant?'

Harriette thought for a moment. 'I was always determined, especially when my parents kicked me out.'

'Where did you go?'

'First I went to my boyfriend's house.'

'Eddie's father?'

'Yes, but I received the same treatment from him and his parents. I was a disgrace.' She shook her head. 'They called me all sorts of names, accusing me of trying to trap their son, that he wasn't that type of boy, that he had a bright future ahead of him and they weren't going to let me "soil" his reputation by spreading lies, touting him as the father. So I ended up sneaking into my best friend's room and sleeping on her floor, but she didn't want her mother to know I was there because her mother and my mother were good friends.'

'Did you have the entire neighbourhood against you?'

'It was a…tight-knit community.' Harriette laughed without humour. 'My parents were incredibly hypocritical. They cared about what the community thought of them but if I'd had a quiet abortion, if I'd agreed to kill my child—their grandchild—*my Eddie*, then all would be forgiven and I could continue living at home. No one, except the three of us, would ever know what had happened but because I'd told my boyfriend, because I'd told his parents and my best friend, I had brought utter humiliation upon them.'

'You have got to be joking.' Felix's entire body was tense with anger at how she'd been treated. 'No one, especially a young, impressionable girl, deserves to be treated that way, especially when it takes two to tango.'

He drew in a breath and forced himself to relax his clenched fists.

Harriette stood and took her empty glass to the bench and poured herself another glass of wine. 'Thank you and thank goodness times have changed.'

Felix walked to her side and placed his hand on her shoulder, looking into her eyes. His touch was warm and for some reason sent a multitude of tingles flooding throughout her body. His brown eyes were such an amazing colour, like a deep rich chocolate with small flecks of gold here and there. Her breathing hitched at the compassion she saw in his gaze. She hardly knew this man but on some level the story of her past had touched him.

'You've done a fantastic job. Not only with Eddie, but following the career you wanted.' His voice was deep, soft and filled with support. He was looking at her as though she should be recommended for sainthood and the thought made her smile.

'I can't believe you put yourself through medical school with no financial help, with no support.'

'I had Eddie.'

'But he was just a child.' A frown pierced Felix's brow.

'Kids are a great support. Eddie was my biggest fan. I was his mummy. His superhero.' Tears pricked her eyes as she spoke, her voice filled with the utmost love for her son. 'Even when things looked as though they couldn't get any worse, when there were days we didn't have enough money to see us through, Eddie would wrap his arms around my neck and tell me I was doing a good job. That I was the best mumma in the world.'

'You're lucky you had him.' Was that a note of envy in Felix's tone? She wasn't quite sure and, even if it was, it disappeared almost instantly. 'He's an amazing young man.'

She grinned and sighed. 'I'm so proud of him.'

Eddie walked into the room and Felix immediately dropped his hands back to his sides. 'You talking about me? How brilliant I am?' Harriette's smile was answer enough. Eddie bent and kissed her cheek. 'Ya did good, Mum, now shift. You're in my way and the dinner will burn if I don't apply my brilliant skills of expertise.'

'Did I mention he also has the gift of hyperbole?' She laughed.

'Uh…where's Chloe?' Felix asked.

'She's in her room,' Eddie said. 'She has the usual three-year-old's attention span—bored after ten minutes. Does she usually have a bath before dinner?'

'Usually, if she doesn't fight it,' Felix grumbled, and was once again treated to the tinkling of Harriette's laughter. He found it difficult to believe she'd been through so much and yet was still, for all intents and purposes, a very happy, well-adjusted person. She wasn't bitter or angry. She didn't feel as though she'd been dealt a horrible hand and why? Because she loved her son and had that love returned.

Was it really that simple? To love a child and have that child love you back? Was that all he needed to do to gain the sort of inner happiness he'd been searching for his entire life?

Felix looked at Harriette, who swept her hand in front of her. 'Go, Felix. Become her superhero.'

'Run that bath,' Eddie added encouragingly.

'Superhero work begins by running baths?' Felix quirked an eyebrow at them, showing Harriette that beneath that gruff exterior he often portrayed there was clearly a mischievous side to his personality.

'Absolutely,' she returned with a wide grin and, with that, he headed off to get Chloe's bath ready.

Once the little girl was bathed and dressed for bed, Eddie served up dinner. Felix sat next to Chloe and cut up her food. 'It might be a little spicy for her,' Felix added after chewing an exquisite mouthful.

'We'll see,' Harriette remarked as they watched Chloe take the first mouthful.

She grinned and swallowed and declared the food 'yummy'.

'Really?' Felix seemed surprised.

'And Eddie had a cheese sandwich all ready to go in case she didn't like it,' Harriette remarked.

'Cheese sandwich!' Chloe declared and put her spoon down.

'You spoke too soon, Harriette,' Felix remarked and Eddie immediately went and retrieved the cheese sandwich, with the crusts cut off and in little rectangular finger-sized bites. 'A fancy cheese sandwich,' he continued and Eddie just grinned. Then Eddie dipped one end of the cheese sandwich into the boeuf gravy and held it up to Chloe's lips. The child immediately ate it and asked for more.

'It appears to me, Felix,' Harriette said a while later when they'd all finished their meals, 'that your niece prefers French cuisine.'

'Ugh. Trust me to end up with a child who has up-market tastes.'

Harriette smiled at him, impressed because his tone held the right level of humour, mixed with the right level of truth and—dared she hope?—a little bit of love towards the gorgeous girl. She had no doubt that Felix loved Chloe but it wasn't a deep, personal love but more one born out of duty. He'd mentioned his father had served in the military and it made her wonder whether that was what 'love' had been like in his household, one of duty and respect rather than one filled with cuddles and laughter.

When Eddie offered to put Chloe to bed—in her own bed—the child willingly agreed but insisted on a horsey ride to take her to her bedroom. Immediately complying, Eddie crouched down and waited for Chloe to seat herself on his back before making clip-clopping noises as he headed towards Chloe's bedroom.

As they stacked the dishwasher Felix couldn't help but voice his amazement. 'Eddie really is quite a natural with Chloe.'

'He's always had a way with people. He just accepts them for who they are and doesn't judge.'

'You, too. You're a lot like that, very personable, very trusting.'

'Ah, but that blind trust can sometimes get you into a lot of deep water.'

'Eddie's father?'

'Exactly. I believed him when he said he loved me. I trusted him when he said that being intimate was the next step in our future relationship, that he wanted to marry me and be with me forever.'

'And yet you still seem able to trust people you've just met?'

'Like you?' When he only shrugged, she continued. 'I have to trust you, at least in a professional capacity. Out here in the middle of nowhere, we're forced into closed quarters. Living here—' she gestured to the house '—working in the clinic, going off on house calls, which out here last for two or three days because the properties are spread out. We need to trust each other, to be open and honest with each other, rely solely on the other person—especially in an emergency. We're not in a large teaching hospital any more, where there are countless other staff members and a plethora of equipment. It's just you and me and our wits.'

'And our training.'

'That, too.' She smiled. 'What I'm trying to say is, the sooner we figure each other out, the sooner we form an understanding of how each other ticks. That's what small-town medicine is all about—getting to know the staff on a personal level, getting to know your patients on a personal level and thereby being able to provide personalised treatment. When someone gets a cold in this town *everyone* gets a cold. Everyone gets sick together, or it comes in waves, and to deal with that we need to be a *part* of the community rather than standing back from the outside looking in.'

'But in standing back, we may be protected from becoming sick ourselves and therefore will be more able to heal the community from the outside.'

'Fair point but that's just not an option. Your patients won't trust you, they won't tell you what's wrong in the first place and then signs and symptoms risk going untreated and causing more of an epidemic that then spreads throughout the wider districts, infecting more people.'

Felix sighed with exasperation and sat back down on the chair, elbows on the table, head in his hands. 'What have I done, coming here?' The question was rhetorical and Harriette stayed quiet but went and sat down next to him. 'I'm not the sort of bloke who enjoys… closeness of community. I've never had it before. Not in my family growing up and not in my working life. I guess I don't need "closeness" as much as others.'

'Everyone needs to be close to someone, Felix.'

He lifted his head and stared across at her. 'Like you and Eddie?'

'Yes. You can have that closeness with Chloe.'

'But she's only three.'

'Almost four,' Harriette added. 'And yes, you can have that closeness with her. Just because she's a child, it doesn't mean she doesn't have the same feelings. She may not comprehend them in the way you and I do, but she has them and she needs you to help her and the only way you can help her is to *become* an integrated part of her life. If you let her in, if you let her break through that heart of yours, which you've clearly had locked up for quite some time now, then your life will change in all the positive ways you've probably never even imagined.'

Felix stared at her for a moment, then shook his head in stunned bemusement. 'How is it you seem to know me so well?'

'I know your type. Eddie's father was a lot like you.'

'I don't think that's a compliment, given he left you in the lurch.'

'And you wouldn't have?'

'If I had accidentally impregnated my girlfriend, I would not have left her to raise *my* child on her own.' His words were vehement and direct and she could see that he meant every single word. 'There are too many injustices in the world. It's important we fix the ones that are within our control.'

'Would you have offered to pay for an abortion?'

'No.' His answer was instant.

'So in your opinion I did the right thing?' She couldn't help the hint of her past inexperienced sixteen-year-old self tingeing her words.

'Of course and meeting Eddie only proves you did the right thing.'

'I think your brother did the right thing by appointing you as Chloe's guardian. Whatever your differences, he knew you'd be able to cope with the situation. That's a compliment.'

Felix leaned back in his chair and laced his fingers behind his head, stretching his shoulder muscles. Harriette tried not to stare, tried to remember why there were sitting here chatting, that she was trying to help him put his situation into perspective. Instead, she seemed to be memorising the way his shirt was pulled taut across his well-defined biceps and how the buttons looked as though they were ready to burst as his chest expanded beneath the fabric. She closed her eyes for a split second, determined to focus and get her over-active hormones under control.

'Once or twice a year,' Felix began and Harriette looked at him again. Thankfully, he'd stopped stretching and was rubbing his temples with his fingers. 'David would get himself into some sort of trouble and I'd either get a call while I was away at medical school, from my father telling me to "handle it" or from the police. The area where David and my father still lived was where I went to high school and two of the police officers at the local station were in my year so nine times out of ten they'd call me first, rather than having to deal with my father.'

Harriette raised her eyebrows in surprise. 'The police didn't like your father?'

'Post-traumatic stress disorder, especially when triggered through serving in a war zone, doesn't bring out the best in people who suffer from it.' He clasped his hands in front of him and placed them on the table. 'My father's moods were erratic. One minute you'd be having a normal conversation with him and the next, he'd be yelling at you to get down under the table, to protect yourself. He'd accuse you of taking his gun, of being in collusion with the enemy.' Felix looked down at his hands and only then realised just how tightly he was clenching his fingers. He forced himself to relax, to take a deep and calming breath.

'David's antics were often more than enough to set Dad off. Sometimes, he'd think David or I were the enemy and he'd hit us. Then, when he snapped out of it, he would apologise profusely, often in tears, begging us to forgive him and not report him.'

'You poor boys.' Harriette's heart went out to the younger Felix, feeling sad for what he'd endured.

'I think Mum hid it from us for quite a while, managed it by getting him onto anti-depressants, which seemed to help with the symptoms, but after her... death, he just snapped. He was never the same, never fully comprehensive of what the life around him was all about.' Felix spoke softly, looking past Harriette as though he was looking back in time. 'Life could have been so different for us all. We wouldn't have been so estranged. It would have made Mum sad to know that that's how things ended up. David and I not talking. Dad turning his back on both of us, declaring us "dead to him", not wanting to talk to us, to have anything to do with us.' His voice was soft, reflective and filled with regret. He was so lost in his thoughts that he was surprised when Harriette put her hand over his, offering support. When he returned his gaze to meet hers, he was even more astonished to find she had tears in her eyes.

'Wow.' The word was soft and she sniffed, offering him a wobbly smile.

'Wow?' He mimicked her earlier response.

'And I thought I'd had a hard life.'

Felix couldn't help but smile. 'I guess we…every-one…has their own crosses to bear.'

'It's how we deal with them, how we allow them to shape us as a person, that matters most.' She rubbed her fingers slowly on top of his in a gesture of support and understanding. She'd been through her own personal hell and she'd conquered it. And yet, he was still surprised at how one simple touch from her was really starting to make him feel better about his past. That sort of thing had never happened to him before. Then again, he'd rarely spoken to anyone about his family. Even with his ex-wife and definitely not with his last girlfriend. So what was it about Harriette that was making him open up, making him tell her things he'd never have thought of telling her?

Was it because she was such a calm and confident woman who, as he'd witnessed over the past few days, was very empathetic towards her patients, the staff and basically everyone she met? Or was it because she had the ability to make him feel as though he was the most important person in the world right now, that all her attention was focused solely on him, that she was *listening* to him.

'Where is he now?' Her soft words brought his thoughts back to what they'd been discussing, even though he was still highly aware of her smooth, soft hand resting on top of his.

'My father?' At her nod, he continued. 'In a nursing home in Darwin. It's one for ex-servicemen and especially those suffering from PTSD and other associated disorders. He has dementia now and wouldn't have a clue who I was. I receive regular emailed updates from his physician and the last one stated that the old man was slowly failing.'

'Oh, Felix. Darwin isn't that far from here. You could go and visit him. Dale could fly you there as soon as you like.'

Felix withdrew his hand from her touch and stood. 'Why would I want to see him? He hasn't spoken to me in years. He told me I was useless, hopeless and a disgrace. He blamed me for my mum's death, he accused me of—' He stopped and shook his head. 'No. I don't want to see him.'

As though he couldn't stay still, Felix started to pace back and forth in front of her. 'Do you see your parents? Especially after the way they treated you? Treated Eddie?' He clearly wanted the conversation turned away from himself and the only way he could do this was to attack her. Thankfully, Harriette recognised this behaviour and answered the question calmly, rather than allowing him to rile her as had clearly been his intention. She knew what emotional pain was like and she knew it could make you do and say things you often wished unsaid.

'Yes. I tried many times over the years and they refused any contact but then, when Eddie was twelve, he ended up in hospital with influenza A. It was the darkest time of my life. Nothing…no hurt, no pain— *nothing*—could compare with the thought of losing my boy. We had to go to Melbourne city so Eddie could receive treatment. I called my parents. I begged them to come to the hospital and…eventually they did. It wasn't a tear-filled reunion and we still don't talk regularly but at least I know I can contact them if I need to and vice versa.'

'You forgave them? After the way they treated you? Treated Eddie?'

She shrugged. 'You just do because otherwise it eats

at you. You end up with regrets and if you leave it too late, those regrets can affect your life.'

He knew what she meant. He had so many regrets but they were to do with his mother, not his father. 'Mother.' He whispered the word, barely audible but somehow Harriette heard.

'You have regrets about your mother?' she asked softly.

Felix swallowed and clenched his jaw as though he was desperately trying to control his overwrought emotions. 'Yes.' He choked on the word and lowered his head to look at the ground, his hands curled tight into fists at his sides.

'Everything changed when she died?' Harriette offered when he didn't say anything more.

'Yes.'

'You loved her.' It was a firm statement.

He raised his head and met her gaze. She could see the anguish in his eyes, could see the sorrow and regret in his face. 'Yes.'

If all Felix was capable of was monosyllabic answers then she would provide him with the easiest way to get through this difficult conversation because now that he'd unlocked the doors he'd obviously kept closed for quite a few decades, she didn't want him to slam them shut again, especially not when his father was dying.

'Do you think your mother would want you to go see him? Even if he doesn't know who you are?'

It took a while for him to answer. 'Yes.' He cleared his throat. He looked so much like a little lost boy that her maternal instincts kicked in and she instantly stood and walked to his side. He remained where he was, body taut, hands clenched, jaw tight. He was still looking at her, still holding her gaze, still trying to shut her out but clearly unable to do so. Harriette was honoured. She placed her hands onto his shoulders.

'Would you like me to go with you?' She held her breath as she waited for him to answer. It was a turning point in his life. Would he choose to heal his past or would he live with regret for ever? He clearly regretted the rift between his brother David and himself. Would he miss the same opportunity with his father? She continued to hold his gaze, not wavering but trying to support him, with whatever decision he made. She silently prayed it was the right one. That he would go.

'Yes.'

The instant he said the word, Harriette breathed out and then, as though it was the most natural thing in the world, she slipped her arms under his and allowed him to draw her close into a hug. It wasn't a hug filled with sensual overtones, although she wasn't unaware of just how perfectly his body was sculpted. Instead, it was a hug between friends—friends who were becoming closer with every passing moment. By agreeing that he wanted her to go with him on this venture, he was showing her just how much he was putting his trust in her.

'I won't let you down,' she whispered against his chest and closed her eyes, his firm, solid arms still enfolded around her.

'Thank you.'

CHAPTER SIX

FOR A LONG moment Felix stood there with his arms around Harriette, unable to believe that this woman had not only managed to get him to open up about his family, and more particularly his father, and was now hugging him close, offering her support.

He wasn't used to people supporting him, being on his side. In fact, every woman he'd ever dared to care about had rejected him in one way or another. Harriette might be saying she'd support him now but she'd leave him in the end. Although she'd offered to come and see his father with him, she would forget about it, or she'd find an excuse.

He stopped the thought before it began and adjusted his arms around Harriette, trying to loosen his hold a little as he became more aware of just how perfectly she fitted into his arms. He tried not to breathe in her alluring scent, tried to remember that she was only hugging him because she'd been emotionally moved by what he'd told her. A woman like her, a woman who appeared genuine and naturally caring, couldn't possibly be interested in a career-hungry surgeon who didn't know the first thing about raising a child.

Felix shifted back a little, knowing he needed to let her go before he started to memorise the contours of her body pressed against his own. Harriette. Sweet Harriette. During the past few days she'd helped him more than she'd realised. Gratitude was one thing but starting to become more aware of her as a woman was a completely different thing altogether.

Harriette lifted her head and looked up at him, concern still reflected in her gaze. 'We'll get through this together. You're not alone.'

He nodded and edged back from her, trying not to be delighted when she took her time sliding her hands from his waist. Was she trying to linger? Could she feel that same awareness buzzing between them?

'We should probably go and say goodnight to Chloe.'

'Uh…' He cleared his throat. 'Yes. Good.'

Harriette walked ahead of him and he followed, trying not to watch the way her hips swayed gently from side to side, trying not to feel bereft because she wasn't in his arms any more. They were colleagues. Yes, he was a man and yes, she was an incredibly attractive woman, but if this whole situation was going to work he needed to get himself under better control. Focusing on Chloe would definitely help and, when they entered her room, they found the little girl all snuggled up in bed, almost asleep. She was still awake enough to know they were there. Eddie finished reading the last page of the book using a boring monotone voice, then grinned at his mother before standing and heading out.

Felix watched in the dim light of the room as Harriette knelt down beside Chloe's bed and tenderly brushed some hair from the little girl's forehead before placing a gentle kiss there. She whispered sweet and soothing words to the child, just as a mother would. Just as his mother had when he'd been little. He could remember her coming into the room he'd shared with David. He'd been almost eight years old and had been begging for his own room. His mother had told him that when they moved to the next military posting, onto the military base, he would be able to have his own room. He'd told her that when that happened, he wouldn't need her to come in and say goodnight to him like this, to brush her hand on his forehead and place a kiss there. He would be too old for that ritual and she need not bother. His mother's answer had been to chuckle softly and kiss his forehead. 'I will always come and kiss you goodnight,' she'd told him. 'You're my wonderful son, no matter how old you are.'

Felix tried to swallow over the dryness of his throat before forcing himself to block out his emotions surrounding his mother. She'd lied to him, she'd let him down and she'd left him and David alone in the world to fend for themselves.

'Did you want to give her a little kiss? She's practically asleep right now.'

Felix blinked, bringing his thoughts back to the present at Harriette's soft question. He looked at her. 'Pardon?'

She smiled and beckoned for him to kneel down next to her. He hesitated for a moment, then did as Harriette had suggested. As he bent down his knee cracked and Harriette immediately grinned. 'Getting old,' he mumbled.

'Aren't we all?' she whispered back.

'Not you.' The words were instant. Harriette continued to stroke Chloe's hair and a moment or two later, the child's breathing evened out into a natural rhythm. 'You don't look old enough to have a twenty-two-year-old son.' He gestured to the sleeping Chloe. 'A child of this age—yes, but the mother of a grown man? Most definitely no.'

Harriette looked at him for a moment, a look of surprise and…embarrassment? Had he embarrassed her?

'Sorry. It wasn't my intention to embarrass—'

'You didn't,' she responded quickly, perhaps too quickly. As they both knelt beside Chloe's bed, side by side, leg near leg, arm near arm, Felix realised far too late just how close they were to each other. He breathed in her scent, allowing it to wind its way around him, to become absorbed by his senses. 'I…er…it was very nice of you to say that. You know, that I look young.'

He was learning not to be astounded or even surprised at her openness. Harriette would talk about any subject with him in an honest way and that promoted a faith in her, the beginnings of trust. Of course, on a professional level, there was already a certain level of trust forming between them, but this was a deep, personal kind of trust and he wasn't sure when he'd last felt that way about anyone.

'Surely you know how beautiful you are, Harriette.' His soft words were a statement and for a long moment they stared into each other's eyes. It was as though time stood still, as though it were only the two of them. That seemed to be happening to him…to them…a lot lately. Would it continue? As he settled into life in Meeraji Lake, would this sensation, these feelings, the attraction he felt towards her continue to grow? Did he want that?

'Well…uh… I guess that doesn't…um…really matter.' Her stuttered words weren't the reaction he was expecting. In fact, he wasn't sure exactly what reaction he'd been expecting but he didn't expect her to stand and walk away. He *had* embarrassed her, or at the least he'd made her feel uncomfortable. Felix turned and watched Chloe sleeping, shaking his head slowly from side to side.

'Women,' he murmured softly but in a way that held such confusion and bewilderment. 'I doubt I'll ever understand you.' He reached and brushed Chloe's hair from her forehead, mimicking Harriette's actions. He hadn't really done this before, watched Chloe sleep. Usually, as soon as she was asleep, he'd collapse with exhaustion.

As he looked at her, gently touched her smooth, soft forehead, he was filled with a sense of...love. He knew he loved Chloe, in the sense that she was his niece and it was his duty to love her, but to be so completely stirred by the emotion, to look at this angelic little person—the same little person who he'd hardly class as angelic when she was awake and causing complete havoc in his life—and have his heart fill with love for her... He paused, then leaned forward and pressed a kiss to her forehead.

The instant his lips touched her baby-soft skina warmth flooded through him and seemed to spread throughout his entire body. A warmth of affection, a warmth of protection, a warmth of devotion. He eased back and stared at the child in complete bewilderment. Even though she'd caused him deep consternation, deep confusion and deep contemplation, even though she'd screamed so loud he'd thought his ear drums would burst, even though she'd turned his life inside out and upside down... Felix loved her. Not because he *had* to love her but because he *wanted* to love her.

He stood and once again stared at the sleeping angel. 'Huh!' Then he turned and stopped short when he saw Harriette leaning against the door jamb. 'I thought you'd gone.'

'It's amazing, isn't it?' she stated quietly.

'What?'

'The moment you're completely overcome with parental love for your child.'

Felix shoved his hands into his pockets, unsure he was ready to discuss the emotions he'd just experienced. They were still too raw and personal for him to talk about, especially when he wasn't even sure he understood them.

'She's my niece,' he murmured as he walked past Harriette, feeling a different sensation—one of close awareness—as he made sure their bodies didn't accidentally brush each other as he headed into the living room.

'She's your *daughter*,' Harriette corrected. Eddie wasn't anywhere to be found so she assumed he'd gone to his own bedroom.

'No, she's not. She's David's daughter. In my mind, she will always be David's daughter and I'll always be Uncle Felix.'

'In *your* mind, yes, but in her mind, she will come to see you as her father.'

'Hmm.' He hadn't thought about it that way before. He sat down in the chair and gave it some serious consideration. 'She'll always know her true parentage. Even if she forgets David and Susan, I'll remind her, I'll show her photos of them, tell her anecdotes about them.'

'Of course.'

'But she'll see me as her father. She'll be my daughter.'

Harriette sat down in the chair opposite and kept quiet, delighted at watching the dawning realisation cross his face.

'Chloe is legally my child, my *daughter*.' He paused and allowed that previous sensation of love, the love he felt towards the girl, wash over him once more. 'I'm not just her guardian, I'm her...*father*!' His mind seemed to race, to connect dots that he'd never noticed before. 'I'd never wanted children before because of...well, because of many reasons but now that it's finally sinking in...' He looked at Harriette. 'I want to be a good father.'

'And you will.'

'How can you know that?'

'Because we're having this conversation. There will be a lot of questioning, a lot of arguments, a lot of love and, believe me, it's all well worth it.'

'But *how* do I do it? How do I become a good dad?'

Harriette leaned back in the chair and grinned. 'Get to know Chloe.'

He waited for more advice but it never came. 'That's it? The wise and sage advice you're offering is "get to know Chloe"?'

'Yep, but *really* get to know her.'

'How?' He leaned forward in his chair and spread his arms wide, his face earnest, his words filled with incredulity. 'How do I do that? No one will tell me how. I've read about a hundred parenting books and articles online but none of them are written out like hospital protocols. None of them say, "Do this and then do that." So what am I supposed to do, Harriette? Tell me, please. How do I get to know her?'

Harriette was laughing at him but not in a mean way, more in a way that told him she was as surprised by his outburst as he was. 'OK. OK. I'll help you. I'll tell you the secret to parenting.'

'There's a secret?'

'Well, there's a few and the first one you need to know is—be interested in what they're interested in.'

'Be interested.' He nodded. 'What else?'

She thought for a moment. 'It doesn't get better, it just gets different.'

'More riddles? What is that supposed to mean?'

'It means that whatever phase your child is going through, it's never going to get better. You can't wait for things to get better, to settle down, because they don't. Just when you think you have a handle on things, when you think you've figured them out, they enter the next phase and—'

'It gets different.' He nodded. 'Anything else?'

Harriette sighed and frowned in thought. 'It's a long time since I've had to do any of these things.'

'So there does come a time when you're done? When the parenting is over?'

'No. When you're a parent, you're a parent for life— if that's what you choose. Eddie is my best friend. I love being with him and I hate it when he goes because I worry about him. That part never goes away.'

'The worry never goes away. Got it.' Felix looked around. 'I should be writing these down.'

'You're a smart man. You'll remember them.'

'But tell me *how...how* do I get interested in what she likes?'

Harriette eased back into the chair and thought for a moment. 'Ask what her favourite book is.'

'Favourite book. Got it. What else?'

'Read stories to her. Ask her which toy is her favourite. What's her favourite colour?'

'She has a favourite colour?'

'Of course she does.'

'What is it? Do you know?'

'You know as well, you just haven't tuned your brain into realising it.'

'You're talking in riddles again.' He leaned back

and crossed his arms in an action that immediately reminded her of Chloe.

'What colour is the backpack she takes to day care?'

'Purple.'

'What colour are the shoes she likes to wear the
most?'

He thought on this one for a moment. Chloe had
a favourite pair of shoes? He pictured the ones she'd
been wearing today...and then realised she'd worn them
yesterday and the day before and, for that matter, she
usually got upset if he tried to make her wear different
shoes that were more suitable to the weather. 'Purple.'

'So...her favourite colour is?'

'Purple.' He nodded slowly, as though he was finally starting to see what Harriette was saying. 'Was
that why she got angry with me yesterday morning?
Because I told her to wear runners to day care rather
than her sparkly purple shoes?'

'Yes.'

'Well, why didn't she just say they were her favourite?'

'Because she's three years old.' Harriette laughed.

'Am I supposed to let her get away with doing whatever she wants?'

'She'll *want* to listen to you if you give her good
reasons to listen.'

'There you go again. Talking in riddles.'

Harriette shook her head in bemusement. 'You can't
cram for a parenting exam. You just learn things over
time.'

'I wish it was an exam. It would certainly be easier.'

'To start with, why don't you arrange a playdate with
her? That way, you're showing Chloe that you're interested in what she's interested in.'

'But what if I'm actually not interested in the same things as her?'

'Then you learn to be.' Harriette's words were earnest, her gaze direct. 'This is too important, Felix. Your relationship with Chloe is more important than your work, than being published. Patients will come and go. Jobs will come and go. Publications will come and go. Chloe is in your life *forever*. She's a constant in your life, just as you're a constant in hers. So start by spending time together. Just the two of you, or invite some of her day-care friends along if you must, but *you* have to be a part of the event.'

'Event? Like what?'

Harriette thought for a moment. 'Uh…what about a…tea party? Sit down and pretend to have a tea party with her.'

'Pretend? As in make-believe?'

'Yes. Use that rusty imagination of yours. It could do with a good oiling.'

'A tea party?'

'Yes.'

'A pretend tea party.' He mulled over the idea.

'Pretend ones are easier to organise and she'll be less fussy about the food,' Harriette pointed out.

'Good point. She won't get cross with me for cutting her cheese sandwich into squares instead of rectangles if it's imaginary.' Felix rubbed his chin with his thumb and forefinger. 'A tea party, eh?'

'Looks as though you're already getting ideas.'

'Will you come?'

She looked at him with excited surprise. 'Do you want me to?'

'Yes. You and Eddie, Chloe and myself.That way, as

it'll be my first time hosting an imaginary tea party, you'll be able to tell me if I'm doing anything wrong.'

Harriette laughed. 'I think Chloe will be the one to tell you if you're doing it wrong. She's very forthright in her opinions.'

'I've noticed.' He closed his eyes for a moment and shook his head.

'That's a good thing, Felix. Just think. When she's older, when guys are interested in her, she's not going to be a pushover. She's going to know exactly what she wants, and she's going to go for it but only if she knows you've got her back.'

'Don't even mention guys. Just the thought of her, all grown up with some pimply, hormonal teenager drooling all over her—' He clenched his hands and shook his head, a protective look in his eyes. Harriette couldn't have been prouder.

'The point is, if she has your support, she'll realise she can do anything in life.'

'And it all starts with a tea party?'

'And it all starts with a tea party,' she confirmed with a bright and happy smile, delighted she'd been able to get Felix not only to open up to her, something she had a feeling he rarely did, but to view his guardianship of Chloe in a different light. He had been blessed with the opportunity to be a parent, to be a father to a grieving, hurting child, and as she watched him declare he was going to go and watch his *daughter*, not his niece, sleep, Harriette was positive she'd seen the imaginary swish of a superhero cape fluttering out from behind him.

CHAPTER SEVEN

IT WAS TWO days later when Harriette received her invitation to join Miss Chloe Jane McLaren and Dr Felix McLaren for a tea party, to be held at half past four in the afternoon, at the doctors' residence. She rushed through her paperwork after clinic and managed to arrive only two minutes late.

'She's here! She's here!' Chloe's excited words filled the house as Harriette stepped inside. Eddie, Chloe and Felix were already in the lounge room where a picnic rug had been spread out on the carpet and a lovely new purple tea set with little white flowers on it, had been set up for four people. Felix stood behind one of the high wing-back chairs, grinning widely at Chloe's over-excitement.

'Look. Look.' Chloe pointed at the tea set as she ran around the edge of the rug with hyperactive delight. 'Uncle Felix bought it for me. For *me* because he said I've been a good girl and it has little flowers on it. Look, Harriette.'

'That's so pretty.'

'And we're having a tea party!' Chloe jumped up and down and clapped her hands, completely and utterly delighted with this turn of events. 'I helped Uncle Felix set it all up and we did it together.'

Harriette glanced at Felix and nodded in approval. 'Very impressive.'

'But the food isn't real but then we can use our 'maginations and have purple tea and orange cupcakes,' the little girl continued, taking Harriette's hand and leading her to a place setting. 'You sit here.'

'All right.'

'And, Eddie, you sit over here.' Chloe led Eddie to his spot, clearly eager to get this tea party underway. 'And, Uncle Felix, you sit over here.' She took Felix's hand and he seemed surprised at Chloe's voluntary act of treating him like the others. 'And I'll sit here because then I'm closest to the teapot and the 'magination food so I can give it all to you.'

'That sounds perfectly lovely,' Harriette said and then held out her cup to Chloe. 'May I please have a cup of…blue tea?'

Chloe giggled but lifted the pot and poured a cup of imaginary blue tea for her first guest. As the party continued they all pretended to eat the vibrantly coloured food and Eddie made sure Chloe drank her imaginary tea with her little finger in the air.

At some point, Chloe even went into her bedroom and came out with two or three soft toys, declaring that Eddie, Harriette and Uncle Felix had had enough and now needed to go into the kitchen because she had other guests coming for her next tea party. The three-year-old amused herself, playing with her toys and the tea set while the adults dutifully went to the kitchen.

'I'll get the non-imaginary dinner started,' Eddie remarked.

'You don't have to cook for us,' Felix stated. 'I'm happy to do dinner this evening.'

'It's fine. I like cooking for my mum and her friends. Makes me feel as though I'm giving her something back.'

'You know you don't—' Harriette began, reiterating what Felix was saying, but her son silenced her.

'Shh.' He held a finger to his lips and glared at her. 'Enough, Mum.'

'Yes, son,' she remarked with a twinkling smile. Felix watched the exchange between the two of them, astonished at how close they really were. Even before his mother had passed away, he'd never been that close to her. Never in his life would he have 'shushed' his mother, but neither would he have laughed with her or put his arm around her shoulders or given her a kiss on the cheek. It wasn't that she hadn't loved her boys, it was simply that she hadn't been the demonstrative type. Her way of showing them love had been to cook meals, to clean their clothes, and to help proofread their homework. Still, she would come in at night, brush his hair from his forehead and kiss him. She did it with himself and David and only when their father wasn't around.

Felix could recall his father berating his mother, telling her she would make the boys soft, that she would turn them into sissies if she kept cuddling and kissing them all the time. Boys needed to be tough, needed not to cry, needed to shoulder responsibility from a young age or they would never grow up to be men, they would grow up to be sissy men. Felix closed his eyes for a moment, wanting to remove his father's dictatorial and overbearing voice from his mind.

Ever since he'd mentioned that his father was in Darwin, Harriette had been trying to figure out a way for them to go and see him and every time she'd brought the topic up, he'd done his best to shut her down. He regretted telling her about his past and especially about his father. He didn't want to see his father, didn't want anything to do with him. Couldn't she see that? The man was a cold, hard-hearted emotionally abusive— and sometimes physically abusive—soldier with dementia. The old man might not know who Felix was but Felix surely knew who his father was and the more Harriette talked about it, the more he started to retreat, to withdraw from the subject and from her, to put some distance between himself and his new colleague. He'd always been a loner and, although he could acquiesce and make room for Chloe in his life, he wasn't about to make room for anyone else.

Was that the reason why he'd had difficulty being demonstrative himself? Because he'd been raised by a cold man and a woman who only felt able to show him some affection when his father was nowhere around? Clearly that wasn't the way Eddie had been raised and with what he'd already learned about Harriette, he knew she'd shown him all the affection she could. She'd shared that affectionate heart of hers with the people of this community, with her patients, with him and with Chloe. It was an affection that promoted easy acceptance, that seemed to make insurmountable problems very easy to conquer.

As he half listened to the easy banter between Harriette and her son he realised that, from what she'd said, her own home life hadn't been that loving. Had her parents cuddled her in public? Kissed her in public? Told everyone how proud they were of their daughter, telling them without agenda or self-importance? He guessed not, because if they had truly loved and cared for Harriette they would never have kicked her out of home in the first place and yet here she was, enjoying that loving, caring relationship quite openly with her son.

He remembered how, when she'd first seen Eddie come down the aeroplane stairs, her eyes had twinkled, her mouth had curved into the biggest smile and her arms had opened wide in order to envelop her most beloved son. He'd never seen a mother behave like that towards her adult child and he'd never seen an adult child behave that way towards his mother. Eddie was more than happy to be seen with her, to spend time with her, to laugh and chat with her friends—whether they be old or young. They accepted each other for who they were, as individuals and as part of a family.

It gave him hope that perhaps one day he and Chloe might have a relationship like Harriette and Eddie. Today he'd been heartened by the way she'd accepted his surprise of having a tea party, of the special tea set he'd ordered online a few days ago and that had been delivered via plane on the daily mail run.

'Where ever did you find that tea set?' Harriette asked him, interrupting his solitary reverie. 'It's absolutely perfect.'

'On the Internet.' Felix shrugged as though the entire thing were no big deal and Harriette couldn't help but laugh and shake her head. Her twinkling eyes said she knew he was being nonchalant, that she knew he would have spent far too much time on the task, determined to get it right.

'Then, I must say, excellent work, Dr McLaren. Perfect choice of colours and pattern in the china.'

'Purple,' he interjected.

'And perfect size. Easy for little fingers to pick up and use.'

Harriette was sitting at the table and Felix joined

her, sitting on her right and trying desperately not to knock her knee as he shifted in his chair. Ever since the other night when he'd held her in his arms, he'd become hypersensitive about how close they were, of whether their fingers had touched, whether their knees had knocked together beneath the table. And every time they did accidentally touch, a shot of desire would ripple through him.

It was ridiculous, of course. Harriette was his colleague and the fact that they lived in such close proximity and worked in such close proximity and…ate meals in such close—

'Are you all right, Felix?' Harriette asked, stalling his thoughts. Her head was slightly tipped to the side and she was looking at him with a hint of concern.

'I'm fine. Why?'

'Well…' She cleared her throat and lowered her voice to just above a whisper. 'You're…uh…staring at me.'

'Oh? Was I? Sorry.' He shifted back in his chair, trying to put distance between them. Chloe was in the lounge room still chattering away to her toys and feeding them imaginary food while Eddie was whistling as he worked, chopping vegetables. There were two other people with them and yet Felix felt as though it were just himself and Harriette…close…together…intimate. What was it about this woman that was making him so aware of her? He'd never had this problem before. He'd always been able to control his libido, to control his emotions, but with Harriette… He shook his head.

'What is it?' she asked again, her concern deepening.

'I don't talk about my life.' The words were almost ripped from his vocal box and he surprised himself at the low determination accompanying them.

'So I gathered.'

'What's that supposed to mean?'

Her instant smile disarmed him once more. 'It means that every time I've mentioned your father in the past few days, you've shut me down. Clearly you regret telling me anything and I respect that.'

'You do?'

'That doesn't mean I'm going to stop in my preparations for us to get to Darwin to see him.'

'But—'

'Berate me. Hate me. Never speak to me again.' She shrugged one beautiful shoulder, the cotton strap of her top falling off, exposing the perfect skin beneath. His gaze honed in on the area where her shoulder and neck met and the tingling in his lips, the need and the desire to taste that one spot, roared through him like a heat he'd never felt before. 'You need to see your father before he dies.'

She was speaking words but the reverberating sound of blood pumping furiously around his body was inhibiting him from processing what she was saying. Good heavens. Didn't the woman have any idea just how desirable she was? Why hadn't she married? Why had she remained alone all these years? Why hadn't any man realised how wonderful, caring and giving she was and asked her to marry him? Perhaps some had? Perhaps she'd said no. Perhaps she'd said yes. In fact, he really had no idea whether or not—

'Uncle Felix!'

Chloe's insistent and impatient tone broke through his thoughts and he'd never been more thankful for the interruption. Thinking about Harriette in such a fashion was something he'd been trying to keep at bay. 'Yes?' He turned to face his niece, who had clearly been calling his name a few times.

'I need your help,' she demanded.

'Manners?' Harriette interjected.

'I need your help, *please*, Uncle Felix.' Chloe's instant amendment, not having a tantrum about being reminded to use her manners, showed him just how far the little girl had come in such a short time.

Felix stood and walked over to Chloe, giving her his attention. One of her toys wasn't able to sit up properly and kept falling into his imaginary food.

'I've already had to clean Captain Gumleaf twice and I'm getting tired of it,' the little girl told him and Felix couldn't help but smile.

'I think a cushion will do the trick.' And he took a cushion off the chair and placed it behind the toy, forcing the stuffed koala to sit up properly and behave himself. The toy had been a present from Eddie, an Australian koala to welcome Chloe to her new country. She loved the toy but clearly had expected better manners from him at her tea party.

Felix decided to stay with Chloe, sitting down on the carpet just behind her toys. It was far safer to be here than to go back to sitting at the table with Harriette. He hadn't responded to her declaration that she was going to force him to see his father. Deep down inside he knew she was right. He also knew if he told her to stop, that he was serious about not seeing his father, she would indeed stop. He didn't want to see his father. He didn't want to face his past, but if he didn't would he end up being as distant and as unfeeling with Chloe as his father had been with him?

Chloe. He sighed with resignation as he watched her. No matter what plans he might have had for his life, no matter what sort of father he would make, it didn't change the fact that this little girl was depending on him and he needed to do his best not to make a mess of things. And that included keeping his libido under control.

He glanced over at Harriette, who was now at the kitchen bench helping Eddie with the dinner preparations. The two of them were chatting softly and occasionally laughing. Felix closed his eyes, allowing the tinkling sound of her sweet laughter to wash over him. He wasn't used to connecting with women, not in such an emotional way as he seemed to be doing with Harriette. He was used to dating, to making sure the rules were clear—that his career came first.

That wasn't the case anymore. Chloe came first and that meant anything he felt for Harriette was irrelevant. If, for the sake of argument, the situation between himself and Harriette progressed, they started dating, started to become serious about their relationship, what would it mean for Chloe? He knew Chloe loved Harriette, even more than she might love him, but he was Chloe's guardian, not Harriette. Besides, he didn't even know if Harriette wanted to be in a relationship where a child was involved. Did she want to have more children or, now that Eddie was a grown man, was she done? There was still so much he didn't know about her, so much he wanted to ask but had no idea how to go about it, given he wasn't used to prying in other people's lives.

It wasn't as though they hadn't talked. They had, because with Eddie here for the past few days, once Chloe had been in bed, the three of them had sat up chatting.

Eddie told stories of his travels, of backpacking through Europe and how he was now learning German as well as French.

'Would you like to go to Germany to cook as well?' Felix had asked one evening.

Harriette's eyes had widened at this news of perhaps having her son live overseas for a while longer but Eddie didn't seem to notice and it was then Felix realised that while Harriette had lived the majority of the past twenty-two years for her son, she had also let Eddie go so he could find his own life. That took courage, especially as they were so close. He remembered her elation at seeing Eddie at the airstrip. How would she cope when Eddie left?

A few days later, when Eddie started to book his flights back to France, stopping in America for a few days in order to break the long journey, Felix noticed that Harriette started to withdraw slightly. She was her usual happy self but the laughter in her eyes dimmed faster. At the hospital, he'd watch as she just stared out into space for a minute or two, completely lost in thought until someone asked her a question. The hugs she gave Eddie seemed to be longer and more intense.

'He'll be fine,' Felix murmured as she stood bravely on the edge of the airstrip and watched as her son boarded the small plane that would take him to Brisbane. From Brisbane, he'd head overseas, every step of his journey taking him further and further away from his mother.

'I know. I raised him to be fine, to cope, to enjoy his experiences.' Harriette's voice hitched in her throat as she waved again and blew kisses. Eddie blew kisses back and then disappeared inside. The stairs were pulled up and locked in place. Harriette looked at the windows, laughing when she could see Eddie making funny faces. The laughter, however, didn't stop the tears from rolling down her cheeks and Felix found himself putting a soothing arm around her shoulders in an effort to support her.

He'd debated whether or not to bring Chloe with them but Harriette and Eddie had both said that if she saw Eddie get on the plane and leave, then she wouldn't be worried about where he'd gone. 'Especially with her parents just disappearing from her life, it's best if she can see that Eddie is OK and not...you know—'

'Dead?' he'd offered and she'd nodded.

'Then she can join in my online Internet chats with him so she can again see that he's all right.'

So he stood there now, his arm around Harriette's shoulders and his other hand holding onto Chloe's as she waved enthusiastically at Eddie and laughed along with Harriette at the funny faces Eddie was making.

That night, he watched as Harriette started to prepare dinner, noticing the slight slump of her shoulders. Felix knew he was supposed to be running Chloe's bath but the little girl was busy chatting away quietly to her toys, especially Captain Gumleaf.

'Can I help you with anything?' he asked Harriette, but she shook her head and sniffed before turning to look at him.

'I'm fine. Thanks.'

'Really?' Felix walked over and put a hand on her shoulder, wanting to comfort her but not entirely sure what was acceptable under the terms of their friendship. What he wanted was to turn her around and haul her into his arms, to wrap his own arms around her and let her wet the front of his cotton shirt with her tears. Even the thought of having a woman cry on him was so unlike him, so unlike the firm, staid and determined surgeon he'd been for so many years. Was it Chloe who had started to first break down those barriers or Harriette? Perhaps it was a combination of both.

'Harriette, he'll be fine.'

'I know. I know he will be, but until he calls me and tells me he's landed in Brisbane and then that he's in the States and then, in a few days' time, that he's back in Paris, then I have the right to worry.' She put down the knife she'd been using to chop the carrots.

'Of course you do.'

'This is what I wanted for him. I wanted him to have all the experiences I couldn't have because by the time I was twenty-two, I had a six-year-old son, was working twenty hours a week as an orderly at the hospital and studying medicine the rest of the time. And I know that was my choice but it was hard and exhausting and I was often so stressed that I would get sick but Eddie was there, helping me, carrying my books, making me a cup of tea, doing more than usual six-year-olds because he had to.' Tears of determination were running down her cheeks as she continued. 'I worked hard so that he could have every opportunity, that he could have money for his first overseas trip, that he could have an amazing set of chef knives, that he was eligible for the scholarship. I did everything I could and now he's living his dreams and I love him for it but, oh, Felix, my heart aches so badly when he's not with me.'

The way she looked at him, the way her heart seemed to really be breaking because she was without her son, tugged at his own heart and then, without even thinking further about it, he found himself reaching for her and enveloping her in his arms. She went willingly, burying her face in her hands as she leant against his chest.

'He's my boy. My little boy.' The words came out as sobs. 'I love seeing him, spending time with him, but I hate it when he has to go, but I know he has to, because he has his own life and I have mine and I worked hard to become a doctor so that when the time came for him to leave me, to walk his own path, I wasn't left alone with no purpose in life. He knows that. He understands and...' Her words trailed off and she allowed the sorrow of having said goodbye to her adult son to overwhelm her.

Felix found himself rubbing one hand slowly up and down her back, offering comfort. The fact that he was enjoying the opportunity to be there for her was something he was going to regard as a privilege. He'd breathed in her sweet, summery scent many times before and it had never failed to have a hypnotic effect on him.

Her body was warm against his, soft and cuddly, and he couldn't deny he liked the way she felt in his arms. It was the oddest thing, allowing himself to admit to such emotions where he usually kept his distance, kept everyone at arm's length, yet with Harriette Jones he was definitely enjoying every moment. He didn't enjoy her pain or the grief at having to say goodbye to her son, but he was pleased she was allowing him to help her.

'It doesn't make any difference how old they are,' she mumbled, shifting her hands slightly away from her face and resting them onto his chest, her face still buried so he found it difficult to properly understand her. 'Whether they're Chloe's age or Eddie's age. Not being with them is the thing that eats away at a parent's heart.'

'Harriette.' Her name escaped from his lips, barely a whisper, and he closed his eyes and rested his chin atop her head, shifting so she was settled more comfortably in his arms. Her tears had stopped and she was now sniffing and hiccupping a little but her breathing was starting to even out. 'You really wear your emotions on your sleeve, don't you, Dr Jones?' he murmured and immediately felt her tense up. She pushed against his arms but he wasn't quite ready to let her go. 'No. No, Harriette, you misunderstood me. That's a good thing. I'm saying that's a good thing because I find it so incredibly difficult to—'

He stopped talking then because she'd lifted her head and was looking up at him with the utmost confusion. Her eyes were puffy, her cheeks were blotchy, her nose was red and her lips…her perfect, ready-to-kiss lips, were plump and parted and definitely ready for him to kiss.

CHAPTER EIGHT

HARRIETTE WASN'T SURE what was happening. She seemed to be frozen in place, looking up into Felix's handsome face. She'd noticed, all too often lately, how he combed his fingers through his hair when he was confused. She'd noticed how he was smiling more and more and how that smile had the ability to make her heart skip a beat. Plus, she'd most definitely noticed the growing awareness between the two of them. Naturally, she'd done her best to ignore it, and while Eddie had been here the goal had been easier to achieve, but now that her son was gone, she couldn't help feeling vulnerable.

She knew Felix wasn't taking advantage of the situation because, even though she'd been upset, she'd been able to see the struggle within him, to comfort or not to comfort and that was all he was offering. Although there might be a physical attraction buzzing beneath the surface, she knew it could never go anywhere because his attention needed to be on Chloe. The attraction was only the result of spending too much time together because ever since he'd arrived in Meeraji Lake, they'd been hard pressed to avoid each other. He needed her help, he needed her to be a friend, to help guide him through the parenting forest, knowing when to chop down a few trees to make something new and when to plant some saplings so that something beautiful would grow in years to come.

She drew in a deep, shaky breath and instantly realised her error in doing so. Where the deep breath was supposed to relax her, help her to get under control, all it did was alert her heightened senses to Felix's earthy scent. It was as though it contained a hint of spice and all things nice and it would be far too easy for her to stay right where she was and absorb everything else about the man. Comfort was one thing, but she shouldn't take advantage of his good nature. He was being nice, he was being a friend, and here she was, momentarily forgetting about why she'd been upset in the first place, her thoughts and tingling senses far too focused on the way his closeness was affecting her.

As though she could no longer remain in his arms under false pretences, she tried to pull back a little more, to break the embrace of his arms holding her tight, but Felix didn't seem to want to let her go. She gazed more closely into his perfect eyes, surprised by what she saw. Repressed desire! Felix desired her? The realisation made her mouth go dry and her heart beat, which had just started to settle to a more normal rhythm, picked up the pace again, although this time it wasn't because she was missing her son. In fact, right now she was glad Eddie wasn't here because the tension that was winding itself around herself and Felix was one of mutual awareness and need. She couldn't even put a name to what she was feeling but, whatever it was, it was something she hadn't felt in an incredibly long time.

But she couldn't. He was her colleague…her colleague with a very firm chest. Her colleague with a delicious spicy scent. Her colleague who was looking at her as though she were the most beautiful woman in the world?

How could he possibly look at her in such a way? Stare at her mouth as though it were perfect? Gaze into her eyes as though he could drown in them? Send out those 'come closer' signals she was picking up on loud and clear?

He wanted to kiss her? Felix wanted to kiss her! The urge was clearly visible in his expressive eyes. The question remained: did she want to kiss him? Harriette had tried desperately not to move her hands, not to allow her itching fingers to spread out and touch his solid chest. She kept them as still as possible because even if she made the slightest movement, the shockwaves of delight at being able to touch him, to explore every contour of his perfectly formed body would—

'Harriette.' Had he spoken her name or had he thought it and she'd somehow tapped into his thoughts?

'Felix?' She tried to whisper his name, confusion evident in her tone, but she hiccupped a little as she spoke, her breath hitching a few times before she sighed and relaxed some more. It was far too easy to relax within his arms, those firm bands surrounding her as though he were never going to let her go. Part of her wished he wouldn't.

'Harriette,' he returned, his gaze flicking between her lips and her eyes. This time she knew he'd spoken her name because she hadn't been able to remove her gaze from his mouth, from watching it move, as though in slow motion, to speak her name. *Her* name. He was saying *her* name and causing her body to ignite with suppressed desire.

The hands at her back started to move in little circles, which only made pure fire spread throughout her entire body, bringing her dormant senses to life. He bent his elbows, then shifted his hands, bringing them up to cup her face. The instant his fingers touched her face, she sighed audibly at the delight he was invoking. Felix was as aware of her as she was of him and she couldn't help but lean a little into his right hand, wanting him to know that she felt whatever it was he was feeling, that it was reciprocated, that she wanted…she wanted…

'Harriette.' Again her name was soft and gentle on his lips, his parted lips, his parted lips that really weren't that far away from her own. They were so close that if she stood on tiptoe and leaned forward a little she… they… 'Why are you looking at me that way?'

She eased back, trying not to feel as though she'd been slapped in the face with his words. 'What way? I wasn't looking at you—' She stopped because she realised she was speaking quickly, too quickly, and that her voice was high pitched for some reason, as though she had something to hide. Had she read his expression incorrectly? Had she been on the verge of making a complete fool of herself? 'I'm not looking at you any particular way. Why would I do that? I wouldn't.' Her words were still too fast, filled with defensiveness. She shook her head a little, then closed her eyes in the hope that blocking him from her view might actually assist with calming her over-flustered senses into some state of normal. 'I was just… I was upset and you offered me—'

Harriette felt his finger land on her lips to stop her from babbling and she quickly opened her eyes and stared at him. There was the slight hint of mirth in his expression but also awareness. 'Let me rephrase that.' He slowly removed his finger from her lips, then rested his hand on her neck, the other one still cupping her face. 'What I meant to say was, why are you looking at me in such a way that makes me want to kiss you?'

'You want to—' She stopped, unable to finish her sentence as the embarrassment she'd felt only seconds ago was replaced by an overwhelming sense of wanting, of needing, of being desperate to feel as she hoped only Felix could make her feel. Her heart rate increased, every sense within her body seemed to tingle with utter delight and all because Felix wanted to...wanted to...

'Kiss you,' he finished for her. 'Yes.'

'Oh.' Clearly they were now openly acknowledging the attraction that had been building slowly between them. Harriette continued to stare at him, quite unsure what to do next. 'Uh...this may surprise you,' she eventually babbled, her words just as fast as before, 'but... um... I have no idea what to do next.'

Felix raised his eyebrows in surprise at her statement but then smiled. 'Do you mean kissing? Or just... in general?'

Harriette shifted a little, feeling highly self-conscious, but all her movements did was to highlight that her hands were still against Felix's chest, splayed out over his shirt, the cotton fibres doing little to disguise his excellent male physique beneath. At the contact, it was as though jolts of heat radiated up each finger and thumb before travelling up her arms and then bursting throughout her body in a frenzied rush of fireworks.

'Allow me to help you with that,' he murmured, and the next thing she realised was that his head was descending towards her own, their breath beginning to mingle, the faintest touch of their lips against each other. If she'd thought there had been fireworks bursting throughout her body before, it was nothing compared to now.

The kiss was soft, testing, tentative, as though neither of them were sure this was the right thing to do but simply couldn't resist any longer. Self-control, it seemed, had taken a momentary vacation but she wasn't complaining.

Felix was kissing her. He was holding her and he was kissing her. He wanted to kiss her. He was clearly enjoying it as the next touch against her lips was firmer than the one before. Nothing mattered at the moment. Not their patients, their living arrangements, their families. It was just the two of them, together…kissing.

He was awakening dormant emotions, making her feel things she hadn't felt in an incredibly long time and…and…her mind was starting to shut down all avenues of logical thought as her heart opened, as butterflies swirled in her mind, as emotions of delight and happiness and lightness and unexpected pleasure coursed through her.

Even when Felix pulled back, resting his forehead against her own, both of them basking in the soft and tantalising wake of having satisfied temptation, Harriette still found it difficult to believe she wasn't dreaming, that this was actually happening.

Felix was talking to her, speaking words of some kind, but her mind was busy wondering if he wanted to repeat the action, but this time to go a little further, to increase the intensity of the kiss rather than keeping it controlled and testing.

At that particular moment, it didn't matter she'd previously told herself she wasn't interested in any sort of relationship with any man because she had far too many other important things to be doing. When the reality of a warm-blooded male who found her attractive was actually staring her in the face, it caused the box in her mind that she'd labelled do not open to open wide and fill her with longing. A longing for companionship, a longing for intimacy but, most of all, a longing for acceptance.

'What do you think?' Felix asked her softly. 'It's the right thing to do. For all of us.'

'Wait.' She shifted back a touch, doing her level best to ignore his warmth, to ignore the sensual pheromones swirling around them, and looked at him. 'I'm sorry. Would you mind saying all that again, please?' She almost added, 'Because I have trouble concentrating when you're this close,' but, thankfully, she stopped herself in time. If Felix was saying what she thought he was saying, the more she guarded her own heart, the better. She'd been heartbroken before and she wasn't going to allow herself to be that vulnerable ever again.

'I said that while this is great, kissing you and wanting to kiss you some more...' He paused and cleared his throat. 'I'm not convinced this is the right time—for you, for me, for Chloe and—'

Harriette instantly dropped her hands back to her sides and stepped away from him, bumping into the bench and hurting her hip.

'Are you OK?' he asked, reaching out a caring hand. She held hers up in defence and sidestepped him, ignoring the pain coursing up and down her right leg.

'I'm fine. Fine. Absolutely fine and dandy.'

'Harriette,' he tried as she walked the long way around the kitchen table in order to get into the lounge room because from where she'd stood, he'd been blocking her exit.

'It's fine, Felix. You're absolutely correct. Even though we may feel an attraction, it's no doubt only because of our close living and working situation plus the fact that we're both helping Chloe, and that's good that your focus is on Chloe. It should be on Chloe and it is so how could I possibly argue with that? Even if I was going to argue, which I'm not because I agree with you. Good decision.' The entire time she'd been talking, she'd walked backwards into the lounge room where Chloe was starting to get bored playing with her toys. 'In fact, it looks as though she needs you now and I should head over to the clinic to finish off some paperwork and—' She stopped and, without bothering to finish her sentence, turned and headed to her bedroom, closing the door firmly behind her.

How could she have been so stupid? How could she have imagined that anything good could ever happen to her? That any man would love and desire her for who she was, no matter what was going on around them. Logically she knew he'd made the right call but, emotionally, the sensation of loneliness swept over her. She should never have allowed that box to open, the box that contained her most intimate wants and desires.

She dragged in a breath. She'd been caught up in the moment. That was all. The box could be shut again and shoved back on the shelf. She could ignore it, just as she had for the past few decades. Harriette knew Felix's first priority had to be Chloe. She, more than anyone, should realise that the child always came first when one was a single parent, and therefore she couldn't fault Felix's reasoning, nor could she hold anything against him. He'd been open and honest with her. How could she fault that? How?

Harriette could feel another bout of tears beginning to rise within her. Loneliness. It had already swamped her once today with Eddie's departure and now she also had to face the prospect that she would always be alone in this world. Yes, she had Eddie but his own life would begin to take up more of his time. He would eventually find a partner, have children of his own, keep pursuing his career, and her role in his life would become even more diminished than ever before and that was when she could give herself up to loneliness. She laughed without humour, remembering how, when Eddie had been little, all she'd wanted was a few hours of alone time, to be by herself, to watch a movie or read a book. It had been her saving grace, that alone time, and now, when she was looking towards her future, all she saw was alone time.

She'd told herself that she didn't want to go down the family road again. She wasn't interested in having more children, and when she'd dated in the past it had been with professional colleagues who were focused on their careers, but even then she'd found them two-dimensional given they didn't have strong family connections to balance them out. That was probably how Felix would have been if Chloe hadn't been thrust upon him. He would have been two-dimensional and even if she had been attracted to him, which, given the way he looked, would have been a definite, she still would have found him two-dimensional. Now, though, seeing him interact with Chloe, making the effort to get to know his niece, to become a permanent fixture in her life, she found him far more attractive. He was changing, learning, accepting and offering love to a child who needed it. What woman wouldn't be attracted to him?

Even though she'd told herself no more children, no more distractions, tonight, for one split second, she'd allowed herself to dream, to see a future with a tall handsome man and his little girl. The images had flashed through her mind like a series of instant photographs and, for one split second, hope had flared strong and firm within her heart, before it was quashed once more.

She closed her eyes and listened, hearing his deep tones mixing with Chloe's higher-pitched ones, both of them laughing. Oh, how it warmed her heart to hear him having a good time with his niece, especially when Chloe still didn't seem too sure of him at times. At least the child was starting to view Uncle Felix in a different light and lo and behold the gift of a tea set had been the avenue to allow that to happen.

She opened her eyes and walked to the mirror on her dresser, looking at her reflection. Good heavens, she really did look a mess. Her hair was more of a bird's nest than normal, her eyes were puffy and her nose was red. And Felix had seen her looking like this? No wonder he'd decided to focus on Chloe rather than pursuing an attraction with a woman who looked as if she'd just been put through the wringer.

Quietly, Harriette opened her bedroom door and headed to the bathroom where she splashed water on her face and added a bit of make-up. She fixed her hair, wrapping it into a loose bun on her head, several tendrils still escaping the bonds because they were too short to stay secured without clips.

'At least it's a bit of an improvement,' she told her reflection and, after taking a few deep breaths, she walked quickly though the house, trying to ignore the sight of Felix lounging on the floor with Chloe near him, the two of them looking at pictures from one of her books. 'Off to clinic,' she murmured, heading straight for the door.

Pasting on a bright smile, she headed into the clinic, greeting her waiting patients with her usual optimism and joviality. She listened to them, prescribed treatments for them and wrote up her clinic notes. Once she was done, she headed to the hospital to touch base with her patients on the ward and to check with Tori that the ED was running smoothly.

'No emergencies,' the nurse reported. 'I've just finished restocking all the rooms and writing out an order form for next month.'

'Sound like fun times.' Harriette sat down in the seat next to her friend and sighed.

'How are you coping?'

'What?' Could Tori read her expression that well? Could she see the feelings for Felix? How could the nurse possibly know what had transpired between the two doctors?

'It can't be easy saying goodbye to him.'

'Eddie!' Harriette breathed a sigh of relief. 'No, it's not easy but I raised a good boy and he knows to contact his neurotic mother the instant he lands.'

Tori looked at her quizzically for a moment. 'What did you think I meant?'

'Nothing. My mind was on the patients I've just seen at clinic.' She waggled a finger near her head. 'How are the wedding preparations going?' She needed to change the subject and fast and what bride-to-be could resist talking about her up-and-coming wedding?

As Tori talked about her latest wedding drama Harriette silently chided herself for having misinterpreted the question. She needed to stop fixating on what had almost happened between herself and Felix.

'Are you and Felix still planning to stop in at Darwin after the house calls?' Tori's question caught Harriette a little off guard and she knocked over a container full of pens at the mention of Felix.

'What?'

'The house calls? You told me you wanted to go to Darwin once you've done the house clinics. It does seem quite logical. You're already going to be working your way up further into the Northern Territory so why not go a little further and show Felix and Chloe a bit of the closest capital city? I'm presuming Felix hasn't been to Darwin before?'

'Not that I know of.' She shook her head, forgetting the planning she'd already made for their trip. 'We leave the day after tomorrow.' Harriette couldn't keep the doom and gloom from her tone. She'd organised it while Eddie had been here and she'd been looking forward to helping Felix mend the fences with his father. Now…now she didn't want to be cooped up in a car with Felix for an extended period of time. And after they'd finished in Darwin, they would be spending three days driving back to Meeraji Lake, stopping and doing district clinics on the way. If she'd thought they were living and working in close quarters now, then it would be nothing compared to the way they'd be forced together during the next week.

Tori chuckled. 'Cheer up. It's not as though it's any great hardship being in such close quarters with Felix. He is one good-looking man…but nowhere near as good-looking as my fantastic fiancé, who is presently walking in the front doors.' The nurse waved to Scotty and went to embrace him.

After offering a brief g'day to Scotty, Harriette headed to the wards to check on her patients, but even as she paid them the attention they deserved thoughts of Felix remained in the back of her mind. She decided to try and do some paperwork as that usually required her full concentration, but it didn't work.

If only they hadn't kissed! What had they been thinking? Well, that was the problem—they hadn't been. They'd given in to temptation and now she had to pay the price, the price of being uncomfortable in his company. Harriette sat alone in her small office and buried her head in her hands as misery, discomfort and loneliness swamped her. 'What am I supposed to do?' she mumbled into the silent room.

She stopped her thoughts and shook her head. A week with Felix, in a car, driving from homestead to homestead and then ending up in Darwin for one night before starting the drive back to Meeraji Lake. It would be so confining, so uncomfortable and yet incredibly intimate. Thank goodness Chloe was going with them. At least the almost-four-year-old would break the tension…or so Harriette hoped. Getting through the next week was going to require her utmost concentration and professionalism because there was no way she was going to let Felix McLaren lure her into such a confused situation again.

Harriette straightened her shoulders, determination coursing through her. She could do this. She'd managed to navigate her way through situations far more difficult than this one. Then again, she hadn't been faced with a man who made her heart race, her knees go weak and her body fill with desire just by smiling at her.

Her shoulders sagged. It was hopeless.

CHAPTER NINE

'ARE WE THERE YET?'

Chloe's voice from the back seat of the four-door utility truck made Harriette smile. She concentrated on driving while Felix turned and addressed the little girl. The rear of the vehicle was packed with everything they would need to hold travelling clinics for the next few days, along with clothes for the three of them and an entire bag of 'stuff' for Chloe, which she'd insisted upon bringing with her. Captain Gumleaf, of course, was sitting in the back with her, strapped into his own seatbelt to make sure he was safe.

'It's only ten minutes since you last asked.' He grinned at her. 'Would you like a drink?'

Chloe screwed up her nose. 'Will I have to go to the toilet in the bush again?'

Harriette chuckled and looked in her rear-vision mirror, reflecting on the look of horror on Chloe's face when they'd had to stop a few hours ago so the child could relieve herself behind one of the native shrubs that was scattered here and there along the way. To say Chloe hadn't been impressed was an understatement. 'There is a good chance that may happen, Chloe, depending on how much you drink.'

'I don't like doing that,' Chloe stated and shook her head as Felix held out her drink bottle.

'You've got to drink, Chloe.' His tone was caring but insistent.

'I don't want to!' She sat in her car seat and crossed her arms with determination, a frown on her face, her little lips puckered in defiance.

Harriette laughed again and Felix turned on her. 'What's so funny? She's got to drink. Out here in the Australian outback, it's imperative to remain hydrated, especially when in a car. The heat outside is—'

'The car is air-conditioned, so we're hardly at risk of overheating, and she's already drunk quite a bit today. I don't blame her about not wanting to urinate in the bushes. It's far easier for you males than us females and, to make my final point, we're only about forty-five minutes away from arriving at the first homestead. Once we're there, she'll eat and drink and urinate in a proper toilet.' She looked over her shoulder and winked at Chloe. 'Isn't that right, princess?' she stated rhetorically.

'Proper loo,' Chloe repeated, naturally translating the word into her English counterpart. She uncrossed her arms and clapped her hands. 'Proper loo.'

'At least she's smiling, now,' Harriette remarked as Felix scowled at her. 'You look just like Chloe,' she said, teasing him slightly. 'All frowny and grumpy.'

'I'm not grumpy,' he stated. 'I'm annoyed. There's a difference.' Without another word, he pressed the button for the CD to start playing, pleased that Erica had given them quite a few different children's CDs for Chloe to listen to on the long drives.

'I've already heard this one,' she stated from the back.

'And now you can hear it again,' he retorted, seemingly annoyed with both the females. He waited a few minutes, until he could hear Chloe singing along with the song, then shifted in his seat so he was facing Harriette. 'I don't appreciate the way you're constantly undermining my authority with Chloe,' he remarked, doing his best to keep his tone level so Chloe couldn't hear him. He'd noticed that the little girl often picked up on undercurrents between Harriette and himself and ended up having tantrums over it, as though thinking that if the two main adults in her life were misbehaving, it was perfectly all right for her to do so as well.

That was the way it had been in the house until they'd left for this trip. He wouldn't say that he and Harriette had had tantrums, per se, but the atmosphere certainly hadn't been one of relaxed joviality as it had been before they'd kissed. Harriette's attitude had been one of polite indifference. She'd arranged to eat out at different friends' houses, saying that she'd neglected her friends while Eddie had been here. That had meant cheese sandwiches for Chloe and a tin of soup for him as he hadn't felt much like cooking. After Eddie's gourmet cooking, his soup had tasted bland and unappetising and he'd kept glancing at the door every time he'd heard a sound, hoping it was Harriette coming home to spend some time with them.

She hadn't. Not at least until rather late into the evening when he'd bathed Chloe and wrangled her to sleep. And when she had come in, she'd walked straight past him, murmured a polite goodnight and headed to her part of the house.

Felix knew Harriette had every right to go and see her friends—after all, the two of them were just colleagues, or at least that was the way she was making him feel. He'd thought they'd progressed past that, that they'd become friends as well. They had, he realised, until they'd kissed and everything had changed.

'I'm sorry,' she replied, bringing his thoughts back to the present. 'I guess it's the mother in me that takes over.'

'I know you know more than I do, but how am I supposed to learn if you keep jumping in and contradicting what I say?'

'I wasn't contradicting—not really. I was…justifying and explaining to her. She has every right to say she doesn't want to go to the toilet in the bushes, even though out here it's almost considered a rite of passage.' Harriette grinned, the ute still speeding along on the endlessly straight road with not a house in sight. 'Still, I will do my best to refrain from appearing to undermine your authority because it *is* important for you to exert it.'

'And you'll try to back off? To let me at least attempt to deal with Chloe on my own?'

'I'll most certainly try and bite my tongue, but only on the condition that if you need help with Chloe, if you feel out of your depth, you'll ask me for help or advice. I can't promise I'll always know what to do but we can work it out together.'

'Can we?' The two words were softer than the others and the tone in them had definitely changed. A prickle of apprehension washed over Harriette, and when she risked a glance at him again it was to find him watching her more intently than before. Clearly they weren't talking about Chloe any more.

'Of course we can,' she remarked, keeping her tone as jovial as possible.

'You like children, don't you?'

For a second, she thought she'd misinterpreted what he was saying. Was this going to become a habit? Was she ever going to be able to figure him out, figure out his moods, or was she always going to be grabbing the wrong end of the stick? 'Uh…of course I do.'

'Would you like to have more?'

This time she turned her head and stared at him for a long moment. 'Me? More children!' He nodded. 'No. No. No.' She shook her head and returned her attention to the boring, very straight road. 'I mean, could you imagine it? Having my kids over two decades apart? That's a bit…strange.' She laughed, then shook her head again. 'It would be funny to see Eddie's face when I told him I was having another child but—no. I've worked too hard for too long to finish my surgical training and I'm so close to being finished.'

'You can have career and family, you know.'

'Like you? How's your career going since Chloe entered your life?'

Felix thought for a moment before agreeing. 'Point taken.' He eased back into the chair as they drove along and Harriette refocused her attention on the road. 'What about men?'

'Pardon?' She stared at him again, wondering if she'd heard him correctly.

'Have you ever had a serious relationship? I mean, apart from Eddie's father.'

'Uh…sort of. I've dated colleagues in the past and not really seriously until Eddie was in his teens.'

'Fair enough, but none made you want to take a trip down the aisle? Have more kids?'

Harriette frowned as she drove along, pleased she had the protection of her sunglasses as she answered his questions. 'I was serious about one guy. Eddie was seventeen, hanging out with his mates and being hormonally obnoxious.'

'Eddie? Hormonally obnoxious?' He chuckled.

'Happens to all of us,' she added, smiling at him.

'So...the guy?' Felix prompted when she remained silent for a moment.

'Right. The guy. His name was Mark and he had moved to the country to work in the hospital for a few years. I was deciding whether or not to specialise in surgery and he just seemed to make my life so much richer. He supported me in my career, he was great with Eddie and everything seemed perfect.'

'And then?'

'And then he had articles published in a reputed journal and was offered a fellowship.'

'Wait. Not Mark Masters?'

Harriette snorted with derision. 'One and the same. Clearly you know him.'

'I took over the fellowship from him.'

'Of course you did.' And there it was in a nutshell. Felix might be putting Chloe first, but his career still came second, which meant there really wasn't any room in his life for Harriette. 'All you career-climbing surgeons know each other.'

'So I take it he left the country hospital for the high life?'

'In the middle of his contract, leaving me short-staffed and overworked. Eddie was devastated.'

'As were you, I'm sure.'

Harriette could only shrug, and before he could ask her any more personal questions she turned up the music a little and began singing along with Chloe.

'Let me know if you're becoming fatigued and I'll take over,' he offered ten minutes later.

'It's not long now and, besides, I'm used to driving long distances.'

'How often are these clinics?'

Although they'd already been over this once, it was clear Felix needed to get a full grasp on the strange situation of taking the doctor to the patients rather than the other way around. 'Once a month. Depending on how many clinics are being held, usually one of us goes out and the other stays in Meeraji Lake.'

'But now that we're both going, Tori and the rest of the staff are holding down the fort? What if an emergency comes in?'

'Generally, because people know we're holding district clinics, they'll travel to the homestead where the clinic is being held. Usually it's closer for them than coming into town.'

'And these clinics are held because a lot of outback people can't, or won't, take time off to visit the doctor even when they're sick?'

'Yes. Outback Australians are made of sturdy stuff and sometimes they think they're immortal. These clinics mean more people can be immunised, especially for things like tetanus, and have their concerns addressed without needing to take a day or two off work in order to drive to Meeraji Lake.' She was starting to slow the vehicle down. He still couldn't see anything around them apart from the odd tree and shrub and a lot of reddish-brown dirt so he wasn't sure why she was slowing down.

'Where are we going?' he asked as she turned the vehicle onto what could only be described as a dirt track.

'To the homestead. This is a shortcut.'

'Shortcut? Are you sure that's wise?'

Harriette laughed at him. 'We can go the long way around and add another hour to our journey?'

'No. No. This way is good.' Felix held onto the hand

grip above the passenger door as the utility truck made its way over ground that appeared to be flat but was in fact rather undulating. He checked Chloe in the back but she seemed perfectly fine with the new terrain. In fact, she was clapping her hands with joy at the bumps and giggling. 'Great. She's a daredevil, just like David.'

Harriette laughed again and continued navigating their way across country. Twenty minutes later, she turned onto a graded gravel road and soon after that she turned into what could only be described as a long dirt driveway, the sign at the turn-off to the homestead the only indication that this was the correct way.

'You'll have to jump out and open and close the gates for me,' she told him, and as he did as she asked Harriette had to admit that the day's driving adventures hadn't been as bad as she'd initially thought. She'd anticipated that it would have been confining in the small cabin of the truck, that Felix's scent would drive her crazy and that the close proximity would be distracting but, in actual fact, she'd enjoyed it. Her embarrassment at having been a fool in his arms a few days ago had decreased and she'd managed to return her spirits to her usual jovial self.

Harriette brought the vehicle to a stop outside the front of the homestead, a lot of cars already parked, people milling around ready and waiting for the afternoon clinic to begin.

'What's all this?' Felix looked out of the window at the plethora of people.

'Patients.'

'I hadn't expected this many. It's like a week's worth of clinic hours all in one hit.'

She grinned. 'Busier than a major hospital, mate.' She switched off the engine and removed the key from the ignition before jumping out of the car and waving to the owner of the homestead. Remembering their earlier conversation about how Felix needed to be the parent with Chloe, she left it up to him to get the child from the car and, instead, Harriette went to say hello to some of the locals she hadn't yet met.

Surrounded by people, they unpacked their belongings from the ute and headed inside where their hosts had set up rooms for a makeshift clinic.

'What do I do with Chloe?' Felix asked as Harriette handed him a note pad and pen so he could write down notes on each patient. She was opening the medical kits and other equipment they'd brought with them, such as tongue depressors, gloves and an array of bandages.

'I think she's already playing with the other children out the back in the sandpit.' Harriette finished setting things up for him before heading next door into her own consulting room to do the same.

'But how do I know she's going to be supervised properly? What if she decides to run away out here?' Felix had followed her, clearly anxious.

'Then you'd best go talk to her, set down some guidelines and find out who's in charge of looking after the children and let Chloe know.' Harriette could quite easily have taken over but that wasn't the way for Felix to learn. 'Communication, in any relationship, is paramount.'

'Right. Right. Good. Talk to Chloe. I can do that. Thanks,' he returned, and as he disappeared from her view she couldn't help but smile at the progress he'd made in such a short time. At least now he was more than willing to talk to Chloe, to interact with the little girl and to ensure that her safety came first.

'Doc?' There was a knock at her open door and when

she looked up it was to find a man in his late thirties standing there with an old towel wrapped around his hand. 'I've just arrived and the blokes outside said I could jump the queue.'

Harriette nodded and ushered him in, closing the door. Clinic time had clearly begun whether she liked it or not, and as she unwrapped the towel she discovered a fencing nail going into the man's hand.

'Here we go,' she whispered beneath her breath as she gathered together the supplies she would need. She treated her patient, giving him a local anaesthetic before removing the nail. She debrided the wound and then packed and dressed it.

'You'll need to have the dressing changed regularly for the next three weeks. I'll put you on the district nurses' roster but when they can't make it to you, you'll either need to get to Meeraji Lake or to Darwin.' Harriette tried to smother a yawn as she spoke.

'You all right, Doc?'

'Just a bit tired from driving this morning. It'll settle down.' She started to write up the case notes for her patient, then asked him to send in the next person.

'How are you going?' Harriette asked Felix a few hours later as they stopped for a drink of cool iced tea.

'Getting through them. There's such a variety of problems. I hadn't expected that.'

She clinked her glass with his and grinned. 'Far more exciting than your average hospital clinic, right?'

Felix pondered her words for a moment, which only made her smile increase. 'What are you smiling at?' he asked, giving her that cute little quizzical smile.

'You.'

'What about me?'

'You like to really ponder things before you speak
or make a decision and that's great.'

He nodded and leaned on the kitchen bench as a few
of the older kids who were around the place came hurtling through. Harriette stepped forward in order to get
out of the way and when she next looked at Felix, she
realised just how close they were. 'And you, Harriette,
like to say whatever it is that comes into your mind.'

'Hey. I do think things through. Perhaps I just think
faster than you.'

He angled his head to the side and regarded her for
a moment; she wished he hadn't, especially as his gaze
dipped to take in the shape of her mouth, lingering there
a second too long before returning to look into her eyes.
Didn't he realise how he was affecting her? How that
long look had brought a mass of tingles to flood through
her body, had caused a wanting heat to wash over her?

She tried to return her thoughts to an even keel, to
ignore the way he was making her feel. Theirs was a relationship that would remain professional and platonic,
with her helping him to learn how to parent Chloe. She
could accept that, but if she was to get through the rest
of this year, working alongside Felix, living in the same
house as him, seeing him become a wonderful father—
as she'd already glimpsed—then she needed to find a
way to keep her emotion under control. There would
be countless more times when they would need to be
this close, where the heat from their bodies would be
combining together, where their scents would blend to
become one heady concoction of desire.

She breathed out, trying not to look at his mouth
but failing miserably, and what she saw there were his
lips curved into a small smile. She looked at his eyes

and saw one eyebrow raised in a teasing but very interested manner.

'You were saying?'

'Uh...' Harriette tried desperately to think of what she'd been saying, of what her last thought was, but all she could remember was how much she wanted him to kiss her again.

'You think faster than I do?' he continued to tease and she realised he knew full well that their present closeness was having a devastating effect on her equilibrium.

'Stop teasing me, Felix.' Her words were soft, intimate and meant only for him.

'Or what?' he challenged.

'Or I may shut you up by kissing you.'

His smile increased, which only disarmed her more. She'd half expected him to take a step back at her words, to put some distance between them, to become uncomfortable at her straightforward speaking. 'I can think of worse punishments,' he countered, his gaze once more dipping to take in her mouth.

Harriette sighed with repressed desire and clenched her jaw to stop herself from leaning forward and following through on her threat. 'Why are you doing this to me? You were the one who said we shouldn't get involved, that we needed to think of Chloe, that you didn't want me undermining—'

Felix placed a finger over her lips to stop her from talking, the touch causing her to gasp, the desire buzzing through her magnifying. 'Perhaps I was...a bit hasty. Perhaps we should—'

He broke off as the owner of the homestead came into the kitchen and he immediately dropped his hand but didn't ease back, still leaning casually on the bench.

Harriette was the one to straighten, to take a step back, to try not looking guilty at being caught in an intimate tête-à-tête.

'Find everything you need?' Paulette asked them.

'Yes, thank you,' Felix answered as he took another sip of his long, cool drink. 'Harriette and I were just discussing a few of the patients,' he offered, as though explaining why they'd been standing so close. 'As this is my first outback homestead clinic, I needed to clarify a few things.'

'Fair enough,' Paulette responded. 'Now, I've had a few problems with people needing to stay the night and the fact is that I've run out of beds. Harriette, I had you and Chloe in the last room at the end of the corridor. There's a double bed in there but, Felix, I don't have anywhere for you to sleep. A lot of the men are dossing down in the lounge room but they've all got sleeping bags with them. Some are sleeping outside in their swags but at the moment the only real bed I have left is the one Harriette and Chloe will be sharing.'

'What?' It was Harriette who reacted. 'None of the couches are free?'

Paulette shook her head. 'I didn't think it right to assign poor Felix to a space on the floor or to a couch, given you've both got to do a clinic first thing in the morning, plus you've been driving. You're both going to be exhausted and—'

'It's no problem,' Felix stated, finishing his drink and taking the glass to stack in the dishwasher. 'Harriette and I can share with Chloe in the middle of us. She'll love that.' He smiled at Paulette. 'You're doing a great job dealing with the gaggle of people here.'

Paulette seemed taken aback at his praise and smiled warmly at him. 'Oh. Well, thank you.' She actually fanned her face. 'How lovely of you to say so.' She glanced at Harriette. 'I can see why he's considered the new catch of the county. Luckily I'm a happily married woman.'

Harriette drained her glass of its contents and went to put it into the dishwasher but Felix took it from her and performed the task. The last thing she wanted was to be discussing how Felix was bachelor of the year; to listen to the gossip that was no doubt already spread right around the district, especially when she'd been contemplating kissing him again.

'Right. Back to work.' With that, she left Felix and Paulette in the kitchen and called her next patient through into her makeshift consulting room. How she managed to get through the rest of the patients scheduled for that evening, she had no clue. With the way he'd looked at her in the kitchen, with the way he'd placed his finger over her lips, causing her breathing to increase and her senses to become even more heightened, it was enough to make her hyperventilate by just thinking about it.

How on earth was she supposed to sleep the entire night in the same bed as him? Of course, from a practical point of view, it was the best solution. They would both get to sleep on a comfortable mattress and awake refreshed in the morning, ready for the next clinic, but, to own the truth, being that close to Felix—all night long—especially with the way he was making her feel, meant she doubted she'd get any sleep whatsoever.

She could always go and sleep in the ute. It would be uncomfortable but she was sure she would actually get more shut-eye than she would being so close and yet so far from Felix. How was it that this man had somehow commandeered every aspect of her thoughts—ex-

cept for the medical professional part? She'd managed
to get her thoughts in order, to simply be colleagues
with Felix, to be friendly but to keep her distance, to
help him with Chloe. That was all she'd been planning
to do for the next year and, hopefully, somewhere in
the process of denying herself, she would find a level
of compatibility with Felix where they could lose the
awkward awareness of each other and achieve a com-
panionable existence.

Not any more!

CHAPTER TEN

BY THE TIME the patients had all been seen and Paulette's husband had barbecued an enormous amount of food to feed those who had come for the clinic or were staying the night, Harriette had to admit she was exhausted.

People were still chatting and eating and drinking, some were leaving to head back to their homes, others were already asleep on the floor in their sleeping bags. With Chloe starting to look as though she would fall asleep at any given moment, Harriette picked the little girl up from where she'd been playing with one of her new friends, and carried her towards where Felix was chatting with a few of the patients he'd treated that day.

It was good to see him mixing with the locals where she'd half expected him to keep himself aloof, separate, superior. He watched her walk towards him, Chloe's head resting on her shoulder.

'Do you want me to take her?' he asked, putting his glass of iced tea down on a nearby table.

'It's fine. I'm happy to put her to bed tonight, if that's OK with you.'

A mild look of relief crossed his face and she realised that he hadn't wanted Chloe to have one of her tantrums when she was eventually put to bed. 'Thanks.'

That was all she needed, his permission—because

there was no way she wanted to be accused of overstepping the mark once again. With a smile and a brief nod in his direction, Harriette headed back to the homestead, where she quickly brushed Chloe's teeth and then got her ready for bed, glad their bags had been put into the room. Once Chloe was settled, Harriette found herself yawning profusely and decided she would follow suit. She doubted anyone would miss her if she went to bed now. Besides, if she could fall asleep with Chloe before Felix came to bed, then she wouldn't have to think about him lying next to her.

After doing her teeth, changing into her pyjamas and plaiting her hair so it didn't get in the way, Harriette climbed between the cool sheets, the little girl instantly snuggling in and wrapping her arms around Harriette's neck. The action helped Harriette to relax, loving the sensation of having a child sleeping next to her. It reminded her of those times when Eddie had had bad dreams, or had just wanted to have a 'sleepover' in mummy's bed. Her little boy. Her precious little boy who was now such an incredible young man, but in her eyes he would be *her* little boy for ever.

Which was why she was astonished by the sensation of feeling as though Chloe were *her* little girl. Since they'd met, she'd been amazed with the way the child made her feel, heightening her dormant maternal instincts. She loved playing with the toys, reading the stories, engaging the imagination, especially during their tea parties. Even though Harriette had been focusing on her career, she'd been desperate to do that because she'd needed to ensure she had a life once Eddie had left her. Now that he was actually living on the other side of the world, she'd needed to surround herself with people, to become a part of a new community, but what she hadn't counted on was Felix.

Felix had changed everything. Not only had he brought Chloe into her life, but he'd raised dormant feelings, ones she hadn't expected to cope with. Before, when he'd been flirting with her in the kitchen, every sense in her body had been heightened and on red alert...alert in case he actually followed through on the desire she'd clearly seen in his eyes.

He was confusing her. He'd told her he didn't want to start a relationship with her and she'd respected his wishes, sorted her head out and decided to make this trip one of friendship and fun. Now, he was saying he'd made a mistake, that he *wanted* to see where things might lead...or was he? She had no idea because tomorrow he could change his mind again, if he so chose, and then where would she be?

'It's too confusing, Chloe,' she whispered to the sleeping child. 'I like him. I really do. I like him a lot. He makes me think, he makes me feel and he makes me want more for the life that I've tried to plan for myself.' Surprisingly, as she whispered the words into the dark quiet room, Harriette found her eyes starting to fill with tears.

'I wanted the "happily ever after" ending all those years ago and I didn't get it, so I never let myself think about it again. I had Eddie and that was enough but now he's gone...he's gone, Chloe, he's left me, and...and...' She stopped, knowing there was no point in upsetting herself. If she allowed her thoughts to continue down this path, she would end up crying herself to sleep and no doubt wetting poor Chloe in the process. Deep down inside, Harriette had always wanted the normalcy of

what society at large called 'a family'. Two parents raising children together.

'Little girl,' she continued to whisper after a moment, her words less broken than before. 'You have
brought laughter and sunshine into my life.' And so has
your uncle, she added silently, and as she listened to the
child's even breathing Harriette found herself drifting
off to sleep, thoughts of Felix mixing with her dreams,
dreams of the two of them walking along hand in hand,
teasing each other, working alongside each other at the
hospital. She pictured not only herself and Felix, together, as a couple, but also with Chloe and Eddie, the
four of them making up a mix-and-match of a family
but a family nevertheless.

Felix had been well aware that when Harriette had gone
to put Chloe to bed, she hadn't returned. He knew because he'd been looking for her, scanning the gathered
group of people for a glimpse of her beautiful face. As
he finally said his goodnights and went to the room as-
signed to them, he found exactly where Harriette had
disappeared to.

How long he stood there by the bed, watching the
two sleeping females who had become so important
to him in such a short time, he had no idea. Chloe was
lying on her back, one arm up above her head, the other
almost across Harriette's face. Harriette lay on her side,
one protective arm curled around the little girl, both of
them breathing deeply. He wasn't at all surprised Harriette had been so exhausted, given that she'd driven
the entire way to the homestead and then done a clinic
on top of that.

She made a little noise, a little sighing sound and a
small smile tugged at her lips. A buzz of protective de-

sire flooded through him and he couldn't help recall the moment they'd shared in the kitchen earlier in the day. He'd wanted to kiss her again, wanted to see whether the chemistry from the first time had been a fluke or whether it was real. If it *was* the real deal, if his growing feelings towards Harriette continued to soar, what would happen then? His life had already been derailed once. Would it matter if it was derailed a second time?

The possibility of a different future, one he'd never considered before—a future of him, Chloe and Harriette, along with Eddie…together as a family—made him tremble with longing. He quickly turned away from the vision of loveliness in the bed and went to brush his teeth. When he returned and contemplated getting into the bed with Harriette so near and yet so far, he felt it better to sleep fully clothed. It was a warm night and he didn't really need covers so, instead, he lay down on top of the bed and tried to relax. He listened to Harriette's and Chloe's even breathing and slowly…very slowly, he drifted off to sleep as exhaustion caught up with him.

A loud scream of delight pierced Harriette's dream world and she woke with a start. 'Chloe!' Her eyes were wide open and every muscle in her body was tense. Chloe wasn't in the bed at all. In fact, no one was in the bed with her. She was all alone but she could see the dint Felix's head had made on the pillow, which indicated he had actually come in and slept. She didn't remember at all.

Harriette stared at the pillow for a second before picking it up and smelling it. Yes. It smelt like him, that spicy hypnotic scent that had often excited her senses. Realising she was being foolish, she returned the pillow and searched around for her cellphone in order to check the time.

She was still looking for her phone when the door to the room opened and Chloe came running in, clambering onto the bed and bouncing on her knees. 'Wake up. Wake up.'

'I'm awake,' Harriette told her, slipping one hand around the little girl and relaxing at seeing she was all right.

'Uncle Felix! She's awake!'

'Excellent,' he remarked as he came in behind Chloe carrying a tray of food. 'Sit up, Dr Jones, as breakfast is served.'

'We made breakfast for you.' Chloe was still bouncing on the bed, clearly bursting with excitement.

'Well, Paulette and her husband did the cooking,' Felix clarified. 'But I put some food on a plate for you and made you a cup of tea.'

'I helped pour the juice,' Chloe stated as Felix lowered the tray onto Harriette's lap, telling Chloe gently to stop bouncing on the bed or the juice might spill. The child did as he asked. 'And I picked the flowers for you from the garden,' the little girl added, and Harriette smiled brightly at the thin-stemmed flowers that were really weeds but looked absolutely delightful in a small glass of water in the corner of her breakfast tray.

'I'm...I'm overwhelmed.' Harriette gazed up at Felix, who was standing beside her, grinning as excitedly as Chloe. The thought was incredibly touching and she could see it was heartfelt, which made it all the more special.

'What's that mean?' Chloe started to bounce again, but when she saw Harriette's juice start to wobble she instantly stopped. 'Oh, sorry.'

'It means that I'm happy,' Harriette clarified.

'Chloe, why don't you put on your purple shoes and go and play with some of the other children?'

'Really? I can go outside?'

'Remember your hat,' Harriette added and held the tray as Chloe scrambled off the bed and located her shoes. She quickly slipped them on and then accepted the hat Felix was holding out to her. 'Bye.' And she was out of the door.

'Oh, to have the energy of a child,' Felix stated as he came around the other side of the bed and sat down next to Harriette. When he didn't make any more effort to move, she turned her head and looked at him.

'Are you just going to sit there and watch me eat?'

'Yep.'

'Have you eaten?'

'Yep. Come on,' he urged. 'It's getting cold. Don't want Paulette's hard work cooking the bacon, eggs and toast to be in vain, do you?'

'No, sir. I do not.'

'I'll keep you company.'

'Gee, thanks.'

He laughed at her words and she delighted at the sound. 'You're certainly happy this morning,' she stated before taking a sip of her tea. 'Mmm. Perfect.'

'You can have coffee before clinic starts but I thought tea might be a nicer, more relaxing way to help you wake up.'

'Thank you.' She gestured to the tray. 'This is very thoughtful.' And it was. Even though she'd spent a lot of time with Felix since they'd met, there were only a few occasions where she'd witnessed the 'real' him, as though he felt the need to keep his inner being hidden from the world. Yet this morning it seemed he was happy to fling open the doors to his inner soul and let the sun shine.

She picked up the knife and fork and began eating the food before it cooled too much. No sooner had she eaten the first mouthful than Felix reached over and snagged a piece of toast from her plate. 'Hey! I thought you'd already eaten.'

'Still a bit hungry,' he mentioned before munching away. And there they sat, Harriette beneath the covers, Felix on top of the covers, eating breakfast together much in the same way they had many times before but never in a bed they'd shared. The intimate setting and the absence of Chloe made Harriette feel highly self-conscious, aware of every movement he made. Some of the dreams she'd had last night started to flood back and, as Felix had featured in them in an even more intimate way than they were presently experiencing, she felt colour suffuse her cheeks.

She quickly finished off her food, then took a large drink of her tea, wanting to be done with breakfast as quickly as possible so that Felix would leave. 'All done,' she remarked.

'You haven't had your juice yet. Chloe will be most upset if you don't drink it all, especially as she slopped quite a bit all over the bench when she was trying to pour it.'

'Oh, the darling,' Harriette murmured as she started unplaiting her hair. 'It was a good idea to include her and let her help, even if she did make a mess.'

'What's that old saying? More of a hindrance than a help?'

'Exactly.' Harriette grinned as she ran her hands through her hair, loosening it up, knowing the plait would have made the tendrils wavy during the night.

'But she enjoyed being included and that's the biggest thing at the moment.' When Felix didn't make any further comment, she glanced over at him to find him staring at her, his mouth open slightly. 'What?'

He managed to close his mouth but then slowly shook his head from side to side. Without another word, he leaned closer and removed the breakfast tray from her lap, placing it on the ground. Harriette continued to work the small knots out with her fingers but still watched Felix's movements, wondering what she'd done to make him stare at her in such a way. His look seemed to be one of confusion, one of incredulity, and she wasn't sure why.

When he nudged the open bedroom door closed with his foot, then sat on the bed, facing her more than before, her eyes widened in surprise. 'Felix? What is it?' Was he about to tell her something private, something personal, something important? She waited.

'Your hair...' Tentatively, he reached out a hand and carefully touched her loose hair. 'You are exquisite, Harriette,' he murmured as he threaded his fingers through the locks. 'Such a great colour.'

She swallowed over the sudden dryness of her throat and tried to talk but seemed unable. In fact, this time, she decided to keep completely quiet. Felix was close to her, his gaze taking in her slightly parted lips before flicking back to stare into her eyes once more.

'I need to know,' he murmured. 'Need to see if this chemistry is real and not just a figment of my imagination.' Even as he spoke, his voice deep and laced with desire, he continued to sift her hair through his fingers. 'Harriette?'

Was he waiting for an answer from her? 'Uh...' She

stared into his eyes, amazed at the intensity she could see there, unable to form any other sort of reply.

'I haven't been able to stop thinking about our kiss, wanting more, needing more.' He stopped touching her hair and instead started caressing her cheek and neck with the tips of his fingers, the touch light and tender and intoxicatingly sensual. 'I've dreamt about you, I've dreamt about us kissing, about us being together and—' He broke off and gazed once more at her mouth, this time running his thumb over the soft suppleness as though he needed to touch her more intimately.

Harriette's lips parted and her tongue slipped out to wet her lips, licking the tip of his thumb. They gasped in unison, the room filling with the tension of unrepressed desire.

'Harriette,' he murmured and began to lower his head, drawing his mouth closer and closer with each passing second. 'If you want me to stop…' His words were barely audible but the sound seemed to boom around them.

'Shh,' she whispered. 'Kiss me, Felix. Kiss me now.'

And as though he needed no further coaxing, that was exactly what he did, bringing his mouth to connect with hers, to explore, to taste, to fulfil the need both seemed to be experiencing. He kept the movements gentle, testing, teasing and tantalising both of them. The taste of her lips held a hint of saltiness mixed with sweetness mixed with perfect Harriette-ness.

She placed her hands on his arms as though ensuring he kept his hands at her face, as though ensuring he didn't pull away, because she simply wasn't ready for him to do that. He was encouraged by her touch and, slowly but surely, he increased the pressure of the kiss, opening his mouth a bit wider and kissing her as he'd wanted to for what seemed like his entire life. No other woman had made him feel the way Harriette did, accepting him for who he'd been, for who he was now and for who he would be in the future. How was it possible that she had such a capacity to care and that she would choose him of all people to care about?

Although their kiss had intensified, she wasn't letting him rush ahead, wasn't letting him speed things up and he liked that, he liked that he could kiss her intensely but slowly, savouring every second, every flavour, every sensation she was evoking within him. She was caring and giving and now she was giving to him. The action only made him want to reciprocate, to make her feel special, to make her feel as though she deserved the utmost in happiness for the rest of her life. Whether or not he was the person to give that to her, he had no idea but the question he'd originally wanted an answer to had been answered in abundance.

With a slight groan, he eased back from her, his hands still cupping her cheeks, his breathing as erratic as hers as he stared into her eyes.

'Yep. It's there all right,' he ground out.

'Uh-huh,' she confirmed as she leaned forward and rested her forehead against his, both of them breathing heavily. 'The attraction is awake and definitely alive…'

'And increasing with each passing moment,' he finished.

Harriette sighed. 'What do we do now?'

'That's a very good question.'

CHAPTER ELEVEN

'CLINIC' WAS THE logical answer to their question even though it wasn't the one either of them wanted. The homestead seemed to be getting louder and louder as the people who had stayed overnight started to rouse and others who had been driving in for the clinic began to arrive.

All too soon, Harriette and Felix were back at work, seeing patient after patient before packing up around midday and driving out to the next property. Chloe kept up a steady stream of chatter as they drove along, Felix taking a turn behind the wheel and surprising Harriette when he reached over and took her hand in his, giving it a little kiss before he continued driving along the straight bitumen road. When she told him to slow down and take another shortcut, he didn't quibble but instead turned off and headed across country, unfortunately needing to have both hands on the wheel again.

It was as though that kiss this morning had opened up the unaired part of Felix. He was being demonstrative, jovial, interactive and, well…happy. Even Chloe noticed the difference in him, laughing as he spoke to her in a silly voice and willingly going into his arms when he went to unbuckle her seatbelt. It was as though he'd been given a new lease of life and that night, when they'd finished the clinic, Felix and Harriette sat out on the porch in rocking chairs and watched the sun set. Chloe was snuggled on Harriette's lap and eventually fell asleep as Harriette rocked steadily back and forth.

'Another busy and eventful day over,' he murmured, shifting his rocking chair closer to hers. She couldn't believe it was only that very morning since he'd kissed her...kissed her in a way she couldn't ever remember being kissed before and seemed, for all the world, as though he was looking forward to doing it again.

'Chloe seems to be enjoying the interaction with the other kids who come to the clinics,' Harriette stated and Felix nodded.

'It's good to see her laughing and smiling and joining in.'

'She deserves happiness.'

'Yes, she does, as do we all.'

'Yes,' Harriette agreed.

There was silence between them for a few minutes, the sounds of the wooden rocking chairs moving back and forth on the wooden porch.

'What do we do now?' Harriette asked softly, echoing her question of earlier that morning.

'I'd like to start by kissing you again,' he murmured and she couldn't help but smile at the suggestion.

'I'd like that too, Felix, but you know what I mean.'

'I do but it doesn't mean we need to figure everything out straight away. We've only kissed a few times and, although I do intend to repeat the action again and again, there's no need to plan a future just yet, is there?'

Harriette pondered his words for a moment. 'I guess as you usually like things all organised and hospital corners, I just thought that—'

'I'm trying to change, Harriette. I'm trying not to

live my life by logic but by emotion. I don't know how I'm going to progress but I know for now I don't want to make firm plans, to organise, to sort things out. I just want to...*feel* and you...you make me feel, Harriette.'

She smiled at his words. 'You make me feel, too, Felix. Like I can't ever remember feeling before and that's a nice thing.'

'See?' He reached over and took one of her hands in his and kissed it. 'Tomorrow, we do our last clinic, then go to Darwin, then head back to Meeraji Lake when we can discuss things.'

'OK.' She lifted his hand to her lips and kissed it in reciprocation. 'For now, though, Chloe's starting to become a dead weight and we need to leave bright and early tomorrow morning.'

'Then we'd all best get to our beds.' With that, he let go of her hand, then stood and carefully picked up Chloe from Harriette's arms. The little girl went without fuss, winding her arms about his neck and resting her head on his shoulder, not waking up at all. 'Shall we?' he asked and Harriette nodded. 'You lead the way as I can't remember which rooms we were allocated.'

'Oh. OK.' She opened the screen door and held it while Felix entered the house with Chloe, then led the way down the quiet hallway of the old homestead until Harriette opened one of the bedroom doors. She quickly pulled back the bed covers so he could put Chloe down. 'I'll get her sorted into her night clothes later,' she stated.

'She hasn't brushed her teeth,' Felix pointed out and, when Harriette shrugged one shoulder, he held up his hand as though to stop her from speaking. 'I know, I know. One night won't hurt.'

'Very good,' she praised as she covered the little girl

with the sheet before turning to face Felix, smiling up at him with delight. 'You're a fast learner, Dr McLaren,' she stated, unable to stop herself from edging closer to him, wishing he would take her in his arms and kiss her goodnight.

He didn't disappoint and slipped his arms about her waist, bringing their bodies into contact. He immediately lowered his head, their mouths meeting in perfect synchronicity as though they really had been designed for each other. They continued to explore but this time he let her guide them through the tumultuous, raging rapids of desire.

'You smell so good,' he murmured as she broke off and pressed soft kisses to his neck, standing on tiptoe so she could reach.

'You taste so good,' she replied before seeking his mouth once more, the intensity of their need for each other becoming heightened with each passing second. When Felix's hand shifted to slide beneath the hem of her top, Harriette instantly stilled.

'Sorry. Too fast?' he murmured against her mouth and she eased back to look at him.

'I…uh…don't want you to take this the wrong way but…having become pregnant at sixteen and bearing the consequences, I'm…er…not in the habit of becoming intimate with someone until I know where the relationship is going.' She kept her words as strong as she could because she *wanted* Felix to continue, wanted to throw caution to the wind and see where it might lead them, but she'd also promised herself decades ago never to let herself be sweet-talked or pressured into doing something she wasn't ready to do.

'You're right. Of course you're right,' he remarked and, instead of pulling away as she'd half expected, he simply slipped his hands back around her waist and dropped a kiss to the top of her nose. 'And of course we need to adhere to lessons learned in the past. I, myself, am usually extremely cautious about the…uh… women I see.'

'Women?' She raised an inquisitive eyebrow and grinned before kissing him on the lips when he started to look worried. 'I'm teasing, Felix. Of course we both have past relationships. You don't get to our age without having them, but the past is the past and although we need to learn from it, we also can't let it dictate our future.'

'So you *do* want to sleep with me?'

'Of course I do but it doesn't mean I will. For a start, we have Chloe to consider.' They both looked at the child sleeping soundly in the bed, completely oblivious to what was happening in the room. 'And I meant what I said. I need to know where things are heading before I can let myself break down that last barrier.'

He kissed her, then put her from him. 'Just as well we're not sharing a room tonight.'

'Just as well,' she agreed and couldn't help but laugh as he took her hand in his, kissed it, then bowed and closed the bedroom door behind him. 'Good night,' she called softly, not at all sure he'd heard her.

'Sleep sweet,' he returned, equally quiet, and Harriette couldn't help but clasp her hands to her chest and giggle with happiness. No matter what might or might not happen between herself and Felix in the near future, for the moment—right for now—she was happy, and happy was good.

The next morning, they were up with the birds and watching the sun rise as they drove. Once more, Felix had been attentive towards both her and Chloe and Harriette was pleased to see the *real* Felix, the man she'd always known was buried deep inside him, starting to venture out. Part of her wanted to know why and the other part simply wanted to accept and enjoy. If she questioned him, she risked him clamming up, which she most certainly didn't want. Instead, she tried to take her own advice and not worry, not try to think fifty steps ahead as she'd conditioned herself to do.

'Have you heard from Eddie? You haven't been able to speak to him online due to having no Internet connection out here,' Felix asked as the sun started to rise in the sky, the greys of the morning changing to muted reds, blues and greens.

'I told him before we left that it might be difficult to contact me but we should be nearing Internet and cellphone range soon so hopefully my phone will buzz with lots of delightful messages from my boy.'

'Eddie! Eddie!' Chloe clapped her hands in the back seat and hugged Captain Gumleaf close. 'I want to talk to Eddie.'

'Hopefully we'll make that happen,' Harriette told her. 'Until then, would you like to listen to some music?'

'Yes. Music! Music!'

Harriette put a CD on, singing along with Chloe to the songs, surprised when Felix joined in, his lovely baritone blending nicely. 'You have an incredible voice,' she told him when the song had finished.

His grin was a little sheepish and he shrugged one shoulder. 'My mother used to like it when I'd sing to her. She told me I had the voice of an angel and I probably did, given I hadn't properly gone through puberty.' He chuckled and Harriette closed her eyes for a moment, not only delighted at the sound of his laughter but also the brightness in his eyes as he talked of his mother. 'I don't remember singing much after she died. I guess I never really had a reason.' He reached out and laced his fingers with hers. 'Until now.' He glanced across at her. 'You make me happy, Harriette.' He kissed her hand then let it go before gesturing to the wide open space they were currently driving through. 'Out here, in the middle of nowhere, I can start to believe that things *can* change, that life doesn't have to be a drudge.'

'And it makes *me* happy to hear you talk that way.' She leaned over and placed a kiss to his cheek, her seatbelt restraining her from doing anything further.

'Do that again,' he stated and she did, but this time when she went to kiss his cheek, he turned his head so their lips could meet.

'Oi! Focus on the road,' she told him and was rewarded with another of his delicious chuckles. Today's drive would take them closer towards Darwin but still three or four hours out of town. The clinic was a small one, for which she was grateful, and tomorrow they would go and see Felix's father. She wondered whether he'd start to withdraw from her as the time neared for him to come face-to-face with the man who had caused him pain. She still had no idea what had transpired between the two of them all those years ago but hopefully they'd be able to restore their relationship before it was too late.

By the time they arrived at the next homestead for the final clinic, it was almost midday and no sooner were they out of the car than they were swamped by a group of anxious-faced farmers who had all been talking together in a group by the barn.

'You gotta come out with us. There's been an accident. The air ambulance has been called but it's gonna take them a while to get here. Get back in the ute,' one man said as he climbed into the back, stopping when he saw Chloe sitting there, looking at him with her big eyes. 'You got a squirt in here, Doc.'

'I know I have.'

'A squirt?' Felix asked, bristling at the other man's high-handed attitude.

'A child,' Harriette offered as Chloe started to niggle. 'It's all right, darling.'

'Sorry, squirt. Didn't mean to scare ya,' the man said and waited while Harriette unclipped Chloe's seat-belt, the child instantly throwing herself into Harriette's arms. 'My kids are inside playing. You wanna go see them?' the man continued and Harriette nodded.

'Good idea. I'll take her inside, Clem, and you can tell Felix what's happened.' She looked at Felix. 'That OK with you?'

'Sure.' He winked at Chloe and blew her a kiss, delighted when she blew one back. Harriette carried Chloe and her bag into the homestead and spoke with Clem's wife, Josie. As soon as Chloe saw the other children, twin girls who were about her age, watching her favourite television show, she instantly wriggled out of Harriette's arms and went to sit down with the others.

'She'll be fine,' Josie reassured her. 'Leave her here as long as you need to.'

'She's become quite adept at playing with other children these past few days,' Harriette remarked as she kissed the top of Chloe's head before walking towards the door. 'Thanks, Josie.' When she reached the ute, it was to find Clem sitting in the front and Felix already behind the wheel, buckling his seat belt. She quickly climbed into the back and buckled up. 'What's happening?'

'Tractor accident,' Clem told her as they drove off

towards the outer paddock, leaving the other men to follow in a different vehicle. 'Aaron Smithfield. He was
coming over for the clinic and decided to drive across
paddock in his tractor. Not the first time he's done it and
it won't be the last. Cuts a lot of time off the journey.'

'Naturally.'

'Tractor got a split in the tyre and when Aaron was
changing it, the jack broke and the tyre landed on him.
Leg's badly broken up. Lucky for Aaron, he had his
cellphone in his pocket and managed to get an emergency call through to report it. Couple of my blokes are
already out there, keeping him conscious and stuff like
that, but from the reports his leg looks badly busted up.'

'Any bleeding?'

'Yeah. A bit.'

'Has he lost consciousness?' Felix asked.

'Don't know.' Clem pointed out to a large tree. 'Head
over there and then turn left at the tree. I've put cattle
grids in so we don't need to get out and open any gates.'

'Good.' The sooner they were able to get to Aaron,
the better, and when they finally arrived it was to discover that Clem's blokes, the men who worked on the
land, had erected a makeshift tent over Aaron in order
to provide some shade from the hot summery sun and
removed the tyre.

'We've sprayed him with some insect repellent, too,'
one of the men said.

'Thanks,' Harriette remarked as she and Felix carried their emergency bags towards their next patient.
'How's it going, Aaron?' she asked.

'Feeling faint, Doc,' he told her.

'Understandable.' She took Aaron's pulse as Felix
hooked the stethoscope into his ears and listened to

Aaron's heartbeat. She checked his eyes and asked if he'd hit his head.

'I don't think so. I may have blacked out at some point but I don't remember.'

'Are you allergic to any medicines?' Felix asked as he took out a pre-measured syringe of morphine.

'Not that I know of, Doc. Not usually the sick type, if you know what I mean, but the wife said I had to come to the clinic and get my immunisations or else I would end up being the sick type and she wasn't gonna have me die from stupidity and leave her alone to raise the kids out here.'

Harriette ran her gloved fingers carefully over Aaron's legs, then reached for the heavy-duty scissors and cut his hard-wearing denim jeans open. Felix finished administering the morphine. 'This will help you.'

'That's a nasty fracture you've got there, Aaron,' Harriette remarked as she exposed the area, shooing away the flies. She could hear Clem talking to some of the blokes, mentioning that they had to make an area for the air ambulance to land safely.

'The closer we can get the plane to Aaron, the better,' Clem was saying. Harriette stared at the fracture for a long moment, wondering if the orthopaedic surgeons would be able to fix the badly crushed tibia and fibula. Aaron's foot had also sustained a few fractures and the area was, generally, a mess.

'How's the femur?' she asked Felix as he inspected the upper part of Aaron's leg, checking the thigh for fractures.

'It looks intact but his blood pressure isn't strong so there may be internal bleeding.'

'I'll get his leg splinted,' she remarked, but first she

put a neck brace around Aaron's neck. 'Need to keep your head still so we don't do any damage to your spine.'

'Yep. Pain's going now,' Aaron said and started to close his eyes.

'Aaron? I need you to stay with me,' she told him. 'Talk to me. Tell me about those kids of yours. How many do you have?'

Felix performed Aaron's observations as Harriette stabilised the leg and his report indicated that, even though the badly fractured leg was a mess, there was obviously something else wrong. Somewhere, Aaron was bleeding internally.

'How long until the air ambulance gets here?' Felix called to Clem, a clipped and urgent note in his tone.

'ETA two minutes.'

'There's a portable stretcher in the back of our ute. Can someone get it, please?' No sooner had he asked, than it was brought over.

'Leg is splinted,' Harriette reported as she once more asked Aaron questions about his family. Aaron, in typically Aussie-outback fashion, was hanging in there, showing he was made of tougher stuff and wasn't going to give in to a little thing like internal bleeding.

'Plus, if I was to die out here,' he tried to joke, 'me missus would have me guts for garters.'

'You're not going to die,' Felix told him. 'Both Harriette and I are trained surgeons and if we have to open you up here and now in order to save your life then you can bet that's exactly what we'll do.'

'Truly? Operate in a field?'

'Plane sighted! Coming in for landing!' Clem yelled, jumping up and down and waving his arms about.

'But if necessary, the plane will do,' Felix added.

'You'll make it to the hospital in time,' Harriette remarked. 'Once we get you in that plane, we can give you some top-up fluids, which will definitely help you feel better.'

'Yeah?' Aaron sounded hopeful. 'I'm not gonna die today?'

'Sorry to disappoint you.' Harriette chuckled. Soon, they had him safely transferred to the plane, both Harriette and Felix deciding to travel with Aaron.

'If we need to operate, I'll need you there,' Felix had told her when she'd said she'd stay and do the clinic.

'Don't worry about your squirt,' Clem told her. 'We'll take good care of her.'

'We'll be back as soon as possible,' Harriette told him before the door to the plane was closed and they were getting ready for take-off. Thankfully, they were able to get some plasma into Aaron, which made a big difference to his status so that when they arrived at Darwin hospital, a team of emergency specialists waiting for them, their patient was whisked away into the care of the trained orthopaedic team.

'So...' Felix asked her as they walked through the hospital. 'How do we get back to the homestead?'

'First, we go to the cafeteria and have a coffee. Then we chat to the local pilots and see if we can't work something out.' As they headed to the cafeteria Felix looked around at the walls and smiled.

'I'd almost forgotten what it was like.'

'The walls or the feel of a hospital?'

He grinned at her words. 'The feel of a hospital. I took leave when I was notified of David's death and then, when Oscar suggested I come to Meeraji Lake, I took a twelve-month sabbatical from my hospital in Sydney.'

'And you'll go back there when you're done in Meeraji Lake?'

'That's the plan,' he stated, but there was a hint of confusion in his tone.

'You sound a little unsure.'

'Well...' He took her hand in his and laced their fingers together. 'There have been quite a few developments in my life and, honestly, who knows what might happen? The fact remains that we're only babysitting the hospital for Daisy and Oscar and when they eventually return, it'll be time to move on.'

'But to where?' she asked.

'That,' he remarked as they sipped their coffee, 'is the million-dollar question.'

'Not back to Sydney?'

Felix frowned thoughtfully, considering the question, but before he could answer they were interrupted when someone called his name.

'Felix McLaren?' A small, white-coated doctor was headed their way, the man having a moustache and a large mop of curly dark hair on his head. 'Felix? Is that really you?'

'Myron? Wow.' Felix stood up, towering over the other man, and shook hands with him.

'What on earth are you doing in a Darwin hospital? I thought you were ensconced in the hierarchy of Sydney General for ever.'

Felix shrugged nonchalantly. 'Times have a habit of changing.' When Myron looked pointedly at Harriette, Felix quickly remembered his manners. 'Allow me to introduce my colleague, Harriette Jones.'

Myron shook hands with Harriette, smiling warmly, and Harriette found she instantly liked the man. He was bright and jovial and clearly held Felix in high esteem. 'Your ears must have been burning,' he told Felix a moment later as he pulled up a chair and sat down at their table. 'As I was only talking about you this morning.'

'Really?'

'We've had a patient come in overnight who requires an intricate hernia repair and bowel resection. I was explaining to my colleagues how you basically wrote the book on that type of surgery and it was a pity you were so far away in Sydney because it would be amazing for them to watch you perform the surgery, just as it was for me all those years ago. So…' Myron grinned at him. 'How long are you in Darwin? Feel like doing surgery?'

'Uh…' Felix looked at Harriette, then down at the table. 'I'm not licensed to practise here.'

'Actually, you are,' Harriette interjected. 'As doctors at Meeraji Lake, we're automatically granted visiting medical/surgical officer status here at Darwin hospital.'

'You're at Meeraji Lake?' Myron seemed shocked but quickly recovered. 'At any rate, it's my gain so why would I bother looking a gift horse in the mouth?'

'Actually, I have a clinic to do, plus I—'

'At least come and review the patient,' Myron interrupted, clearly not wanting to hear any excuses from Felix. Felix looked at Harriette.

'Why don't you go and I'll organise our trip back to the homestead?'

'Are you sure?'

'You don't need to ask my permission,' she told him, and before he walked away she saw that bright spark in his eyes, that lightness to his step and realised that, even though he'd made the sacrifice to work at Meeraji Lake for Chloe's sake, it was a shame that he wasn't able to do what he clearly loved, which was dealing with the difficult cases and saving lives.

He might not want to head back to the big city after

his stint in the outback, but she couldn't see him *not* working in a hospital environment. He seemed to have come alive ever since they'd set foot inside the hospital and, although Darwin was nowhere near as big as Sydney or Melbourne, it was still a fairly decent size as far as cities went. He'd be able to work shorter hours, perform difficult surgeries and still spend time with Chloe. Plus there were some excellent schools here in Darwin so Chloe would be well catered for with her education.

And what would she do? Would she return to Melbourne? The opposite end of the country? Would she stay? Move to Darwin? Start afresh…afresh with Felix and Chloe?

Trying not to be swamped with an air of despondence, Harriette pulled out her cellphone and called the air ambulance and Royal Flying Doctor Service to see if anyone was heading towards the homestead where they were supposed to have started clinic almost an hour ago. There weren't any flights scheduled at the moment but they promised to give her a call if things changed. Next, she called Clem's homestead to check on Chloe and to give them an updated report on Aaron's situation.

'Aaron's brother, Paul, has a chopper on his property so he's going to fly Aaron's missus to the hospital in about two hours' time,' Clem told her after she'd had a chat with Chloe, who seemed quite happy. 'So if you and Felix want a lift back to pick up the squirt, then Paul can bring you back then.'

'Sounds perfect,' Harriette agreed. 'Sorry about the clinic. Looks like we may have to postpone it.'

'Already taken care of. People will either need to make a date in Darwin for treatment or wait until next month for the next clinic. It's no sweat, Doc.'

'Thanks, Clem. See you later on, then.' After she

disconnected the call, Harriette tried calling Eddie but only got his voicemail so left him a message saying she missed him. She could really do with listening to some of Eddie's adventure stories right now. Anything to take her mind off how Felix was starting to tie her in knots.

She put her thoughts on hold and went in to the ICU, which was where she presumed the sick patient would be located. Sure enough, there she found Felix, a gaggle of nurses, registrars and interns gathered around him as he pointed to a set of patient X-rays on the large viewing box. He was explaining the intricacies of the procedure and some of the interns were furiously writing down notes. Myron was beaming from ear to ear, as though he'd done the impossible and snagged the biggest fish around and was proudly showing him off for his friends. Felix was…famous. Or, at least, in medical circles he was. She thought back to his first day in Meeraji Lake and wondered if Patrick realised just how brilliant the surgeon who had removed his appendix really was.

When Felix glanced over and saw her standing off to the side, he raised his eyebrows in greeting before returning his attention to a registrar who was asking him a question. Harriette waited patiently, listening to everything he was saying, and when he was done, and had been thanked for his time, he walked over to Harriette, a large grin on his face.

'I'd forgotten how much fun teaching could be. I always enjoyed educating the students…and registrars,' he said pointedly and winked at her. 'I could help you study when we get back to ensure you pass those end-of-year exams with flying colours.'

'Uh…yeah. Thanks.' It was a generous offer and she knew she should be more grateful but what she really wanted from Felix wasn't a study buddy. What she wanted from Felix was the man deep down inside him, the man who had opened up to her, the man who, she realised in that split second, had stolen her heart. She wasn't the type of woman to give her heart easily, but the fact that Felix had most certainly made an impression, and one that had caused her entire being to swell with love for him, was a miracle in itself. Stunned by the realisation, Harriette continued to stare at him, completely dumbfounded. It wasn't until he waved his fingers in front of her face and called her name that she snapped out of it.

'Sorry.'

'You were miles away.' He indicated that they should leave the ICU so the staff could continue their work.

'Look at you,' she said as they headed back into the main corridor. 'You're loving it, aren't you?'

'I have to confess I am. I mean, I love the work in Meeraji Lake, it's a different pace and I've loved the travelling and the hectic clinics, but I do love a hospital atmosphere. It feels like home.'

'And speaking of home, or rather getting back to the homestead where Chloe is, we can get a lift with Aaron's brother in a few hours' time.' She explained the situation and Felix seemed fine with it.

'So we have a few hours to waste away in Darwin, eh?'

'We do.' She bit her lip for a moment as a thought entered her mind, unsure whether or not he'd go for it. 'Would you…uh…like to go see your father?' The frown that pierced his forehead was instant and she quickly continued. 'It means that after we pick up Chloe, we don't have to come back here and can instead head back to Meeraji Lake.'

He thought on this for a moment, his eyes darkening, and she felt guilty for quashing his happiness. Although, she rationalised, he'd known all along they were going to be seeing his father. 'Why not get it over and done with?' They were walking through the corridors and Harriette wasn't sure he even knew where he was going. What she did know was that his stride had increased, had become more determined, frustrated, much the same way he'd walked around Meeraji Lake when he'd first arrived.

'You need to see him, Felix. You agreed.'

'Do I, though? I've been doing fine for decades without any input from him.'

'He's dying. That at least deserves our compassion. He's at the end of his life with regrets and, besides, apart from Chloe—'

'He's all I have left in the way of family,' he finished as they came to the front doors of the hospital. Sighing heavily with exasperation as though he knew she was right, he walked directly to the kerb and hailed a taxi. One instantly pulled up into the designated taxi rank and he opened the rear door for Harriette. 'Shall we get this over and done with?'

Not about to look a gift horse in the mouth, Harriette slid into the taxi and was pleased when Felix got into the back beside her. As they buckled their seatbelts, he gave the taxi driver the name of the nursing home. They remained silent in the back of the cab and although Harriette wanted nothing more than to take Felix's hand in hers, to give it a little squeeze, to reassure him, he kept his arms crossed tightly over his chest.

They arrived all too soon and, where he'd been quick to get in the taxi, he took his time getting out, paying the driver and thanking him for his time. Harriette waited on the footpath outside, feeling even more antsy when she saw the darkness in his face, the mask of protection, the closed expression. Here was a man she most certainly never wanted to meet in an abandoned alley and, swallowing over the lump in her throat, she held the door open for him.

It was something he needed to do, she knew that, he knew that but…perhaps it wasn't. As they spoke to the nurses at the desk Harriette wondered whether she hadn't made a mistake in urging him to see his father.

Grim faced, they were taken through to a private room where Mr McLaren senior was lying in a bed, an oxygen tube near his nostrils and hooked around ears that seemed too big for his leathery face. Harriette had seen death many times and she could easily recognise that Felix's father didn't have long for this world. At that moment, she *was* glad they'd come.

'It's good you've come. He took a turn for the worse this morning and we were just debating whether to call you, to see if you could come today instead of tomorrow, when you walked in the door. It's fate,' the nurse said as she brushed a soft hand over Mr McLaren's forehead.

'He's not in any pain?' Felix's words were brisk, professional, detached.

'No. We've made him comfortable.'

He nodded, then thanked the nurse, asking for some time alone with his father.

'Do you want me to go, too?' Harriette asked softly when the nurse had left. Felix's answer was to shake his head. He picked up his father's hand, as he would any patient, and checked the pulse.

'Dad?' Felix's deep voice seemed to reverberate around the quiet room but there was no response. 'Dad?'

he tried again, a little louder this time, and gave his father's hand a little squeeze.

'What do you want?' the old man grumbled and opened his eyes, staring unseeingly at Felix before finally focusing. 'Oh. It's you. Come to watch me die, eh?'

'Do you know who I am?' Felix asked, knowing full well that dementia patients sometimes became confused and, in his father's case, along with the shell shock, it was inevitable. Still, there was the chance that this was a brief moment of clarity and Felix wanted to be sure.

'Of course I do. You're Felix.' The words were hoarse but gruff and the old man glanced around the room. 'Where's David? Has he come to switch off the machines, to watch me die?' His father jerked his hand out of Felix's grasp, the brisk action causing him to cough.

'Easy, there.'

'Don't tell me what to do,' Mr McLaren managed to say between coughs.

'David's not here.'

'Then who's that? Your wife? I remember you getting married. Didn't realise she was so good-looking.' He raised his bushy eyebrows in a wolfish gesture. 'Come here, toots, and grant an old man one last kiss.'

Harriette smiled and stepped forward, obliging by kissing Mr McLaren on the cheek.

'At least you did something right, ya good-for-nothing son. Where's David? Has he come to switch off the machines, to watch me die?'

Felix glanced at Harriette briefly, both of them knowing that momentary lapses in memory were more than common at this stage. 'No, Dad. Didn't the nurses tell you? David and his wife, Sue, passed away.'

'David, eh? Gone?' He coughed. 'Soon you'll be the only one left. All alone. Just like you always wanted.

You always thought you were better than us, with your fancy medical school. You ran away after driving your mother insane.'

'Dad… I didn't.' Felix clenched his jaw and tried not to look at Harriette, pain and mortification flooding through him. It was out now. The main reason why his father hated him. The old man was positive Felix had caused his mother's death, but as Felix looked at his father he knew that the one who had driven his mother to the point where she'd taken her own life was the man before him.

Felix shook his head. 'This was a mistake. I shouldn't have come.'

'No.' His father's voice sounded, a little clearer than before but still just above a hoarse whisper. 'You're useless. Just like *her*. You look like her, you'll wreck your marriage, you'll push people away when they try to help and God help any kids you have because you'll make a crappy father just like she made a crappy mother.'

'I'm done.' Felix shook his head then shoved his hands into his pockets and walked around the bed, heading for the door.

'Felix, wait.' Harriette tried to reach out to him but he avoided her touch and stormed past. She stood there for a moment or two, listening to the old man's raspy breathing. She jumped when the door opened and Felix stalked back into the room.

'Don't you ever talk about my mother that way again. She was a decent, hard-working and caring woman. *You* were the one who berated her to the point where she'd felt she had no option but to end her own life, leaving us alone, leaving us…leaving us…' He stopped, unable to continue.

Mr McLaren rasped in another breath, then out again, coughing a few times before the next breath.

'You were a rotten father and I would rather be like her, with all her weaknesses, than anything like you.'

'That's where you're wrong, boy. You're like both of us.'

'No.' Felix's tone was vehement. 'I am *nothing* like you.' He shook his head. 'You're… You're… You're not worth it. You are *not* worth it.' Then, without looking at Harriette, he stormed from the room again. Mr McLaren took in another raspy breath, coughed twice… then didn't breathe out.

'Mr McLaren?' She pressed her fingers to the carotid pulse, but didn't feel anything. She gave him a little shake and called loudly, 'Mr McLaren? Can you hear me?' No response. No pulse. She pressed the button for the nurse and then checked the old man's pupils. Fixed and dilated.

A moment later, a nurse came into the room.

'He's passed,' Harriette announced. 'Forty-five seconds since his last breath.'

'Are you a doctor?'

'I am, but best get your own doctors to call time of death. If you'll excuse me.' Harriette headed out of the room and looked around for Felix. He was nowhere to be seen. She headed out of the closest door and found herself walking towards a lovely little garden, where people could come and walk with the residents or spend time together as a family.

'Felix?' she called but received no response. She walked further into the garden, following the path. 'Felix?' she called again, but when she rounded the next corner she found him sitting on a bench, elbows on his knees, head in his hands. She sat down beside him but didn't say anything. She just waited.

'Has he passed?' he asked about five minutes later.

'Yes.'

He lifted his head but didn't look at her. 'I'm sorry.'

'No. You had every right to say to him what you—'

'Not that. I'm sorry I let you talk me into this. It was a mistake.' With that he stood and walked away.

CHAPTER TWELVE

'HI, MUM.' THERE was a slight delay as Eddie's voice came down the line. 'I'm back in Paris, safe and sound.'

She sighed with relief. 'Good to hear.'

There was a pause on the other end of the line, then, 'What's wrong?' There was no hiding anything from Eddie. He knew her far too well.

'Oh, Eddie,' she gasped, then blurted out the whole story of how they'd had an emergency, then they'd gone to see Felix's father and that Felix had blamed her for everything. 'And then…then…' She stopped and blew her nose. 'Then when I arrived back at Darwin hospital, it was to find that Felix had agreed to perform the surgery for the patient he'd consulted on and that he'd be doing it with loads of people watching so they could observe his technique, and that's fine but it's the way he spoke to me. It was as though I was a stranger, as though we hadn't spent any time together, as though… as though…' She stopped and sniffed.

'Where is he now?'

'He's still in Darwin.'

'Where are you?'

'Chloe and I are back in Meeraji Lake. We managed to get a ride back in a helicopter two days ago.'

'That would have been exciting for Chloe but...Felix left her?'

'He calls her on the phone every day, talks to her. She thinks it's great. Just like you and I and, besides, he did tell her he'll be back in a few days. He's going to stay and monitor the patient in case of complications.'

'That's logical.'

'I know. I know it is but, oh, Eddie. I've blown it. I've wrecked everything by pushing Felix to see his father. Honestly, Mr McLaren was horrible to Felix. He knew exactly who he was and he said some awful things. And then...and then... Felix blamed me, then walked away. He left me there. Left me at the nursing home. Dismissed me. Looked at me as though he didn't know me at all.'

'Mum. Mum.' Eddie tried to get a word in and finally succeeded. 'I know things seem dire now but Felix will come around. He's hurt and he has a right to be. He doesn't have the right to take it out on my mother, though, and I'll be making sure he apologises to you for that.'

'It's OK, darling.' She sniffed then smiled, pleased her boy was protective of her. 'But, Eddie, what if he doesn't come around? I love him. I love the stupid, idiotic man and there's nothing I can do about it and I have to work with him for the rest of the year and then there's Chloe and—'

'Mum!' Eddie's words cut her off and even with the delay due to the fact they were on opposite sides of the world, it still managed to silence Harriette. 'Chillax. Take it a day at a time. Go and spend some time with Chloe. Focus on Chloe. Oh, and isn't it Tori and Scotty's wedding soon?'

'Yes.'

'Go and be girls together. Do your nails. Play with hairstyles. You've never had a little girl to play dress ups with.'

Harriette sniffed again then smiled. 'True.'

'Go and be a mum to Chloe. You already love her as though she was your own. She needs you now and if Felix needs to take a few days or a week to sort his head out, then give him the space he needs. The poor bloke's already had quite a few hectic and confronting months.'

'True.' She sighed, feeling calmer than before. 'Thank you, Eddie. Sleep sweet, darling.' Harriette ended the call then blew her nose once more before going to the bathroom to splash water on her face. She could be there for Chloe…and Felix. Even if he ended up breaking her heart in the process, surely it was worth the pain? Wasn't it?

Three days later, Harriette still hadn't heard from Felix and she was doing her best to hide it from everyone— except Eddie, but at least she could face him in the privacy of her own room. Felix had called her phone and immediately asked to speak with Chloe so he could say goodnight to her, and apparently, according to Erica, he'd called the day care a few times to speak with Chloe during the day.

'At least he's keeping in contact with her,' Erica had said yesterday when Harriette had gone to pick the little girl up from day care. 'After losing her parents, he wants to make sure she knows he's only away from her because he has to do important doctor work in Darwin.' Erica had sighed. 'That poor man, the one Felix stayed behind to operate on,' she clarified. 'He's had several complications but last time I spoke to Felix, he felt the man was finally stabilising, so that's good.'

In fact, it seemed Felix was keeping in contact with everyone in the town except for her. Tori had mentioned that he'd called to check on a few patients and to say he was getting a lift to Clem's property and would pick up the ute Harriette had left there. 'He's going to drive it back to Meeraji Lake and said he'd try his hardest to get here in time for the wedding,' Tori informed her.

Even in the pub where she and Chloe had eaten dinner the other night she hadn't been safe from talk of Felix. Patrick had been showing off his appendectomy scar.

'Just look at that neat scar. Perfect stitching, from Doc McLaren. Did you know he's a famous surgeon, published in journals and sought after by doctors all over the world? And he operated on *me*. *Me!*'

By the time the day of the wedding arrived, the whole town was buzzing. Tori and Scotty were getting married in a large marquee next to the community centre. Chloe woke up in a bad mood and had a tantrum when it was time to put on her pretty dress.

'I don't want to wear a dress to the wedding and Uncle Felix said he would be here to get dressed up with me and he's *not*.' The child stamped her foot and crossed her arms huffily, pursing her lips together in a pout. 'I want Uncle Felix. I don't want you, Harriette.'

'Not you, too, Chloe.' Harriette sighed and left the child alone to calm down while she finished getting ready. She'd chosen to wear a lovely floral dress with ribbons for shoulder straps, a fitted bodice and a flared skirt. Eddie had brought it over from Paris on his last trip, knowing that Tori and Scotty would soon be getting married.

So now, as she dressed in her pretty outfit and slipped on her shoes, which had a small heel so she wouldn't sink into the grass, she reminded herself to take a photo and send it to Eddie. She'd just finished piling her hair on top of her head and was about to start putting her make-up on when Chloe came into her room, still with her arms crossed, still huffing and still not in her pretty dress.

'I want Uncle Felix!' she demanded.

'Would you like to put some make-up on for the wedding?' Harriette asked, trying to distract the child by holding out a lip gloss. 'I have a purplish one in here which will look lovely on you.'

'I don't *want make-up*!' Again the little foot stamped in protest. 'I. Want. Uncle. *Felix*.' She yelled his name throughout the house and Harriette didn't blame her. She wanted Felix here too and, although she'd already tried to explain to Chloe just why Uncle Felix wasn't here, she didn't have the energy to go through it all again.

'Me, too.' Harriette put the lip gloss down and sat on her bed. What was the use of looking this pretty if Felix wasn't here to admire her? To compliment her? To share the event with her? For the past few nights, ever since he'd been so dismissive, she'd ended up crying herself to sleep, her heart breaking in the worst way possible. It was far more painful than the broken heart she'd had at sixteen when Eddie's father had dismissed her. It was worse than when Mark had abandoned her for his career.

Seeing Harriette so despondent seemed to somehow snap Chloe out of her tantrum and she quickly climbed onto the bed beside Harriette.

'I like Uncle Felix. He's funny,' Chloe stated.

'Yes, he is.'

'He's really good to me and he gives me tea sets.'

Harriette smiled and kissed the little girl's head. 'Yes, he does.' In the end, it didn't matter if Chloe attended the wedding in her grubby shorts and T-shirt with her purple shoes on her feet and purple hat on her head. It didn't matter. Nothing mattered because Felix wasn't here to share it with them.

'I miss him.' Harriette sighed.

'Me, too,' Chloe agreed, mimicking Harriette's previous tone exactly. They both sat there for a while, content just to be. When the screen door to the house opened, neither of them moved, Harriette expecting whoever it was to call out a greeting, but nothing happened. Perhaps it was the wind that had banged the door...but there was no wind today.

Frowning, she stood and headed out into the lounge room and stopped still when she saw Felix standing there, his back to her as he peered into his part of the house, clearly looking for Chloe.

'She's in my room.' Harriette's tone was firm and impersonal even though her heart was pounding with delight. He was here. He'd come back for Chloe and that really was all that mattered. His relationship with the little girl was paramount and although she'd convinced herself that that was all she cared about, she knew as soon as he looked at her that she'd been lying to herself.

'Harriette—' He stared at her for a moment, as though drinking her in, as though needing to have his fill. The look in his eyes, one of desire and need, sparked a small light of hope within her.

'Uncle Felix!' Chloe had clearly heard his voice and came hurtling through the house, her arms open wide. Felix quickly bent down, his own arms open wide, before he scooped her up and held her close, breathing in the little girl's scent and kissing her cheek. 'I missed you, Uncle Felix,' she told him.

'I missed you, too, gorgeous girl,' he remarked, then, when she pulled back, she reached out a hand and touched the three-day-old growth of whiskers covering his face.

'You look different.'

'Sorry, princess. I haven't had time to shave.' He shifted Chloe in his arms and looked across at Harriette. 'I drove straight through after picking up the ute from Clem's. I wanted to be here.'

'For the wedding?'

'Not particularly, but don't tell Tori that. No. I just wanted to be here…with you two.'

That spark of hope grew bigger but Harriette still stood her ground. 'You can't treat people that way,' she told him, knowing he knew full well what she was talking about.

'I know. I'm sorry.' He held her gaze for a long and intense moment but Harriette needed more. As though he could read her mind, he turned to Chloe. 'Why aren't you wearing your pretty dress?'

'You promised that you would get dressed up and we could go together, remember?'

'Well, I'm going to talk to Harriette and then go and get ready so we can go to this wedding together.'

'Like we planned?'

'Like we planned,' he confirmed. With that, he put the little girl down and she ran to her room to get changed. 'Just as well the dress is one she can pull on over her head and doesn't need help from us,' he stated as he quickly crossed the distance between himself and Harriette. She'd thought, with the way he'd walked, that he was going to scoop her up into his arms and kiss her full on the mouth but he didn't. Instead, he kept his hands by his sides and lowered his head for a moment before meeting her gaze.

'Harriette, I'm sorry. I was wrong to treat you the way I did because, stupidly, I let that cranky old man who called himself my father get to me. Just as he always used to.' He paused. 'As you may have gathered, my mother took her own life, unable to live with him… or indeed the rest of us.'

'Oh, Felix.' Her heart broke for him. 'That would have been devastating for you.'

'I was already at medical school but David went off the rails. Naturally, Dad couldn't take responsibility for anything and so blamed the two of us. Then I had David blaming me because I'd left home. He kept saying that if I'd been there, Mum would have been able to cope.'

'Is that why you didn't speak for so long?'

'Yes, but thankfully, as we grew older, we realised it wasn't our fault. Poor Mum. She simply couldn't see any other way out of the mess which had become her life. For so long, I thought if I let people get close to me, too close, that I would end up being pushed over the edge like her or losing my mind like him.'

'And now?'

'Now I realise I'm my own man. My circumstances are different from theirs and I don't have to run from the past any more. Seeing the old man helped me realise that. I can write my own future.'

'Oh, Felix.'

'You keep saying that,' he remarked, looking at her. He held his hand out to her and she immediately took it, Felix sighing with relief that she hadn't rejected him.

'That's because your pain is my pain. Can't you see

that? When you hurt, *I* hurt, which is why I'm so sorry I forced you to see your father.'

'It wasn't your fault, Harriette.'

'But you said—'

'I know what I said and I'm ashamed of my behaviour, the way I spoke to you, the way I left you. Harriette…' He linked their fingers together and drew her closer, looking down into her upturned face. 'Can you ever forgive me?'

She reached out and touched his cheek, delighted when he leaned closer, coveting her touch. 'Of course I can. I already have.' And she had. 'You see, Felix…' She took a deep breath, surprised at the nervousness she felt. She knew it was the right time for a declaration of her feelings, she needed to tell him, but how would he respond? 'I…um…'

'Love me?' he prompted when she had difficulty continuing.

Harriette met his gaze and saw the question there, as though he was desperate for her to confirm it. 'Uh… yes. How did you know?'

'I didn't. I could only hope because I love you back. I love you so very much, my sweet Harriette.'

Now he drew her close and pressed his mouth to hers as though saying the words wasn't enough, he needed to show her as well. 'No woman—no *person*,' he clarified, 'has ever made me feel the way you do.'

'And what way is that?' she fished.

He grinned and kissed her once more. 'You make me feel as though I'm capable of so much more. You make me see myself in a different light. You make me want to be a better man, a better parent to Chloe, a better… partner for you.'

'Oh.'

'Don't be alarmed. We don't have to rush, don't have to decide on anything right now, but I've had a lot of time to think over the past few days. I'm not sure I have it all figured out but that doesn't matter because we need to figure it out together. We can live near Darwin or another small town where there's a decent-sized hospital for me to work in. I don't need accolades for my work but I do need you and Chloe. We need to discuss our future, the three of us. Chloe needs to add her own opinion.'

'Because children have opinions. Maybe not fully formed but they have opinions nevertheless.' Harriette kissed him.

He returned the kiss, then looked at her again. 'Does this mean you're happy to become Chloe's mother?'

'Happy? Being a mother was the best thing that had ever happened to me and now that Eddie's off overseas, living his own life, I tried, I tried so hard not to be lonely, to focus on my career, on moving on with my life, but I was failing miserably...until you and Chloe burst into my life and filled it with sunshine once again. So of course I want to be a mother to Chloe. I already love her as though she were my own because she is just so loveable.'

'Are you sure?' His tone was earnest. 'Because... because you said you didn't want to have any more children.'

Harriette chuckled. 'No. I meant I didn't want to give birth to any more children, but if you're happy with just Chloe or you may want to adopt in the future, I'm fine with that.'

'Really?' He eased back a little and looked deeply into her eyes as though he needed to see the truth of her words reflected there. Then, as though he finally realised she wasn't dressed in her usual scrubs and that her hair wasn't falling about all over the place, his gaze drank her in. 'Wow. Dr Jones. Wherever did you get such a dress? You look absolutely stunning.'

'Paris, *mon cheri*.'

'Eddie. I should have known.' Felix kissed her neck, enjoying the way her hair was piled on top of her head, providing plenty of easy access for him.

'By the way, he's mad at you for upsetting his mother.'

'I figured as much.' He drew back and looked into her eyes. 'I'll speak to him later.'

'But he also told me that you didn't mean to hurt me and that you'd come to your senses eventually.'

'Hmm. That boy of yours is smart.'

'Yes, he is.'

'Just like his mother,' Felix whispered and kissed her once more. 'So what do you say, Harriette? Let's forget the past of our upbringings and forge ahead together with our future.'

'So long as you promise never to dismiss me again, because that's what hurt the most, Felix. I've been dismissed by everyone I've ever loved, except Eddie, and I didn't care for it.'

Felix shook his head in shame. 'I will spend copious amounts of time making it up to you.'

'Good. I'm looking forward to it.' With that, she wound her arms around his neck and kissed him soundly, glad she hadn't put her make-up on yet.

'You're not changed!' Chloe's voice stopped them in mid embrace and they both froze, wondering how the child would react to the two of them kissing in front of her. Felix was the first to speak, reluctantly slipping his arms from Harriette but reaching for her hand, as though he needed to be touching her.

'I'm sorry, princess. I'll get changed in just a moment but first, can you come here? Because Harriette and I want to ask you something very important.'

Chloe frowned at him but gave in and walked towards him, still a bit huffy. She was wearing her pretty dress but she'd put it on backwards and Harriette couldn't help but smile at the child as Felix bent to scoop her up. Then he placed his free arm around Harriette, drawing the three of them together.

'Chloe, I know your mummy and your daddy have gone to heaven but what do you think about having a new mummy and daddy?'

'A new one? You can do that?'

'Yes. Yes, you can.' He kissed her cheek, delighted at her response.

'Then I want you to be the daddy and Harriette to be the mummy. *Now* can you get changed?'

'So simple,' Harriette whispered as Felix dipped his head and kissed her.

'Yes, it is. Harriette Jones—' He stopped and let Chloe down as she was wriggling so much he was afraid he might drop her. 'Harriette Jones,' he began again. 'Will you do me the honour of becoming my wife and Chloe's mother?'

'I will. And will you, Felix McLaren, do me the honour of becoming my husband and Eddie's father?'

He grinned at that and nodded. 'I'd be delighted because that boy could surely use some discipline.' Both of them laughed, but stopped when Chloe huffed and whinged again. 'All right. All right, I'll get dressed.'

'Come on, Chloe. Let's go put our make-up on.' And that was what they did, Harriette even managing to get Chloe's dress on the right way before they left the house.

Chloe walked in the middle of them, holding their

hands. 'Family, family,' she sang as she wiggled her way up the path towards the large marquee. 'Come on, Mummy.' She giggled at the word and smiled up at Harriette. 'And come on, Daddy.' She looked up at Felix and laughed some more, as though her words were the best in the world.

And they were.

* * * * *

*If you missed the first story in
Lucy Clarke's* OUTBACK SURGEONS *check out
ENGLISH ROSE IN THE OUTBACK*

*And if you enjoyed this story,
check out these other great reads from
Lucy Clark*

STILL MARRIED TO HER EX!
A CHILD TO BIND THEM
DR PERFECT ON HER DOORSTEP
HIS DIAMOND LIKE NO OTHER

All available now!